PERILOUS PASSION

Tré held Jane's hand in his. Exerting slight pressure to pull her forward, he was inexplicably drawn to touch her hair, her brow; his bent fingers skimmed the curve of a cheek soft as a rose petal. She did not pull away.

He lifted her hand to his mouth, a courtly gesture that was seductively potent. Lips grazed the back of her fingers; he heard a soft inhalation and turned her hand over. He pressed his mouth to her palm while he held her gaze.

The smell of mint filled his nose, mouth, and lingered. Working lower, his lips found her wrist. The sleeve of her bliaut brushed against his jaw. He imagined her naked beneath him, ivory skin lush and warm. His thumb tested her wrist, leaving a red mark.

He watched it fade, a faint flower. Anticipation rose, ached; the hunger was back, stronger this time, a rush of heat like fire through his veins, scalding and destructive. If he allowed it, she would destroy him. . . .

ALSO BY JULIANA GARNETT

The Quest

The Magic

The Vow

The Scotsman

JULIANA GARNETT

THE BARON

BANTAM BOOKS

New York   Toronto   London   Sydney   Auckland

THE BARON

A Bantam Fanfare Book/December 1999

FANFARE and the portrayal of a boxed "ff" are trademarks
of Bantam Books, a division of Random House, Inc.

ISBN 0-553-57628-3

Published simultaneously in the United States and Canada

Bantam Books are published by Bantam Books, a division of Random
House, Inc. Its trademark, consisting of the words "Bantam Books" and the
portrayal of a rooster, is Registered in U.S. Patent and Trademark Office and
in other countries. Marca Registrada. Bantam Books, 1540 Broadway, New
York, New York 10036.

PRINTED IN THE UNITED STATES OF AMERICA

OPM   10 9 8 7 6 5 4 3 2 1

To Stephanie Kip, my wonderful editor. Thank you for your encouragement and support and for making such an important difference. Most of all—thank you for your patience!

ACKNOWLEDGMENTS

This book could not have been researched without the generous hospitality given me by four people: Salvator and Jane Harris Merola and Clive and Pip Harris. Along with Rita Burke (who planned my itinerary and saw to it that we got on the right trains), they enabled me to explore to my heart's content, braving the M5 and accompanying me as I clambered over ruins and trod forest paths in the rain, and descended into caves with video and digital cameras. To all these marvelous souls, I offer my heartfelt gratitude and a promise not to return for at least six months.

And to Amelia Bomar, who can find absolutely anything when it comes to research books and medieval trivia. The medieval archery book is a treasure. You're a wonderful friend with a magnificent library. . . .

I

BRAYETON, YORKSHIRE

DECEMBER 1210

A gust of wind snagged a cloud on the topmost turret of Brayeton Keep; gray shadows crept down the hillside. Bare oak branches clacked together like an old man's teeth, a desolate sound splintering the silence.

"Are you going to die too, Papa?"

The hesitant whisper filled with misery caught his attention; her breath was a cloud of vapor-frost in icy air. Childish lips trembled slightly as Aimée looked up at her father.

Robert Devaux, third Baron of Brayeton, ignored the dignity of his position and went to one knee. The ground was raw, damp, with a thin coating of hoarfrost over the new grave. Errant flakes of snow powdered his dark hair.

He put comforting hands on the small shoulders clad in a red wool mantle, bunched the material beneath his fingers. Eyes as green as his own lifted in a silent plea for reassurance.

A smile felt stiff on his lips. "Not if I can help it, my treasure."

"But Maman died. Now Tricket." A quiver betrayed her grief. "Promise not to die, Papa!"

Awkward, clumsy, his thumb scraped over the track of a tear frozen to silver on her cheek. How could he answer her? How to explain to a child beset by grief for her pet dog that he could not promise immortality?

Helpless, he looked past her to focus on the high stone walls of Brayeton Keep, cold and forbidding in winter, a sentinel on the horizon. It guarded land held by the Devaux family since the time of the Conqueror. He was only an extension of the power signified by his title, the latest to hold it, another descendant of a Norman tenant in chief who had won glory and land with the might of his sword.

"Aimée, look." He turned her gently, pointed to the wind-whipped banner atop a turret. "Do you remember what that is?"

She nodded, hood slipping back so that a curl of golden hair escaped. "Yes. It is the Devaux pennant."

Still on one knee, he pulled her to him, folded his arms and mantle around her to keep her warm. "It has flown over our land since the time of my great-grandfather. He was the first to devise the Devaux crest, the raven against a field of gold—"

"The *sable* and *or*," Aimée interrupted in a childish treble of Norman French. "Madame Marie told me."

"You are very smart to remember your lessons."

"I am nearly six, you know." Pride erased some of the grief in her voice.

He held her tighter against his chest. "You are a big girl now, Aimée. Do you recall what else Madame Marie told you about the pennant?"

Her head bobbed. "When it flies, the raven is home." She turned in his embrace, regarded him with a faint frown. "I hope you stay longer this time, Papa."

"So do I, my treasure." Unexpected guilt scourged him; he silently cursed his overlord and the king impartially for their demands on his time and coffers. They commanded too much. Welburn wracked him with constant demands, and King John was no better. They would plunder Brayeton if he did not put a halt to it.

Aimée hiccuped; he managed a smile for her, hooked a finger under her chin to lift her face. "Madame Marie was to teach you the family history. Can you recite the names of the barons who have held Brayeton Keep?"

"Oh yes, it is easy." A dimple flashed briefly in a cheek made pink by wind. "They all have the same name as you—Robert Devaux. You are the third baron, and when you were a little boy, your cousin called you Tré instead of *treie*. Some people still call you Tré. I call you Papa."

"As you should. Here is what I want you to remember: as long as there is Brayeton Keep, there will be a Devaux. As long as there is a Devaux, none of us will ever die."

For a moment she digested his assurance with quiet solemnity, then frowned. "Madame Marie said that since the king is ex—excommin-icated and all the priests sent away from England, we will die unshriven of our sins."

He hid a smile. "The priests are not sent from England, only barred from performing their duties."

"Madame Marie said worms will eat us all one day."

"Shall we let the worms eat Madame Marie instead?"

Aimée giggled. He rose and took her hand to lead her back up the hill. She broke away, moved to the grave, and bent to place a holly sprig upon the mound. For a moment she stood still, a forlorn little figure that seemed suddenly older than her scant years. A brisk wind flapped the loose edges of her mantle with a popping sound, knocked heavy branches together in the towering oak. The hill that was so lovely in spring was now stark, bleak, with no remnant of beauty. A fitting place for a grave, guarded by the shadow of Brayeton Keep, overlooking a valley that would come to life again in May, as immortal as England.

Aimée turned, went to him, and tucked her hand into the curve of his palm; fingers curled tightly into his as she looked up at him.

"Tricket is a Devaux, too."

"Yea, so she is."

"I shall miss her."

It was said with resignation and sorrow, but not the grief of earlier, and Tré nodded. Death was a part of life; it was a fact he had learned young as well.

His own mother was a vague memory. There had been a brother and sisters, but none had survived. Only he and his father had been left out of their once numerous family, two strangers with a common goal: Brayeton's endurance. It was his alone now, a legacy to pass on to his own heirs.

Aimée's mother had died of childbed fever, another loss regretted but not mourned. An arranged marriage, a union formed to link lands more than hearts.

It had not been a happy union. His bride had found him too harsh, she said, too sparing of pretty phrases, and ignorant of a woman's desires. It was true; he knew that of himself. He had little time for wooing, was too impatient to try. An arranged marriage suited him well, for it had been decided when he was still a boy. He had not known or missed love.

Until Aimée.

A squalling infant at first held no charm for him, but he had found himself fascinated by the sweet child with bright curls and happy laughter. She was everything he was not: fair where he was dark, merry where he was somber. A gleeful sprite of a child who brought the miracle of laughter into his life and changed him forever.

Perhaps it was the novelty of such a creature, unspoiled by life, unaware of the darkness in men's souls, that drew him. Whatever it was, she had captured his heart. Above all else, he would keep her safe.

Evening mist curled in gauzy streamers through trees and brush, whispered over the lowered drawbridge stretched across a moat frozen in winter. Aimée skipped over wood planks, distracted now from her earlier turmoil as they entered the keep.

Sir Guy greeted them by the fire, a towering blaze that lit the great hall; he glanced up, smiled at Aimée, and gestured to the woman who stood to one side.

"Madame Marie awaits your pleasure, duckling."

"I shall stay here."

Tré put a hand atop her tousled curls, caressing the bright strands. "Duty calls, Aimée. One who has not learned to obey cannot earn privilege."

A faint sigh greeted his gentle chiding; she nodded, a brief regret before surrender. "Shall I see you on the morrow before I leave, Papa?"

"Most assuredly, my treasure. You will not be gone long before you return. York is far more exciting than Brayeton, and you will be well cared for until I come for you."

"Grandmère and Grandpère would be pleased if you were to stay too, Papa."

He doubted it; his late wife's parents blamed him for their daughter's death. But he said nothing of that, only bade her a sweet night's sleep before she left in the custody of Madame Marie.

When she was gone, he turned to Guy, saw in his face that he had grim tidings. "What news?"

"Another village destroyed, stores burned and churls slaughtered." Guy held out a cup of wine. "Welburn's men were seen leaving, yet we have no way to prove it. A peasant swears he will strike again on the morrow."

"*Merde!*" Steel tinged a soft promise: "The faithless earl courts harsh reprisal. Should he come again with sword and death, he will rue it."

His gaze shifted to the fire, where flames danced. Two years. A long time for a man to bear rancor for a mistake. His overlord, Pell Ewing, Earl of Welburn, had vowed vengeance upon his Norman vassal for the death of a favorite horse. No appeasement was accepted; a deadly feud was sparked by an accident.

It was time the feud ended; his villeins bore the brunt of his dispute with Ewing. Too many losses, too much time spent defending Brayeton land—too much time wasted in appeals to a king who cared only for his quarrel with the pope, nothing for the barons who supported him. Now he would levy his own justice.

"*Ad noctum*—Into the darkness." Sir Guy indicated the Devaux shield hanging on the wall and the motto painted on wood. "It fits you well."

Devaux regarded Sir Guy with a half-smile. "It was my great-grandfather's motto."

Guy grunted acknowledgment. "Ah. The first baron. He was like you, no doubt, dark as the night and just as grim."

"I am not grim, just too busy to ply foolish maids with pretty words and wine."

"It would do you good if you did." Guy raked a hand through his fair hair until it stood up on end like a cock's comb. He yawned, eyes thinned against the glare of the fire. "After the warning you sent him, Welburn is still fool enough to ravage Brayeton villages. Do you think him bold enough to strike again on the morrow, or is it only a false tale?"

"We will know soon enough."

Sparse light glinted from a rising sun veiled by trees along the banks of the River Ouse. Traces of snow laced tufts of brown grass; blood turned white drifts to pink.

It was more brutal than he had anticipated. Two of his best men lay dead on the field, crumpled into shapeless forms. Welburn's dead littered the field, as well, but there was no sign of the earl. Guy had pursued the men who fled.

Black smoke boiled into the sky; the stench of charred flesh permeated the air. Only the skeletal outline of a dwelling remained. It had been set afire with the peasants locked inside, their screams unheeded. Too late to save them but not too late to deal justice to men responsible for such horror—save for one.

Welburn: Saxon by birth, old enmities of race ruled his judgment. It was not truly the loss of a horse Welburn begrudged, but the presence of Normans on land that had once belonged to Saxons. A hundred forty-four years since William the Conqueror had invaded England, yet hostility still raged against Norman rulers. Futile hatred.

Damp wind curled over him as he regarded Welburn's dead. He should have been satisfied at the victory; he was not. There was nothing to indicate that the men had come at the earl's mandate. No distinctive livery here, none alive to be questioned. It would require more than dead peasants and soldiers to levy proof of Welburn's perfidy.

A drumming of hooves interrupted his preoccupation, and he glanced up. Guy approached, driving before him two men on foot. Bare headed and bloodied, they stumbled, fell, were jerked upright by ropes wound around their middles.

Dismounting, Devaux plunged his sword tip into the chewed earth at his feet, splayed his legs to stand at the edge of the small clearing and wait. Proof came to him with dread in their eyes. . . .

Foam flecked, Guy's steed snorted, nostrils flared red and wide as it was reined to a halt in front of the baron.

"They claim to have knowledge should we spare them, my lord." Hazel eyes gleamed behind the noseguard of Guy's helm; satisfaction curled his lip. His huge courser danced sideways a step, tightening the rope enough to unbalance the prisoners. Pained oaths rent the air, and pleas for mercy betrayed cowardly natures.

Hired Flemish mercenaries—unscrupulous butchers. Tré regarded the bloodied men coldly. His fingers tightened on his sword hilt; blood still glistened red on the wicked blade.

"Stand up and speak. I would hear what Welburn pays men who slay the innocent."

Awkward, they lurched to their feet; lips hung slackly, fear burned in their eyes. Paid assassins, the scourge of England.

"My lord Brayeton . . ." A croak, breathless and shaky, emerged, then trailed into quivering silence.

Tré's sword flashed upward; mud sprayed in an arc. His eyes were hard, mouth taut. "If you have knowledge to impart, do it ere my blade severs your tongue."

"Hold!" A hand came up swiftly; a thin ray of sunlight flashed from the suspended blade. In a panicked rush, the mercenary blurted, "The earl seeks only his just rents—"

"I levy my required fees. He has no cause for this. It is a choice he will rue as well as you. . . ."

The sword point lowered, pressed against the Fleming's throat—a promise of his fate. The prisoner blanched.

"My lord—you look to avenge the wrong deed, when there are outlaws who even now destroy your treasure."

"My treasure?" Amusement laced his words, held the sword at bay. "I do not think even the Earl of Welburn fool enough to besiege Brayeton Keep."

"Nay, but Saxon outlaws would waylay a baggage train to York readily enough, if told it carries treasure."

For an instant, it was beyond comprehension. Even when Guy swore foully, Tré did not dare let his mind absorb the implications. It was not until he was mounted and spurring his steed down the muddy track toward York that the enormity was inescapable.

Aimée . . . my greatest treasure. . . .

II

WINDSOR CASTLE

FEBRUARY 10, 1213

1

Dark eyes regarded Tré steadily; rings flashed in torch- and candlelight as the king waved him forward. The chamber was near empty, save for a scribe and the king's steward.

Tré approached the dais where John sat in an unkingly sprawl; he did not bow his head or bend the knee, but stood silent and still while the king spoke to his steward. Heavy tapestries covered the chamber's walls, richly embroidered, a blur of red and gold behind the dais.

It was cold; Tré's boots were muddy, but he had taken no time to don clean garments when summoned by King John. In truth, he had been given no time to do more than accompany the guard sent to escort him to Windsor, a dire omen that set his jaw and his temper.

King John, Pell Ewing—two men of the same ilk. Greedy, ruthless warlords. Nothing mattered to them but their own goals. Not even the life of a small child—whose loss he blamed on king and earl as well as Saxon outlaws.

Over two years since Aimée died—not so long ago. Yet a lifetime....

"Lord Devaux, Baron of Brayeton."

The scribe's gruff announcement jerked him from harsh memory to the present. Tré looked up, met the king's gaze with a steady stare. John's eyes narrowed slightly; thin lips twisted at the blatant refusal to bend knee or head.

"You took overlong to answer our summons, Brayeton."

Petulance marked the royal face and tone; one hand came to rest languidly upon the carved chair arm. Tré stood silent. Tension thumped in his belly.

John's expression eased into a mocking smile. Jewels winked as he chewed a fingernail, halted to say abruptly, "The Earl of Welburn has been deseisened of his lands and title."

Savage exultation flared, but Tré did not allow it to show in his face or words. "Indeed, sire."

"Yea, indeed, my lord of Brayeton!" The king leaned forward in his bolstered chair. "What say you to that?"

"It is a grave misfortune, sire."

"A misfortune?" John gave a bark of laughter that held no humor. "Misfortune for Ewing, or for yourself?"

"I am not allied with Pell Ewing, sire."

"No, you are not. Yet it has come to our attention of late that you have withdrawn from our service. You paid knights' fees and shield tax, but did not answer our summons to Nottingham. Explain your reasons to our satisfaction."

"My lands require much of my time, sire." Salvation lay in half-truths; survival prompted him to remind the king, "I have just returned from your campaign against the Welsh."

It was waved away as inconsequential. "We need more assurance of your loyalty. You have no family, no hostages to offer us, only an oath of fealty that you have not yet sworn."

Tré held his tongue; not even to avoid censure would he swear an oath he was not certain he could keep. It would be treason should he break it. More danger lay in perjury than in refusal.

The king's steward stepped forward, murmured in John's ear, then stepped away. Tension prickled down Tré's spine; the new wound in his side throbbed, raw and unhealed, a constant ache, compliments of a Welsh sword.

John turned back, mouth curled in a nasty smile. "We have seized Welburn lands for the crown. Ewing is your overlord, a proven traitor, alive only because he has fled to Ireland. He named you as conspirator. Show me good cause to allow you to remain free, my lord Brayeton."

Anger sparked, was swiftly tamped. "Sire, you are aware of my long feud with the Earl of Welburn. Would you accuse me of treachery on his word alone?"

"Can you prove your innocence?"

"I have not heard specific charges, sire. If I am to be accused, I demand my rights as baron to a trial before the Council of Barons."

John regarded him through hooded eyes; mockery tucked the corners of his mouth. "The council meets at Nottingham Castle. As we just met in September, you will remain in our custody until the next council meeting."

A clank of weapons and armor from the guards entering bespoke the king's intent; Tré tensed. Few men left Windsor's dungeons alive.

Coolly, he said, "Sire, the Barons of Brayeton have served England's kings since the time of the Conqueror. Imprison me without trial and you will earn the enmity of even your allies. Do you court more enemies when you are beset on all sides?"

King John frowned, glanced toward his steward again, and chewed his fingernail for a moment. Then he sat back, narrow shoulders pressed against wood and gilt.

"Your lands are forfeit until charges against you are put before the Council of Barons. Unless you prefer prison, you may be of some use, my lord Brayeton. We are in need of a High Sheriff of Nottingham."

Surprise and outrage rendered Tré silent for a moment. Wily John—if he could not extract one oath, he would secure another. An appointment to sheriff would bind him to uphold the very laws he hated. A refusal would result in his imprisonment. He sucked in a deep breath.

"I thought the position occupied, sire."

"Not," the king said harshly, "for long. Eustace de Lowdham has misjudged me. His greedy hand plunders my taxes. He fails to catch the outlaws who poach Sherwood preserves and steal from royal coffers. You have proven your worth in pursuit of the Welsh—prove your worth as sheriff, and lands and title will be returned to you in time."

Tré's eyes narrowed; dust motes danced in gray bars of light filtering through the open window. It was a subtle trap. Far easier for John to be rid of an appointed official than to risk alienating all his barons by eliminating one of their own without proven cause.

Disaster loomed. Until this moment he had not known how complete was Welburn's hatred of him. Cunning earl, to destroy an enemy with a simple accusation—tempting a king who coveted rich lands for his war against Philip of France and the pope.

Far better to compromise than lose all. . . .

Silence stretched, grew heavy and dense. Impatient, John snapped, "Decide, my lord Brayeton."

Bitter words burned his tongue: "If I am not trusted to be baron, am I trusted to be sheriff?"

"A landless baron wields little enough power. You will be a warning to those who consider treason—evidence of our resolve, and our generosity in allowing you life and liberty."

The king beckoned to his scribe, looked back at Tré. "Arrive in Nottingham before the first Sunday of Lent. Serve us well, Devaux, and we shall reward thee well. Fail us, and lose all."

Devaux—I am already stripped of title and rank. . . . He swallowed rage and unwise comment, held his tongue when John's eyes glittered with malicious satisfaction.

Brayeton Keep, gone in the blink of an eye, seized for a false accusation. Now they belonged to King John: the stone keep where he had been born, and a hillside where two graves lay beneath an old oak.

Aimée. . . .

Memory veered from the sharp pain, barricaded itself behind familiar grayness: hollow, empty of soft emotion, a vast desolation where it was safe. Where the anguish of loss could not reach him.

Ad noctum—Into the darkness.

2

Rain glistened on the domed helmets and chainmail of Norman soldiers entering Nottingham Castle beneath the jagged iron teeth of the outer gate. Hooves pounded like brittle thunder. Vapor rose from steaming hides of muscular coursers near as fierce as their riders. The clatter of sheathed weapons was muffled but ominous. It was suddenly loud in the outer bailey, a warning to those within that the unknown would soon be upon them.

Jane, widow of Hugh de Neville, drew the edges of her fur-trimmed mantle more closely around her. Nervous fingers tugged at the hood to cover her hair. There had not been time enough to don a wimple when word came that the new sheriff was near Nottingham at last. It had taken too long to coax her cousin into readiness, leaving her just enough time to club her own light brown hair into a plait and tuck it beneath her hood as they hastened from nearby Gedling to the castle. Rain misted her lashes. She blinked it away as she peered through the drizzle and jostling crowd toward the approaching Normans.

A contingent separated from the others to enter the middle bailey. A banner flew damply in the wind, snapping like the crack of a whip above mailed heads to announce the sheriff's arrival. Tension knotted in her stomach, twisting. So close now.

Beside her, Lissa made a sound of impatience and shoved roughly at the man in front of them. "Oaf! Beware of where thou trod!"

" 'Ere now!" the man protested, but moved from her path. It opened up a hole in the throng, so the cousins had a much better view.

It was more crowded than Jane had anticipated; barons, freedmen, and merchants were allowed into the middle bailey to greet—or confront—the new sheriff. Saxon English and Norman French commingled in wanton intercourse of language, one ancient, the other the speech of the Conqueror. All of Nottingham had turned out. Now narrow streets held little more than cold wind and dread as citizens packed into the castle bailey; their collective support or resistance would be determined by the actions of the new sheriff.

Shivering as much from anticipation as the icy gusts that tugged at warm wool and skirts, Jane craned to see as the Normans drew close enough for her to pick out individual men instead of a blur of steel and arrogance.

Which one is the high sheriff?

There was no mace of office to identify him, no gold-linked chain of office worn around the neck to mark him as the king's man.

But as the column of horsemen garbed in black and gold tunics slowed their mounts to a walk, she knew. He was *there*, flanked by other Normans, yet distinctly separate.

At her side, Lissa heaved a long, appreciative sigh. "It has been a long time since I have ridden something that big and magnificent...."

Jane shifted her gaze from the Normans to her cousin. "I assume you mean the horse," she murmured, and Lissa laughed.

"I could be speaking of the steed, of course—both are fine, muscular animals, sleek and dark and dangerous."

"Mind your clacking tongue. Would you have others here remark upon your vulgar wit?"

A serene smile and shrug were ample evidence of Lissa's indifference to the warning. Her silk wimple fluttered in damp folds against her lovely face as her gaze returned to the line of Normans. "Do you think *he* is Devaux?"

Jane knew which man she meant without asking. Iron-shod hooves struck sparks on the uneven wet stones as a splendid black steed pranced arrogantly forward. The Norman in the saddle was even more impressive.

A negligent hand curbed the restive gait of the courser before it trod upon eager citizens; there was steel in the light grip that even the willful nature of the huge beast recognized. Snorting, nostrils flared in dangerous crimson flowers, the stallion obeyed the unspoken command and halted only a few feet from Jane. Her gaze moved in wary fascination from courser to master.

An eloquent centaur, spare of motion and expression, features devoid of all but regard for the animal, he seemed not to see those crowded among the barracks and stone walls of the bailey. The only sounds were the brisk rattle of military accoutrements. Fraught with suspense, the abrupt absence of conversation paid homage more to the bearing of the sheriff than to the apprehension of the people.

She understood completely.

Unencumbered by heavy mail, broad shoulders and a thick chest were encased in a flowing surcoat of ebony wool. Fine gilt tracery formed a stark pattern on the front, emblem of his rank and heritage. Soot-black hair was neatly trimmed in Norman fashion; rain-dampened strands fell forward over eyebrows that slashed across his forehead. He had a strong face, angular as most Normans', with high carved cheekbones and a chiseled mouth that looked as if it had never known a smile.

Jane stirred uneasily. Unexpected appreciation of his masculine features fluttered briefly before she thrust it firmly aside. *Pray, let him be different from the last high sheriff. . . .*

She slipped one hand beneath her mantle, skimmed the rose-colored velvet of her cotte until her searching fingers found and curled tightly around a length of finely wrought gold chain. She drew the small gold cross at the chain's end into her palm and rubbed her thumb over the carved surface.

Since de Lowdham's departure, the undersheriff left to

mete out justice in the Saxon borough had been just as harsh.
It did not bode well for Nottinghamshire if this man proved to
be as merciless as had been his predecessors.

The crowd shifted, closed ranks to block her view of him;
Jane rose to her toes to peer over the heads in front of her. The
tang of fresh horse droppings was on the rising wind; spurs jangled and curb chains clinked in brittle song. Servants' rouncies
snorted, pawed stone, backed into sumpters loaded with baggage. The horseboys came running to take charge of the
animals.

The spell that had briefly gripped the crowd was broken,
melded into chaotic babble. Anticipation rose sharply as the
high sheriff lifted his head to survey the bailey with a raking
glance. Arrogance was evident in every sharp angle and line of
his powerful frame. He looked competent—and ruthless.

Jane sucked in a sharp, disappointed breath.

A horseboy held on to the reins of the fractious courser as
the sheriff dismounted, betraying a slight stiffness of movement where she had expected more agility. Yet when he turned
to face the barons lined up like wet crows on a hedge row, he
exhibited no infirmity.

Slowly drawing off his leather gauntlets, he surveyed them
all with a lifted brow. "I did not foresee such a welcome, my
lords. To what do I owe this unexpected reception?"

The pretty consonants and vowels of Norman French were
more of a growl on his tongue, the fluid language of the Conqueror bludgeoned into blunt inflection. Jane pushed forward
to stand behind a baron she had known since childhood. A
silent glance of disapproval was eloquent with his belief that
females should remain in their place. She ignored it, her attention on the sheriff.

His breath formed frost clouds as Devaux waited for a reply.
A brow angled sharply upward when no one came forward to
answer him.

"Is there no spokesman?"

The drizzling rain made a soft hissing sound. Norman
knights shifted, weapons clanking. When no Saxon summoned
the courage to step forward or speak out, coarse laughter rippled through the Norman ranks.

Devaux's lip curled in undisguised contempt. "So I thought. Get you home before the rains reduce you to naught but sodden curs."

It was the shaming laughter from Norman ranks as much as the sheriff's contempt that prompted her; Jane elbowed past Gilbert of Oxton. Her voice rose to be heard above the clank and clatter of the guards:

"My lord high sheriff, we come to ask that you listen to our concerns and give us redress."

Rising wind muffled the words so that they sounded strangely distorted. Lord Oxton turned to look at her. Chagrin was evident on pale, sharp features, his Saxon English roughly familiar:

"Lady Neville, 'tis not necessary for you—"

"No, what you mean is that it is not *proper* for a lady to speak out thusly." Impatient, she shrugged off the restraining hand he put on her arm. "Yet who else will have the courage to speak if I do not? 'Tis certain none of these brave barons can summon nerve enough."

Her stinging barbs found accurate marks. Several Saxon barons suffused with angry color, but it was the sheriff who commanded her instant attention:

"Step forward, my lady, so that I may view this Saxon with enough courage to demand amends."

His Saxon English was fluent, a warning to any baron who might think Norman scorn of the language gave them an advantage.

Jane tensed. Dread coiled in her belly. It would be impossible to walk without stumbling; sudden realization of the notice she had brought upon herself rendered her immobile. Her tongue cleaved to the roof of her mouth, uncooperative and clumsy.

But I am the daughter of a valiant Saxon knight, widow of a Norman baron, and no man can shame me unless I allow it—

Her chin rose with a determined tilt. "Indeed, sir, 'tis not courage that prompts me to speak, but justice."

"Justice?" A straight brow winged upward; the mouth she had thought too harsh to smile tucked inward with wry humor. "A strange word to find on English lips."

"Not so strange, my lord, but certainly a word found too infrequently in Norman hearts."

For an instant, their gazes locked. Distracted, taut with uncertainty, Jane had a brief impression of eyes as hard and green as emeralds; the wary gaze of a cat lurked beneath a brush of wet, black lashes.

"I find your assertions intriguing, my lady." The words were smooth, the voice a low rasp. Rain hissed on stones and bare heads. "Such a mettlesome adherent of justice requires an introduction. What is your family name?"

Hunting eyes, keen and watchful, waiting for an answer and a misstep. . . . "My late husband was Hugh de Neville, the king's Baron of Ravenshed. My father was Rolf of Ashfield, loyal knight to the Lionheart."

"Neville was your husband?" He paused, finally adding, "I knew him, Lady Neville. He was a fine man and valiant knight in his day."

"Yea, so he was, sir. His death is most grievous."

The words were steady enough, though there was a curious crumbling inside as she said them. Hugh's loss had been painful but not unexpected. It was the desolation she had not foreseen. There were times she felt so alone. . . .

A low rumble of thunder sounded in the distance. The rain began to worsen. It struck the bailey with increasing force, pinging loudly against metal helmets and shields.

Devaux gave a terse order for the barons to accompany him into the hall, then turned to Jane and held out his arm.

"You will do me the honor of being my guest, milady."

It was not a request but a demand. Though she bridled at his arrogance, she placed her hand on his arm. Eyes followed her: Oxton's angry, others' shocked, Lissa's round with awe. Trapped, Jane did not betray her own dread.

Her slight stature was dwarfed by the towering Norman. She had never felt more keenly vulnerable than she did at that moment. Her fingers lay lightly on his sleeve; beneath rich wool was ample evidence of taut muscles and strength. It was daunting, a suddenly inescapable feeling of walking into a lion's lair—no less daunting than Nottingham Castle itself.

High curtain walls of buff-colored sandstone fifteen feet thick rose in concentric circles to protect a castle studded with gates and turrets. In daylight, crenelated stone battlements resembled jagged teeth gnawing at the sky; at night, some said 'twas the devil's backbone.

A massive precipice of sandstone provided the natural advantage of unscalable height. Forbidding rock cliffs and the River Leen bounded the south side. Between the River Leen and the River Trent in the distance lay only vast meadows, now browned by winter sear and thin traces of snow—a bare expanse with no tree or structure to obscure the view of possible enemy approach. The fortress was intimidating, brooding over town and countryside like a great, hulking bird of prey, slitted eyes keeping watch from high towers.

Tense, cold, blinded by icy rain, Jane was grateful to see the great hall loom ahead. She stumbled slightly on the bottom step. An arm immediately went around her waist to steady her, then lingered. Imposing, silent beside her, Devaux's strides were lithe and sure as they ascended the steep, rain-slick stone steps and moved into the stark shelter of the guard room.

Blinking rain from her lashes, Jane dropped her hand from his arm and stood shivering. Her rich mantle was sodden, clinging to her body in heavy folds. She pushed back the hood, scraped a hand over wet, curling strands of hair fraying from her plait, discomfited that she had not taken the time to garb herself properly. She no doubt resembled an alewife, hardly a recommendation for her status as a baron's widow. Only a thin coronet of twisted gold wound with blue ribbons to match her eyes held back wet hair from her forehead.

The guard room was gloomy, close, smelling of rain and mud and dank stone. Lifting a hand, Devaux beckoned. A steward rushed forward to remove the damp mantle from her shoulders as her cold fingers fumbled to unfasten the clasp.

"Allow me, milady," the steward murmured, and slid it from her shoulders before he turned back to the sheriff. "My lord sheriff, Sir Gervaise sends word that he awaits your immediate presence in the antechamber."

Brittle silence was followed by a soft reply that did not

disguise the steel beneath it: "Does he. He will wait longer ere I heel like a hound. I will escort the lady to the hall. Take her mantle to dry by the fire."

Devaux turned, his shadowed gaze studying Jane's up-turned face so intently that she had to smother an inexplicable urge to smooth her hair. *He unnerves me. . . .*

"It is warmer by the fire, milady. Come. I will hear more of your complaints."

Silent, she inclined her head in an agreement she did not feel; disquiet stirred within her at this separation from the barons.

"My mantle," she said, reaching for it when the steward turned to go; he held tight to it, gave her a quick smile of apology.

"It will be safe, milady. I shall not lay it too close to the flames."

He was gone before she could halt him, weaving swiftly through the throng of damp barons and Norman guards now crowded inside. Devaux waited, an unsettling presence, a solid wall of Norman hostility at its finest; she could not think how to disentangle herself without insulting him, to her future detriment.

"Are you contemplating ways to escape me, milady?"

Startled at his astute observation, her head jerked up. Heated embarrassment burned her cheeks. "Yes," she said bluntly, and was rewarded with a faint suggestion of a smile at the corners of his hard mouth. His brow rose.

"Am I so hated, then?"

"Only what you represent, perhaps."

"Which is law and order. Would that Saxons could perceive the necessity for it."

His sarcasm stung; she drew in an angry breath. "It is not law and order which is so detestable, but the arbitrary manner in which it is measured. Outlaws visit devastation, yet roam free while honest citizens are gathered up and threatened with imprisonment for life if they do not fight for a king who cares nothing for them."

"You do not bandy words idly, I see." Though sarcasm still tinged the remark, it was diluted. He looked at her thoughtfully, then after a moment took her by the arm again to move beyond the heavy curtain separating the guard room from the great hall.

Cavernous, with high ceilings and hazy light, the hall was crowded with barons and noise; double doors were thrown wide to allow easy access. Trestle tables stacked against the walls were being taken down and put into place by beleaguered servants. She was cold without her mantle, the rose velvet cotte scant protection against the chill. Her feet were wet, squelching on muddied rushes and stone as she walked beside him.

At a gesture from the sheriff, those by the fire abandoned a low bench; he waited until she was seated before he sat beside her. It was warmer there, the pool of heat welcome. Acutely aware of him beside her, she tugged the hem of her cotte up to her ankles, wiggling her feet as the delicious warmth from the fire spread under her skirts.

He adjusted his sword, then stretched out long legs clad in tight-woven black chausses. Supple calfskin boots rose to his knees. Tiny splinters of light caught in the gilt emblem on a tunic shortened for riding; the embroidered shape of a raven was recognizable now.

A raven—Celtic symbol of darkness and despair. . . .

The pleasant smell of wind and leather mingled with the scent of wet wool as he turned to look at her. Unexpectedly, her pulse began to race in a most unseemly manner at his steady regard. The knot in her stomach tightened. Her lungs grew starved of air, so that she had to breathe in deeply to fill them. . . . He was most disconcerting.

"Who is your escort today, milady?"

"My cousin, Lady Dunham of Gedling."

"Then you have no protector."

Danger loomed, couched in the simple statement. "I was not aware I needed a protector here, my lord sheriff."

A straight brow rose. "Have you no mirror?"

There was subtle mockery in the question, and to hide her sudden confusion she looked away from him to survey her surroundings.

The hall had changed little since last she had been there.

Banners and huge iron rings of candles were suspended from the high ceilings, which were buttressed by stone columns. No woven hangings softened the walls, only shields and battle-axes were displayed against stone. Thin, polished hides stretched over the high windows allowed in ribbons of gray light, but torches set into a dozen metal sconces provided the most illumination; their indiscriminate sparks singed the skin, hair, and garments of those too near them. Servants bustled down wide aisles, vanishing behind latticed wood screens, only to reappear with platters of food for the long trestle tables set at right angles to the dais. Somewhere a lute player coaxed bawdy ballads from his instrument.

Clearly a fortress and not a home; yet, if not for the uncertain hazards of the new high sheriff, it might have been festive in those last days before Lent commenced.

Beside her, Devaux shifted position. His strong hands were splayed on his knees. He was brusque now, the mask of courtesy dropped. "You have grown suddenly timid, milady. A Saxon trait. It is expected, but I thought better of you."

Stung, she swung her gaze to his face, openly stared at him. "I am not responsible for what you expected, my lord sheriff."

"No." The hard line of his mouth eased. "You are not."

He baited her. She had risen to it far too easily, but would not give him the satisfaction of looking away, of yielding to the demand for a submission she knew he required. She would not be as the others, cowering under Norman rule. As he had said, *It is expected.*

But it was more difficult than she had imagined not to look away, to hold his gaze while he willed her to yield ground. Silent struggle was freighted with determination and something else, some small spark deep inside that ignited a mute appreciation of masculine symmetry: wide-spaced eyes, a straight nose, well-formed lips, and clean-shaven angle of jaw that projected stubborn determination. Ancient Northern forebears of his race had left him the legacy of height and muscle.

Daunting, daunting man—fearsome in his pride, more dangerous in his silence. . . .

Still holding her gaze, he said, "By Sunday next, the king has commanded that all English ships return to their home ports. I am bade summon all who have done homage and fealty to the king to meet with horses and arms at Dover by the close of Easter. It is my duty to ensure that those within this sheriffdom join the king or suffer reprisal."

Her brow rose. "Indeed, it should pain you greatly to visit new woes upon the land, my lord high sheriff—though I think it does not."

After a short, sizzling silence, Devaux said, "You intrigue me, Lady Neville."

Her hands clenched in rose velvet.

"Why? Because I say what I think? Or is it because I spoke up when others would not?"

"Both. You should be at home weaving cloth or governing servants, not meddling in the affairs of men."

His ridicule stung and she stiffened. "The few servants I have left to me after the conscriptions into royal service can weave without my supervision, but you are right, my lord—I should be at home. It is evident I have wasted my time and yours by coming here to plead for succor."

"Not necessarily." There was an intensity to his gaze that took her breath away. "I will weigh your pleas most carefully, milady. But do not mistake contemplation for weakness. I tell you plainly that I am the king's man, here to mete out justice in his name and restore order to the shire."

"That is all any man or woman could require—justice. I pray that you are what you claim to be, my lord sheriff."

"I claim to be nothing." His tone was flat and rough again, his eyes narrowed slightly. "I was appointed sheriff. I will do my duty as bade to by King John. It would behoove these barons to believe that the king wishes them to be content. Should you have occasion to relay that information to the unhappy barons with you, it would be better for all."

"I am not a messenger, my lord." Anger overrode caution as the first brief flare of hope was quickly extinguished. *Does he think me so naive as to believe that he has only the best interests of Saxons in mind?* Tartly: "I do not presume to tell others what to think, but expect them to make their own judgments, just as I have done."

Tense silence lay between them, while in the hall, music

rose from lute and harp; men laughed and hounds barked. A log popped in the fire, sparks like tiny shooting stars forming a glowing arc. She was aware of it all, as she was aware of her thudding heart and slowly warming feet; paramount was the man before her, who held in his hands the power of life, death, and freedom.

He rose to his feet. A faint, ironic smile pressed at the corners of his mouth. "No, milady, I see that you are not a messenger. A pity. It would save so much time and trouble."

"Perhaps, but I doubt it would be to my advantage."

This time his smile was genuine. "You are as sharp-tongued as you are sharp-willed, Lady Neville. I commend you for your spirit, if not your civility."

She would have answered sharply again, but took a deep breath instead. Prudence now seemed the wisest course.

"My lord sheriff." The steward appeared, his cough a polite interruption. "Sir Gervaise grows most anxious to meet with you as soon as possible."

"No doubt. Lady Neville will wait here for my return, Giles. See to her needs." With that unceremonious farewell, he was gone, stalking across the great hall with his long, loose stride while she stared after him.

Another polite cough snared her attention, and she heard Giles ask if she needed a cup of wine.

"No. Bring my mantle."

A pause, then, smoothly: "It will be brought to you upon my lord's request. Shall I bring the wine?"

"Yes. Bring the wine."

Uncertain, angry, Jane sat with her feet still to the fire's heat, torn between flight and compliance. Any other time, she would have abandoned the hall despite his order. Yet now she hesitated.

Conversation ebbed and flowed in the crowded hall like sea tides, washing over her in anonymous waves. Occasional laughter sounded sharp and strained. Only Normans were at ease here in this hall barren of English pride.

Rich scents of roasted meat teased the air and empty bellies; Jane gazed resentfully at long tables set with lavish food and silver nefs. They thrived at Ravenshed because she husbanded their food supply carefully; a meager harvest could be ruinous. She always had enough food, and coin to buy more, yet the freedmen who owed her rents would suffer grievously if she forced them to pay. Taxes were too high, too frequent, on everything from bread to water to wood. Her coffers were slowly draining of coin.

Across the hall, Saxon barons stood uneasily in a loose group. Lords Oxton and Creighton looked tense; there was no sign of her cousin, who had undoubtedly been sensible enough to go home to Gedling. The sheriff's men milled about with casual deliberation. There was no overt threat, yet the air reeked of intimidation, evidenced by mailed guards bearing heavy weapons, discreetly stationed by the doors.

It was suddenly overwhelming. Giles was gone to fetch her wine; no one seemed to notice her now that the sheriff was absent. Jane rose from her seat before the fire with unhurried grace. Her shoes were almost dry; her cloak could be forsaken. Rushes crackled beneath her feet as she crossed the hall and left through iron-fortified double doors.

Icy rain had turned to snow, frosting stones and walls in white lace caps. The middle bailey was filled with the sheriff's men, black and gold livery stark against the paler sandstone and snowy curtain. Intent upon warmth, food, and rest, none gave her more than a second glance as she moved from the middle bailey through the gatehouse, then across the expanse of outer bailey and high barbican that guarded the outer moat and portcullis gate. She was free.

Nottingham closed around her when she quit the castle. Vendors had begun to close their stalls in Market Square. Her feet slid a bit on the steep grade leading from castle rock. Dark alleys staggered between the half-timbered buildings that hunched over streets softened by falling snow. The cold masked the strong stench of offal, human and animal, that usually clogged the air. She heard the Watch marching, boots crunching on icy mud as they patrolled the streets.

Shivering, she waited in the shadows behind a leaning alehouse until they passed, then made her way toward Goose

Gate. In resonant tones, the bells in St. Mary's tower tolled, marking Nones. Winter light was sparse and weak, disappearing rapidly in the waning of day.

She blew on her hands to warm them, regretting the loss of her mantle. Gedling was less than a mile past the town walls, but it would be a frigid walk once night fell. Her darkening mood suffered as much from bitter realization as from the cold.

Nothing had changed. Only drastic measures would save England from the king's rapacious demands . . . and from the new sheriff.

3

Gervaise Gaudet was waiting in the antechamber with barely concealed hostility when Tré entered. Light flickered over a fair man of medium height, richly garbed. The window was shuttered but the room was well lit, with several candle racks staggered at intervals along the walls. Carved chests squatted on each side of the door; a scarred table bore a flagon of wine and two silver cups. Gaudet stood beside the table, a cup in one hand, resentment simmering in his hot eyes.

Bone-deep weariness threatened, lapping at the edges of Tré's endurance. He ignored the sullen gaze and customary niceties:

"I am aware that you are the cousin of my unfortunate predecessor, Gaudet, so do not waste your time or mine with hostilities. The king saw fit to appoint me sheriff instead of you. It does not have to make us enemies."

"No?" An angry smile played on Gaudet's mouth. "Yet Eustace was not yet deposed from his position when you were appointed. A strange coincidence, perhaps."

"So it would seem." Tré watched him for a moment, the taut set of his jaw, the barely restrained hatred that vibrated the hand holding his wine, and recognized futility in more attempts at civility.

When the silence stretched ominously, Gaudet stirred. "If you think the Saxons will comply with your edicts, you are much mistaken. They will not do so willingly. My cousin found that out to his sorrow, when he attempted to force them to pay their lawful taxes."

"Eustace de Lowdham's error was in keeping the monies he collected, not in forcing reluctant barons to pay them. Surely blood kinship does not outweigh common sense so much that you do not recognize that."

Pale eyes narrowed to thin slits in Gaudet's fleshy face. He was not a tall man, but projected a sense of height and power due to his brawny frame. His chest swelled with anger as he spat, "A lie! Not only was he put to the trouble of bringing to heel the most defiant barons, but Eustace was beset by outlaws along the way. If you want to hold *your* position, you had best keep in mind that you cannot tender monies to the king that outlaws have stolen from you—"

"Your concern is touching, but you need not fear for me. I will deal most harshly with the outlaws."

"It is said that you harbor a hatred for outlaws—especially Saxon outlaws."

"Men who listen to gossip oft find themselves in dire misfortune when they repeat it."

It was said softly, with no inflection or particular emphasis, but his point was well taken. Gaudet grew silent.

Impatient now to conclude the first meeting with the Saxon barons, Tré turned toward the door. "We will discuss your duties later. Attend me tomorrow."

It was not an auspicious beginning to his tenure as sheriff. First the barons, now Gaudet. He would not be surprised if he was confronted by a scullery wench before the night ended.

In the hall, Saxon barons milled about with furtive glances and uneasy courage.

The lady has more mettle than do they, Tré mused. It was a trait that altered his first impression of her, for impassioned courage imbued average features with a rare beauty. Integrity made her dangerous. Lady Neville was a lively adversary, worthy of both caution and admiration.

His gaze roamed the crowded hall, but there was no sign of her by the fire or at the table. Hardly surprising, but definitely annoying.

"Where did she go, Giles?" His soft tone was deceptive, halting the passing steward in his tracks.

"I know not, my lord. When I returned with her wine, she was not by the fire. I did not think she would leave without her mantle."

"She left the garment behind?"

"She did, my lord."

"Fetch it. Then find Sir Guy and send him to me."

Giles departed hastily. Noise overwhelmed the hall, bouncing off high walls and the ceiling. The stench of unwashed bodies was oppressive. A smoky haze permeated clothes and stung the eyes. Tré moved toward the dais. Conversations died; he felt the speculative scrutiny as he maneuvered down the trough between tables.

They watch, furtive as rats in a granary, and as constant . . . enemies in all the shadows.

When he reached the dais he took his place behind the long, linen-covered table reserved for the high sheriff. The hall was quiet now, with only occasional laughter from the direction of the guard room. The Normans present were more at ease, but the English watched him with rapt intensity.

They wanted answers to questions when he had none for them. None they would want to hear. He resented the Saxons' carping and whining, their insistence on justice when all England lay groaning under the weight of John's heavy hand. How could he give them what he did not have himself?

The edge of the huge carved chair pressed into his legs and beckoned comfort, but he did not sit. Not yet. He waited as the silence grew complete and the barons nervous. Then he gestured, an expansive sweep of one arm that encompassed the entire hall.

"Answers are best sought on full stomachs, my lords. Do you be seated at my table."

Wary glances were exchanged. The smell of roast meat and honeyed sauces was tempting. He sat down as if it were any banquet; a sewer rushed forward bearing a silver ewer filled with scented water and a towel to dry his hands. It was a signal for dishes to be served.

No cloths draped the lower tables, but jugs of wine and cups were in good supply. The Normans did not hesitate, but found seats on the long benches flanking the tables, until only a few places were left. Finally the Saxons joined them, bunching at one side in a segregated group.

Tré leaned back against feathered bolsters that still bore the blue and silver of the former sheriff. It was his habit to eat sparingly. When he looked up from his trencher, Guy was weaving through the crowded hall to reach the dais and the chair next to him.

"There is dissent among the barons. They thrash about like rabid weasels." Guy folded his long frame into the stark wood that formed the smaller chair. "Or did you notice?"

"Your humor is misplaced." Tré indicated the hall with a tilt of his head. "All of Nottingham is a hornet's nest."

"Fill their cups again. Enough wine should give even dour Saxons a sense of humor."

"Enough wine may put the barons at ease."

"Nothing but the tomb can do that." Guy eyed him for a moment. "Where is the lady?"

"Gone. Fled into the night like a frightened hare."

Guy laughed softly. "You would frighten any woman, but I had not thought that one would be so easily terrorized."

Irritated, Tré did not reply. He scraped a thumb over the curved stem of his cup. It was plain, with simple lines that fit his hand, and he lifted it to drink.

Light from torches and branches of candles gleamed on Guy's pale hair as he lifted his cup, restless eyes peering over the brim. "It grows late, even for Saxons."

Tré set his cup on the table and stood up. Heads turned toward him and voices subsided into low mutters, then silenced in tense expectation.

"My lords," he said evenly, "my purpose in Nottingham is simple. King John has appointed me sheriff to guard his interests, and also the interests of Nottingham's citizens. I will do so. In return, you will supply me with men and arms for your king. By Easter."

Mistrust already reflected in the sullen faces of the Saxon barons swiftly altered to outrage. Tré's gaze fell on russet-haired Gilbert of Oxton. He said with deliberate emphasis:

"Bring your individual concerns to Guy de Beaufort, who sits at my right hand. He will have my scribe appoint a time to any man who wishes to express his discontent to me."

Oxton snapped, "It grows difficult to tell tax men from out-laws, save the color of their livery."

"Not so difficult," a companion retorted, "for outlaws leave us enough to eat, while the king's men do not!"

Dissension rumbled, growing louder; across the hall, Nor-man guards watched with wary readiness.

Tré spoke sharply: "You complain of outlaws that prey upon your lands. You plead for my aid to be rid of them. Why should I lend my arms to your cause, when you do not lend yours to mine?"

"You are the sheriff!" Oxton burst out. "It is your duty—"

"Exactly. As it is your duty to aid your king and your coun-try." Silence fell. He surveyed flushed, angry faces. "Aid me, and I will aid you."

When no one spoke, Tré indicated that the meal was over by beckoning the sewer to come forward with the ewer of scented water and a towel to dry his hands. It was the signal to clear the hall; the metallic clank of his guards' weapons con-vinced the barons that there was no more to do or say.

Sprawled indolently in the low-backed chair, Guy glanced up at him. Mockery lit his hazel eyes. "That went well."

"I fully expect Oxton to withhold taxes."

Guy tugged at the gold chain holding his dark blue mantle on his shoulders, then straightened in his chair to frown down the length of the near empty hall. "If he does, the others will join him."

"I expect that as well." Tré turned to leave the dais, but a sudden pain in his side jerked him to a halt. For a moment he could not draw a deep breath and was forced to take shallow gasps of air.

At once, Guy was solicitous, his deceptive indolence vanishing as he leaped up. "*Merde*! You are as white as a pall. . . .Has it broken open again? I will bring the surgeon."

"No." Breathing was difficult, tortured, the pain a fist that would not release him. Blindly, he put a hand on the back of the chair to maintain balance. "It will pass."

"The wound is not yet healed, and will likely kill you if you break it open again." Guy's voice was taut.

Tré sucked in air between his teeth; the pain began to ease, slowly, intermittent now. "Let it be. It will heal."

"Yet it has been over a month since you were able to wear even a hauberk." Low, intense: "Curse John for sending you here on the devil's business—"

"Guy." Softly, a warning reminder that ears were always attuned to treachery. It was enough.

Slowly, he released the back of the chair, ignored Guy's offer of a hand, and stood up straight. The pain receded. Even his body betrayed him, refusing to obey commands to heal.

More to disguise his infirmity from prying eyes than anything else, Tré stopped the young steward passing by the high table: "Giles, you have been remiss. Deliver to me the mantle the lady left earlier."

Giles paused, said, "I put it aside for you, my lord, as you were engaged in business. I will deliver it at once."

"A lady?" Guy studied him with open curiosity. "It is not like you to be so hasty in forming new friendships."

"Not *a* lady. Lady Neville of Ravenshed."

"Ah."

A wealth of innuendo lay in that one word, and Tré had no intention of allowing him to expand upon it. Giles returned with the mantle; a faint fragrance of mint wafted up from blue wool as Tré held it out to Guy.

"Keep it safe until it can be returned to the lady."

"Which you will do personally, of course."

"Of course."

4

May 1213

Jane followed a narrow track that was almost invisible, a dun-colored ribbon snaking through primeval wood where spring left scant sign of its arrival. Scattered buds of blue and yellow blossoms brightened the grasses but scorned graceful feathers of bracken; wind soughed in branches of gnarled, twisted trees with knotted faces older than time.

It was raining; but in Sherwood's depths, rain fell more softly. It was shadowed, silent, reeking of ancient specters. The heavy air was wet against her face, mist dripped from the woolen edges of the hood pulled over her head. Her hosen and jerkin were green—a whisper of color against surrounding shades of olive and umber that rendered her invisible.

Feet clad in laced buskins trod carefully, cushioned on aeons of forest debris; silence reigned king in the forest, a royal presence disapproving of interlopers.

Just ahead was the Cockpen Oak, where Fiskin waited for her. A vine snagged her foot, and she paused. In one hand she held a longbow, an unfamiliar weight now, when once it had been frequent. That was years before. Another lifetime. Another person. The maid she had been then had long since vanished. A childless widow remained, a score and seven years of age now, a veritable crone.

Her palm slid along the sleek length of the bow, idly testing. Five feet of Spanish yew, carved from the heart of a seasoned log and fashioned without joints; horn nocks clamped in place with a thin length of twisted flax permeated with beeswax, a resilient bowstring for arrows made of ash and fletched with goose feathers. Lovely, lethal, cherished as much for the giver as the gift; a trick of nature had lent her the talent to use it well.

The redolence of wet, chewed earth filled the air. Her breathing was soft, a faint haze in front of her face to dissipate in the mist. It was densely wooded beyond this track, quiet oblivion amidst tangled vines and creepers. The leafy, thick crown of the Cockpen Oak was barely visible; it presided over a small clearing near the Edwinstowe Road.

The fluty trill of a plover rent the air and propelled her forward. When she neared the massive girth of the Cockpen Oak, Fiskin grinned out at her from the deep cavity scoured by time and nature. She smiled.

" 'Tis a little late in the year for a plover. A jackdaw is the proper signal." Her criticism was no more dampening than the rain that failed to penetrate the lush bower of leaves that spread almost to the ground.

"Oh." Fiskin emerged from the oak. He brushed clinging leaves from his rough woolen jerkin. "But not so late this year, milady. Winter forage was scarce in the fields."

"Forage was scarce all over England." She gestured to the road with her longbow. "Do the others wait?"

"Yea, milady, in the verge along the Birklands road. The bracken there is high as a man's head already, for the trees are thinner and let in the light."

Tension tightened the muscles in her shoulders and down her back, knotted in her belly and knees. She bent a glance down the indicated track. Nothing moved, save shuddering leaves struck by rain.

Fiskin gazed wistfully at the bow she held; his eyes were dark blue, hair the color and texture of straw thatch, his frame slender as a sapling.

"I could shoot it, milady." He gestured to the bow. "If a gentlewoman can bend the yew . . ."

"No."

He let the eager hand drop to one side and tugged at his forelock in belated servitude. It was a gesture Jane disliked; a frown pleated her brow.

"There is no need for that, Fiskin. I merely meant that you could not draw it without tutoring. Today is not the time." She glanced down the empty road again. "Nor the place."

"Do they come, milady?"

"It is hoped they do. Now go. See to Will and the others, then return to Ravenshed."

He was swift, a fleet hare bolting down the road, heedless of the slick mud that turned ruts into mires. She was alone again, with only her thoughts for company.

Her footfalls were muffled on the grassy verge as she picked a path free of mud; the tree loomed in majesty, low branches stretching out twenty feet from the trunk on each side. A squirrel frisked along a branch as thick as a man's chest, its protest accompanied by a twitch of red tail.

She braced a hand on the fissured bark; it was cool and damp under her palm. A furring of powdery green residue grew where the trunk was wet. Peering inside the shadowed cavity that had so recently hidden Fiskin, she saw with pleasure that it was as large as it had seemed when she was a child.

Inside, she felt it close around her, a musty shroud of ancient patience, mocking the fleeting lives of men. She had come here with her uncle. So long ago now, the time and the man gone the way of all; a vision lost, a legend faded. There were still times she thought it but a dream.

Then she would remember—a scrap of conversation, a shaft of sunlight through dappled leaves, the winding of the horn—and she would know it had been true.

She knelt on one knee, her hands around the longbow, so cool beneath her palms. He had given it to her. The gift angered her mother; she had heard them later, when they thought she was asleep, their voices raised, one in protest and the other in defense. In the end, she had been allowed to keep the longbow, though she did not know what had been said to arrange such a miracle.

Braced with arms on her bent leg, she gazed out from the oak and waited. It was so hushed and still that she knew the moment he came; she heard the heavy step, and smiled. *I knew he would not fail me.*

Abrupt shadow obliterated the light from without. From the dark came a familiar voice: "Be ye in there, my lady?"

"Yea, John Lyttle, I am here. What of you?"

Soft laughter preceded the immense form that stooped, peered into the cocoon of bark and decay, then put a huge foot inside. The rest of him followed, agile for so large a man. Set into a face bearded with red-gold and marked by years were bright blue eyes and a wide grin.

"I never thought to see ye again in the belly of an oak."

She smiled, foolishly pleased to see him again, greatly relieved he had come. "It has been a long time."

"Aye. Too long. My bones ache with age." He shifted; legs encased in cross-gartered hosen and boots bent beneath him to lend more room inside the hollow. One hand scratched along his bearded jaw in the speculative habit she had forgotten. "Is this a fool's dream we ply?"

"No." She drew in a deep breath that smelled of damp wood. "It can be done."

Thick fingers stroked the beard that had sprinkles of gray amidst the red-gold. "Aye," he said at last, pensive and heavy, "if Robin were still with us. He is not."

"Will came. And Alan of the Dales. They brought others who weary of empty bellies and purses."

"I saw them." He grunted, boots shifting on the thick cushion of moss and deadfall inside the tree. He smelled of wet wool. " 'Tis dangerous, my lady."

"Yea, so it is. When did Little John begin to mewl an old man's complaints?"

"When I became one." He paused. "Or thought I would live long enough to see the prince become king."

"We are still here."

"Not all of us."

He did not have to say the name again; she knew it well, had heard it since infancy, loved it since she was old enough to follow the laughing woodsman who was uncle, earl—and the outlawed Robin Hood.

"No. Not all of us." She curled her hands more tightly around the sleek yew of her bow. "But enough of us. Here. Today. With the means at hand to thwart the sheriff."

"My lady—"

"Tax men come along the Birklands road. Four of them. Only four. There are ten of us."

"Nine." Resignation clenched his jaw. "If I stay, ye must go."

"You need my skill." She waggled the bow. "I will stay safely in here, but my arrows will fly. Even soldiers cannot endure a swift arrow through mail—and these are garbed as monks."

"Monks? Not soldiers?" John's brows knitted. "The new sheriff is either bold or witless."

"He thinks to disguise them, but Tuck sent word that these monks wear leather hauberks beneath their robes."

"And they travel through Sherwood." John shook his head doubtfully. "I had not thought Devaux foolish. Ruthless in seizing monies and men for the king's service, but not so foolish to send only four men through Sherwood laden with silver."

"You have been talking to Will."

"Aye, that I have. He said nothing about monks. He said soldiers. Normans. The sheriff's men and thus the king's as well. We would hang if caught."

"If caught." She put a hand on his arm. Taut muscle flexed beneath her fingers. "Children go hungry because the outlaws take what little the king leaves. If we take the sheriff's monies, he will pursue those outlaws at last."

"What will this serve? Killing the sheriff's men will only bring more Norman wrath upon the land."

"There will be no deaths. Not even Normans will defy the threat of a cloth-yard arrow. The tax monies will be yielded. When the sheriff returns from Canterbury, he will be reminded that the justice he speaks of can be a two-edged sword."

A brief image spun before her, of green eyes in a hard face, a competent hand upon her arm; she shivered.

"Desperation." Her voice sounded strange to her, as hollow

as the tree. She looked at John, saw comprehension in his gaze. "Will came to me in desperation and hope. I could not think what to do. This"—she curved a hand toward the road—"was all that made sense. The sheriff is absent from Nottingham to present the king with a muster of who has obeyed royal summons and who has not. Only a small garrison remains behind, too few to guard the tax men."

"I fear ye have allowed Will Scarlett to endanger more than empty fields with his notions of bravery. He ignores obvious perils, and prates of yesteryear." John heaved a great sigh; broad hands splayed on his bent knees, fingers curling into wool hosen. "I brought my bow. And my staff. But I will not use them until ye are gone from here."

"Am I not to meddle in men's business?" Her tone was taut as a bowstring, bitter with the memory of the sheriff's taunt. "Robin taught me well. I am capable."

"Aye, yet—hark now!"

Jane rose to stand in the high cavity of the oak. She was unprepared for the hissing *s-swwooosh* and solid *thunnnk* as an arrow found its mark in the ridged bark of the oak. John leaned out, a big hand closing on the vibrating shaft. Peacock feathers fanned from the slotted vane, wound fast with red twine.

"The time to flee is gone. They come." His glance was probing. "Be ware. Even four Normans can be deadly."

"I know." Her gaze shifted to the greenwood beyond the oak. "Will has planned carefully."

"I have suffered Will Scarlett's botched plans before, milady. Look to thy safety, and I will be at thy back."

He left her, ducking to leave the hollow, shoulders as wide as a bull's draped in Lincoln green. Stooping to lift his bow from where he'd propped it against a birch, he trotted across the clearing to a gloomy bower of shadows that swallowed him in a single step.

Jane settled into the hollow; she took up the bow and leaned into the yew to seat the bowstring. Fingers plucked it like a lute. It hummed softly. She extracted an arrow from her quiver and held it loosely.

Save for a fine mist, the rain had ceased. No wind stirred

leaves or fern or damp, heavy air. Beyond the oak, a faint shimmer of leaves betrayed waiting men armed with weapons her coin had purchased. The sound of hooves on mud drew closer. She slid the tip of her tongue along the ticklish feather fletching, then nocked the arrow and waited.

Expectation made her hands tremble; the blue steel of the bodkin arrowhead quivered.

Loose it easy, steady and yet sharp. Do not wink with one eye and look with the other. Stand as straight and firm as the oak. . . . Nay, draw not with the strength of the arm, but of the body, little Jaie. . . .

Robin was with her still, his remembered advice a familiar echo.

She smiled, reassured, and saw the first rider emerge from the leaves curtaining the Birklands road. A deep breath, reflexes directing her, she gripped the bow with her left hand, the arrow still loosely nocked and held with the first three fingers of her right hand.

Do not draw too soon, Jaie, or the arrow will not cast as it should.

Three more horsemen trailed the first; false monks with hoods pulled up passed beneath the dripping trees. Abruptly, a white-fletched arrow hummed in warning, digging into the mud in front of the first courser. The animal neighed, reared, plunged to one side.

Lay the body to the bow, Jaie—draw from thigh and hip as much as from the arm.

Jane brought up the bow, stood with left foot a bit ahead of her body's curve and the bow held vertically, while her right hand drew back the string and arrow until knuckles and goose-feathers grazed the angle of her jaw. An instant's pause before her fingers snapped free, then arrow left string in a sizzling hiss. It was a smooth motion with an imperceptible pause—tension released the moment the arrow was free. Five more followed swiftly, a shower of deadly ash to join the cloth-yard arrows being fired so quickly that there was scarce a pause in the loud humming until the monks were ringed by a prickly barrier.

"Leave the coffers and go in peace," came the demand from dense foliage—Will's voice, harsh and determined. "No harm will come to you."

Shadowed faces, skittish horses, and a flurry of brown-robed Normans milled in the newly barricaded road. Low debate was quickly followed by the unfastening of straps that held the coffer atop one of the horses; the sound of the chest landing in the middle of the rutted track was brittle and weighted.

"It is all we have." The voice was muffled by his cowl. "Do you steal from the church?"

Laughter, then: "Why not? Even the king steals from the church. And I have no patience with fat and gluttonous monks when my own belly gripes." Another arrow flew, singing into the grassy verge along the road. "Be on your way. The tithe has been paid for this day, Brother Monk."

Lowering the longbow, Jane expelled breath from her lungs in a disbelieving gust. The tax men turned their mounts in haste, spurring toward Edwinstowe. It had been far easier than she had dreamed. No fierce Norman resistance, and now the coffer lay abandoned. A veritable fortune, if Will was right; taxes from Welbeck Abbey and villages along the way to Nottingham, wrung from citizens already bled dry. Their return would be welcome.

She leaned against the misshapen arch of oak hollow and observed the road, empty of all save bristling arrows and Norman silver. In the silence a raven beat heavy wings and settled atop the stark horn of an oak that had been blasted by lightning. A shadow separated from the density and became distinct as Will Scarlett moved from the trees onto the road.

Caution marked his step, the bow held loosely in front of him, an arrow nocked for swift use. Nothing stirred, not even echoes from fleeing Normans. Will knelt beside the coffer. A heavy lock dangled from an iron clasp, clunking against wood and studded leather. He rattled it, cursed, and called for Little John.

"Lend thy great strength, ere we spend all day here."

"Bring it with us," Little John said, emerging from the wood to stand beside Will. "It can be opened later."

Will shot him a frown. "It is too clumsy and heavy to carry with us, and will be too obvious. We brought hemp sacks to bear the coin more easily. Can you not open this accurst strongbox?"

"Aye, move thy arse from my way, and I will see it done so we may be swiftly gone." As Will complied, John lay aside his bow and quarterstaff to kneel in the road. Iron and wood stoutly resisted even his impressive strength; his muscles strained and his face grew red with effort as he sought to pry open the hinges that held it fast shut.

Jane remained at a distance, while men she recognized came from the wood to lend their advice and might. A faint smile plied her lips. Alan's girth had thickened with the years, but he was still a comely man. Clym of the Clough knelt beside Little John, nudging aside William l'Cloudisely in his impatience to open the coffer.

Familiar companions; reminders of childhood days spent with Robin: trodding greenwood paths in her uncle's shadow, eager for his company despite her mother's despair at her rebellious daughter's bent for adventure, rather than mundane lessons that more befitted the only daughter of a Saxon knight.

Indulging reminiscence, she came lately to the sight of riders approaching. A ringing shout and the Normans were upon them, swords flashing death and vengeance in the gloom beneath the tangled trees. No mere four monks now, but a contingent of soldiers in full armor. Norman crossbows twanged with bolts quickly spent and useless. Peril lay more in the weight of horse and rider skilled in dealing mortal blows; lethal blades and hooves expertly cleaved a path among the scattering outlaws.

It was quickly done; some few escaped into the trees, while others were brought to heel with savage efficiency. Four lay motionless; crumpled green and pooling crimson in the road.

When it began, Jane had instinctively melded into the dark obscurity of the Cockpen Oak. Heart hammering and mouth dry as fuller's earth, she watched in horror. Fingers clutched futilely at a bow no longer practical. Save two, her arrows lay broken and splintered under iron-shod hooves.

A Norman horse danced, blurred black against green held

in check by a mailed hand. She recognized first the steed, then the rider, and foreboding turned her blood to ice: Tré Devaux. Not in Canterbury, nor even Nottingham, but here on the Edwinstowe Road to visit defeat upon their hopes.

Disaster. . . .

5

— 🌿 —

"Bind them." Still mounted, Tré regarded the bloodied men standing in the road impassively. Eager, agitated from the fray, his destrier sidled onto the grassy verge until curbed by a patient hand. Defiance stared back at him from the men being shackled. He smiled.

Deliberate Saxon English, mocking: "Let them walk to Nottingham. The sight will give the good citizens of the shire ample time to ponder the wisdom of outlawry."

One of them—a giant of a man with fair, shoulder-length hair—regarded him with baleful eyes. "The good citizens of the shire have had ample time to ponder Norman thievery. Be ware, lest ye meet them in Sherwood glades not yet infested with pet curs who heed the call of coin instead of honor."

"Honor? Strange word on the lips of a man so recently engaged in plunder. Heed thy own advice, Saxon."

It was enough to silence the brigand; blue eyes flashed chagrin, and the bearded jaw clenched. He radiated fettered power, evidenced by the quarterstaff splintered against a Norman helmet, shattering more than the wood. A broken pate was not the only injury inflicted on his men. Several of them bore smashed noses and snapped bones, surprising in that the struggle had been brief and overwhelmingly in Norman favor.

Most had fled or died; only these men had stayed behind, unyielding in the face of inevitable defeat. Three live outlaws, four dead—a good day's work.

Guy moved close, his mount fractious. "Shall we give chase to the rest?"

"Futile, in this wood. They have gone to ground like weasels. By this time, they are halfway to Cuckney."

"A village named for the king, I trow, as John makes it a habit to cuckold husbands."

The jest eased Tré's mood. In the distance a mutter of thunder promised more rain. As he nudged his mount toward a large tree across the road, he said over one shoulder, "They still hold a Horn Fair each October in honor of the king and the cuckolds."

Guy's laughter followed him. He dismounted beneath the spreading branches of the most massive tree he had yet seen, a leafy giant more worthy of the title than yon outlaw.

It would be a lengthy journey back when his bladder was full. There was much yet to do. His return from Canterbury was too recent for him to have tended to duties neglected in futile service to his king.

John. A blight on humanity. If nature had done its task properly, the king would have been stillborn.

He stepped to one side of the tree, lifted the edge of his tunic to unfasten the cords of his chausses. Boots sank into forest debris: leaves and twigs too swollen with damp to snap beneath his feet.

Relief from the pressure of his bladder was attended by pattering on leaves beyond the toes of his boots.

Two months had passed in Nottinghamshire, months of constant harrying and attendance to the king's demands for men and monies, resources torn from citizens already burdened by taxes and winter's depredations. Yet he was sworn to it. He had as little choice as they, though it would not be believed.

A slight sound to one side distracted him; he looked up from the business at hand to feel the cold press of steel against his bare throat. Instinct urged instant retaliation, but common sense intervened. He wore no mail coif, having donned the garb of a monk. His leather hauberk fit from neck to knee, hardly protection against a bodkin arrowhead in the throat.

Heedless of the danger and silent command, his bladder continued to empty.

Soft, faintly mocking, a hoarse demand issued from the shadowed depths of a hood: "Whilst I have no wish to disturb you, my lord sheriff, I must ask that you release my men."

He cleared his throat; steel moved with the spasm, then nudged a little harder so that his reply was constricted into a single, "No."

Harder now, steel against flesh. From one corner of his eye, he glimpsed hood and shadow. Beyond the arrow's length, deadly promise: "You *will*, ere you sport a new hole in your throat."

At last his bladder emptied. *Of all the positions and places to be in . . . .*

Freer now, he focused on the bowman's voice. The words were couched in gentle Saxon English, not the rougher tongue of peasants and outlaws. Soft tones. A Saxon youth of good family, perhaps, flushed with outrage against anything Norman.

Evenly: "Put down the bow, young master. Go quietly, and I will not offer hindrance or pursuit."

It was reasonable to expect his suggestion would be accepted; two dozen Norman soldiers and an accomplished knight were within fifty feet. Review of the situation would demand an intelligent concession, even from a Saxon youth.

Unbelievably, the bodkin dug more firmly into his skin until he felt it tear; warmth oozed down his neck. His jaw set. The youth was beyond his grasp. No man was swift enough to halt a loosed arrow.

"Call to them. Tell them to free the outlaws." Steady, insistent, oddly familiar, the voice from the hood drifted on the air currents between them. "I have nothing to lose by slaying you should you refuse."

It was true. Blood had been drawn. He had no intention now of allowing this insolent bowman to escape. Silent, immobile, he weighed his options. Flight from an arrow was impossible; it would transfix him before he could do more than turn. He had seen men pierced through heavy metal armor and leather, with no more resistance than wet bread. English bowmen were legendary for their effectiveness.

Even against mounted Norman knights.

"I expected better from a well-spoken Englishman," he said to gain time. He gauged distance and reach, plotted a swift turn and swerve to one side. . . .

A reminding nudge of the arrow. "I am not responsible for what you expected, my lord sheriff."

Coupled with the tone, recognition exploded in his brain. *It cannot be. . . .*

Yet the phrase was the same, well remembered these last two months, as was every word she had uttered his first night in Nottingham. But it was impossible. A knight's daughter—a Norman baron's widow—swathed in Lincoln green and determination, holding an arrow to his throat.

Then, irrationally: *I still have her mantle. . . .*

Carefully, he released fistfuls of wool so that his tunic covered groin and opened chausses. The bodkin prodded a bit harder.

"Time flies, my lord sheriff. As swift as an arrow."

A pointed reminder. The irony did not escape him. He decided then. Behind him he could hear Guy and the others, no doubt too involved in their own thoughts of victory and the promise of food and ale at journey's end to take notice that he had not yet rejoined them. If they glanced up, they would see the grazing destrier that blocked their view of him and his unexpected companion.

"Slacken the pressure so that I might call out," he said, and felt hesitation in the hooded figure. He knew she wondered if she could trust him. He could have told her she could not.

But he remained silent, and when at last she eased back slightly, he called to Guy, "Release the outlaws."

A sound of astonishment answered him, rife with disbelieving protest. "Did I hear you right?"

Like the crack of a whip: "You heard me give the order to release the outlaws. Do it without delay."

There was no debating that tone. It was one of command, learned from his father and a hundred other men used to power. It earned instant obedience, as he expected it to.

He waited. Aware of her beyond the arrow, he noticed now what he had been too chagrined to notice before: a faint teasing scent of mint drifting on the damp wind. It was familiar, too; marked in winter months when clothing and bodies reeked for want of washing. She had worn it then, a light fragrance that permeated her mantle as well. The garment hung on a pole in his private chambers, meant to be returned but the errand delayed in his pursuit of the king's business.

Perhaps it was time to return it.

Motionless, silent, he was aware of the freed outlaws in the road, their amazed laughter, then louder hoots when it was discerned that he had been accosted when emptying his bladder. No doubt it would be all over Nottinghamshire ere night fell that the sheriff pissed away his chance to hang the outlaws.

A twig snapped underfoot, surprisingly dry in the moist forest, and the bodkin left his throat. He did not move. He had no intention of trying to halt her flight.

Then they were gone, vanishing back into the greenwood whence they had come like so many shadows. Guy strode to him as he was retying the cords of his chausses.

"Merciful God, you must have good reason for letting them go free!"

Dryly: "Yes, I prefer only one hole in my throat."

An impatient hand waved the remark away as trivial. "We had them by the ballocks."

Hitching up the waist of his chausses, Tré said, "I was in a fairly similar situation. It was not to my liking."

Some of Guy's fury abated, and an unwilling grin widened his mouth. "This tale will be repeated, I fear."

"I am certain of it." He walked to his destrier, ran a light hand over the sleek hide, then mounted. "We may turn that to our advantage."

"Ah." Guy looked up at him with sudden comprehension. "I see. Before a sennight passes, all of Nottingham will know their names. The outlaws will not be able to resist letting it be known who escaped—or who held you at arrow's point."

"Perhaps." He nodded. "We may learn the names of the giant and the others, but I do not think we will hear the name of the boldest outlaw bandied about."

"No?" Guy followed as Tré nudged the stallion into a walk. "A modest fellow, is he. Unusual for an outlaw. They seem to prefer boasting of feats only imagined." He reached for his destrier and took up the reins. "I wager you are wrong. That outlaw will brag of his deed over the length and breadth of England ere long."

It was most unlikely.

As they started down the road back to Edwinstowe it began to rain, a downpour that turned the already muddy track into an impassable mire. Miserable, wet to the skin despite mail and tunics, the bedraggled Normans rode in disconsolate silence with their wounded and the coffer used as outlaws' bait.

Rain dripped from the visor of Guy's helmet. His eyes were a pale gleam behind the noseguard. "How do you intend to catch the outlaws again?"

"I think," Tré said softly, "that I shall let them come to us."

"A surrender?"

"Of sorts." He flexed his fingers to ease the throbbing ache in his hand, ignoring the rain streaming down his face. "First, we must return a lady's mantle."

6

Ravenshed Manor perched high on a rounded hill that over-looked fields stitched with stone fences and tall hedges. A line of trees formed a ridge on the horizon, lower than the manor and from a distance seeming a mere thicket.

A ribbon of road marked by ruts and time curved from the manor, winding past Ravenshed's estate toward the King's Great Way, an ancient Roman road swooping near straight as an arrow to Nottingham. It was a rare day; sunlight warmed sodden meadows and treetops—and reflected from domed helmets in the distance. Normans approached at a swift pace.

Fiskin saw them first. He raced to the kitchens behind the manor house shouting alarm at the top of his lungs. "Milady! Lady, they come!"

Jane looked up as he jerked to a halt just inside the kitchen door. Breathless and flushed, tunic awry and leather shoes covered with mud, he put her in mind of a dabchick.

"Who comes, Fiskin?"

But she knew. It was not unexpected. Her fingers tightened involuntarily on the sprig of dried mint in one hand; fine pieces powdered the table.

"Normans—and th-the sh-sheriff!"

She looked down, smoothed the scattered crumbs into a bowl, then brushed her palms together.

"Calm yourself, Fiskin. You have muck on your shoes. Dena will scold if you spread it on the floor she just swept clean."

She lifted another sprig of mint that was to be tucked into clothing and linen chests to deter moths and fleas; it was stiff, dried from the preceding summer, still fragrant.

"What shall we do, milady?" Staring at her, eyes wide in a pale face splotched with freckles, he waited for her answer.

"I shall greet them when they reach the manor, but I do not intend to fly down the road like a goose girl. Do you go and fetch Enid to the kitchen. She should come and be with her mother."

Still outwardly calm, she left the kitchen and stepped out into the courtyard. Light spread pleasantly over stones and walkways; it pricked her eyes. *I should be garbed more properly, as befits a lady of the manor.*

It would not matter. What did a condemned gentlewoman wear on the way to her execution? A clean kirtle and linen coif would be required, perhaps. A coif—she put a hand to her head, fingers grazing loose hair. Absence of appropriate headgear was becoming an evil habit; she tucked the mint she still held into her frayed plait, then smoothed her hands down the soiled front of her bliaut. No time to change into a clean cotte. She would meet her doom in garments stained with evidence of housewifery—an irony that her mother would surely have appreciated. . . .

She held tightly to her composure. Her safety—if there was any—lay in her rank. And deception. It would never do to betray any hint of guilt. There lay destruction.

Yet it was much easier to plan than to achieve. When Devaux dismounted in front of the fieldstone manor house, her trembling legs threatened to deposit her in a heap on her own threshold.

He cannot know . . . he cannot know.

Hands folded calmly in front of her, she waited in the open doorway of her hall as he approached. A barrier, polite but not welcoming.

Dark features betrayed nothing; bare of helm, in black tunic and chausses, he emanated power and purpose. He moved easily, long strides eating up the few yards until he stood before the shallow steps leading into the house.

"Greetings, my lord sheriff." Coolly civil despite the flutter of fear that rattled her tongue: "To what do we owe this honor?"

He rested one foot casually on the bottom step and looked up at her. She had a brief impression of intense green beneath black brows.

"Your mantle."

She stared at him blankly. He gestured; a tall, blond Norman stepped forward with a hooded cloak draped over one arm. In the courtyard behind them, a dozen men garbed in the sheriff's black and gold livery began to dismount and walk their horses to the shallow trough of water beside the well. Hooves clattered loudly on cobbled stones. Fitful sunlight bounced off helmets, chainmail, and intimidating weapons, but failed to define eyes glinting behind helmet noseguards.

Her gaze shifted back to the length of dark blue wool that dangled from the blond Norman's arm.

"Oh," she said in sudden recognition, "yes. My mantle. How kind of you to come this far to bring it to me."

"I did not come this far to be kind."

The blunt words heightened her fears, but she merely smiled and lifted a brow. "I see. Whatever your reason, my lord, I am pleased to have my mantle returned."

She held out a hand for it. The blond Norman hesitated, then at a gesture from Devaux relinquished it to her with a faint smile. He had a pleasant countenance. Pale hair longer than the norm brushed against mailed shoulders to frame his face; unobstructed by helmet or heavy nasal, hazel eyes were direct and humorous. He briefly met her gaze, curiosity a muted gleam in his eyes.

"Your servant, milady."

Devaux shifted position, one foot moving to the shallower step of the threshold. His boots shone dully. "I would speak with you, my lady. In private."

Her heart thundered, but the smile on her lips did not waver as she shook her head. "I am afraid you have caught me at a most inconvenient time, my lord sheriff. My household is not prepared to offer hospitality to such an esteemed guest, and—"

"Lady Neville, you misunderstand me. This is not a polite request for the pleasure of your company."

He left her no option. With as much calm as she could, she said, "Grant pardon, my lord. I was unaware you had come on such an errand."

He did not reply; no indication of why he had come eased her apprehension. Fully aware that he was close behind her, she went into the house. When her eyes adjusted to the change from light to soft shadow, she saw Dena staring at her from a doorway, her eyes wide and frightened. Calmly, she directed, "Dena, bring us refreshment."

"Aye, milady." Dena's scared gaze flicked to the tall Norman and away again. Age and generous weight made her awkward; she dipped toward the sheriff in the slightest of curtsies and turned stiffly away.

Devaux was silent, all loose-limbed grace and resolve. The knot in Jane's belly grew tighter; she drew in a deep breath for courage as they entered the hall.

Lime-whitened plaster walls were washed with ocher light that fell through latticed windows; timber posts formed a double line down the middle of the hall to support the ceiling. A new stone fireplace filled one wall, drawing smoke up the chimney with wonderful efficiency.

She heard him behind her, his feet crackling on clean rushes. She *felt* him behind her. A presence, silent but seeming to fill the empty hall; he intimidated her. She curled her hands into fists at her sides. If he had come to arrest her, she was powerless.

When she turned around, Devaux was frighteningly close. The light that streamed in through the windows in irregular squares left his face in shadow.

"You smell of mint, milady."

It was unexpected; mundane and harmless. At a loss, she fumbled for a reply that would not sound inane or guarded.

When nothing came to mind and the silence stretched, one corner of his mouth tucked slightly inward. Not a smile, but an acknowledgment, perhaps, of her disconcerted state.

A little awkwardly, she put a hand to her throat; her fingers grazed the small, smooth globes of the prayer beads she had put on that morning. Cool stones that signified an appeal for redemption; unanswered pleas in pretty futility around her neck.

Devaux watched her. The silence was unbearable now. Words crowded her head, clogged her throat with misery and fear. *He knows.*

How? What had betrayed her?

She wanted to speak, to pierce the heavy stillness with her defense. Still, no words would come; her tongue was weighted with guilt.

Not guilt for the attempted robbery—but for the result. Four men had died. Even with her eyes wide open she could see them lying in the road, green jerkins soaked with blood. *Perrin, Oswald, Adam, Wace.* Names put to men to be mourned. Brave men all.

While she had fled with John, Will, and Alan—fading into the greenwood and abandoning the dead—their souls had gone prayerless into eternity. Yes, guilt weighed heavily, rendering her incapable of coherent thought.

"Are you praying, milady?"

Startled, she shook her head. "Nay, I do not."

"No?" He reached out; his hand curved around hers where she held the beads, lifting her fisted penance. "These are prayer beads, are they not?"

"Yes, of course they are."

"For what do you pray, milady? Deliverance? Temperance? Patience?"

The back of his hand brushed over the bare skin above the edge of her bliaut. He held her hand still, engulfing it in brown, corded tendons and capable determination.

"I pray for tolerance, my lord."

"Ah. Tolerance. A noble prayer. Not"— he drew a finger along the curve of her cheek— "unsurprising in a woman of your character."

She strove for insouciance to hide the reaction his caress provoked: "It would intrigue me to hear what would surprise you, sir."

A step back; his hand fell away, and she could breathe again.

"It would not take long in the telling. There is little that surprises me now." He paused. Swooped in with deceiving simplicity: "Save the folly of outlaws."

There it was: Accusation. Arrest. Execution.

The inevitability made her desperate. She felt shaky. In a faint voice, she said, "Time wanes, my lord."

"So it does. Time flies—swift as an arrow." He closed the gap between them, palming the dangling end of her prayer beads. His voice was a soft, ruthless reminder. "Four men were killed on the Edwinstowe Road yesterday. Outlaws, all."

"Do you wish me to pray for their souls, my lord? Or did you purchase prayers at Saint Mary's for them."

Too close, too close . . . I cannot breathe with his hand against me.

"Outlaw souls do not concern me." His eyes burned into her, an intensity that compelled her to look at him though she tried to resist. A muscle leaped in his jaw; his voice was taut. "I have more tangible concerns. Three men escaped my custody yesterday. I want them."

I want them. A simple, *I want them.* He expected compliance. He expected her to deliver them.

"Perhaps they will surrender, my lord," she said when she could trust her voice not to crack.

"I rather think they will." A tug on the beads to bring her closer, escalating heartbeat like thunder in her ears, and— "You may convince them of it."

He waited. Expectant again, certain he would hear her agreement.

She was outraged.

The lassitude that had gripped her vanished. Renewed by fury, she saw from the sudden thinning of his eyes that he knew it, too.

"Release me, my lord sheriff." Her voice lashed him, and to her surprise, his hand opened to free the beads.

"Beware a hasty tongue," he said then, calmly, the only sign of displeasure his narrowed eyes.

"My tongue is rarely hasty. Sharp at times, perhaps, but some find the truth unpalatable. So it is now—I will not convince anyone to surrender to you, nor to any Norman, for I would never be able to wash the blood from my hands."

"And have you tried washing them today, milady?" Soft reminder, brutal in its way, and she steeled herself.

"Say plainly what you mean. Do you have proof of guilt? Have you come to arrest me?"

Strangely placid, she waited for his affirmation. It did not come. He stared at her, and a faint smile played at the corners of his mouth.

At last he said, "No, I think not."

7

Tré watched emotions flicker across her face. It would avail him little if he arrested her. He had hoped she would be more . . . amenable. She was not. The disquiet and dread that first attended her had vanished, replaced by stubborn anger. Determined rebellion.

It was faintly surprising to discover a facet of his character he had never suspected: He admired a female with courage enough to defy him. Not foolish defiance that would gain nothing, but calm, intelligent disregard for consequence that defined great strength of character. It was a trait he had found more in men than in a woman; had *never* found in a woman, he amended.

Yet even that was not the reason he did not intend to arrest her. She was still useful. She knew the outlaws. More important—the outlaws knew her. There would come a time when outlaws and lady would meet again; he would not be forced to spend wearying days in the saddle searching forest and field for sign of them when they were bound to save him the bother by drawing near the lady. Moths to a flame. . . .

He saw her wary relief and smiled. "You are a baron's wife, my lady—a Norman's widow. There would be an outcry from here to London were I to arrest you. Saxons claim you as their own, and Normans are fiercely protective of their rights."

It was true. Alone, that would not have saved her from retribution. Yet, he needed her; a lure to be used in much the same manner as the coffer had been, only more precious for her vulnerability. If the outlaws did not rise to that bait from fear, they would come for loyalty. But he would save that tactic for last, if all else failed.

Easy enough, to send out patrols across the shire in a conspicuous effort to snare the outlaws, while all the time the lady would be watched. He would set men to hide in the surrounding wood, spies to report a lady's treachery. A pity that she was faithless.

For she was lovely, this lady of Ravenshed, a realization just remembered. Not, perhaps, in the conventional sense: no mane of blond hair that was so highly prized, no haughty pride to render a swain hopeless with despair. But he had never been a man who admired such things. He left that to the poets and minstrels, the knights of song and leisure. It was not for him.

For him, perhaps, the understated elegance of this lady who now gazed at him with dignity and courage. A lady with eyes of intense blue below delicate winged brows, light brown hair a shimmering loose drape around a face of ivory character. Pristine. Sculpted by a master hand. Clean of line and uncluttered with the excesses of life. Yea, a rare beauty; a treasure; worthy of love were he so inclined.

But he was not. He had made the mistake of loving too well, and it had nearly destroyed him. Not the love, but the loss of it . . . the end of a life that had set him on this path to destruction, to the ruin of all he had once prized. It was not an error he intended to make again.

Yet it did not keep him from wanting this lady—if not for love, for pleasure. She had lingered in his thoughts; a fleeting memory to intrude at odd times, a swift vision of curving cheek, smooth brow, lips a soft rose color that drew his mind to sweet diversion.

As now.

Inconvenient lust, importuning and impudent, rising to

unsettle him. He wondered if she recalled the details of their last meeting, when he had stood with lifted tunic and she had held a barbed arrow at his throat. Few things left a man feeling more exposed, chagrined.

A sound beyond Lady Neville snared his attention, and the servant hove into view, a silver tray held carefully before her.

Jane turned, something like relief briefly crossing her face as she beckoned the woman forward.

"Dena, place it on the table. And bring a knife for the cheese, as I have left mine in the kitchens."

"Weaponless, my lady?" His mockery drew her attention again, as he intended. "I feel much safer now."

"That would be a grave mistake, my lord. Wine?"

He flicked a glance to the cup she lifted. Lightly: "Is it safe, or should I have a taster drink first?"

Deliberately, she put the cup to her lips and sipped. His gaze shifted to her mouth; a glimpse of good teeth, white and straight, save for one that was slightly crooked. The imperfection was somehow endearing, even more alluring. His body responded with a swift, aching erection.

She gazed at him over the rim of the cup, then held it out. Wine beaded her lips, ruby against rose, wet and gleaming with temptation.

He took the cup when he wanted to take her in its stead, and held it in one hand, ignoring the fierce surge of lust that rocked him. Necessary restraint, learned in years of deprivation; a benediction and a curse.

Her gaze was expectant, a bit curious. He sought, then found, the thread of conversation.

"Should I summon your servant if you fall to the floor in a frothing swoon, milady?"

"That only happens when the poison is particularly virulent." She paused. "Or when the wine is sour."

An attempt at levity, hard-won from the look of strain in her eyes. He rewarded it with another smile, this one more sincere. A sip of wine, then two, and he gazed at her over the cup's silver rim as she held her own cup in both hands, long, well-shaped fingers curved around the bowl to hold it steady. He wanted to see her drink again, the lips to part, a glimpse into forbidden territory. He wanted it fiercely.

"Sweet," he murmured, and when her brow lifted: "as new wine should be."

She pressed the cup to her mouth; lips parted on silver to drink daintily. Her throat worked, creamy skin tantalizing above the square neck of her bliaut.

"What will you do, my lord?"

Pleasant reflection vanished at her words, bringing him back to the reason he was there. The brief interlude was over.

"Arrest the outlaws when I find them. And I will find them." Another sip of wine, a delay while she absorbed that, then a casual shrug of one shoulder. "It is inevitable. I have been charged with their apprehension by the king. I will do my duty."

Her tongue lapped at a drop of wine shimmering on the cup rim, riveting his attention. Distracted, it took him a moment to digest her comment: "It was told to me that you are not in the king's good graces, my lord."

"Doubtless," he said, watching her mouth while heat pooled in his groin, "you have been ill advised."

"Yet you have lands in the north. An estate of your own. You are a baron in your own right. The office of sheriff cannot avail you more than do rents from freedmen and vassals. Unless you are as the others, of course, enriching your own coffers at the expense of citizens and the king."

"That," said Tré softly, "would be dangerous as well as foolish to suggest. I am amazed at your temerity."

"And I yours, my lord." A flush pinked her cheeks, made her eyes bright. "You visit evil acts on men of your own rank, and exhibit no shame or remorse. I should not have been surprised that you would do worse to those of lesser rank."

He recognized the tactic for what it was, a diversion from the topic of outlaws. "Of late, my lady, I am among those of lesser rank. My lands are at the king's discretion, as are all of our lands. You would do well to remember that ere you find yourself in like straits."

"Then it is true." She studied him with wide eyes, as blue

and shadowed as woodland pools. "The king dispossessed you."

"Let us say that he is merely safeguarding my estates until my business in Nottinghamshire is done." His tight hold on the stem of the silver cup loosened, and he moved to set it on the table. His fingers were cramped, and he flexed them. "I intend to conclude that business as swiftly as possible."

Harder now, an edge to his tone, he turned and said, "My patience has its limits, as does my generosity. I freed the outlaws. If they surrender to me, they will be shown mercy."

"It was not generosity that freed those men," she said, "but the point of an arrow at your throat. I daresay your version of the tale differs from the other being told."

"It may." A tight smile felt frozen on his lips. He still wanted her. Contention did not ease the need, nor did her impudent reminder of his position. Situations changed: One day he would be liberated from the hateful bonds of service he performed for the king. He was a patient man because he had to be, not because he chose to be.

"Are you through baiting me, milady?" he asked when she fell silent. She did not answer, and he smiled. "I have set my men to a search of your estate. For tax assessment, of course. Do me the honor of escorting me outside."

Outrage was plain on her face, and he did not blame her. It was an outrage to be so misused. No more so, however, than the outrage of having a bodkin tip leave blood on his throat while desperate men were set free to rob and kill again. Not for the first time, he wondered if she was as adept with the longbow as she was with her contempt for the law.

He put a hand on her arm to guide her; her spine was rigid as they crossed the hall. At last, the ache in his groin eased.

They passed the servant, Dena, who had returned with the cheese knife and looked after them apprehensively as they went out to the courtyard. It was bright after the shadowy gloom of the manor house, and he squinted. A glance found Guy lounging against a low wall that enclosed a small garden.

A slight shake of blond head and a shrug; no outlaws had been found there. But he had not really expected it.

"I have made inquiries, my lady," he said, and put out a solicitous hand when she stumbled on a loose cobble. "Your late husband left the largest estate to a cousin also named Hugh. These lands were left to you to be held in security against the crown. If you do not remarry, the church receives your dowry grant while you retain dower rights."

"I am well aware of the terms of Hugh's will." Coldly; a distinct chill replaced her heated passion of earlier. "I cannot see where it is a concern of yours."

"Ah, but it is. It occurred to me that you may be in dire need, thus explaining why one might feel compelled to— thievery."

A deeply drawn breath was audible. She turned to face him with her back to the stone manor house, a gracious abode and a refuge.

"If you have proof of my complicity with outlaws, arrest me."

"Jésu, these challenges. Did I accuse you?"

"With all but the words."

Bold lady, bold enough to lie in wait in the greenwood. His first impression of her had not been altered by this knowledge of her duplicity. There was a bit of larceny in every soul, whether it was admitted to or not. Integrity was defined by a personal code of ethics.

Still, it was gratifying to think her goal was not more personal gain but a desire to lend misguided aid to those she deemed needy of it. A glance at the manor house proved minor neglect but not need. A husband's hand would set all aright in short order.

He frowned, and she mistook it for his response to her claim.

"Do you deny it, my lord?"

A moment's recollection of her earlier remark, and he said, "Of course I do. If I had proof to arrest you, I would have done so." A lie; necessary, but with this woman, strangely awkward on his tongue. Did honesty beget honesty?

A dog barked and a harsh Norman command silenced it; her gaze flickered toward the soldiers waiting just out of hearing. He was not above intimidation. If it gained him his ends he used it.

"Then. . . ." Uncertain hope in her voice.

"Then you have been warned of outlaws nearby. If any are seen, send a messenger to Nottingham ere you find your household suspect." He paused to allow the silent threat to sink in, and saw from the sudden light in eyes quickly veiled by her lashes that he had succeeded.

"If any are seen, my lord, I will send a messenger."

Nodding, his gaze drifted again to the manor house. Sunlight picked out a loose shutter, a few broken cobblestones in the walled courtyard, overgrown shrubbery. Clouds of ivy swarmed up walls to the thatched roof and cascaded over the front door. At one side, gardens were laid out in neat squares and bisected with paving stones; fronds of mint, basil, sweet fennel, and pennyroyal waved in a light breeze.

A faint fragrance wafted toward him: fresh mint from the lady. He breathed deeply. The sunshine was warm against his face, welcome. A relief after days of rain and grayness that made his hands stiffen and his injured side ache.

He flexed his fingers, idly, letting the moment drag on too long. It was pleasant just standing in the sunlight; it was rare leisure. The domestic sounds of chickens and sheep were a low murmur, the sweet scent of mint and woman close and oddly soothing.

"Warm tallow will ease the stiffness, my lord."

Wary, surprised, he looked at her. "Tallow?"

"I have used it before. It is an old remedy. Dip your hands into a pot of warm candle tallow—not too hot. Leave them only a moment. When they are cool, peel away the tallow and your hands will be eased of stiffness."

"Will they?"

Caught, lured by the sunlight and an unfamiliar sense of domestic tranquillity, he took her hand in his, heard her soft, drawn breath as he scraped his thumb over the hill of her palm. Long fingers, shaped nails; slight traces of rough skin lent evidence of their use. He thought of the strength it took to bend a longbow, of these hands fitting arrow to string, and smiled.

"Deceptive . . . soft hands. Unlikely that they have known much stiffness, milady."

It was acutely humbling. Her hand lay like a white dove in

his dark palm; calluses roughened his skin, earned in years of wielding a sword. Not for him the purchased spurs and title of knight, he had been knighted in battle at twenty; in the thirteen years since there had been few days without a weapon in his hands.

"My husband . . . Hugh. His hands often ached."

His thumb pressed into her skin. He thought of her wed; remembered words of grief for her husband. A year since he had died? He tried to summon a clear memory of Hugh de Neville and failed. He had known him well by reputation, met him on occasion, a long time ago.

But he would remember Hugh's widow . . . had remembered a dozen things about her after having seen her but that one day in Nottingham.

Mint teased him; he would never smell it again without thinking of her.

He still held her hand in his. Exerting slight pressure to pull her forward, he was inexplicably drawn to touch her hair, her brow; his bent fingers skimmed the curve of a cheek as soft as a rose petal. She did not pull away.

Brown lashes quivered over deep, blue eyes; her lips parted slightly.

He lifted her hand to his mouth, a courtly gesture that was seductively potent with this woman. Lips grazed the back of her fingers; he heard a soft inhalation and turned her hand over. The pads of her thumb and fingers were raw; unaccustomed to the snap of a bowstring, perhaps. There was a blister in the cup of her palm. His eyes lifted to her face, caught the fleeting shadow of guilt. Deliberately, he pressed his mouth to her palm while he held her gaze.

The smell of mint filled his nose, mouth, and lingered. Working lower, his lips found fragile blue veins beneath the pale skin on her wrist. The sleeve of her bliaut brushed against his jaw. He imagined her naked beneath him, ivory skin lush and warm beneath his hand. His thumb tested her wrist, leaving a red mark.

He watched it fade, a faint flower. Anticipation rose, ached; the hunger was back, stronger this time, scalding. If he allowed it, she would destroy him.

Abruptly, he released her hand.

A desultory breeze curled a strand of ash-brown hair over her face to tangle in her lashes. Her hand lifted to brush it aside, a graceful movement of arm and wrist that was both eloquent and dangerous.

A dog barked again, and the shouts of Normans and Saxons mingled. Welcomed distraction, shattered expectation, and the thread of tension snapped, freeing him.

He drew a deep breath, said merely, "My lady," and turned on his heel.

Long strides took him to his horse, and he mounted while his men scrambled hastily to their steeds. In a loud clatter of iron-shod hooves on stone, they left Ravenshed Manor, passing Lady Neville where she still stood motionless and wide-eyed in the courtyard.

Once through the arched gate and over the wooden bridge that stretched across a narrow moat, he turned his mount toward Nottingham with grim resignation. He had come to chasten, and returned chastened. It was a moment he did not care to repeat.

8

— ❧ —

When they reached the wider road of the King's Great Way, they settled into a steady pace that would quickly traverse the near twelve miles to Nottingham. For a time they rode in silence, broken only by the muffled smack of hooves on still-wet ground.

Guy nudged his bay mount into a less jarring gait that brought him alongside Tré's huge black. "Ravenshed is a fine manor. Prosperous, I would think."

A negligent shrug and disinterested reply: "True. The tariffs are ample."

Gnawed by curiosity, Guy cast about for another topic that might draw an explanation of the day's work. "There was no sign of outlaws. We searched so well, I was near done in by a furious rooster and an irate sow. Even poked haycocks with our swords, to no avail. What did you learn from the lady?"

"I did not go there to learn anything from her. It was a warning."

Guy fell silent again. He waited until they had drawn ahead of the others to say, "Can you be certain it was Lady Neville who held you at arrow point? She does not look to have strength to draw a hundred-weight, though I do not doubt she has the mettle."

"The lady," said Tré with a quirk of his mouth, "can be deceptive." He paused. "Perhaps a sixty-weight bow would be more suited to her."

Guy laughed softly. It was difficult to envision the elegant lady drawing a bow of any kind. A good bowman drew a hundred-weight easily, but only after years of practice. Could a slender woman manage it?

But he said none of that. It would avail him nothing but an ironic arch of brow or a caustic comment, and he could do without both. It was a pleasant day, with rare sunshine pushing back the gray that usually washed the English skies. He would have preferred a leisurely perusal of female charms to a fruitless ride.

Yet, he had seen Tré Devaux kiss Lady Neville's hand, and that was worth something. If he pondered for hours, he would not be able to recall the last time he had seen the Baron of Brayeton be so politic as to kiss a lady's hand. Any lady's hand. It was not a gesture that came easily to Devaux.

Most of his dealings with women were conducted with impatience or disdain or both; Tré took a woman when he needed one, but it was casual. Gone were laughter and any hint of softness, melded now into a nature that took necessary risks with his life—and none with his emotions. It was hard to equate the man he had known with the man he knew now: a man who would not name his horse or dog because he might lose them. Tré Devaux closed himself in—and everyone else out.

They paused near Papplewick when one of the soldiers complained that his horse was lame, halting by a decent-size cottage planted by the roadside. A small grove of trees beckoned with shade and respite. While a rock was dislodged from an iron-shod hoof, others dismounted to dip a ladle into a bucket of water. Beyond the simple dwelling, cattle grazed or chewed the cud in a broad field; a dog barked lazily for a moment, then wandered away in disappointment when they paid it no attention.

The yeoman owner of the house came out to greet them respectfully, if a bit nervously.

"I have fresh milk, my lord sheriff," he offered in Saxon English, "if you are so inclined."

While Tré declined, Guy accepted eagerly and followed the farmer to a small shed. Chickens pecked the dirt clean of insects, clucking irritation when they were interrupted by the intruders. A young maid with a grain pan in her arms stood in barefoot silence among the fowl, staring at the Normans with as much awe as fright.

It was a household scene similar to that at Lady Neville's, but on a smaller scale. No sprawling demesne with moat and walls, but a small parcel with thatch-roofed huts strung in a haphazard circle like broken paternoster beads.

Guy took his time, sipping sweet milk from a wooden cup, idly reflecting on the country charms of the blushing maid with flaxen curls and a fresh face. A soft breeze blew, carrying a blend of strong scents on the currents: cattle, grass, sweetly cloying blossoms scattered on apple branches. Smoke from the house lent a sharper tang to the air.

Childish voices broke into his reverie, and he glanced up.

Two young boys played nearby, clad in rough tunics and smeared dirt, whacking at each other with sticks obviously meant to be swords. Guy smiled. He recalled doing the same when he was young, before he reached seven and was sent to foster in the same castle where Tré Devaux had been sent. It could have been they, twenty-five years before, when life had still been new and England enjoying relative peace under Henry II.

"No," one of the lads was complaining, "I always have to be Norman! 'Tis my turn to—"

"Ye do not know the bow well enough, Wat," the other interrupted. He held up a small, crude bow and slender sticks that Guy supposed were meant as arrows. "Ye have to be the best to be Robin Hood."

"But I weary of being the sheriff!" Truculent, hands on hips and wooden sword still clutched in his fist, the lad stuck out his jaw. "Robin always slays him. I want to be Robin Hood this time. Robin is noble and brave, the most famous outlaw ever. All know the Sheriff of Nottingham is treacherous, no braver than a mouse. . . ."

In tandem, the maid and her father turned to the boys, both voices urgently bidding them quiet. The lads glanced up, round faces reflecting their sudden fear when they saw Guy. The boys dropped their wooden swords. Guy looked around, though he knew who was behind him.

"I will have a cup of milk, yeoman," Tré said calmly. When it was held out to him with a trembling hand that spilled creamy white over fingers, he lifted a brow. "Your sons play at interesting games."

"My lord sheriff . . . they are children who know no better than to repeat such false tales."

"So it seems. I stand here very much alive."

"Before God, my lord sheriff, it was not you they meant but a former sheriff. 'Twas years ago, when King John was still prince . . . only a legend, after all. A tale—"

"A tale of a famous outlaw who slays the sheriff?"

Tré angled a brow skeptically; Guy recognized the glint in his eyes.

"Famous, yet I have never heard of him. Unless—would he be a large man, taller than any other? Broad of chest and light of hair, and handy with a quarterstaff?"

"Nay, my lord sheriff, that would be Little John. He is—or was—one of Robin's men. But only tales, my lord. Do not blame my lads for being children. They play, 'tis all, a simple game."

Tré sipped milk from the cup. "A simple game for children, yes, but there are those who would play it in a more dangerous fashion. A coin for your milk, yeoman."

A shaky hand accepted the coin, but a look of strain marked the creased face that watched them turn to leave. Guy felt it, saw fear in the maid's eyes as well, and was bemused.

"A child's game," he said to Tré as they returned to the horses, "What manner of game boasts an outlaw victor over a sheriff?"

Tré turned to one of the guards. "Oliver, have you heard of an outlaw named Robin Hood? Or one called Little John?"

George Oliver, captain of the guard, nodded. "Aye, my lord, that I have. Heard of both of them, though it has been a while since any have seen Robin Hood. Some say he is dead, and others—"

"Others say what?" Tré prompted when Oliver fell abruptly silent.

"Others," Oliver finished, "say that he is only biding his time until it is right to return."

"Return . . . as an outlaw?"

"My lord, it is a tale. I heard it as a youth, though I never saw Robin Hood, nor even Little John." He paused. Doubt shadowed the honest face and intelligent eyes. "I will say that if ever I was to mark a man as Little John, it would be the giant we took prisoner at the Cockpen Oak."

When they were mounted, Oliver rode close again. "My lord, it came to me that the one to ask would be Lady Neville."

"Lady Neville?"

"Aye, my lord sheriff. She would know the truth."

"What *truths* would those be if these are just tales for the credulous, Captain Oliver?"

Guy recognized conflict in Oliver's face before he said bluntly, "It was not mere tales that slew Guy of Gisbourne, and Hugh Bardulf, who was then high sheriff, my lord. 'Twas fifteen years ago or more, but I can remember other tales as well. Lady Neville knows the truth."

"Why would Lady Neville know the truth?"

"She is Robin Hood's niece."

Ominous silence descended; opaque eyes regarded Oliver impassively. "Then I shall ask the truth of her."

Captain Oliver nodded and turned his mount back to ride with the guard. A muscle leaped in Tré's jaw, betraying tension. Guy studied him cautiously.

"The lady may know the truth, but will she tell us?"

"She will tell it." Tré nudged his steed to a faster pace; hooves sent soft dirt spraying behind him in a wide arc. "She dare not refuse me."

As they neared Nottingham, they passed several off-duty soldiers gathered in Rock Yard at the foot of the castle rock, drinking new March ale from the brewhouse and tossing dice. Most wore the livery of the high sheriff, but sprinkled among them were the scarlet and yellow surcoats of Gaudet's livery. This was neutral ground; though the land belonged to the castle, land rights belonged to the Priory of Lenton.

Out of habit, Guy swept an assessing glance over those gathered in front of the inn built into the rock. A monk in the

company of one of Gaudet's men exited beneath the sign pro-
claiming it to be The Pilgrim. Wary resentment flashed at the
mounted Normans; hardly a surprise coming from a Saxon, or
from the monk, in light of the king's persecution of the church.

When they had scrabbled up the steep hill that led to the
castle and passed through the gatehouse, Guy broke the long
silence. "Do you mean to send for the Lady Neville?"

"I mean to send her a message." An oblique glance warned
of listening ears, and Guy lapsed into silence.

They dismounted in the middle bailey as horseboys came
running for their mounts. Tumult reigned briefly, left behind
as they entered Tré's quarters. The heavy door shut out light
and noise, enclosing them in welcome gloom lit by candles.

Guy poured wine for both of them, held out a cup to Tré.
"What message will you send the lady?"

"A message she cannot misinterpret." He took the cup,
drank, lowered it to say softly, "She will tell me all I want to
know about her uncle."

9

A ragged half-moon hung low in the darkening sky, shedding a hazy glow over the fields. Insects hummed; the sleepy cooing of a turtledove drifted uphill from a hedgerow thick with new growth. An erratic breeze wafted the sweet, heady scent of May trees up the grassy slope to curl around the garden bench where Jane sat with abandoned needlework in her lap.

Nottingham lay in the distance, castle lights eclipsed now by summer leaves that hid the brooding fortress. On a clear night in winter, it was easily visible from Ravenshed Manor. A chief advantage of the manor was its position on a hill; it was high enough to give ample warning of riders approaching along the road. At night, manor torches promised safety behind the stone walls.

But safety was a rare commodity of late. Her hands tightened on the half-mended garment in her lap; she drew in a heavy breath that tasted of wood smoke and night air. In the week since Devaux had come to Ravenshed, the pursuit of the escaped outlaws had escalated.

No word from them since the Cockpen Oak. . . . Are they well and safe?

It was increasingly difficult not to fret for the fate of Little

John. For Will Scarlett and the others, blending in would be easy; for a man of John Lyttle's size, it would be near impossible. She bitterly regretted having asked his aid. How much better it would have been if she had just quietly given coin for the weapons Will Scarlett needed, and not involved a man long removed from dissension.

Should disaster befall him, I am responsible. . . .

A bitter truth, to know that she may well have cost a man his life, and certainly cost him hard-won amnesty.

The peaceful, familiar sounds of serenity mocked her. The night was calm, cool with soft winds that summoned memories of more pleasant times. She thought of her parents, dead since she was but thirteen years of age. A fever, swift and capricious, left behind a skinny, rebellious maid yet took robust parents and two healthy brothers. It had also left her a ward of the king; another twist of fate found him dead within a year after, victim of a chance arrow while besieging a castle in Châlus.

And when the Lionheart died, so too did Robin's heart and spirit. . . .

Robin—beloved uncle, warrior-earl—left England and grieving niece behind to continue the Crusade for Richard.

A useless cause, noble in concept, villainous in deed. Anger still troubled her at times; men left, never to return, not knowing or caring what happened to those who loved them.

Yet, anger for past deeds was a vain emotion. It availed her nothing and only clouded bright memories. It was an emotion she could not afford to indulge, and in truth, the years had been kinder to her than she had expected.

Chosen for her by King Richard, Hugh de Neville had been a caring husband, though much older. She had been fifteen, he forty when they married; a loyal Norman knight and a Saxon maid, old enmity woven into a tapestry of hope for England. It had pleased Richard, thus pleasing Robin.

Yet no one ever listened when I said it did not please me, the small, irritating voice reminded.

She could not really blame her uncle; he was duty bound to his king by love as well as honor. And it had been for the best, as Hugh loved her and she had grown to love him. Perhaps Robin had been wise after all. Their marriage bound together the lands of Blidworth, Ravenshed, and Ashfield. A tidy parcel even with Blidworth now inherited by Hugh's cousin; enough to lure more barons than she cared to consider when Hugh died. The year of mourning was nearly finished, and with it, the time granted to make a decision: nunnery or marriage.

Neither appealed to her.

Soon, she would have to choose. Perhaps Marian would give her advice. . . .

Chaaack! Chaack! Chack!

The familiar signal came abruptly, piercing the night and her reverie. A dog barked nearby, and others took up the baying chant. Hair prickled on the back of her neck; her hands tightened in her lap, the darning needle pricking her thumb.

From the shadows, Fiskin suddenly appeared; his face pale and indistinct, like a disembodied moon.

"Milady! Come quickly!"

"Is the gate locked?"

"Aye, 'tis locked and barred. Come. Come with me."

Abandoning the mending, she followed Fiskin. He moved swiftly, almost running so that she had to lift the hem of her kirtle to keep up. Her breath came fast; she knew the path well, for it led to the orchard.

The apple, pear, and cherry trees smelled sweet; branches slapped at her in sharp rebuke when she failed to duck. Just ahead, Fiskin came to a stop at the back wall that circled the manor estate.

A large shadow separated from the rest, visible only by the distant glow of torch- and moonlight.

"Milady. . . ."

"John!" Relief flooded her. "You are safe."

"For the moment." His tone was wry, weary. "The Talbots are out. Hard on my heels. I dare not linger."

She went to him, swiftly, taking his hands in hers though he shook his head and tried to avoid it. They were damp and sticky. Her heart thumped. "You are wounded."

"It is nothing . . . the dogs. The sheriff's men took Rowan and Shandy. I go to join Will and Alan. We were somehow betrayed. They narrowly escaped capture."

She turned. "Fiskin, go quickly and bring food. Have Dena put in some salve and strips of clean linen as well. Fly swiftly now, for there is not much time."

Little John gently pried loose her hands, and she heard grim satisfaction edge the words: "They nearly had me in the dales, but I killed one and wounded two . . . curse them. I have been fleeing the daylong since they found me in the hills above Newstead Abbey."

"It is my fault you are hunted. I should have left you in Hathersage to live quietly, and not endangered you thus."

"Milady." Softly: "As lovely and dear to me as thou art, if I had not wanted to lend my aid to Will Scarlett, I would not have come. I knew the risks. I knew them twenty years ago, when I joined with Robin."

"This is different. Robin is—not here."

Silence fell, freighted with sorrow and acceptance. A heavy sigh slipped into the air between them. Little John made a gesture like a shrug and waved his arms in despair.

"Would that he had never gone on Crusade. We will never know what happened to him. Not even Lady Marian knows. If he had only lived. . . ."

Jane did not comment; the moment was steeped in sadness, then passed with the return of Fiskin.

Panting, he held out a heavy leather pouch. "Bread, cheese, salve, and linen, milady." He sucked in a quick breath. "And half a roast chicken saved for pie."

John laughed softly. "Dena knows me well. If she were not already wed—"

In the distance could be heard a faint, baying howl, and Jane pressed her hands against him. "Go," she urged, "for I hear the Talbots give voice. If they have found your scent. . . ."

"They will lose it again unless they can swim." John took the leather pouch, and in the glimmer of light through branches and shadow, his eyes glinted. "Be Brother Tuck still at Rufford Abbey?"

THE BARON 79

"When last I heard from him. Fly swiftly now, John Lyttle, and I will pray for thy safety."

"See to thine, milady, for the sheriff is relentless. He has snared men this past week. He hunts dale and hill."

"And the forest."

At that, a soft laugh: "Nay, not Sherwood. The wood is too thick, and he knows it. Others—the outlaws who prey on innocents—have gone to ground in Thieves Wood. It would suit me well were the sheriff to arrest that scurrilous lot, for they ravage with random acts. 'Tis why I go to the caves."

"May the Virgin keep thee safe, John Lyttle."

He was gone. A soft farewell lingered on the breeze when he was on the other side of the wall, his seven-foot height mastering it with ease.

She waited in the shadows, but the belling of the hounds did not draw near. Night sounds were all she heard: the familiar lowing of sheep, rustle of birds, stomp of hoof. It was quiet again, safety in the barren night.

She returned to the garden bench and knelt, looking for the mending she had ignored earlier. It lay on grass damp with dew, and she sighed, shaking it. The bliaut made a snapping noise, suddenly loud.

A dog barked, and another, all the manor dogs taking up the chant. She rose to quiet them, then heard Edwin cursing, and halted. There was a yelp, a whine, and peace was restored.

Jane laughed softly. Her relief was mixed with anxiety for John's safety; she prayed he would reach the caves. Salvation lay in Sherwood's vastness.

Her kirtle hem was wet and cold against her ankles where it had dragged through the grass. Lifting her skirts in one hand, she cradled the mending under her arm and returned to the house.

Fiskin appeared again from the shadows beside the door; she started, almost dropped the mending.

"Must you do that, Fiskin? It is most annoying, when—"

Urgently: "Milady, riders approach!"

A cold chill pricked between her shoulder blades.

"You saw them?"

"Edwin—"

No other assurance was needed. Dena's husband possessed a keen eye. She nodded.

"Alert the others. And send Edwin to me."

Fiskin disappeared again, melting into the shadows like a wraith. When Edwin reached her, his broad face was creased with anxiety.

"Milady, it is Normans."

"Normans?" The knot in her stomach twisted more tightly, but her voice was calm: "Summon Ulric and the others to guard the gate. You know what to do."

"Aye, milady."

They were after John, of course. Jane discarded a score of defenses as inadequate; she desperately wished that she were better at lying. It was not a thing that came readily to her. She prayed fervently that Devaux was not among these Normans. His cold eyes would pick apart her every half-truth, deboning it as efficiently as Dena picked clean a chicken for pie.

It was late; purple shadows had long since deepened to dense blue. Soon, the skies would be agleam with light even near midnight. But it was not yet the second week of May, and darkness fell before the Compline hour.

In the courtyard, Edwin and the stablemen assembled with crude weapons: scythes, pitchforks, and stout staves. Even Fiskin bore a weapon.

Jane waited at the manor house, outwardly composed while her insides churned with apprehension. She could see the gate from where she stood on the stone steps. It was sturdy oak, thick and well hinged, barred against intruders. It would not keep out determined men, but it would hinder them long enough to hide, should it be warranted.

A heavy thud of hooves on the moat bridge, then the pounding of a mailed fist on the gate rent the night. The dogs set up a racket again and were quickly hushed.

Fiskin opened the wicket with a fumbling hand and demanded querulously, "Who awaits there?"

The challenge was swiftly answered, and Jane, standing on the top step with hands clenched tightly in front of her, felt her stomach drop when the answer came curtly:

"The Lord High Sheriff of Nottingham. Stand aside, you

witless knaves, and yield entry. The sheriff is sore wounded and needs attention."

Fiskin glanced around, and at a nod from Jane, Edwin bade him open the gate. The bar slid back with a grating protest. The gate swung open.

Men seemed to fill the night, their mail glinting in the wash of torchlight. Spurs rattled and sheathed swords clinked as some of the men dismounted. Jane sucked in a deep breath, her hands knotted so tightly that her fingers felt numb and cold.

Then she recognized Guy de Beaufort, his pale hair a beacon in a restless sea of shadow and silhouette.

"Lady Neville, we impose upon your hospitality." Again, it was not a request but a demand.

"You said the sheriff is injured, Sir Guy."

The men moved fully into the light; Devaux hung slackly between Guy and another man.

"He is, milady. We were close-by, so brought him here."

There was nothing she could have said to stay them even if she had attempted it; she bade them bring Devaux into the manor house to be tended. He was only half-conscious, bare head hanging low and swaying from side to side.

"This way." Jane indicated the steep, narrow staircase that led to the second-floor bedchambers.

Guy eyed it and shook his head. "Do you not have a place any closer? He weighs at least fifteen stone in all this armor, and feels more like twenty."

"Bring him in here."

They followed her to a small room used as a storage area near the back of the house. Dena scurried ahead and readied a rough pallet of bed linens and rags on the floor, and the sheriff was lowered gently.

"Where is the hurt?" Jane knelt beside him, her hands already swift efficiency as she tugged at the buckle of his sword belt. "I see no head wound."

"His side. 'Tis an old wound, newly injured. No, this side— let me doff his armor or you will make it worse."

Jane lifted a brow when he pushed her aside. "I am used to tending wounds, sir."

"Perhaps, but not *his* wounds." A swift frown bent toward

her as he deftly unfastened the leather sword belt and beckoned to a man-at-arms to assist him. "I know there is not a Saxon in all of Nottinghamshire who would not leap at the chance to do him in."

"Probably not, but do not think me fool enough to do harm to him while he is here. I am not such a simpleton as to think you, or even the king, would allow that to pass without reprisal."

Easing Tré free of the metal hauberk and coif with some effort, Guy let them drop in a clinking pile to the cold stone floor. He sat back on his heels and looked at Jane. Hazel eyes stared deeply into hers for a long moment, then a faint smile curved his lips.

"No, I suppose you are not that witless. His wound is grievous. Are you skilled?"

"As skilled as most women who must tend men foolish enough to wield sharp implements. Remove the rest of his garments while I fetch herbs. He is feverish."

She rose to her feet, not waiting for his response as she left the storeroom. Dena and Enid came swiftly to her side, the older woman nervous, voice a low whisper:

"Milady . . . the Normans have two prisoners with them."

Rowan and Shandy. There was nothing she could do for them now.

"We must see to ourselves, Dena, and give no offense or we will end as badly. Hasten, for we have much to do."

When Jane returned to the storeroom with her pouch of medicines, Dena bore a tray with cups and mortar and pestle; Enid brought a heavy cauldron of boiling water. They placed the items on the floor near the pallet, then withdrew to allow Jane near. She knelt once more beside the wounded sheriff.

He had been stripped to his braies. Divested of his garments, he looked younger than his years; unexpectedly vulnerable. His body bore the marks of his profession, healed scars from previous wounds crisscrossing his chest and belly like so many hedgerows. Yet it was the wound in his side that gained her immediate attention: the deep gash oozed corruption. She turned slightly.

"Enid, fetch a jug of old wine from the cellars. Fiskin is to bring me six eggs."

Guy made an inarticulate sound. "Eggs? Do you feed him or heal him?"

"It draws poison and cools the fever of the flesh. Move back, sir. You are in my light."

Guy swore softly, a curse in Norman French that brought up Jane's head to stare at him so coldly that he flushed.

"Sir Guy, you brought him to be treated, did you not?"

"Only because we were close."

"But you brought him here. Trust in my skills if not my loyalty. Feel free to watch. Do not get in my way lest 'tis your wont to bury the sheriff before a sennight passes."

"It is that bad?"

She gestured to the wound; crimson fingers spread out like the marks of a hand. "If he had not broken it open to release the poisons, he would no doubt be dead ere much longer. Even so, the poisons may still lay him low."

Silence fell. Devaux's breathing was a harsh rasp. Light from a rack of candles danced across the wall. Guy held her gaze until the tension stretched so tautly that she thought he would refuse. Then he blew out a heavy gust of air, cheeks puffed with the effort.

"I am not skilled at these things. He would not allow any surgeon near. . . ." He flicked a glance at Tré, then at her again. "Yet there is no other choice. If not you—nothing."

"Then as I am better than nothing, let me work."

Guy nodded curtly. "But I linger to watch, milady."

"As long as you do not interfere."

Jane turned her attention back to the wound; a pang of dismay clenched her stomach. For all her confident words, it might well be mortal. Her hand rested on Devaux's ribs; his skin was hot to the touch. His chest rose and fell rapidly. His eyes had not opened, though black lashes beat thinly like the wings of a trapped bird. Even though her reward might be a writ of arrest, she could not allow him to die without doing her best to save him.

Putting aside all other thoughts, she concentrated on

cleaning the wound with old wine that smelled strong. At one point, Guy and a man-at-arms were employed to hold him down, for he began to thrash about in his feverish state, muttering and throwing his arms about wildly.

"Aimée. . . ." The name erupted from his throat as if in agony; for a moment Jane paused. The sheriff's face twisted in a tortured grimace. "Ah, God—*Aimée!*"

She looked up at Guy; he gave a slight shake of his head. "She is long dead now."

"Hold him," she said then. Guy used his weight to pin down the sheriff's shoulders with both hands while she held a rag soaked in mandrake to Devaux's nose. It worked, slowing his restive movements.

By the time Fiskin returned with the eggs, Jane had thoroughly cleansed the open wound with a mixture of herbs and hot water. She mixed egg whites in a shallow bowl, then gently spread the sticky paste onto the bruised, torn flesh and bound it with a wide strip of linen around his middle.

"Do not remove this," she said to Guy.

"Until when?"

"Until I do it." She met Guy's quizzical gaze with a faint smile. "It draws. He must have rest. The hurt must be allowed to cleanse and heal, or it could yet kill him."

"So I told him when he was first injured. He would not listen." Guy looked worried; he raked a hand through hair dampened by the weight of his helmet until it stood up in short golden spikes atop his head. "I will sleep next to him."

"Then I will have my servants prepare another pallet. When was he wounded?"

"Three months ago. This last, just this afternoon." He looked up to meet her gaze. "In the dales."

Her heart thumped a warning. "That is not far. It is fortunate you were so close to Ravenshed."

"It was the outlaws who brought us here. We routed some of them from hiding."

She thought of Shandy and Rowan, only names to her, but men known to Little John.

Guy's gaze was steady; he waited for her response, and she

could think of nothing that would not sound foolish or too well informed.

Finally: "The barons will be most pleased to have the shire rid of outlaws."

"We do not," said Guy slowly, "do it for the barons. It is for the king."

"Of course." She wiped egg from her fingers with a cloth. "The new wound most like did him a service. His blood is near poisoned. A weaker man would have died long ago."

"Should you not bleed him to rid his body of poison?"

"No." Jane shook her head. "The evil humors are gone."

"A surgeon would bleed him yet."

She folded the sticky cloth in her hands. It was true. A surgeon would bleed him; Brother Tuck would not. She trusted Tuck, for he was oft right in these matters.

Devaux lay more quietly, yet there was a tinge of gray beneath his normally dark skin. She shrugged.

"You will do as you like, of course. If you bleed him, you will undertake his care yourself. I will not be held liable when he dies, as he surely will if you bleed him."

"Lady, you have a sharp tongue."

"So I have been told." She stood up. "I shall brew a potion to ease his fever and pain. Shall I administer it, or do you take responsibility?"

"I take responsibility for him regardless of your actions. He is more than my liege—he is a friend."

"I yield liability most willingly."

When she returned with the bitter brew of mandrake and wine, Devaux was restless again. It took great effort to pour the contents of the cup down his throat, and Beaufort was sweating when it was at last emptied. The man-at-arms nursed a split lip and black eye; Guy gingerly felt his bruised nose.

"When he recovers, I shall demand ample retribution for this."

Jane smiled as she gathered up the herbs scattered during the struggle and motioned for Dena to remove them. "I shall leave this flagon of potion, Sir Guy. Give it to him again before first light. He should rest easier."

"Pray God he does, for I do not think I will hold out much longer. He is much stronger than a man with his wounds should be."

Jane was not surprised. Devaux emanated strength, even delirious and half-conscious. Sweat-sheened skin was of a darker color than most, bronzed as if from the sun. Long limbs were muscular, lean yet powerful even in repose.

Inexplicably, her cousin's words returned to her in a rush. Lissa's mocking jest that the sheriff and his courser were "fine, muscular animals—sleek and dark and dangerous," summoned an uncomfortable and disconcerting heat.

Escaping prying eyes, she retreated to the bedchamber she had shared with Hugh. Empty now of all save memories. The wide bed lay in shadow, curtains drawn around in velvet protection. A knight's bed, massive and wide, her marriage bed. Twelve years she had slept in that bed. Gone from maid to matron in a single night, she had learned that the romantic tales told by minstrels were just that—romantic tales.

Later had come love for Hugh. Never had it been the fevered passion and breathless anticipation of the poets. No tempestuous emotion that swung her from despair to bliss in a single instant, but the steady burn of constancy. At first she had been disappointed. Then she had come to realize it was comforting. Security lay in her husband's arms, if not the sweet ardor she had once dreamed of . . . yet even that would vanish in time.

Hugh died, an old man, ill at the last and appreciative of tender care, leaving her with regrets and no children. He had made a bad bargain, after all. Yet he had never complained, never felt that loss as did she, it seemed. If he had, it was not mentioned. Sweet Hugh . . . he was missed. He had made her feel competent, graceful; never a beauty like her cousin, she had blossomed under Hugh's gentle love. He had taught her confidence in her abilities if not her beauty and she was grateful for that.

She leaned her head against the wood frame of the open window; beyond the manor, moonlight washed silver and gray over sloping field and dense wood. In the courtyard was the sound of men settling for the night—Normans, with horses, weapons, and vengeance. She should have been wary.

Yet, in the lady's chamber, she stared into the night and thought of a long-limbed body and the passion she had never known. She thought of Tré Devaux.

10

—🌿—

The cock crowed twice before Jane rose. A dream lingered:
vivid images of Devaux. Intense, disturbing, the dream stirred
unfamiliar sensations, a sense of heavy waiting, of wanting. It
left her strangely flushed.

In lucid day, would Guy de Beaufort see her depravity?
Would it be apparent to all who glanced her way? Long had
she lain awake, strangely restless; vague yearning for something beyond her ken pricked her so sharply it had been nearly
cockcrow before she slept at last.

Only to dream. . . .

Fumbling, eyes scratchy from lack of sleep, she made her
morning ablutions and left the chamber to seek out Guy de
Beaufort. He would expect it.

She met him at the door to the storeroom where Devaux
lay. Bleary-eyed, haggard, his grim expression sparked alarm
that he put to rest with his first words:

"He is restless still. He burns with fever. I fear he has lost his
mind."

"It is to be expected. I will see—"

"Milady—" Guy put out a hand to stop her. "I had to tie him
to keep him from tearing open his wound again. He pulled
away the bandage, but I rebound him as best I could."

"I understand. Little you may credit it, Sir Guy, but this is not the first wounded man I have tended. Have you forgotten the Welsh wars? My husband was wounded more than once. I learned at an early age which wounds kill swiftly, and which heal slowly. Will you allow me to pass?"

Guy stepped aside but followed hard on her heels as she entered the storeroom. It smelled of spilled wine and candle tallow.

Devaux was bound at both wrists; loops of leather were stretched and secured to a heavy chest that stood against the far wall. Guy had tossed a light cover over him.

Muttering, he twisted and turned as far as the confines of the leather would allow; his muscles flexed against the restraints. Norman French was guttural and incoherent, his words indistinguishable.

Jane knelt at his side. A light touch of her hand on his cheek found it cooler than the night before, though still warm. She glanced up at Guy.

"His fever wanes. Perhaps he should be moved. It would be easier to tend him in a bed."

"I do not relish moving him."

She stood up. "Nonetheless, it must be done."

Guy sighed heavily. "I will need to fetch more men. He is too unwieldy for two men to manage."

"It seems only one man is available if you mean yon man-at-arms. He sleeps."

Grunting, Guy moved to the dozing soldier and kicked him awake. The poor man went sprawling, blinking owlishly up at Beaufort when he snapped out an order:

"Fetch three more men from the stables to help move the sheriff."

Lurching to his feet, the soldier nodded. He cast a wary glance at the restless Devaux as he left the room.

Jane followed his glance; heat flooded her face. The light cover was kicked free. At some time during the night, the braies had been removed. Devaux lay bare as the day he was born, candle glow washing over him in unerring clarity.

Boldly defined, potent male in unexpected beauty, a sculptured promise of raw power and passion . . . a warrior-baron, invulnerable until now. It was disconcerting and beguiling; she inhaled sharply. The tight coil in the pit of her stomach moved lower and blossomed, heat a live thing, insidious and powerful. Unfamiliar, unwanted response, rendering her defenseless.

A slight cough, a shift of booted feet on stone, and she jerked her eyes from the sheriff, mortified and flushed. Guy de Beaufort gazed at her with lifted brows and bemused eyes. There was no comment she could make that would not be too obvious a defense, so she merely turned away and moved from the storeroom with silent, desperate dignity.

Dena waited in the corridor. Her matronly face was creased with curiosity and anxiety, her eyes were strained. "Is all well, milady?"

"Yea, take Enid and ready the front bedchamber for the sheriff. They are moving him there."

"Yea, milady. Shall I fetch your herbs?"

"I will do it." It would give her time to recover her poise. But as she gathered the basket and pouch of herbs and measured them, mixing and grinding with mortar and pestle, her hands trembled slightly. Absurd, that it would affect her so. He was not the first naked man she had seen; though intimate only with Hugh, she had tended other wounded men. It had necessitated seeing them in exposed circumstances; neither unusual nor remarkable.

"Milady?" Enid stuck her head around the corner of the small nook where Jane was mixing the herbs; her young face was frightened. "One of the Normans calls for you."

Jane wiped her hands on a cloth as she returned to the storeroom. Guy met her just outside.

"Have you a potion to quiet him? He has knocked the men about so, they fear to go near him. I cannot do it alone."

"Yea, I have potions to summon deep sleep, but—"

"Give it to him. Or give it to me and I will give it to him. He is too unruly for us to manage this way." Guy bent his head toward the storeroom. "In his fever, he has fair wrecked the chamber. I do not think we will be able to get him up that staircase unless he is asleep."

"Perhaps I can—"

"No."

A bellow came from the storeroom, followed by a sharp cry of pain and the sounds of a scuffle. Jane pondered the options. To sedate him would take a powerful draught and the danger of overdoing it was great. Dare she risk it? Slowly, she shook her head.

"It is difficult to judge just how much to give a man at times. Even big men oft can bear only a small amount, so that—"

"Start with a small amount then," Guy snarled, "but for the love of all the saints, give me *something* to quiet him! I fear he will tear open his wound again, and that will end him."

It was an excellent point. Jane returned to her store and took down a familiar concoction brewed from her precious supply of poppy seeds. Dark, vile-smelling, it was powerful and often dangerous. Her hand trembled as she measured out an amount in a shallow cup. Enough to summon oblivion but not death . . . too little better than too much.

She took it to Sir Guy, who disappeared into the storeroom again; the sounds of struggle escalated, then faded.

Guy emerged at last, a new rip in his tunic and his breath labored, but grimly pleased. "He drank it, though if he ever remembers what I said to him, I may need some of that potion myself."

A faint smile in response, then: "When he is claimed by heavy sleep, take him to the chamber on the second floor. Dena has readied it for you."

"And where will you be, milady?" Guy put out a hand when she turned to go, and she paused to look back at him.

"Where should I be?"

"It is best that you not leave Ravenshed for now. If you have needs, ask them of me. Until the sheriff recovers, no one may leave or enter the manor, save at my discretion."

"How dare you come to my home and presume to give me orders as if you command here, sir!"

"Lady Neville, for the moment, I do command here."

The quiet reminder was uncompromising. It served as a warning: Ravenshed was occupied by Normans, susceptible to Norman rules and retribution.

She thought of Little John, Alan, and Will, prayed they had made good their escape, and nodded calmly.

"I see, Sir Guy. If it pleases you, I shall retire to my daily duties, lest I give offense by withholding food or giving drink that is inadequate."

His eyes thinned a bit; his mouth tightened. "You will receive proper recompense for your hospitality."

"Hospitality? I am not hostage, but hostess, then. Is that correct, Sir Guy?"

For a moment he stared at her, then shook his head. "He was right, I trow. You have a most wicked tongue, milady."

"If you mean the sheriff, his tongue was honed well upon me, so I do not waste remorse for any of my words to him."

A grin widened his mouth. "Aye, fighting cocks are not so entertaining as would be the two of you. If I were not fearful of my own safety, I would set you one at the other."

"There is no need of that. When the sheriff wakes, he will take up the reins of intimidation from you."

"Doubtless." He glanced up and past her to the quiet hall where none moved except for a hound seeking rest among the rushes. "It would serve thee best, milady, to bide thy tongue at times. Truth will be a better ally than deceit."

The warning lay between them; a promise. A prophecy. She wondered why he had ventured it. Temptation reared; a need to know the sheriff's intentions, but it would be a mistake to ask this man.

"Truth," she said, "is a two-edged sword, Sir Guy."

"Yea, but an unwise lie is always fatal."

There was no answer that would not betray her, and she lapsed into silence marked by tension. It did not linger long, for he turned away to summon a man-at-arms.

"Tell Captain Oliver to secure the perimeters. He is to report to me should anything be amiss." A pause, a glance at her, then to the guard: "Have the prisoners been taken?"

"Yea, Sir Guy. An escort left before cock's crow to take them to Nottingham."

Jane stood impassively, though she could not help a jolt of dismay. Rowan and Shandy had not been among those outlaws who ravaged the lands, but only joined with Will in the ill-fated attempt to recover monies the sheriff's men had so brutally seized. Harrowing, that honest men would pay such a price for desperation.

"I must gather more herbs to tend the sheriff," she said when Sir Guy turned back to her. "Am I given permission to do so, or shall I begin the prayers for his soul?"

He did not miss the sharp bite of mockery; a faint smile curved his mouth. "Do not sharpen your tongue on me, Lady Neville. It will avail you little. Save your efforts for the sheriff. He will give you measure for measure." A pause, then: "I will have a man escort you wherever you wish."

She nodded, stiffly. When she returned to the small corner of the kitchens where she prepared herbs, the sharp smell of mint and bay leaves was pungent; the lingering scent of poppy juice still hung in the air.

For a long moment she stood silent and motionless. The familiar sounds of the house were invaded by the alien noises of the enemy; rattling swords, clink of mail, hooves on stone rent the serenity she had come to expect.

Yet it was the serenity of harmony she most missed, the knowledge that she was inviolate and safe. Nothing was safe now, and had not been for longer than she could recall.

She retrieved a basket and left the kitchen; a guard waited, a silent presence at her side as she crossed the courtyard. The gate was open, wood planks bridged the moat and led to the fallow field beyond the hedge. There she gathered an abundance of chickweed under the watchful eye of her Norman guard.

Ignoring him, she tucked the leafy plants with tiny white flowers into her basket. It was useful for fever and, as an ointment, to draw the heat and corruption from wounds.

Morning light fell on the beads of heavy dew and thick blades of grass; dew wet her feet and the hem of her cotte as she moved along the hedgerows. Beyond the unharrowed field lay a bristle of trees and brush, dense and shadowed.

The discordant *chack!* of a jackdaw pierced the air, and her hand tightened on the basket handle. John? A signal? She waited, tensely; a soft breeze lifted the hair that escaped from beneath the silk edges of her caul. It blew in a caress across her cheek, and she caught the errant curl with a slightly shaking hand.

"Milady," the guard prompted when she remained unmoving and silent, "are you done?"

She rose to her feet. "Yes. We can return now."

The familiar gloom of the hall enclosed her as she entered. The sudden change from morning light to darker interior left her momentarily blind and she paused; she did not know she was not alone until the voice came out of shadows:

"It is a pleasant day, milady."

"It could be, Sir Guy."

Soft laughter; as her eyes adjusted, she saw his fair hair gleam in the shadow beneath the stairs.

"Relentless lady. He is asleep."

"I brought herbs for his fever."

"Is your care of him out of concern or a desire to be rid of us?"

"It would be impolitic of me to reply with a lie when I have been advised to speak only truth, Sir Guy."

"Yea," he said, laughter still in his voice, "it would, indeed."

He moved into the light; this Norman was not as dour as the sheriff.

"Where are your other servants, milady? Are there no yeomen pledged to your service? Your fields lie untilled."

Behind the pleasant tone lay a quest, and she revised her brief impression of him as the less dangerous man.

"I have no yeomen left. There are not ten of us who remain here. The king's summons left me with barely enough to tend our garden and beasts. There are no men left as guard. None hiding to leap upon you, or gone to join the outlaws."

His steady gaze told her she had answered his question; a smile hovered on his mouth. "You are direct."

"It does not waste as much time."

"Another truth. Let us hope you are as full of truths when Devaux awakes."

"Is that a warning, Sir Guy?"

"It is whatever you take from it." He paused. "I find you intrepid. For your sake, I hope you are not foolish."

Jane considered a reply, but discarded it as too reckless.

She moved past him into the small chamber with her basket of chickweed. Dena had already pulled some cabbage and cleaned the leaves in preparation.

"I knew you would make a poultice, milady."

"Yes. Here. Strip the chickweed while I crush the leaves." She busied their hands to engage their minds, unwilling to field questions she knew would come. She had no answers for them, did not want to dwell on the possibility that stared her in the face.

"With all these bloody Normans about, 'tis not easy to do what must be done—" Dena looked frightened when Jane shushed her.

"The walls have ears, Dena. Is Enid with Edwin?"

"Yea, milady. Safe with her father. I do not like the way some of those Normans look at her."

"Keep her close. No harm should come to her. I do not think Sir Guy would allow it."

Hopeful assurance, and based on what she'd observed of the blond Norman, not without reason. There had been no evidence of villainy; the soldiers were disciplined and not destructive. Perhaps it was not as bad as it seemed.

The poultice was soon ready; Jane cleaned her hands and smoothed the skirts of her cotte. It was plain, rose velvet absent of embroidery or gilt. A concession to vanity was the gold mesh caul she wore, her hair coiled over each ear inside the glittering net; her only jewelry was a gold cross on a long chain.

As she ascended the stairs, the damp hem of her garb tangled about her ankles and wet her hose. She had neglected to change shoes; they squelched soggily with each step.

The corridor at the head of the stairs was long and narrow; it stretched the length of the house, with rooms off it like the teeth of a comb. The master's chamber was large enough to encompass a fourth of the second floor; the others were smaller, but all had windows facing the courtyard. Hugh had redesigned the upper story so that one no longer had to go through one room to reach the other. The corridor took a bit off the size of the rooms but lent privacy where there had been none. A rare privilege.

Light filtered through a closed shutter in the room where

the sheriff lay. She entered quietly, shoes scraping softly on wood floors that creaked with every other step. The chamber was gloomy and smelled of old wine and herbs. Tré Devaux did not stir, save for an occasional mutter or grimace.

Sir Guy leaned in the open doorway. She was aware of him behind her, watching.

"You should get some rest," she said as she set down the tray on a broken table that wobbled beneath the burden; a casualty of the sheriff's thrashing. "You will be no good to him if you fall ill."

"When he rests, so will I."

Shrugging, Jane moved to Tré's side. He was cooler to the touch, but still warm. "Open the shutters," she said, and, after a pause, Guy moved to the window.

Sunlight spilled into the room, chasing shadows to the far corners with gleeful efficiency. Jane lifted the light cover and peeled away the bandages. The wound had begun to heal, though it was still red.

With swift, soft hands, Jane cleaned the wound again; she smeared an ointment of crushed chickweed leaves and wool grease against it, then covered it with a large cabbage leaf.

"I will need your aid," she said without glancing around, for she knew that Beaufort had resumed his position in the doorway. He lent his strength so that she could bind Devaux, wrapping long strips of linen around his middle and tying them snugly.

"It looks better, milady."

She smiled. "It should. The surgeon who cauterized it was incompetent."

"Why do you say that?"

She glanced up at him, saw the frown on his brow, and said, "It should have been washed with strong wine before a hot iron was applied. Any decent surgeon knows that."

"It was not a surgeon who treated him." His tone was defensive. "There was not time. There rarely is on a battlefield."

"I see."

Silence, then: "You do not see. A woman never sees. I thought a baron's widow different from the others."

She stood up, gathered herbs and linen strips in her hands.

"If you mean that I do not understand why men must be ever chasing death, you are right. I do not. I never will. It is foolish, reckless, and accomplishes little."

Hazel eyes cooled to frost. "It wins kingdoms, milady."

"And loses them again." Her brow lifted at his soft curse. "King John has lost all of France and Normandy. Men have died to regain it, yet it is still lost. England is under an interdict by the pope for the king's refusal to accept his appointment of Stephen Langton as Archbishop of Canterbury, yet all John thinks of is war with Philip of France. Futile battles to regain lost kingdoms, while England is scoured clean of men, arms, and food, left too weak to stand against her enemies."

"Treason, milady?"

"Disgust, Sir Guy, at the waste of lives."

"Strange words, coming from the widow of a valiant knight such as Sir Hugh."

"Hugh was valiant, but constant warfare took its toll and ended up killing him far too young."

"He was past fifty, to my recollection. Not young at all for a knight."

"Not for a knight, no. But for a husband, yes." Lifting the tray, she turned to leave.

Then Guy said softly, "All men are not as your husband, milady."

Though she gave no indication of hearing him, her step faltered as she continued out the door, his words ringing in her ears. No, all men were not as Hugh. Yet women were left behind, forced to fight or lose all. She had struggled since Hugh's death, nearly a year of balancing like a juggler's dog in the effort to keep her home. There were moments when she bowed beneath the burden, yielded to utter despair, yet knew she must rise the next day and continue the struggle. It was not in her to submit.

An errant ray of afternoon light poked persistently through half-closed shutters, marched boldly across the floor to paint the bed and resting sheriff.

Jane watched idly. It was quiet now, Guy downstairs with

the other Normans. She was to observe Tré Devaux, alone and trusted; a dubious honor for a pointless task. If he awoke, all would know it swiftly enough.

Yet there she was, perched in an uncomfortable chair with no bolsters, listening to him breathe. She thought of the name he had called out, wondered who the woman had been to him. Wife? Lover? He seemed too harsh a man to carry a memory. Somehow, it made him vulnerable.

Jane settled her cheek into the cup of her palm and propped her elbow atop the damaged table to survey Devaux more closely. Easier to stare at him now that he was asleep. Awake, nearly impossible. . . .

His face was bathed in half-light from the window; an odd golden wash of color spread over features softened in sleep. It muted the harshness, the mockery she usually saw there. A small scar etched his jaw, pale against dark beard stubble. His lashes were long, thick, black; his nose was straight and strong, without the Norman curve to it she had come to expect. His mouth—

She stopped there, before her mind lured her to more dangerous contemplation.

Below, she heard familiar sounds of the manor: Dena scolding an errant servant, Edwin tending to the repair of a harness, his hammer tap-tapping against the leather. Over all that, the foreign sound of Norman soldiers milling about the courtyard. Much quieter upstairs, where only the gentle swish of a breeze through open window occupied the room.

Time passed. Edwin's rhythmic tapping was a lulling song; light through the window slanted over bed and walls, pricked her eyelids with an invitation to close.

She yawned, stretched, fought the urge to sleep. Her gaze drifted about the room, ocher washed in light, shadows held at bay. Mail draped over a chest; boots stood in a corner, one fallen over, the other upright. Good leather, scuffed from use. A wide belt, sheathed sword, his chausses.

Bed ropes creaked. He shifted, muttering softly, but did not wake. She turned to look at him again; heartbeat in her ears a sudden, loud song.

The cover had slipped, inched down with his restless movement. Fine dark hair furred muscle, taut skin, the span of his linen-bound ribs, a silky ribbon that dipped below the edge of sheet.

Jane sat as if frozen, seized by abrupt apprehension. Breathless. Agitated . . . *anticipation.*

He moved again, a foot pushing at the linen, and it slid away with a soft rustle. Lower still; fabric folded over an unmistakable bulge.

An invasion, an intrusion of privacy and decency and her own ethics. . . . She should cover him or look away. Or both. She should—

Another creak of bed ropes and a turn; the cover fell away to pool on the floor. She sat still. Sunlight licked his body in erotic detail; seductive, sensuous, elegant male, potent and breathtaking, beautiful enough to bring tears to her eyes.

Silence spun, stretched, dissipated when she released her breath in a rush of air.

Outside, a dog barked. Voices rose—she recognized her cousin's imperative tones below in the courtyard, indignant, demanding. An unexpected—and timely—arrival. Dream fragments spinning away, she moved at last to retrieve the sheet.

She lifted it, stood to settle it over him in a snap of white. It floated down gently, a whisper of sound and air, billowing gracefully to drape in capricious mischief on his thighs and not his groin.

What if he wakes?

Her fingers closed on the edge of linen just as he moved; the side of her hand brushed over his member. Instantly, his body reacted with the predictable response: rising, strengthening, potent proof beneath her palm.

She was shocked. Silk-sheathed steel nudged her hand insistently. *So hot. . . .* A low, fierce groan from him when her fingers closed in convulsive reaction. *Wrong, dangerous, wicked. . . .*

Uncertain, churning with confusion, a tight, throbbing knot of flame blossomed between her thighs. It spread, devoured her. . . . He slid into her fist, a luxurious thrust accompanied by a low mutter that was suddenly terrifying.

She snatched her hand away, reached gingerly for the cover,

pulled it up and over him. Slowly, the pounding in her ears abated, the song dying, the fire turning to ash, sanity returning; hands knotted into her skirts.

He slept still, a satyr washed in gold and shadow, a reminder of vanished hopes and tarnished dreams. Slept, while she burned with unholy thoughts.

11

His head ached abominably, as if hammers were steadily pounding inside it. His skin itched. Tré sipped ale and eyed his untouched pottage. He hated the thin broth with parsnips, leeks, and turnips. He wanted meat and wine, not an invalid's fare.

"You are still weak."

Guy's reminder was waved away impatiently. "You need not fear I will die soon. I would have to feel much better than I do now, for I am like to starve."

An insolent grin widened his mouth as Guy pointed out, "You have recovered more swiftly than expected."

"A week is not swift—"

"Four days. Not a week."

"Four days is overlong when Gaudet is left in command." Shifting, Tré swallowed a groan that came with the movement; a sharp knife thrust in his side. It left him breathless, lightheaded; he narrowed his eyes against the late-afternoon light streaming through the window opposite his bed. "Take this tray and pull the shutters."

Guy took the tray from him. Impatience gnawed Tré, as sharp as the pain.

Wood creaked, a dull thud as the shutter thumped against the window frame. Abruptly they were in soft gloom; he managed to shift position. It cost him. Silent, jaw clenched, he watched Guy move about the chamber, shoving furniture against the wall, repositioning a chair.

A glance, a shrug: "When you must rise, you will not need to dodge these chests."

"So I am considered a feeble cripple now. Enough. We leave on the morrow."

Guy turned, leaned back against the wall with arms crossed. He shook his head.

"It is not worth it, Tré. I sent Oliver to Nottingham. He will keep Gaudet on a short leash until our return."

"Oliver is only captain of the guard. He can do nothing should Gaudet foment trouble."

"He can do more than you, should exertion kill you." Blunt, the words lay between them for a moment.

Tré's hand knotted in the linen sheet, crushing it. "A few days more," he said finally. "Only a few. I weary of lying here listening to nothing."

Guy shrugged. "At least you do not have to contend with two females. Lady Neville has a sharp tongue, and Lady Dunham is even worse."

"Dunham—the cousin from Gedling." A smile formed at Guy's obvious irritation. "Did the lady come to Ravenshed just to annoy you?"

"I begin to think that true. She takes far too much pleasure in bedeviling me. At least Lady Neville only speaks her mind when pressed."

"Yes." He paused, thought of Jane, and nodded. "She does speak her mind at inconvenient times."

"Most inconvenient. I thought to learn from Lady Dunham what I could not discover from her cousin, but Lady Neville interrupted."

"What news in that quarter?"

"Nothing more on the outlaws. The giant, Little John, has disappeared entirely. Gone to ground like a fox. Tales are still told of this Robin Hood. Do you think them the truth? These Saxons lie boldly, with not a flicker of an eye."

"As would we."

Wryly, Guy grinned. "Yea, as would we. Yet I do not understand. They moan of outlaws' depredations, then hide the thieves when we go in pursuit."

"I have been pondering that." Tré eased one leg up to bend his knee, relieving pressure on a backside sore from lying abed. "It seems there are the outlaws who prey upon Norman and Saxon alike. Then there are outlaws who prey only upon Normans. These last, do the Saxons favor with vaunted tales of courage and nobility."

Guy grunted in disgust. "They would not prate of courage had they seen the giant flee the Talbots."

"No." A pause. "Yet they might if told he laid me low first, then killed two of the dogs before escaping."

Silence fell. Memory of that night was still sharp despite the potions he had been fed: The giant rising up out of dense shadows, quarterstaff a whoosh of deadly sound before striking true to send him from his horse. The baying of hounds, shouts of his men, and pursuit cut short was more hazy. But the giant—that image burned clear: anger in his light eyes, bearded face bellowing rage and frustration, the force of emotion behind powerful arms.

If he had not ducked, the blow would have killed him.

"I want that man," he said quietly, and saw in Guy's face a similar desire. "Little John. I want him taken alive. I want an answer to the tale of Robin Hood. I want," he added, "to speak with the Lady Neville."

"It will avail you little. She gives away nothing. If her servants know, they do not tell either."

"If her uncle is truly this outlaw, it explains much. Yet it does not explain *her* presence in the greenwood."

Guy pushed away from the wall where he had been leaning. "It is evident the lady is willful."

"Do you recall the lessons of our boyhood, Guy? How did our masters curb stubborn defiance?"

"With stout rods; but I do not think you mean to do that with this lady."

"No." A soft laugh, then: "But I do mean to show her who is stronger."

"It might be better to *wait* until you are stronger. At this moment, the lady could best you in a wrestling match."

"I do not propose to wrestle her. Fetch her to me, Guy. There are more methods than strength of arm to gain an end."

Still dubious, Guy paused in the doorway to glance back at him. "You are not yet fully healed—"

"Fetch her, Guy. She will not attack me."

"It is not assault that concerns me." With a wry twist of his mouth that left no doubt as to his meaning, he left, leaving the door open behind him.

Tré leaned back; he contemplated a shaft of hazy light that pierced a chink in the wooden shutters. Dust motes floated in the persistent beam, drifting in lazy layers. His eyes burned, and he closed them.

He must have dozed; when he opened his eyes again, Jane stood beside the bed. Hands were folded calmly in front of her. Her rose cotte was plain, simple and unadorned save for a gold cross that dangled from a thin chain around her waist. A silk wimple fluttered slightly when she moved, a soft pink frame around her face.

"Be seated, milady."

"Are you certain? It was just this morning that you evicted me from your sight."

It was the sort of comment he had come to expect from her: audacity swathed in courtesy.

"I grew weary of poppy juice and vile potions," he said evenly. "You seemed determined to keep me insensible."

"Indeed I did, my lord. Awake, you seem bent on your own destruction."

It was the perfect opening. He smiled, saw her eyes widen a bit as he said, "As do you, milady. It is a matter of concern to me that you persist in a course that can only cause you disaster. Be seated."

A touch of steel in his tone, and she sat, perching on the edge of the chair as if poised to flee, the hare from the fox, alert to danger.

Tré studied her face at leisure; he let the moment draw out and increase her tension. Lovely brow, clear eyes, seductive mouth . . . he remembered too well his last visit to Ravenshed, and the overpowering need he had felt for her then.

Her hands twisted in her lap; slender fingers clasped together and drew his attention. He thought of her hand on him, cool, competent, arousing—her touch had lured him from drugged slumber. It was not a dream, though he had thought it was, then. The soft touch of a hand on him, a whisper of air, an instant, aching erection that found no ease in a brief grasp.

Gone too soon, leaving behind an empty chamber and raging need. No, not a dream . . . this lady of Ravenshed had held him in her hand, an intimate touch that had nothing to do with his injury. He was certain of it.

Eyes half-closed, he stared at her from beneath his lashes until she began to fidget, unclasping her hands and smoothing a nonexistent wrinkle from her skirt. Her hands clasped again, knuckles white and strained. He waited. She would break the silence first. . . .

"You summoned me for a reason, my lord?"

No reference to disaster. She avoided it, knowing what he meant.

"Yea, Lady Neville, I did. The outlaw Robin Hood—tell me what you know of him."

A pause, barely perceptible, a careless shrug; then: "I know what all know. In the days when John was still prince, he was outlawed, then pardoned by King Richard. Ballads were sung, tales were written. Most were exaggerated, some with a bit of truth in them. Robin has disappeared like the tales."

"Has he."

It was not a question but a challenge, and she recognized that.

"By all reports, my lord."

"Yet I believe you know differently. Do you not? Is there not more about this Robin Hood? Is he your kin?"

He left her no room for evasion, only for a direct lie. Lie or truth, she would tell him what he wanted to know.

Silence was a sticky web of indecision; she sat like stone, staring at him, conflict obvious on her eloquent face and in her shadowed eyes.

"Yes. He is my uncle," she said finally. "*Was* my uncle. He is dead now. Gone for near fourteen years."

"Gone? Or dead? Different things, milady."

"Dead!" Suddenly fierce, her hands tightened into fists in her lap. "Gone on Crusade to honor King Richard but never returned—sliced to ribbons in a pagan country, all to—"

She halted. Her lips pressed tightly together. He let the silence claim her again, a calming absence of response or demand. When color replaced her pallor, she released a soft breath. A sigh that was oddly poignant.

"It is painful . . . to suffer the loss of someone dear. It is common, I know; yet, on occasion, the loss is—particularly difficult."

Words stuck in his throat. No smooth reply meant to lure her to the truth would form; nothing could be summoned to ease the moment, her pain, or his own sudden stark memories.

Aimée. . . .

Softness and light . . . gone. Lost to him forever. An emptiness nothing could fill.

It was residue of the drug that made him vulnerable enough to recall the past, left him exposed to scouring pain. He sucked in a sharp breath; it raked his wound, welcome and familiar, drowning the other pain, which had no ease.

When he could speak, the memories were banished back to the netherworld where he kept them safe and untarnished.

"Yea, milady, we have all had losses."

Neutral, calm, as if from a distance he heard his voice; safety lay in detachment.

Her lashes flickered, a swift glance at him; if not for the tight quiver of her hands, he would have thought her emotion false.

"So we have, my lord."

"If Robin Hood is dead, and the tales with him, where then lies Little John? Will Scarlett? Alan of the Dales and Clym of the Clough? Their fame spreads of late."

She did not reply; her silence was answer enough.

He nodded. "As I thought. Perhaps your uncle is dead, but not his companions-in-arms." A lengthy pause while she digested the challenge, then: "Sir Guy came upon a longbow in your hall, milady. Five feet of Spanish yew."

Her eyes lifted to his, steady, calm. "Is it so rare to find a longbow in a Norman knight's home, my lord? Search further, and you will discover pikes, swords, maces—"

"*Five feet* of Spanish yew, my lady. Not six feet. A bow for someone your height. I remember Hugh de Neville. He was a tall man, a man who would draw a six-foot bow. This bow is light, with a sixty-weight draw to it."

Calmly: "It is not Hugh's. Even Normans must know that bows are made to fit growing youths."

"Yet I see no sons about."

Color drained abruptly from her face. "No, my lord, you do not."

Her tone had changed subtly; she answered his questions without lying, yet told him little. He already knew the few facts she admitted to—not even the veiled threat that he had proof of complicity was enough to shake her.

Dignified, composed, she allowed him scant hope of forcing from her the names and locations of the men who had been with her in the wood. Still . . . they would come here to her. Little John had come to her that once; they had tracked him here, though the dogs had lost his scent. He would come again, should he perceive the necessity. Yet, to use this woman in such a manner would be profane.

His head ached. His eyes were scratchy; his skin felt hot beneath the light cover. There had to be another way. It would never be enough to capture the outlaws who preyed on both Saxon and Norman; he wanted those who purposely flaunted Norman authority. Flaunted *his* authority. King John would hardly be impressed with a sheriff who could not capture outlaws even when their names and faces were well known.

The king. . . .

Cursed spawn of hell: temperate in nothing, inflexible in all. Ruler of England, tyrant of men, confiscator of lands . . . of Brayeton.

Brayeton: sloping hills, fertile marshlands. . . . His eyes closed, blotted out the chamber, the filtered light, and the lady; hid the mounting frustration that could betray him. *A baron, and I am reduced to holding public office, reduced to the king's bidding like a hound.* It was galling.

For a moment he floated, without direction save resentment. He was aware of the lady sitting beside the bed; her breath was soft, her silence loud.

Oddly, he understood.

This silence was different from the last, a subdued moment without tension or pain. A wave of dizziness crept closer, inexorable, remnants of potion reclaiming him. He resisted the stealing of his senses; *Not while she is here. . . .*

His eyes opened. He groped for words to dismiss her before he unmanned himself, but lost his tenuous grasp of anything that made sense. His vision blurred; her face smeared to a pale oval, shimmering. Abruptly, it faded. From a distance, he heard her voice floating through the mist:

"My lord sheriff . . . are you unwell?"

No . . . yes . . . I am sick to the soul and there is no cure for it.

Her face swam into his field of vision again; brows knitted in a slight frown, wet lips parted. A heady fragrance teased him, seemed to fill the world—mint. Sweet, piquant mint. It surrounded him, imbued him with a mystifying feeling of serenity.

His arm lifted slowly, the movement weighted, as if under water; he caught her chin in his palm. Pale skin, flawless as new snow, his hand a dark intrusion against such purity. He had a brief impression of wide eyes that mirrored light from the window; he pulled her close, then covered her mouth with his. She breathed a soft exhalation of surprise. He swallowed it and deepened the kiss. She tasted of mint, of enticement. He wanted her with a ferocity that was startling in its intensity. He must be delirious, drugged, deranged.

Yet, in his delirium, incited by poppies and raw need, he could lose sight of everything but this woman. It would be so easy . . . too easy.

He put his tongue into her mouth; a shudder went through her, a muffled moan. The tiny sound sparked heat in him, a searing fire surging through his body. Months of denial evaporated like morning mist; he was hard, ready for her, ready to ease himself in her velvet warmth, an act that would save them both, if only for a little while.

Then she wrenched away, the sudden loss leaving him bereft and throbbing. He sucked in a deep breath, sanity returning with air for his starved lungs; his vision cleared, blood beat more slowly, his body eased.

His lashes lowered, blinked away shreds of fog still clouding his mind, and the dizziness passed. Jane stared at him. Eyes, blue shadowed, unblinking, regarded him steadily. Suddenly, he felt a fool, compelled to belittle his lack of control.

"A moment's dalliance. I meant nothing by it."

"Did you not?" A pause, rife with scorn, though her voice shook a little. "I am grieved to hear it, my lord. I thought you a better man than to yield to baseless impulses like a common cur."

Anger, chagrin, summoned a wave of heat that burned his face and throat. He stared at her, eyes slightly narrowed; it was not undeserved.

"You have a wicked tongue, milady."

"So I have been told. May I take my leave now?"

He was suddenly drained of energy to continue the conversation, or even to remain awake.

"Take your leave. And take with you my vow that I will find and arrest the outlaws. Whether Robin Hood or Little John, I will destroy them."

"You chase empty shadows, my lord. Robin Hood died on Crusade. Only legends remain alive."

"Then I will destroy those as well."

Cold, calm, the promise neither silenced nor intimidated her. Her brow lifted, her lips curving into a faint smile.

"You will never destroy the legends. It is all that is left to England now—pride in our champions. That is what you Normans do not understand, will not understand." She turned toward the door, then paused to look back at him. "I pity you for your empty soul."

The door closed softly behind her. He stared at the blank expanse of English oak. The silence was bleak. The echo of her words revolved in his head with mocking accuracy. How had she known? What had betrayed him? What chance word or deed had exposed his secret?

It was true—his soul was empty. Had been empty for a long time. An abyss, a dark place; it yawned before him if he looked, but he knew better than to look. The desolation was too much to bear.

I pity you for your empty soul. . . .

He was lost, lost, drowning in misery and emptiness; he did not know how to save himself—did not know if he wanted to save himself. Nothing eased the pain he carried like an open, raw wound; how ironic, that the wounds of the body were so much easier to heal than the wounds of the soul. . . .

12

— ❧ —

Guy saw Lissa of Gedling in the small garden off the side of the manor house; she was perched on a stone bench with a lute cradled in her lap. Long fingers plucked the strings with a quill plectrum to produce a light melody that was unfamiliar. Her head was bent; a wimple of green silk draped in folds around her face, shrouded mystery as he approached.

"A lovely tune, milady."

Her head tilted, a smile curved her lips. "Do you like it, sir?"

"Charming. I do not think I have heard it before."

She laughed, a light trill of sound. "No, I expect you have not. It would not be a song Normans would appreciate, I think."

Amused, he thought, *A song of victory in battle.* "Will you sing it for me? I enjoy all music."

"If you like." She paused; her fingers glided over the strings gracefully, a ripple of music, then a swift glance. Amber eyes gleamed like gold coins. "It sounds better in English, so you will pardon me."

Guy shrugged. Though he used it little, he understood the language well. English was a crude tongue compared to

Norman French. His long legs bent to deposit him on tufted grass at her feet. His gaze drifted; eyes drawn to the luscious expanse of white skin visible above the square-cut neckline of her bliaut, riveted on the suggestion of shadow between her breasts that lured his attention more than the song. For a brief moment he was immersed in the luxury of envisioning what he could not see. A delightful interlude on a pleasurable day, a recess from the tedium of inactivity.

Lost in pleasant reverie, it took a few moments for the words of the song to seep through his sensuous haze. His head jerked up as she sang:

". . . When Robin came to fountaines abbey whereas that fryer lay, he was ware of the fryer where he stood, and to him thus can he say . . . 'I am a wet weary man,' said Robin Hood, 'good fellow, as thou may see, wilt beare me over this wild water, for sweete Saint Charity?' "

Guy put up a hand to stop her. "Milady, 'tis not wise for you to sing so provocative a song in this company."

Her hand stilled on the lute; her brow rose. "It is not usual for Normans to speak English. Most disdain it as a crude tongue."

"As do I." His jaw hardened at the scorn inherent in her tone. "While most of the men with me do not understand the language, the sheriff does. It would not be to your advantage to be heard singing such a melody."

He thought she would be intimidated; he misjudged her. She only laughed softly. "Perhaps your sheriff needs to broaden his knowledge. Shall I go and sing it to him so he will learn the nature of the men he pursues?"

"Only at grave risk, milady." He sat back on his heels, staring at her in appalled fascination. "Do not make the mistake of thinking your sex will save you, for he does not discriminate—"

"La, I have rarely seen the man who discriminates when it comes to sex, sir."

"You will find," Guy said carefully, "that Tré Devaux is not like most men."

"So I have seen for myself." One hand stroked up and down the slender neck of the lute, a suggestive motion that took him aback. A faint smile curled her mouth, then Lissa leaned forward, her voice soft: "He is a most well-favored man—but so are you, Sir Knight."

The forward movement made the neck of her bliaut gap; creamy skin, soft globes of ivory flesh, sweet temptation visible beneath the bodice. A flirt of pink nipples, just a glimpse, before she straightened. Immediately, his body reacted; any reply snared on his tongue.

"Thou art quiet, Sir Knight," she murmured in English. Her eyelids lowered, lashes fanning her cheeks, bold, an invitation and a suggestion. "Do I offend thee?"

The tip of her tongue swept out to wet her lips, an intoxicating swipe that made him think of things he knew he should not.

Desire surged, hot and strong, rendering him incapable of getting to his feet lest his erection be noticed. His knees pressed into the grass, weight balanced on the balls of his feet—it would be so easy to reach for her, pull her to him. A haycock or shadowed corner; it would not matter, save she was a lady, wed to a Saxon baron. If he touched her, his life may well be forfeit.

Still, he wanted to cover that wet gleaming mouth with his own, cup her round breasts in his hands and taste them until she yielded all. . . . He wanted to push her skirts up and put himself inside her.

Lissa rose to her feet, the lute dangled from one hand as she smiled down at him.

"As my music distresses thee, I will cease. Wouldst thou accompany me to the house, Sir Knight?"

Temptation . . . indecision; he hesitated. Dimples flashed in both cheeks, winsome and more innocent than the lady. She leaned toward him. Loose material afforded an ample view of generous breasts, rose-pink and cream. A whisper in French: "I will tell no one of our . . . conversation."

The implications were obvious. He lurched to his feet, angry that she would so tease him.

"There is nothing to tell, milady."

"Is there not?" A sideways glance, a smile. "Perhaps you are right." She straightened, half-turned, cast a long glance over one shoulder. "There is still time to change that, Sir Knight."

Guy did not move; he stared after her as she crossed the courtyard and took a path by the garden. Tense, taut with need, he watched her slow progress: slender hips, pale head touched by sunlight, green wool kirtle the color of new leaves—unrestrained desire. Uncomplicated by emotion or the need for reassurance; with Lissa of Gedling, there would be no need for pretty words or false declarations. She was everything the priests warned against.

The hall was illuminated by the hazy glow of candle racks; shadows of gold and jet danced on whitewashed walls. It was quiet, empty, save for Jane and Lissa.

Softly, so that her voice would not carry beyond the hall, Jane murmured, "Lissa, what were you thinking?"

A wool-clad shoulder lifted in a shrug. "It was amusing, and I have been bored of late."

She sounded petulant. Faint signs of discontent edged her tone and brow. "Sir Guy is handsome and young, not like Walter at all." She leaned forward; anger replaced the petulance. "At least he is not some blowsy tavern slut, such as those Walter favors."

That was the crux of it. Jane did not reply for a moment because there was nothing she could say to refute her cousin's accusation. It was well known that Walter of Dunham preferred low company to that of his young wife.

At last she said with a helpless wave of one hand, "You may have erred in this. Sir Guy is not some doting swain who will languish upon your whim. He is Norman, and a knight. It would be unwise to dally with him as you have with others."

A soft laugh with the comment, "He is a man like all the others."

"No, Lissa. *Not* like all the others. You dallied with mere boys. Guy de Beaufort is the sheriff's trusted man. He is no beardless youth to despair at your frown, weep at your anger.

There will be no love sonnets written in praise of your golden hair and breasts like pears, no songs sung beneath your bower in hopes that you will bestow upon him the favor of a single smile. You have misjudged your man this time."

"I think not." In the denial crouched uncertainty, and Jane pressed her advantage.

"Leave him be, Lissa. He is not like to fall in love with you."

"And what would you know of love?" Lissa's brow arched; her mouth tightened. "You are a widow in mourning for your dead husband and wasted youth. You have not known love, nor are you likely to. For you will be the nunnery or another loveless marriage. It is all the choice left to women unless they seize the moment and take what pleasures they may."

"As you have done?" Stung, as much by the truth as the cruelty of her cousin's words, Jane continued, "I see no joy in your life, but only unhappiness. With every man you take, do you find joy as well as pleasure? I think not."

Lissa's lower lip quivered; a glaze of tears silvered her eyes. "No . . ." husky, pained, "I have no joy in my life. It only seems fair for me to take what few moments of stolen pleasure I can."

A sigh escaped as Jane leaned forward to embrace Lissa. They clung for a moment, then parted, awkward and uncertain.

"I understand," Jane said at last. "I do. I just—worry about you." She took Lissa's hand between her own, held it fast. "You are dear to me. I want no harm to come to you."

A pause; then, in a rush of words: "I fret for your safety as well, Jane. Devaux means trouble for you. Why else would he be here?"

Because she could not confide the truth without endangering others, Jane shook her head. "The sheriff will leave when his wound is healed."

"Yet—" Lissa frowned, blurted, "He asks too many questions. There are rumors, Jane. Rumors that Robin Hood has returned."

"Returned?" Jane stared at her, swallowed a laugh when Lissa swore it was true.

"Walter told me it was Robin Hood who held the sheriff at bay by the Cockpen Oak—he heard it from a man who was there."

"One of the outlaws?" Jane shook her head. "It is only a wish, not the truth."

"How can you be so certain?" Lissa's eyes narrowed. "Did the sheriff tell you?"

"He does not tell, he demands to know. If it were true, he would not be asking us if Robin Hood is alive."

"Oh." Lissa sounded disappointed. "I suppose that is true. A pity. England could use a champion right now."

Silence fell between them, an easier silence now than before. Candles flickered, smelling of the herbs Jane put in the molds to lend them sweet scent; she must gather more. Her supply had dwindled since the sheriff's arrival. He lingered yet. When would he leave?

He should depart Ravenshed soon. His wound was near healed, his strength returning. Heat rose in her face and throat, as it always did when she recalled his kiss. Scalding illumination, a rare discovery of the lack in her life. Never had she been kissed as he had kissed her. Never.

At first Hugh had been careful with a young, untried maid; when she was older and more desirous of ardor, the pattern of their lives was set. It was a lack she had never felt keenly until now. Until now, when she recognized all that was missing from her life, and added another regret to the growing list.

She sat calmly in the familiar closeness of her hall, as alien in her own body as if she were in a strange land. How different her life might have been . . . and yet, she should not waste time on empty regrets. It availed her nothing.

Flames danced on the hearth; orange, red, and blue tongues greedily gnawed oak to charred embers.

On the morrow, she would go out to gather more herbs. While she did, perhaps she would bring in some sprigs of ivy to garnish the house. Dena swore that the plant guarded against evil and protected those within. It was foolish to believe in such tales, but then, in these times, it could not hurt to err on the side of caution.

A sudden draft bent the flames and made a peculiar hollow

moan in the chimney. Jane shivered. Dena would say it was the *bean sidhe's* warning, and that it presaged a death.

She thought of Little John. Tré Devaux meant to hunt him like a wild hart, run him to ground and take him alive. Yet he would be taken only to be hanged, a warning to all in Nottinghamshire that outlaws were marked for death.

There was nothing she could do to stop it. Nothing.

13

Restive, chafing at enforced inactivity, Tré paced the floor of the small chamber that overlooked the courtyard. He had counted the floor planks—sixteen from bed to window, attended by as many creaks of his weight on wood.

His mouth twisted. Reduced to counting planks, the idle desperation of an invalid.

Invalid in name only now; his strength had gradually returned, though he was plagued by bouts of irritating weakness.

"On the morrow," he said to Guy, sprawled in the flimsy frame of a chair, "I will be hale enough to sit a horse. I have been absent an entire sennight—seven nights in which Gaudet has had full rein. It is long enough."

Scrubbing at his jaw with one hand, Guy lifted a brow. "Yet Gaudet's daily courier assures you he has all well in hand, and that you are to tarry as long as you need."

"That alone makes it imperative that I get back before he sells the mace of office." His gaze came to rest on Guy; a gold-tinged brow and wide grin mocked him, and his tension eased. "He has no doubt changed the locks on all the doors."

Guy laughed softly. "Not even Gaudet is so foolish."

"No." He glanced out the window; sunlight graced the day. "Yet if he could find a way to be rid of me, he would do so."

"If he could find a way." Guy rose from the chair, stretched lazily like a great tomcat, then scratched his chest with an idle hand. "But there is no way for him to rid himself of you. He is still under King John's sharp eye."

"As am I," Tré pointed out dryly. "Gaudet would take advantage quickly enough, should the chance arise."

"Assuredly. Yet we have imprisoned outlaws, you raised the taxes and men John demanded, and have kept the barons quiet. What more could the king ask?"

Silence fell; Tré leaned a shoulder against the wood frame of the window. A warm breeze filtered through the open shutters. He shrugged.

"With John, all can—and no doubt will—be asked. He waits only for a mistake to seize the moment and have me arrested." He raked a hand through his hair, shook away stiffness in his side. "The last message from him demanded that I arrest and execute the Sherwood outlaws."

"No doubt Gaudet sent him word of the disaster at the Cockpen Oak."

"It would suit him well to see me fall." A patch of sunlight shifted on the far wall; he watched it for a moment. "Now that the pope has offered King John a compromise, the interdict will be lifted."

"So the king will be once more reconciled with the church, and give up his war against Philip of France?" Guy shook his head. "He only purchases time to plot."

John had no qualms about breaking faith with church or pontiff, if it suited his needs. On the surface, the king's truce with Rome was beneficial to all. Yet it smacked of subterfuge.

He glanced at Guy. "What men are left here?"

"All but those under Oliver's command. Word from him is reassuring. Nottingham is quiet for the moment." Guy joined him at the window, glanced out, and leaned an arm on the wall beside the frame. "I think it too fine a day to waste inside. Nottingham is the morrow. Today, we are here. What say you to a tour of the garden?"

"A tour of the—" Tré lifted a brow, followed Guy's gaze, then shook his head. "Go, if you must. I linger here."

In an instant he was gone, the oak door left ajar behind him.

Tré's gaze shifted back to the courtyard below his window. It had rained the three days past, but today it was clear and bright; a soft sun spread abundant light on field, wood—and the lady in the courtyard.

Lady Dunham occupied a bench beneath a stone wall that staggered crookedly around the courtyard. Bright blue garb was a merry splash of color against drab, gray stones, an invitation in silk. With a tilt of her head and a smile, she welcomed Guy to the bench, sliding to make room for him beside her.

So much alike, the two of them, both fair-haired and comely, with easy manners. Amusing company, with jests and light words, a diversion from long hours spent in compelled inertia while healing.

Far different from Lady Neville, with her sharp tongue. The memory still burned:

"I pity you for your empty soul. . . ."

In that instant, he had seen himself as she saw him: a husk of a man, only going through the motions of life. It was an illuminating discovery.

He scraped a hand over his jaw; beard stubble rasped beneath his palm. He needed a shave. His hair was too long. No matter how much mint he chewed, he could not rid his mouth of a bitter taste.

No matter what else he thought about, he could not rid his mind of her haunting accusation. . . .

Abruptly, he wheeled about. A tour of the garden was preferable to being alone with his memories. Guy would have to suffer his company. He snatched up a jerkin, soft leather of dark green that had been produced for him in lieu of leather hauberk or mail. He did not want to think about who had worn it before; it was better than discomfort or nakedness.

Descent of the narrow staircase was a bit shakier than he had considered it would be; too much time abed had left him weak. He moved through the empty hall; the doorway loomed just ahead.

He paused on the threshold. Sunlight hit him with blinding intensity. After so many days inside, it took a moment for his eyes to adjust to the onslaught. A fresh breeze carried the fragrance of roses and mint; chickens clucked busily; new lambs bleated.

Mundane details, ordinary life far removed from kings and castles. Peace and promise of life's renewal replaced strife and intrigue; it could become a habit, if he allowed it. But he could not. His life was not one of rural peace. Even if he wanted to retreat, the king would never allow it, never trust him not to raise arms in rebellion against him, as his overlord had done.

A hand shaded his eyes as he moved down the steps and across the courtyard. Guy smiled welcome, a little wryly, while Lady Dunham watched his approach with wary eyes. She cradled a lute in her lap.

His hand dropped from his eyes; he acknowledged Guy's greeting before his gaze shifted to the lady. It was an awkward moment that begged for ordinary comment: "Do you play the lute, Lady Dunham?"

"Yea, my lord high sheriff, I do play. I am most adept at ballads, should you care to—"

Guy jerked to his feet; he held out a hand to the lady. "You do not want to abuse an invalid, Lady Dunham. Come. You promised me a walk in the garden."

A faint, mysterious smile curved the lady's mouth as she rose gracefully. "Very well, Sir Guy. I think you will enjoy a stroll among the roses after all."

Slightly bemused by Guy's uncharacteristic gruffness, Tré watched as they turned toward the garden at the side of the house. It had not escaped his notice in the past days that the lady had taken up with his knight; it was not a matter of concern to him, save that the lady was wed to a Saxon baron. Guy could be trusted not to be a fool. It was the unknown quality of the lady that might prove troublesome.

Across the courtyard by the stables, several of his men worked at repairing harness and cleaning their weapons. Guy had set them to worthwhile tasks to occupy their time and keep them from restlessness. Boredom was often the bane of a soldier's life. As it was his, of late.

Tré followed a narrow path at a right angle from the house,

entering the garden plot behind the kitchens. A soft wind carried the aromatic scent of rue. Lush new vines of peas and beans clambered over poles crossed and tied to bear the weight. Next to these, straight furrows of colewort nudged spindly stems of tansy and angelica, both herbs strong scented, as was the sweet mint drooped over whitish rock borders.

He plucked a leaf of mint, rolled it between his fingers as he walked, releasing fragrance from the bruised leaf. It was a sweet mint, excellent in food and for cleansing the palate. It tasted strong on his tongue.

He wandered by the kitchens, saw the older servant— Dena?—staring at him from the doorway; flex of her knee, a courtesy he acknowledged with a slight nod. She was older, careworn in face and body, devoted, he had noticed, to her mistress. Lady Neville seemed to inspire devotion.

An established orchard ranged behind the kitchen, dipped down a slope to end abruptly at a high wall that enclosed the manor. Apple, pear, and cherry trees were in bloom. The air was full of fragrance and promise. Spring: a new beginning.

A sense of peace enveloped him. It was unexpected, and unwanted. He could not afford to indulge such luxuries. It would make him careless.

A faint mewling drifted on the breeze, and he paused. It came again, more loudly this time, and he looked up. A rustle in the branches of a cherry tree shivered the pink blossoms; the cry sounded again.

Parting leaves and flowers, he saw the source of the noise: a tiny gray kitten, stiff fur and wide eyes, mewled protest and fright. It clung tightly to a branch, claws dug into bark. A pink mouth opened again to emit another pitiful cry. From the ground not far away, an answering cry pushed the kitten to further effort.

Tré glimpsed a quivering of tall grass, saw the shape of a cat slip behind a tree trunk. He glanced up at the kitten again; the mews had altered to panicked screeches. The mother cat paced, afraid but unwilling to abandon it.

He reached up to the branch, grabbed fur and fright, and was promptly bitten. Claws and teeth levied damage as he swung the kitten to the ground much more gently than he thought it deserved. With a last, indignant hiss, the kitten joined its mother and was gone.

As he inspected the damage to his hand, he heard a soft laugh behind him. His mouth flattened. Must she always be near at his most vulnerable moments? He glanced up.

"Obviously a Saxon kitten."

"Yea," Jane replied, "but we think the father Norman."

"On what grounds do you base that assumption?"

"He invaded the stableyard, promptly conquered all rivalry, then made it his home. Let me see your hand." She took his wrist despite his resistance, turned his hand over to inspect the scratches. "None of these are deep."

Sunlight glinted in her hair; the familiar scent of mint emanated from her. He closed his fingers around her arm when she would have pulled away. "A fierce little thing."

"Yes. I fear the gray kitten will be much like his sire."

"I meant you, not the cat."

"Really?" Blue eyes glanced up, looked away quickly. "I have never been called fierce."

"I am amazed. Perhaps none dared say it to you."

"But you, of course, dare." Laughing now, lips worked to suppress it. "A stalwart Norman, as always."

"Stalwart? Yea, I suppose I am. A bit worse for wear now, but alive."

"Like Graymalkin—the Norman tomcat—you must have nine lives, my lord."

"Not anymore. Most of them have been used in the past few years. I cannot have many left." He paused; the moment was in danger of becoming comfortable. Deliberate malice: "Little John's quarterstaff near took another one."

The smile left her face and eyes. He almost regretted having said it. Yet it was true; he waited, and when she did not offer a reply, he looked up and beyond her to the flowering fruit trees.

"The dogs tracked him to these walls that night. I was past knowing it then, but Captain Oliver pursued him. For a time, the scent was lost in a stream. It was found again just beyond this orchard, on the north slope."

Calm, revealing nothing: "And was pursuit successful, my lord?"

Only the tense set of her mouth gave any indication of turmoil, and after a moment of long silence he said, "No. It was not. As you no doubt know quite well."

"I know only what you deem necessary to tell me."

"If that were true, you would be ill informed, indeed." He released her arm and she took a step away. Tension was back; it writhed between them, alive, hissing with suspicion and frustration. Familiar, a safe barrier. . . .

Instead of fleeing as he expected, she remained quiet and still beneath the cherry tree. The wind soughed through the branches; they clacked softly, a chiding sound that loosened a few creamy blossoms to flutter free and garnish the crown of her head.

The tension began to ease with her silence; he thought it must be a gift, her ability to create peace amid turmoil. The tight knot in his belly loosened. The air smelled sweet again, rife with cherry blossoms and mint. He could breathe more easily now, without the pain it sparked in his side.

This was dangerous territory. Far safer to be angry, to keep her at arm's length. Foolish, to allow soft sentiment to dissuade him from a course set long before he had met Lady Neville. There was no place for any sentiment in his life.

He marshalled his resistance, forsook the gift of peace she offered, again found words that would lash it to ribbons: "We return on the morrow to Nottingham. In short time, I expect to have the outlaws in custody."

"And then your life will be once more restored to peace and harmony. Or will it, my lord?"

How did she know? Reproof and reminder: His life would never be peaceful or harmonious. He drew in a deep breath that made his wound ache.

"No, but I will have done what I set out to do."

"That must afford you a great deal of satisfaction, my lord."

His jaw set. "It will when it is done."

Blue eyes named him liar; she was wrong. Why would she not believe that of him? He could hang every outlaw in England and not lose a moment's sleep over it.

He put a hand on her shoulder; his fingers dug into blue wool. "I do what I have to do, and suffer no remorse for grown men who summon their own justice. I do not visit war upon women and children. Even those who have defied the king's demands for taxes have been dealt with fairly. I do not imprison wives, widows, or the elderly. Nor do I allow my men to plunder. Any man of my guard who conducts himself in a vile manner is dealt with by me. I brook no misuse of the innocent."

He paused, saw argument rise to her lips, and said, "I know there are men of the king's guard who do not abide by the same rules of conduct. I have no control over them or their actions. I can only govern my own and the actions of the men in my command. But neither will I allow men outside the law to flaunt my authority."

"Typical Norman arrogance."

His mouth tightened. "It has little to do with Norman or Saxon differences. Outlawry is not tolerated."

To his surprise, she suddenly agreed. A deep indrawn breath, a nod, and the acknowledgment: "Yea, you are right, my lord. It should not be tolerated."

Wryly: "I had not expected such easy victory. You leave me at a loss."

"I am pleased to hear it." She moved back a step and his hand fell away from her shoulder. Shadows flickered over her face, and she refused to meet his gaze.

"Is it your habit to give in so easily when wrong, my lady?" He could not resist the sally, driven by a perverse urge to keep her close when he knew she meant to retreat.

"I would not know," she replied to the space beyond his left ear, still not looking at him. "It does not happen often."

"Ah. And you complain of Norman arrogance."

At last: a faint smile and glance at his face. Her lips recovered first, pressed again into a thin line before she glanced away.

"Perhaps Normans are not alone in their conceit."

"No," he agreed, "perhaps not."

"Easy surrender. . . ." Eyes flicked toward him again, spread fingers smoothed down her sides. A nervous gesture; she was immaculate as always. A simple light wool cotte of blue skimmed her frame, bound around her waist by a plain girdle that held a ring of keys; the keys tinkled lightly with her restive motions. No wimple or coif hid her hair; it was held back from her forehead by a plain circlet, caught in a single braid down her back.

"Not a surrender," he said. "A concession."

"Is that not the same thing?"

"No. I do not surrender all, but I yield to you the point."

"Small differences. . . ."

"Yes. Very small." He was suddenly impatient with this fencing of words. Gone was the need to keep her at bay; he wanted to hold her—to crush her into submission beneath him, to spread his hands in her glorious hair and taste her at leisure. Desire beat in him now, hot and swift and strong. If he gave in to it, he would be lost.

Yet even as the thought formed, he reached for her. His hand cupped the back of her neck, thick plait beneath his palm, silken fibers in a rough caress. Under the pressure, she swayed toward him, eyes a startled blue, lips parted in a swift inhalation.

He ignored her slight resistance and the silent chiding that warned him against it—he took possession of her mouth. Her lips flattened beneath his, parted, allowed him entry.

Hunger sharpened. It drew his belly tight, moved lower to his groin. Heat surged, ignited into raw flame that turned resistance to ash. He leaned his weight into her, pressed her back against the stout bole of the tree. The branches shuddered; pale flowers fell in a fragrant drift.

He felt her surrender; it was a tangible thing, a soft sighing breath, a loosening of muscle and will, a crumbling of resolve. He wanted it, yet he did not. Her surrender could destroy them both.

Angry, at himself and at her, he pushed against her with his body, felt the sweet softness of her curved thighs tremble, her breath shudder. It was arousing; for a moment he lost the anger, found in its place a desperate need to feel soft skin beneath his hands instead of blue wool.

One hand moved to caress her while his tongue explored her mouth, intent, excited. She made a faint sound when at last he encountered female flesh instead of wool, his palm raking aside folds of cotte to slide over her bared shoulder. Something ripped; he heard it, the parting of a seam. Unexpected bounty—his hand shifted down, found and embraced the fullness of a breast. Thumb and finger closed on thin linen and a beaded nipple, teasing it into a tight knot.

Jane broke free of his kiss, arched back against the tree, but he held her with his other hand beneath her chin to keep her from twisting away. His body throbbed, stiffened to full arousal, pressed against her belly. He damned the three layers of clothing between them, captured her mouth again. Blood pounded in his ears. He felt her quiver. His thumb and finger plucked at the nipple still. A moan vibrated low in her throat. She was his for the taking. . . .

For both of them, it was a defining moment of discovery.

Sharp sensation curled inside her as she shuddered in reaction to his touch and kiss. She should push him away, but the fire that had been building inside her burned away caution. She was consumed with it; her body acknowledged his touch; heightened sensitivity beneath his questing hand.

Awkwardly, she twisted free. Her hand lifted to his face, fingerpads grazed beard stubble, touched him lightly on the jaw. Fiercely seductive, strength and determination pressed hard against her so that she could feel the rigid shape of his need prodding her belly. Her eyes closed; she remembered the feel of his body in her hand, silken heat and steel, proud Norman baron demanding her attention.

His hand closed in her hair; tugged at the plait. Her scalp burned at the pressure that brought her chin up; lips burned beneath the ferocity of his kiss. There was anger in it, frustration mixed with need. She felt the throbbing in him. Her breasts were swollen and tender, pushed against his chest; the bruising pressure of metal grommets on his jerkin was sharp. Everywhere their bodies touched, she burned. Between her legs, the pressure blossomed into a relentless ache that bordered pleasure and pain.

The kiss ended abruptly. His breath was hot, harsh against her ear; he pressed her face against his leather jerkin and sucked in a sharp breath.

"Someone comes."

At first, the words made no sense to her. She absorbed them slowly through the haze that surrounded her. Then she understood as he took a step back and released her.

She put a hand to her mouth, touched swollen lips, then to her shoulder where the seam of her cotte was torn. With swift efficiency, he tucked the frayed edges together to cover bare skin and linen kirtle.

She glanced up. His face was sharp, features defined by a dark flush and skin stretched taut over cheekbones and chiseled jaw. A flash of green smoldered beneath lowered lashes; he briefly met her gaze, then looked away. Tension vibrated.

Her lungs were aching for air. The intensity was frightening; yet more frightening was the melting surrender that had turned her resistance to mere shadow.

The smell of cherry blossoms was suddenly too sweet, a cloying fragrance that permeated everything. Nausea rose. Chilled despite the warm sunlight streaming through tree branches, she shivered.

His tone was flat, neutral: "Sir Guy approaches."

Her gaze shifted past him to the front of the orchard, where Sir Guy was just coming down the path. Tré did not touch her, but his body was a barrier that kept her from sight.

"You are composed?"

She glanced up, nodded. "Yea, I am."

A faint smile pressed the corners of his mouth. "It is female advantage that leaves my reactions more exposed."

Involuntary glance down, a flush heated her cheeks, and she stifled a laugh. "I do not complain."

"No. I see that." A pause; Guy drew closer. Bonds of intimacy had been forged between them now. She felt Tré's unaccustomed turmoil. It shadowed his eyes, tinged his words with graceless effort: "I will not see you again. I leave on the morrow."

"Yes. I know."

Lame response, formed without thought or emotion, only an understanding that had not been there before. But he knew her thoughts, briefly met her eyes, a swift glance that burned like dragon's fire.

He met Sir Guy on the path, steered him away. She did not

move from beneath the cherry tree. It supported her, knotted bark against her spine a welcome brace. There was a weakness in her legs, a crumbling of her knees that refused to bear her weight alone.

He was leaving. With him would go the tension, the unbearable anxiety—the drumming excitement. Ravenshed would return to normal. Long days of routine tasks, hopefully uninterrupted by tragedies great or small. Days would settle around her again, comfortable and endless. Her life would return to the same rhythm as before he had come.

And she did not think she could bear it.

14

— ❧ —

May 20, 1213

"You were gone overlong, my lord. I took it upon my own head to make decisions." Gervaise Gaudet's hand curled into a fist atop the table; his eyes blazed as he stared back at Tré.

"Then you can take it upon your own head to undo them. I do not condone indiscriminate killing of prisoners, outlaw or no. All men are allowed justice."

"Justice? Such as that shown in the forest? Those men are wolf's heads—murderers, rapists, and vermin. Outlaws by even their own standards."

"Mark me well, Gaudet—" Tré kept his tone even and soft so that the undersheriff had to be very still to hear him. "Convicted outlaws will be hanged with due process. You are not judge and executioner—unless you wish to feel the weight of my own justice upon your neck."

Silence fell; a torch hissed and sputtered in the iron cresset on the near wall. None near enough to hear the sharp words dared move for fear of attracting attention.

"Do you threaten me, my lord?" Gaudet asked at last. His tone was mild despite taut white lines carved on each side of his mouth.

"I do not threaten. Betimes, I promise, but I see no need for idle threats." His meaning was well marked, and as the pale eyes flickered: "Your place here is only as secure as your prudence keeps it. You have no more power in the Norman borough than any castellan."

Light glittered on the chain of office Gaudet wore around his neck like a badge of pride, polished and preening against crimson velvet. A tuft of beard on the narrow point of his chin quivered with suppressed anger; a muscle leaped in his jaw. "I am appointed by the king to sheriff of the Saxon borough of Nottingham, a man of consequence."

"Until you overstep your bounds. In your recitation of self-consequence, do not forget that you also have sworn to uphold your duty of obedience to your superiors. King John himself made the distinction of high sheriff mine, Gaudet."

It had to be galling. To a man of Gaudet's pride and ambition, the bitterness of seeing the position he wanted go to another would be doubly harsh when accompanied by the shame of his cousin's failure. It would be made worse by the knowledge that the man to whom the position was given made no secret of the fact that he considered it a demotion in rank.

His point made, Tré gestured Guy forward. "Join us, Sir Guy. We must discuss the king's visit. John sends word that he will be in Nottingham by Saint John's Eve, on his way to Clipstone Palace to hunt. As Sir Gervaise took the liberty of forming a reply to him"—a lifted brow and glance at Gaudet made him writhe in his chair—"we are now committed to a celebration in the king's honor."

"A celebration!" Guy checked angry astonishment at a warning glance from Tré, then smiled grimly. "I see."

"No," Gaudet snarled, "I do not think you do see. The king enjoys a hanging. We have outlaws to hang. Hangings always draw a crowd. It stands to reason it would impress the king to conjoin hangings and observance of Saint John's Eve. Especially in light of his reconciliation with the pope."

"Yea, an apt manner to mark a saint's feast day and reconciling with the church," Guy muttered wryly. "Hanging outlaws."

Tré leaned against the table. Thin light almost pierced the

windows overhead; it was gray outside, raining again. Musty gloom pervaded the hall and chilled his bones.

The thought of the king was more chilling.

"It might," he said slowly, and saw Guy turn to stare at him with narrowed eyes, "be to our advantage after all."

"I said it would be." Gaudet sounded as waspish as an old woman. "It will please the king."

"What will please the king is to have his coffers full and all the outlaws exterminated." Guy slung one foot onto a hard bench; his eyes were cold. "We have neither."

"That is hardly my fault." Gaudet lifted a brow; his lips thinned. "Nor is it my responsibility. I have done my duties as prescribed. It is the high sheriff's duty to rid the shire of outlaws and collect the king's taxes."

Tré put up a warning hand when Guy loomed over Gaudet with a hand on the hilt of his sword. "Leave it, Sir Guy. He is right."

"He baits you!" Guy gestured to Gaudet angrily. "It would not surprise me to learn he sent an invitation to the king to come, knowing John will not be pleased."

"Nor would it me. But there are ways to deal with men of deceit." He waited until Gaudet slid his wary gaze from Guy to him, then smiled. "Treachery begets treachery."

Rising to his feet, the undersheriff bared his teeth in a feral smile. "As you should well know, my lord. It was treachery that gained you the position of high sheriff."

"Yea, but not of the sort you mean. If not for the treachery of my Saxon overlord, I would not now be here. He has lost all because of his treason. Be ware, lest you do the same."

Silence greeted his warning, then Gaudet pushed past him to quit the hall in a flurry of red and yellow garments.

Guy muttered, "He will do you a serious harm if he is not watched."

"Even watched, he manages."

Guy nodded agreement. "So the king arrives. We have a month to deplete the shire of outlaws and fill the king's coffers. Again."

"Yet Gaudet has lent us his aid, though he may not know it."

"By inviting the king?" Guy looked incredulous.

"Yea, by inviting the king to a celebration." He pushed away from the table. "I will explain while we see to the king's apartments."

They left the great hall; directly across were the kitchens, with his own apartments taking up the rest of the curtain wall. Cobbled stones were slick as they crossed the middle bailey to the gate that led to the upper bailey and the royal apartments. Rain misted carved lions on each side of the gate, drooled from stone fangs bared in savage warning. A unicorn reared in frozen posture against the drawbridge; chains clanked a hollow protest as the gate was lifted for them. Below, a moat trickled sluggishly, giving off a stench that not even fresh rain could abate. A steep flight of stone steps led to the upper bailey, encompassed by four towers and high stone walls.

"It is hard to reconcile yielding up this castle even to King Richard," Guy muttered when they passed beneath the high tower, which guarded the entry to the upper bailey. "Yet it held out only three days."

"You met Richard once. Would you hold it against him?"

Guy laughed softly. "I would not have tried. What plan do you have to thwart John?"

"See this?" He indicated the newly constructed tower. "It is part of John's plan to strengthen the defenses and refortify the castle. He knows it may be needed. There is more."

They entered the round tower; it was set amid the royal apartments, with chapels, guardhouses, and granary strung within the protection of fifteen-foot-thick walls. This was the highest part of Nottingham Castle. It perched atop the summit of sandstone that jutted up from the feet of the King's Meadows, with rocky toes dipped in the River Leen.

Inside, there was dark gloom unlit by torch or window. A thin slit gave the only light, a weak stream of gray that barely cut the shadows. Tré did not take the coil of stone steps that led to the top. The toe of his boot nudged the floor, counted four stones, then another before catching on a small projection. He knelt; fingers grazed an iron latch worked into stone, tucked beneath the low-hanging rise of stairs.

Over one shoulder: "Are any close-by?"

"Nay." Guy sounded hushed, anticipating. "None come near."

Tré curled his fingers into the iron ring and gave a tug. It grated roughly, stone on stone, shifted only a bit before he tugged again. This time the stone lifted; a rush of musty air swept up and over him. Infinity yawned black and endless.

"A cellar?" Guy sounded disappointed.

"More than that, Guy. Here. Light these." He produced two candle stubs, and Guy lit them from the torch at the entry.

When he returned, he muttered, "We should wait until dark for this."

"No. The light would be more easily seen then. We do not go far." He slid into the opening, looked up, saw Guy's face, and grinned. "You are one of the few who know of this. Step carefully. Do not look so distrusting. Not even Gaudet knows this exists."

"Knows *what*—" Guy's voice bounced eerily and was swallowed by gloom as he followed Tré. He glanced around; disembodied by enveloping blackness, his face was a collage of stark shadow and pallid light. "It is a tunnel."

"Yea, it is that. It leads to the river."

"To the River Leen?"

"Past the brewhouse and under the Rock Yard. It is a natural tunnel, I think, a bit improved upon. It goes through castle rock . . . take caution."

"How did you find it?" Guy spoke in a hush; it did not matter, for his words were quickly smothered in shadow. Underfoot, the sandstone proved to be precarious footing. The tunnel dipped away sharply, disappeared in darkness.

"It was an accident."

"It is not well known, then?"

Tré held his candle higher; a draft guttered it to leave only Guy's candle burning. Above them, the steps were a soft buff shimmer.

"No. It is meant for only the king to know."

"A way out. . . ."

"Built after Richard's siege, I do not doubt. It has been here longer than the tower." He indicated the shaft. "It ends just above the river."

Breath formed clouds in front of their faces; even in the dark, he saw that Guy understood the implications inherent to the tunnel's existence. It was a way out, but also a way into the castle. Dangerous knowledge in the wrong hands.

Once outside the tower again, he stood in the shadow of the wall where the rain did not reach. Above them, on the top battlements, guards kept watch.

"The king anticipates civil war." Guy phrased it as a statement of fact. "He plans for it. He means to use Nottingham as a military base against his own barons."

"Yea, I believe he does. It explains his need for money and fortified walls where the French are not likely to come. If cornered here, he has a way out—and a way in."

Beyond the castle, a northern bailey was already partly enclosed by wooden palisades. Another defensive wall.

"And the king comes in a month," Guy said softly. "Does war against the barons begin so soon?"

"It could. If it does, we will have a way out."

Thunder rumbled in the distance; beyond the high walls of the upper bailey, the King's Meadows stretched to the River Trent, the water only a faint haze below a wooded ridge. London was a long way away, yet had never seemed closer.

"What do we do about the outlaws?" Guy paused. "You said you have a plan."

"Gaudet has been kind enough to solve that problem for us, though he would be grieved to hear it."

Grinning, Guy joined him on the steep descent to the middle bailey. "Then I am doubly curious to hear your solution."

"It is simple enough. We will invite them to the king's celebration."

15

First light would come early now with the waxing of summer strong upon the land. Jane stood in the darkness by the stable wall. She wore a loose tunic and hose beneath a black robe; over that, a red hood with a bell sewn to the long tip. It was a leper's garb, a worthy disguise that should see her safely unaccosted on her journey.

The silence was dense around her as she led a rouncy from the stable, an old beast that would cause little comment, and mounted astride. Rufford Abbey lay a goodly distance from Ravenshed; she prayed Brother Tuck was still there.

Crumpled parchment crackled when she moved, scratching tender flesh, tucked inside her tunic to keep it safe. It bore the sheriff's seal, broken now, delivered by castle courier, a command disguised as invitation: A tourney and banquet to honor the king—her presence was required. It was formal, detached, no hint of what had passed between them; a question unanswered.

Did Devaux seek her out—or warn her?

Fretful uncertainty dogged her; she was no good at this sort of thing, useless with double meanings and intrigue. So few she could trust—Little John and Tuck. Still, wiser heads to offer advice.

The leper's bell jangled, sounding loud as she turned the plodding horse eastward from Ravenshed. Narrow lanes were deserted; there was no sign of soldiers or that she was being watched. The clink of bridle chains softly accompanied the bell bobbing against her back, both echoing in the darkness that blanketed the verge.

Jane was well away from Ravenshed when it grew lighter. The sun rose over hills and wood; gray melded to pearl, grew sharper, burned away the early mists shrouding the greenwood. Light warmed the road and her back, bright by the time she reached Bilsthorpe. The hamlet spread on a promontory, ringed with wood and silence. No one approached her as she passed through; few would approach a leper.

Finally the walls of Rufford Abbey hove into view; the gates were open. She dismounted, changed her leper's garb for the simple robe of a penitent, and led the weary rouncy down the long track to the abbey. White-robed Cistercian monks worked busily; the abbey's infirmary, stables, workshops, and wool mills helped sustain monks and lay brothers. With the king's recent depredations against the church now ended, abbey life was returning to normal.

An order of silence allowed no conversation between monks and lay brothers. Visitors were required to keep their tongues while present.

It was a requirement Jane had no trouble meeting, as her voice would betray her gender should she speak.

There was no sign of Frère Tuck. She lingered alone outside the west wing. The lay brothers' frater just off the kitchen separated it from the choir monks' frater. A bell signaled the main meal, and lay brothers and monks entered the refectory. Tuck was not among them.

Disappointed, she gave in to her rumbling stomach and stepped into the vaulted chamber. Thin light threaded through stone-arched windows to illuminate gloom. No lamps were lit, or words spoken as lay brothers retrieved spoons from a carved niche in the wall and seated themselves at the long tables set up in a double row. In the south wall, another niche held a crucifix and a glowing candle.

A prayer was said; the silence was broken by the shuffling of feet and clack of wooden spoons against bowls as they began to eat. While a monk read to them from the Holy Book, they ate silently; Latin words were a familiar drone.

She kept her head down. Thick circular pillars braced a groin-vaulted roof, graceful as angel wings. The stone floors were cold and damp, and she was grateful for the buskins warming her feet and legs. The pottage was thick and savory with leeks, turnips, and meat; brown bread and ale were provided.

The reading from the Holy Book ended with the meal. All rose and filed from the refectory in silence. Jane trailed behind. As she stepped into the light again, blinking at the sudden change, a hand took her elbow. The silent pressure of pudgy fingers guided her to one side, then back into an arched doorway.

A long, narrow parlor just off the frater closed around her; here there was conversation in low tones. Brothers sat on benches placed along the walls.

"Tuck!"

"Aye." In a tone rusty from disuse, he reminded softly, "Here I am called Brother Robert. We have not much time. Talk is permitted only at certain hours, and only in here."

"I must talk to Little John—can you take me to him?"

Consternation briefly creased Tuck's round face; he hesitated, glanced around, then smiled. "Meet me after Nones by the church in Wellow."

"I will be garbed as a leper—"

"Yea, I know." Laughter edged his voice, a glimpse of the old Tuck she had once known. "A disguise that fools no one. I will find you after my duties are done."

A thousand different thoughts crowded her mind; time passed slowly until she saw Tuck again, coming at last along the narrow track that led from the abbey to the tiny hamlet of Wellow. His stout frame was a familiar bulk, sandaled feet plodding the rutted road with confident grace despite his size. A grin split his face as he saw her waiting beside the rouncy.

"A leper with a horse. Most entertaining."

She laughed softly. "A monk with a big belly is even more so."

"Ah, it is a cross I bear most willingly." Brown eyes regarded her shrewdly, peering into the shadows of her hood. "Your beauty increases with the years."

"And your tongue grows more glib. Tell me news of my aunt."

He fell into step beside her. "Lady Marian—Sister Mary, now—is well. She is content to remain cloistered away from the secular world, yet at times the world invades even convents. She sends her blessings."

Marian. Her aunt by marriage, wife to Robin. For years she had sought refuge in a nunnery, shut away from the world and contact with even those who loved her. Only Brother Tuck remained in touch with her, and that limited. Oddly, tears stung Jane's eyes. Marian was her last link with family; all others were long dead.

Tuck gripped her arm, his voice kind. "Walesby is not far from here. The caves are close. I shall go with you."

"A monk and a leper." She laughed, though it had a taut sound to it. "We are an unlikely pair to pass notice."

"Steady, my lady. You are made of sterner stuff than to wither now. Your mother would be fair proud of you, to see how strong and lovely you have grown."

"My mother?" Memories returned, vague and frayed with time, blurred visions of a dark-haired woman who smelled of mint. "My mother would be horrified," she said with a faint smile, "if she knew what I have done."

"You speak of the fray at the Cockpen Oak."

Wryly, she nodded. "Yea, I do. You have been told of it, I see."

"Milady, all of England has heard of it by now, though few would guess the hooded outlaw who held the sheriff at bay with a single arrow is a slip of a maid, and not the return of a fabled hero."

Amusement eased her brief gloom. "Lord Dunham swears Robin Hood has returned."

"Yea, the tale spreads far from Sherwood. Even in the abbey we hear news. It must gall the sheriff to be so humbled."

Startled, she realized that she had not thought of Devaux's chagrin, only her own emotions. Of course it would shame him—he had been bested, not only by an outlaw but at an awkward moment. Laughter at his expense would be far more humiliating than the escape of the outlaws.

It put him in a different light. Beneath his harsh exterior lay brief impulses of kindness; she had seen it, in the gentle hand that returned a kitten to its mother, in his patience with an elderly servant who tried even her patience at times. Could she have wronged him?

Oh, I do not know what to think . . . he confounds me with kisses, yet leaves without a word. Is he kind, or ruthless? Or is it all a farce? A pretense to gain his own ends?

Tuck put out a hand to guide her from a misstep in a rut, looked up with a smile. "You are much like your mother."

"I am nothing like my mother." Despair etched her tone. "She was a lady. My earliest memories of her are steeped in warnings that I would one day disgrace myself if I did not behave as a lady should. It seems she was right."

Tuck fell silent; his breath was labored as he walked, footsteps heavy beside her light ones. Finally he said, "It is no disgrace to come to the aid of those being abused, my lady. Never forget that. Your mother would not have forgotten it."

"No." She inhaled the scent of wild roses and sweet creeper. "She would not have forgotten it."

It was late afternoon when they reached the shallow River Maun where it wound lazily through sloping meadows dotted with poppies. A breeze made ripples in the grass like sea waves, a soft rustling sound. The warm sunlight and wind in her hair was a benediction; it eased her fears as she paused, listening to the murmur of the river beneath red sandstone bluffs. To one side was a deep, cool greenwood that separated Walesby from the river.

"The wooded path," Tuck puffed, and pointed to the right where a stretch of thick trees parted slightly.

Jane pulled the rouncy to a halt. It blew noisily; the sound carried, brittle in the muffled silence of the wood. She leaned against the horse and felt heat beneath her palm.

"Which way lies the cave?"

"They will come for us." Tuck bent slightly with his hands spread on his knees. "We will wait here." He wore a rough brown-robe instead of the white wool of a Cistercian; it covered his ample frame to the ankles.

Folding her legs, Jane sat beneath a tree on a lush tussock of green, pushed back the hood to free her hair. Tuck moved to sit beside her, grunting as he lowered himself to the ground.

"I grow stiff with age and fat," he muttered. Sweat made fine rivulets from his temples, wetting a dark fringe of hair beneath his tonsured pate. "It is as well that I am removed from secular life. I fear I would soon expire from exertion."

Jane managed a smile. Tuck asked no questions, sensing, perhaps, that she would confide in him when ready. She plucked a sprig of grass; the leper bell chimed softly with her movement. The rouncy began to graze, blowing softly in the long grasses.

Rasping calls of wood pigeon and dove trilled among thick leaves. Tuck struggled to his feet, then held out his hand. "Don the leper's hood, my lady."

She took Tuck's hand and rose to her feet, eased folds of hood over her head and tucked long hair beneath the wool.

It was not long before she heard the low hoot of an owl and then another. A glimpse of green leaf-shiver was swiftly followed by the parting of branches.

A man dressed in Lincoln green beckoned from the thick line of bushes and tall, waving tufts of grass. Unsmiling, unfamiliar, he looked from her to Tuck, then nodded.

"Leave the horse."

Silent, he led them deeper into the trees, until the path narrowed and seemed to disappear. Birds twittered overhead; twigs snapped underfoot as they entered a tunnel of interwoven tree branches.

When they emerged, it was at the bottom of a steep slope. A raw red sandstone bluff rose abruptly like a crude fortress. Scarlet bursts of poppies crowned the bluff; blue forget-me-nots bunched beneath the trees. Violet blossoms of ground ivy lent a strong scent to the air.

Tuck sucked in huge gusts of air; his face was as red as the sandstone. She put a hand on his arm and he managed a grin and slight shake of his head.

"What ho!" came a laughing voice, "A fat monk!"

Wheezing: "Yea, and a lady. Watch thy evil tongue."

Then John appeared; his broad frame rose out of nowhere in front of Jane, grinning when he recognized her. "The leper is our lady!"

She smiled. "Yea, a leper come to visit rogues and thieves. I am pleased to see thee safe, John Lyttle."

"Aye, milady. Why would I not be safe?" A wide grin accompanied the hand John put out to help her navigate the slick, wet grass and rocks that edged the river. "This way—'tis sound footing here. Come along, Turtle Tuck. To the caves!"

The musty smell of damp earth swallowed them; as her eyes adjusted, she saw with some surprise that the cave was deep. Niches had been carved by time; layer upon layer of them in the soft sandstone provided natural hand holds and shelves for candles to be set. Fur pallets lay on the floor by the ashes of a fire.

Tuck's wheezing reverberated from the striated walls. Candlelight licked them with a soft rosy glow. John paused, indicated a low shelf of soft rock with a wave of one hand.

"There are no bolsters, but 'tis not so bad a seat, milady." His gaze shifted to Tuck; his grin widened. "Ye brought your own padding. What brings ye here afoot?"

"Penance," Tuck gasped out as he sprawled on loose sandstone in a shower of sandy grit and pebbles. He took in a noisy gulp of air, blew it out again. "I have . . . not suffered . . . enough yet."

Soft laughter met his complaint; John shook his head. "Then ye have come to the right place for penance, Brother Tuck. There are none of the comforts of home here."

Beneath his light banter, Jane heard the wistful tone. She caught his eye when he glanced her way; his smile faded.

"What news of my home in Hathersage, milady? I fear it will be seized ere long, with me not there to protect it."

There was no comfort she could offer. Regretful, she shook her head. "I have no news."

Tuck's wheezing eased. Tactfully, he said, "We bring news that will amuse you well enough, John Lyttle. 'Tis said that Robin Hood has returned, though we know 'twas our lady here who confronted the sheriff. Rumor has it that outlaws will once more rule Sherwood."

John's eyes widened; he slapped a knee with delight, guffawed loudly. "Aye, and 'twas well worth being outlawed to see the look upon the sheriff's face when our lady Jane held a bodkin arrowhead at his throat!"

"Ah, I regret I was not there." Tuck shook his head, gave a lengthy sigh, spread fat fingers on his knees to lean forward. "But now there will be trouble. The king is to come to Nottingham."

" 'Tis not the king who scours wood and dales with his cutthroats." Humor faded from John's face. Huge hands curled into fists. His voice shook with rare ferocity. "I should have killed him when I had the chance."

"There would only be another to replace him, possibly worse. Devaux is relentless, but not cruel." Tuck frowned, rubbed at a crease over his nose with a pudgy finger.

Jane leaned forward, urgency creeping into her tone. "I did not dare send a messenger—I fear the king's visit hides a deeper motive for the tourney."

Parchment crackled as she withdrew the message she had received, fingers shook slightly as she smoothed it, offered it to Tuck. As John could not read, the monk read aloud: "It is required that Lady Neville of Ravenshed be present in Nottingham Castle on the twenty-first of June to attend a banquet and tournament in honor of His Royal Highness—"

Tuck halted, looked up, fingers crushing parchment in his indignation. "Honor a king who has scourged the church with fines, imprisoned clergy, defied the pope? A travesty! All of England has been under an interdict for four years because King John refused to approve Pope Innocent's appointment of Stephen Langton as Archbishop of Canterbury—no priests have been allowed to conduct Mass, marriages, or even last rites, yet now we are to ignore these depredations and *honor* the king with a banquet? A perversion, I say!"

Jane nodded grim agreement. "It rings false. I did not know what to make of it, so seek your advice. Proclamations have been read in village market squares, inviting entrants to the tourneys, while barons are expected to attend in the king's honor. Saxon, Norman—all are summoned. I fear there is more to this than meets the eye."

Silence fell. She drew in a deep breath, blew it out again, softly. "It reeks of treachery. A tourney with sumptuous prizes tempts outlaws to attend, or rob those who travel to Nottingham. I fear he tries to trap you."

"And ye worried we would rise to the lure?" John chuckled. "Nay, 'tis naught to worry about, milady. 'Tis too obvious a snare."

"Have you thought," Tuck said slowly, "that it may well be a trap for *you*, milady?"

Silence gathered in the corners like shadows. Bitter regret seeped into the cave, almost tangible, a ghostly presence. Other ghosts lingered; his name was not mentioned, yet Robin's memory was sharp and hovering. Jane shut her eyes against it. Tuck's words echoed, a litany to haunt her like the old ghosts:

Have you thought it might well be a trap for you . . . ?

III

❧

NOTTINGHAM CASTLE

JUNE 21, 1213

16

Sunlight flooded the middle bailey, tinged turrets a rich gold, caught in pennons fluttering on battlement walls. Tré saw her standing across the crowded bailey beside a white palfrey; rose-colored silk veil lifted softly in the wind that always blew over the summit of Nottingham Castle. Her face was turned from him, pure profile as serene as if carved from alabaster.

He cursed softly. What was Lady Neville doing there? It was dangerous in Nottingham, more so for this lady than most. Robin Hood's niece would find her welcome strained when the king arrived—with recent rumors of the outlaw's return to Sherwood, King John's mood might turn vicious.

His gaze shifted to the elderly baron at Jane's side. Lord Creighton bore himself with dignity, white hair long and brushing velvet-clad shoulders in the Saxon style. The bailey swarmed with barons and their retinues: horses, dogs, and servants, blurs of color and sound created chaos. Avid eyes everywhere . . . if he sent her away, it would be marked by all, yet temptation was great.

Even as the thought formed, he strode across the paving stones of the bailey. Her servant saw him first; Dena nudged her mistress.

Gracious as a queen, Lady Neville inclined her head in greeting when he reached her side.

"My lord high sheriff, how kind of you to invite me to the festivities and banquet."

It sounded stilted, formal and practiced; he ignored it. "I did not invite you, my lady."

Uncertainty flickered in her eyes, faded into opaque blue. "No? There must be a mistake—"

"I did not make the mistake." His mouth thinned in irritation. "You should not be here. It is not safe."

Her chin tilted upward, lips firmed into a taut line. "If it's not safe, my lord, then there are many here who should be advised of their danger."

"Enough, Lady Neville. I am in no mood for the polite jab and feint that passes for conversation with you. Why did you come here?"

He had almost betrayed himself—an unwelcome surprise that he would venture warning or concern. Yet with this lady it seemed natural—another unwelcome revelation.

Familiar challenge gleamed in her blue eyes. "Is it so amazing that I would answer the summons to Nottingham for a tournament and banquet?"

"A summons?" He put a hand on her arm, fingers closing just above the elbow. "I would speak with you in private, Lady Neville."

"Speak freely here, my lord. Dena is a trusted servant, and Lord Creighton—"

He turned abruptly, swept a glance over Dena and Lord Creighton. "Lady Neville will return shortly."

Creighton sputtered a protest, but the servant had more sense; silent, she made the sign of the cross over her breast.

Devaux escorted Jane to a corner away from horses and crowd. With a hand still on her arm, he said grimly, "I find your presence here unwarranted."

"And I find your incivility insulting!" Anger threaded her words. She glared at him from under brows pleated in a frown. "I was sent a summons—a demand, if you will—to be here."

His eyes narrowed. He asked, though he already suspected the reply: "Who delivered it?"

"It was a castle courier, but your seal bound the message." Uncertainty was back in her voice, faint but definite. "You—did not send it, my lord sheriff?"

Gaudet. It would avail him much to discover Gaudet's reasons for luring Lady Neville to the castle under false pretenses. His jaw tightened, a curt reply:

"No, I would prefer you were still at Ravenshed."

Chagrin replaced uncertainty, stilted words in a voice like ice: "Your courtesy is boundless, my lord. Had I known I am not welcome, I would have been most content to remain at Ravenshed."

Calmly, he surveyed her flushed face. Her reaction seemed genuine, yet trust eluded him. It was not his nature to believe easily. He released her arm and looked away. A throng of men and horses swarmed into the bailey. Nottingham was already crowded; silk pavilions sprouted like weeds all the way to the Trent. King John's royal retinue would soon overflow the grounds.

"Milady, when the king arrives, dissension arrives."

"Then nothing has changed since last I had audience with King John."

A tart observation of truth. He smiled slightly. "I imagine it has not. One of the king's greatest gifts is his ability to create turmoil wherever he goes."

"A birthright not limited to kings, it seems."

His brow lifted. "Is that directed at me, milady?"

"Indeed, you are more clever than you appear, my lord."

He should be irritated; subtle insults usually annoyed him. Yet he understood her chagrin, recognized that he had offended her. Tact was not one of his virtues.

He cupped a hand under her elbow, escorted her from the shadow of staved structures built against the stone wall separating the middle bailey from the inner moat. The great hall was directly across from the square stone gatehouse and drawbridge; he steered her around it. There, thick grass and dirt cushioned their feet. The Royal Mews housing falcons and hawks lay on the north side; at the rear beneath the shade of huge trees and mossed wall was the common chapel. Gravestones dotted consecrated ground; none came here, and it was quiet. Tumult was muted and distant.

Releasing her arm, he freed her to sit on a low bench beneath the spreading shade of an oak. Lady Neville would not meet his eyes, but kept her gaze at his chest and throat. He watched her silently, waiting.

Long, graceful fingers folded in her lap, soft but capable; hands that had held a bow with ruthless intent, then nursed him to health with infinite tenderness. An enigma, this lady of Ravenshed. . . . She looked up at last.

"If you have a matter to discuss with me, my lord, be so kind as to do so. I am to meet Lord and Lady Dunham at the middle gate ere long."

"They will wait."

Lashes lowered; cheeks grew pink with ire. He smiled. Too easy to bait, this lovely lady who haunted his nights and invaded his waking hours—he had not expected to see her again this soon. It took him off-guard, left him floundering for a plausible reason to make her leave—and a better reason to let her stay.

"Lady Neville, your safety is in question."

Eyes widened; light gleamed through the silk wimple to shadow her face. "Why, my lord?"

"If you stay for the banquet, the king is quite likely to take umbrage at your presence. Rumors of Robin Hood and his men run rampant through the shire. But you must be well aware of this."

Coolly holding his gaze, she nodded. "I have heard the rumors, of course, my lord."

She gives nothing away. . . .

His mouth twisted wryly. "No doubt you are well aware of the reasons for those rumors."

"It is possible that such rumors began when you pursued the outlaws—"

He cut off an explanation both knew skirted truth. "Yet even more possible is that the rumors began when Little John and Robin Hood's men were set free from arrest by a hooded figure some prefer to believe is a dead outlaw."

An awkward silence fell; he thought of the garrison of soldiers positioned along Sherwood roads, waiting for outlaws bold enough to ambush travelers to the tournament. A daring ploy, executed by Captain Oliver, who knew Sherwood near as well as the outlaws. A trap to spring shut on Little John, Will Scarlett, and Alan of the Dales. . . .

But what of Lady Neville? A complication, a diversion— possible disaster. Gaudet's trick, perhaps, but he must learn the truth before the king's arrival.

But now, without betraying the careful net cast about Nottingham, he could only accept Lady Neville's presence without more comment. To draw attention to either of them could warn the outlaws she still protected.

He sat beside her on the narrow seat. His sword clinked softly on stone. She eyed him quickly, then looked away.

"I had thought we had an understanding now, my lord."

Dangerous emotion beckoned, a disconcerting urge to tell her how welcome he found her unexpected arrival—it was irritating and baffling. A complication he did not need.

"Why would you think that, Lady Neville?" A safe distance was required, deliberate resistance to the lure inherent in her eloquent eyes, in the sweet fragrance of mint that clung to her hair. She could be dangerous to him—so why this impulse to protect her?

"We did part in understanding, did we not, my lord?"

To say no would be an obvious lie. Too obvious a lie. Agreement would leave him open to a risk he did not intend to take. He did not look at her; his gaze riveted on the stone wall of the great hall. Moss furred its crevices, a bright green against soft sandstone. He splayed his hands on his knees, black wool tunic bunched beneath his palms.

"Your hospitality was most generous, my lady."

"Perhaps one day I can say the same of yours, my lord sheriff."

A gentle rebuke for his rudeness. Unwillingly, he looked at her, then wished he had not.

Regal and alluring; infinitely elegant and achingly seductive, a woman to honor, not to insult—the reasons did not matter. For the first time in more years than he could name, regret curled inside him, a burning ache.

Bitter realization, facing the man he had become—once a knight sworn to courtesy, loyalty, truth—now a mockery of those vows. Honor lost, along with any semblance of humanity he had once possessed.

She rose to her feet, silken grace and fragrant mint. He stood to put a hand on her arm; fingers crushed rose wool but not delicate wrist bones as he held her lightly. Honest concern betrayed him.

"My lady, it would be safer for you to remain at the castle."

"I hardly think that necessary, my lord sheriff." She did not look at him, staring past him to the bailey. "I am to meet my cousin and her husband. Arrangements have been made."

It did not lessen his resolve; he regarded her gravely, a command cloaked in courtesy: "Honor Nottingham with your presence, if you will, Lady Neville. It will be easier for me to guard you well if you are here."

"Guard me? Am I truly in danger?"

"Less danger here than on a Sherwood road rife with outlaws—lest you forget."

His blunt reminder of past transgressions did not go unheeded. She drew in a sharp breath. He released her arm, stepped back to allow her to precede him.

She accompanied him across the bailey; feathers and flutters came from the Royal Mews as they passed. A falconer fed hawks and gyrfalcons bits of raw meat, greeted by fierce screeches and loud whips of great wings.

At the gatehouse, he saw his steward and beckoned him near. "See to Lady Neville's servants, Giles. She will be staying in the castle tonight."

Wind fluttered the silk veil against her face; she frowned in dismay. "What of Lady Dunham?"

"Your cousin is welcome to stay with you here." He flicked a glance at the steward. "See to it, Giles."

"Aye, my lord sheriff." Giles hesitated, then said, "All of the chambers are full, my lord. Perhaps Hugh de Baliol would give up his bed for the lady."

"Put out one of the Saxon barons. The lady will be comfortable in Lord Creighton's chamber. Remove him with all due diplomacy."

As the steward departed, Jane turned angrily. "It is hardly necessary to keep me here, my lord sheriff. Or am I your prisoner?"

"Should you be? Have you committed yet another crime for which you should be arrested, Lady Neville?" He caught her arm when she pivoted on her heel to walk away, turned her back to face him. "Five men elude me still. Do not make the mistake of thinking I have forgotten them or abandoned my determination to see them hang. They are outlaws. Any who consort with them are tainted with the same foul brush—if you have influence, it would save your pretty neck to use it."

"Do I look to be a traitor?" She jerked free, her words an angry hiss. "Consider your own deeds, my lord sheriff—a baron accused of treason—but do not judge me by your lowly standards!"

Stave walls rose behind her; shadows cast by morning sun and high wall shrouded her face. Yet, contempt was plain in her eyes and tone, conviction built on a lie. To refute the lie would resemble a plea for compassion—inconceivable.

"Do not confuse the issue, my lady." Seeming indifference masked the inexplicable sting of her accusation. "We speak of *your* actions, not of mine."

"Do we? I think not. You would have me betray men who have earned pursuit by a sheriff bent on vengeance rather than justice. Far more honorable to wait in Sherwood with drawn bow than to sell souls to the devil for the sake of land and coin. More outlaws reside within Nottingham Castle than without, it seems."

Harsh words that cut to the quick. *I pity you for your empty soul,* she had once said to him. Reluctant truth, hated certainty. A man with a soul could not exist in the world he inhabited. It would destroy him.

Yet he was set on his course and there was no turning back from it. Brayeton was all he had left now, the only purpose in his life. Survival meant more than breath in his body and a beating heart. But he had forgotten the reason for it. . . .

Hooves clattered on stone, dogs barked, soldiers gave harsh orders. A tide of people surged around them, unnoticed by either until now. Tré glanced up, aware at last of their public position, where any straining ears might overhear.

"A crowded bailey is no fit place for such a grave discussion, my lady. Let us retire to a more private site for the continued purging of your spleen."

"I am done."

"I," he said softly, "am not."

His chambers lay in the wing behind them; he steered her forward, skirting the occasional pile of horse droppings. He reached around her to open the door; it swung inward allowing a gleam of light to illuminate the interior.

Prosaic chamber, stark, empty of personal signs of his inhabitance of it. Silence greeted them, dense and familiar; with the closing of the door, gloom descended like velvet, unbroken by an open window in the rear stone wall. A faint draft penetrated, miraculously free of moat taint or smoke.

"You still consort with outlaws despite my warning." It sounded loud in the soft gloom, drawing the lady's immediate attention. Deliberate provocation, an indirect probing for confession or denial—he wanted to be wrong. Yet she said nothing, no admission or disavowal. "They will all be caught, your John Lyttle with them. An inevitable fate for wolf's heads."

Lips parted slightly, then curved in a derisive smile. "If Little John is caught by your men, my lord, it will be a miracle."

"Because he yet eludes us?" He moved to the side table, took up a flagon of wine, poured two cups. "It is a mistake to underestimate my captains or me, my lady. If I do not personally chase deer through Sherwood, that does not mean I am unlikely to have roast venison. There are many ways to dispose of vermin. Wine?"

He held out the cup, but she stared at him and did not move to take it. He set it on the table.

"It occurs to me that you came to Nottingham not to see the tournament or answer a summons, but for more devious reasons."

When she stood still and silent, he frowned, put the lip of the cup to his mouth; it tasted slightly of wine and spices. The air was heavy with anticipation, with suppressed emotion. He felt it, tasted it as tangibly as the cinnamon and ginger in the wine.

Strangely disillusioned when he had thought he had no illusions left, he set his own cup on the table, moved toward her, and saw her eyes widen. He cupped her chin in his palm, fingers curved along her jawline. So fragile, delicate; it would be so easy to tighten his grip until she cried out for mercy.

He smiled, saw from her eyes that she knew the direction of his thoughts.

In a silken purr to hide the menace, he murmured, "Are you sent to persuade me to thoughts other than outlaws, sweet lady? You tremble. That is not an auspicious beginning if you are to play the part of Salome. Do you know that tale?"

Stiff, almost a whisper: "I know the tale."

Her skin was soft, warm, a bloom of velvet flowering in his palm. His thumb slid along the curve of her cheek, deliberate and dispassionate, touched her mouth, caressed the smooth tumble of lower lip.

Softly: "Then distract me. Dance with veils. If you are to be granted my head on a platter, you must first entertain me."

"That . . . is not the way the tale goes, my lord."

"Close enough, Jane of Ravenshed. Close enough." His hand closed on her jaw, skin dark and profane against such white purity; beauty marred by hostility.

Betrayal cut deep. It wounded, reached down into that part of himself that he kept inviolate—yet she had breached it.

Faint white marks reddened beneath the pressure of his hand and he loosened his hold. She drew a deep breath.

"Are you afraid, Jane?" Softly, animosity cloaked in the warmth of concern—his tone as conversational as if the reply did not matter.

"No—yea, I am afraid."

"Ah, the truth at last. I begin to think you capable of it after all."

"I have told you the truth." Soft dignity imbued the simple statement with sincerity. He wanted to believe her. Yet it was more likely she had come for her own purpose than for Gaudet to have summoned her to Nottingham.

"Why do you persist in thinking me a fool, Lady Neville? Do I seem so monumental a simpleton to you?"

"You have . . . never seemed simple." A slight quiver in her voice belied her outward composure.

"Yet you flaunt deeds and accusations with impunity. It would behoove you to guard your tongue if not your actions."

"Do you threaten me, my lord?"

His voice was a soft purr that widened her eyes in the candlelight. "Yea, my lady of Ravenshed, I most certainly do. Take it as a warning or a threat as you like—but heed my words well, ere your missteps see you undone."

"It is not so easy, my lord. It does not matter what I say. You pick it apart, flay my words and intent until I do not recognize them. . . . Pray, leave me be."

He released her; faint marks remained where he had held her face in his palm. Desecration.

"If it is your desire to be left alone, you should have remained at Ravenshed."

" 'Twas an ill wind that blew you to Nottingham, my lord sheriff. Far better to endure blatant atrocity than subtle extortion—much easier to recognize the devil by horns and cloven hooves than by false protests of obligation."

"And you would have intimate knowledge of demons, my lady?"

"Not until I met you, sirrah! You ignored cutthroats to pursue men who only sought to retrieve what the sweat of their labor had earned—then condemned them for doing what you now do. Theft is theft, by any name."

"Ah, now we have the heart of it." Dangerous now, the predatory urge returned. He wanted to crush her; he wanted to force the truth from her, force her to admit that she schemed against him. Most of all, he wanted her to see him for what he was—not a sheriff, a baron, a Norman and an enemy, but a man who did not deserve another betrayal.

He caught her arm, held it when she would have twisted free. She put her other hand against his chest, and he put his own over it to trap her fingers against him.

"Do you feel that?" He pressed harder when she just stared up at him. "It beats, just as does yours. No, you will hear me out—" Her trapped fingers stilled under the pressure of his palm. "I am a man, Jane of Ravenshed. My heart beats, my blood flows. I am capable of reason. I am—a man."

The last two words were soft, almost a whisper. Desire gathered power, beat through veins and body in a thundering rush.

Sudden awareness lit her eyes; her lips trembled, parted on a husky, "What do you *want* from me?"

He knew what he wanted. Awkward lust, importune desire—he wanted her. He wanted to feel her under him, feel her body close around his—

The words would not form. His hand moved, grasped her chin, held it as he kissed her. Sweet lips, parting under the pressure of his mouth, offering refuge and release. He tasted mint. He tasted the beginning of surrender.

Ruthless, determined, driven by need and a desire for something beyond even the yielding, he deepened the kiss. He was done with waiting; he discarded denial.

He kissed her until he felt her legs crumble. He caught her weight on one arm, held her against him, hand splayed on her back to pull her into the full force of his erection. Frustrated violence throbbed; he shuddered with the ache.

Restraint vanished. He heaved her into his arms, heard her gasp against his mouth. Three strides took him across the chamber to the door leading to his private quarters. A swift kick, the door swung wide, and he slammed it with a boot heel against oak. It was loud, reverberating like a clap of thunder.

This chamber was small; a massive bed stood against one wall. Wine-colored draperies framed it, rich and flowing from ceiling to floor, tied back on one side to reveal a high mattress.

He felt her shift in his arms, a moan, a shove of one hand against him in a halfhearted protest as he crossed to the bed, dumped her onto it, and followed with his body over hers. His weight rested on bent arms. Bed ropes creaked; his sword belt clanked softly. He unfastened the buckle and shoved aside belt and weapon without releasing his hold on Jane.

She was soft beneath him. He snared her hand when she caught at his arm.

"Oh no, milady. Oh . . . no."

Lacing his fingers through hers, he pushed her arm back into the mattress and rich bedding. With his free hand, he traced a path from her cheek to her mouth. She suddenly lay still, staring up at him. The light there was filtered by the heavy velvet draperies. It was close, warm, intimate; nothing intruded. Just the two of them existed in this world.

He bent to kiss her. Her mouth opened under his, heated and tasting of mint. He drank deeply of her; relished the soft yielding of lips, need transferred from him to her and given back. . . . She was his, and this time he meant to have her.

"Milord. . . ." Soft, confused, a bit breathless, her head turned, her voice wafted past his right ear. He turned her face back with a finger, found her mouth again.

"Tré." His lips traveled across her cheek to her ear; he blew softly, felt her shiver, said, "Lord Devaux, third Baron of Brayeton."

"You are lord high sheriff—"

"A travesty." He took her mouth again, lingered, felt her breath fray into ragged rhythm; he lifted his head. Huge eyes, dark blue and shadowed, gazed up at him. He traced a winged brow with one finger, fought for control to slow what should not be hurried. There was a strange hitch in his voice, the words husky and meaningless, an exercise in self-control: "I am a baron, milady."

Her tongue came out to wet her lips; his attention shifted. He slid his thumb over the path her tongue had just taken, spread moisture over both lips, bent to kiss her again.

Heat engulfed him. He lowered his weight, pushing into her so that her thighs parted. Soft female . . . sweet cushion beneath the hard throb of his body; his erection rubbed against his linen braies. He wedged himself more closely against her, felt her thighs spread wider under his weight. The hem of her kirtle slid up as his hand raked along her leg. She trembled.

His fingers found the silk ribbon garter tied above her knee; he tugged. Silk slithered over his hand to puddle on the bed. He looked down; white thigh curved beneath his palm in luxurious texture. He curled his fingers into the edge of her hose, slid them down, felt her reflexive withdrawal.

Before she could speak, he bent, covered her lips again with his own, kissed her with fierce demand. Blood beat a rapid thunder in his ears; he ached, taut and ready, urgency coalescing with desire. Slowly, her hand lifted; fingers touched him tentatively, plying along his jaw, a mere whisper as of butterfly wings. He turned his head, kissed her fingertips.

"I yield . . ." softly, on a breath, her words slid between them, "only what I wish to yield. . . ."

17

Lost in a private world inside the velvet draperies, nothing mattered but soft murmurs and sighs. Bereft of speech, of coherent thought, Jane was acutely aware of him over her, dark face shadowed by bed canopy, eyes a pale gleam.

Madness to yield, impossible to refuse. . . .

Tré bent, touched the tip of his tongue to the small pulse that throbbed in her throat. Her hand stilled in his hair when he moved lower; her fingers convulsed. His weight pressed her down, held her without effort. Magnificent male, splendid in his potency, terrifying in his anger—beguiling in rare restraint. She felt his hands at the laces of her bodice in efficient seduction, then a brief hesitation.

Unexpected tenderness rocked her at this glimpse of uncertainty. Black lashes lifted on emerald fire, a hungry glance that stole her breath. She felt deprived of air as her undergarment slid free. A chill draft puckered her nipples. Her breath escaped in a long sigh of pleasure when his lips claimed first one, then the other.

Fervent heat pooled in her belly, spread lower, an aching throb between her thighs. Irresistible lure kept her eyes open, watching him. Long lashes shadowed his cheeks as he glanced up with a fierce smile, recognition of her need and her surrender marked in his eyes.

Blood rushed to her face, a scalded flush. She would have turned away but he trapped her, hands a light pressure on her shoulders.

"Too late, m'lady. Too . . . late. . . ."

He was right. She recognized it, knew it had gone too far to end now. And did she really want to end it? Delicious sensations, exquisite violation—long anticipation answered.

His kiss was harsh, but hot need swelled at his touch. Bare breasts were against his chest, abrasive wool scouring sensitive nipples already hardened into peaks. It made little difference that he accused her of betrayal—she recognized it for what it was. A reason to erect barriers between them, the ploy of a desperate man. But the truth was revealed in his eyes, in the urgency of his hand on her, and all else faded away. All that mattered now was the bruising pressure of his body against hers, the taste of him.

Her hands splayed across his back, fingers curved into black tunic. Yearning drove her, the need to cherish and hold him, to burn under his caress. The secret pleasure that blossomed between her thighs moved her hard against him, as if they could become one.

She felt him groan; powerful muscles shifted beneath her hands as he pushed away from her, braced his arms to stare down at her.

"Curse you . . . I should arrest you and end this. . . ."

But he did not stop; he pressed his mouth over hers again. Her lips opened, tongue meeting his, tasting wine and need. His hand found her breast and teased the nipple between his thumb and finger, summoning urgent sighs from her. The kiss deepened until even the tumult outside the chamber faded to nothing, until not even the winding of a horn penetrated the draperies around the bed.

Impossible to think, to reason, to do more than *feel*; sparks ignited wherever he touched her. She tried to catch her breath. He released her mouth, a sudden desertion; her hands stretched, closed on air, then curled into fists.

His fingers splayed over the swell of her belly. Flesh quivered beneath his palm; he dipped a finger into the dent of her navel, worked the heel of his hand down to press against the crevice at the juncture of her thighs. She caught her breath as his hand tangled in soft, silken curls, a gentle tug.

"Beautiful lady . . . sweet mystery." A hoarse sound, words cracking on the last note. His gaze lifted with a probing question that she could not answer. Then his hand moved lower, slipped on damp folds, stroked her until she writhed and arched upward.

For Tré, this was illumination, a discovery of emotions he yet resisted. Tenderness was unfamiliar to him; the lady's surrender unexpected. Raw lust had become aching need. . . .

He felt the trembling in her, the vibration of flesh and muscle as he held her thighs apart with his hand and body. Still kissing her, he slid a finger inside her; warmth closed around him, deliciously hot and inviting. He raked his thumb over the top of her cleft, relished her shudders as she clutched his hair, her hips pushing into his stroking hand.

The ache consumed him, mixed with anger at her betrayal— a confusing mélange that drove him to possess her. He lifted his tunic, jerked at the tapes of his chausses and braies to release himself. Throbbing, urgent, he replaced his hand with his rigid member, poised for a moment at her entrance.

She gave a little gasp that he quickly smothered with his mouth and a hard, savage kiss. A swift thrust and he slid inside her; her delicious heat threatened to take him beyond control. His breath came in harsh pants as he restrained the urge to surrender only to his own need.

"Sweet lady," he breathed against her shoulder when she twisted beneath him, "do not move . . . not . . . now."

Resolve weakened, frayed, wobbled; he held tight to it. He cupped her hips, fingers on soft flesh. Excitement surged through him, tempered with hard-won restraint.

He lifted his head, stared at her through his lashes, formed a silent, desperate prayer for the strength to resist the new, raw emotions that surged through him.

Tré lost himself in her body, touching her, tasting her, sliding into her bit by bit, slow, erotic anticipation. He wanted ardent response from her, wanted her pleading for what only he would give her—he wanted her all to himself, now and always, an unformed resolution that had eluded him until now.

Her head tossed on the fur bedding, hips shoving toward him, taking him in, an urgent, silent plea for it all . . . her soft, strangled sighs escalated into urgent cries.

He drove into her harder, each thrust a shuddering ecstasy that took him ever closer to his goal. He used her body to ease his own torment—the fierce desire he had denied since the first day he had seen her in the rain-drenched middle bailey.

It was all swept away now, caught up in this maelstrom of physical hunger—and an emotional need he could not escape.

She strained beneath him; her legs curved over his back and she lifted into his powerful thrusts. His head lowered, arms braced to bear his weight, tension drawing tighter and tighter until his face ached with the strain. He breathed through his teeth, harsh pleas for air. She cried out softly, her back arching, head tilted in a shimmer of gold and silk, lips swollen from his rough kisses now parted in ragged gasps.

Beautiful lady . . . elegant and sensual . . . lovely sweetness and surrender. . . .

This time, when he rocked against her with growing urgency, she met his thrusts with her own. She gasped his name and her body jerked, he drove into her, a fierce thrust that ended in a heavy tremor and groan of ecstasy torn from his throat. It washed over him in a drowning wave, then gradually subsided.

Slowly, he pressed his face into the bed beside her, his breath coming painfully. He felt her legs tremble, knees lifted on each side of his waist. She was heat and softness beneath him; as the urgency drained away, so did resistance. He was strangely depleted of everything that was familiar. Lassitude stole over him; an alien weakness close to tenderness invaded his body.

He did not want to feel tenderness. He did not want to risk emotion of any kind. Never for a woman . . . but Jane of Ravenshed was not just a woman. She was different from all others he had known.

She had the power to destroy him, and he knew it.

•   •   •

At last, soft sounds from outside penetrated the dark wine drapes around the bed. Jane heard them, muffled and distant, as foreign to her as her own actions. Tré Devaux lay atop her still, his weight resting on his side, an arm still thrown possessively across her. He was silent, awake, eyes open beneath black lashes. She felt him watching her.

She should flush with shame. The hem of her kirtle was up around her waist; her laces were undone to reveal the white linen smock beneath. Shameless . . . for she did not care.

Wonder seized her instead; a sharp, piercing sweetness that she acknowledged with a sense of gratitude. In the four months she had known Tré Devaux, she had never penetrated the barrier he kept between them. Yet now, in the moment of greatest intimacy, she realized that the barrier was slowly fraying.

He made it so difficult to know him. Now she had lain with him, a mortal sin in the eyes of the church.

He shifted slightly, gathered her body into his. His braies were open, flesh warm and languid against her thighs. As his hand moved, shaping the mound of her breast with light, kneading motions, his body stiffened, prodded against her inner thigh with utter sensuality. Heated flesh rubbed over parts still sensitive and quivering; she moaned softly when he lifted over her.

His hand moved to touch her face, turning her to look at him, and the breath caught in her throat. Dark, wicked beauty; Lucifer's son. Temptation and seduction.

"You are beautiful," she whispered, and saw his eyes widen in surprise.

"An unlikely compliment, sweet lady. Sir Guy is known as the pretty knight, with a troubadour's face and charm. I am too dark, with too many battle scars."

"Perhaps, to some. Not to me." She touched a faint scar on his brow, worked her fingers along it in a gentle caress. "It is not the outer scars that concern me."

A shudder went through him; he took her hand, kissed the fingertips leisurely.

Her lungs ached, her breath emerged in a trembling sigh. He leaned over her, eyes glittering, knees spread between her thighs, stretching taut the wool of his chausses. Her heartbeat loud in her ears, the world was narrowed to the two of them again, closing out the muted sounds beyond the chamber.

His wool tunic was soft beneath her hands as she gripped his arms, her fingers curved over taut muscles to hold him as he moved forward. His head arched backward. Thick and strong, the column of his throat corded with effort as he pushed against her slowly, slipping inside, stretching her until the fullness was almost more than she could bear.

Liquid heat surged through her veins, made her nipples tighten; the muscles in her thighs quivered, and the ache in the pit of her belly and between her legs pulsed with every beat of her heart. Her hands opened and closed, fingers wadding wool in convulsive knots.

He filled her; he filled her body and her world. His dark head bent, face intense and taut, arms shaking with strain as he held her hips steady for his thrusts. His powerful shoulders were bent forward; his fingers tightened on her. A shudder, another push of his body into hers, growing tension and exquisite pleasure. He put a hand between their bodies, raked his thumb over the damp, aching center of her, looked up from beneath his lashes when she cried out.

A faint smile touched his mouth. His lashes lowered again and he slid his thumb over her in dazzling strokes as he moved deeper, a shivering pleasure sweeping through her.

She could not breathe. The air felt weighted, too thick to drag into her lungs. Her body quivered, arched toward him, accepting his hard, savage lunges, seeking the delicious sensation he summoned with his hand, until finally the world wheeled and dived, and she gave herself to the consuming release with a soft cry.

In that moment he held her hard, pinned her with a final thrust that drove them both deep into the mattress in a loud groan of bed ropes. A hard shudder racked his body, he muttered something guttural, and lowered his weight onto her slowly.

Panting for breath, she became aware of his increasing

heaviness, went to push at him just as he rose to one elbow; a faint smile curved his mouth.

"Chérie . . . sweet little bird . . . dainty as a jaie. . . ."

Her fingers dug into wool and flesh. "As a—jaie?"

"Yea." He traced the tip of his finger over the damp path his tongue had washed around a linen-shrouded nipple, touched her hair. "The comparison to a bird offends you?"

"No." A soft laugh, her fingers spread against his face to hold him. "It does not offend me."

Little jaie—as Robin used to call me . . . "You remind me of a small, saucy bird," *he had teased her then,* "as cheeky as a jaie. . . ."

So long ago. Now there was hope for peace in Nottingham but it would come with a price—did she dare trust Devaux? No words of love, no promises offered, only the commitment of his body had been given. Did he yet love his dead wife, the name he had called out when wounded—

"You frown—what has you thinking so hard, chérie?"

His soft murmur caught her off-guard, summoned truth instead of discretion. "I . . . wondered about your wife."

Heat scalded her cheeks when he stared at her; his eyes narrowed slightly.

"Old memories need not be renewed."

Fool, fool to betray myself . . . I am so clumsy with these unfamiliar emotions.

A shoulder lifted in an attempt to retrieve her dignity as she lapsed into silence. It was an intrusion; the barriers were still between them—frayed, perhaps, but not vanquished.

He pushed a loose strand of hair from her brow, tucked it back into the gold mesh net over her ear, rolled onto his back. For a long moment, he stared up at the shadowed canopy then said in a low murmur. "It was an arranged marriage. She said I—frightened her."

Hollow tones were carefully devoid of emotion. It must yet sting. Compassion swelled, but remained unuttered. It would be unwelcome. She remained silent, yet it puzzled her, that he would call out for a woman he had not loved.

After a moment, she dared to glance at him. Strain cut

grooves on each side of his mouth; a desolation creased the corners of his eyes.

Shocked, she reached out a tentative hand, touched his chest. "Milord?"

His head turned; lashes lowered to hide bleak shadows. "There was a child. Aimée. Slain by Saxon outlaws."

Barren tones, a recitation of the past, betraying no emotion— if not for the brief glimpse of torment in his eyes she might have thought he did not care.

He held up his hands, stared at them, flexed his fingers in idle exercise. His conversational tone chilled her as he said, "I hunted them down, every last man who had been there that day, every foul villain who had dared touch what was mine. Before I was done, they prayed for sweet death to claim them. I would do it again."

An involuntary shudder racked her; he glanced at her, lowered his hands. "You would do the same, my fine lady of Ravenshed. Do not judge me."

"No—I do not. . . . I would do the same." Her unconvincing whisper drew a faint smile from him, a gesture lacking real amusement.

"I pray you are never put to the test. It is not a pleasant thing to lose one's soul."

18

Guy de Beaufort squinted against the bright prick of sunlight in his eyes. A rare English day, warm enough to ease the constant chill in his bones. Soft wind blew the stench of coal fires and raw iron up the steep slope to the lower bailey.

Nottingham Castle stretched its stone turrets to the sky, snagging an occasional cloud. Inside the bailey, booths and stalls crowded close to the walls. An air of festive chaos reigned. Vendors hawked their wares, boasting of the freshest eels, the finest pastries, the most beautiful silks.

Restless, Guy moved to a small square where jugglers performed, dancers moved to the music of flutes and lyres, wrestlers sweated and strained; a trained bear with a wide leather collar danced clumsily to a tune from a gittern. It amused Guy only for a short time before he moved on; waiting always scoured his temper.

He climbed the circular stairs to the outer walls. Mail-clad sentries patrolled the battlements, far removed from the excitement, sullen eyes forced to watch it. Guy felt no sympathy for them; by Matins, most of them would be drunk on new ale and puking in their boots.

From this vantage point he could see to the River Trent. It was a dizzying view. Between the castle and the river lay a sea of silk tents and fluttering pennons, brilliant colors of barons and knights camped in comparative comfort in elaborate pavilions; the inns were full, lodgings crowded, and freemen and villeins sought shelter in caves or the surrounding woodlands.

Church bells struck the noon hour as Guy left the walls to wait by the middle gate. He was to meet Tré there. He leaned back against the rough wood of the stave wall; the sturdy construction, heated now by sun, felt warm against his back, even through his tunic. He crossed his arms over his chest, squinted against the light.

Thick black smoke boiled up from smithy fires, drifted on the breeze to sting eyes and nose; across the bailey, bowmen practiced, the *swisssh* and *thunk* of arrows hissing toward straw butts a constant sound. He watched them idly, mind leaping ahead to the morrow when he would fight in the tourney. A welcome change from inaction, a chance to fill his purse with something other than the king's meager coin. It was the best way for a landless knight to acquire wealth if he was skilled enough.

Impatience rose apace with the sun. There was no sign of Tré. Time crawled, the sun rose higher; when it straddled the east tower, he left the gate for the middle bailey. Tré might be in his chambers, waiting just as impatiently.

Shadow swallowed him as he moved through a gatehouse filled with echoing voices as the guards kept the flow of people under minimal control. With the crowd, he passed under the lethal iron spikes of the portcullis raised by huge winches at each side. His eyes narrowed when he stepped out into the light again, adjusting slowly.

"Who are you looking for, Sir Guy?" The soft voice was light against his ear; he turned to see Lady Lissa. Her brow lifted. A faint smile was on her lush mouth as he surveyed her, a sweeping gaze that took her all in.

She wore a sideless surcoat of gold samite tied with silk laces at the hip, revealing form-fitting silk beneath. The low, round neck displayed a tantalizing expanse of creamy skin and rounded bosom. Her beautiful face was framed by blond hair bound in a gold mesh caul and cap.

"You," he lied, and saw by her widening smile that she did

not believe him for an instant. There was no need for illusions with this lady; she had few of her own to muddle a man's pleasure. He returned her smile, felt a flash of heat that had nothing to do with the sun. "I was searching for you, milady."

"Yea, so you say, but I know better." She tapped his chest lightly with a slender oak stick. He glimpsed entwined figures of mythical dragons and griffins intricately carved into the wood. "You do not have the look of a man searching for a woman. I know that look well, for I have seen it oft enough."

A slow grin, a shrug that hitched up one shoulder. "I do not doubt that. You are the most lovely woman I have yet seen in all of Nottinghamshire."

An arch of her brows, a slight smile on rosy lips: "Yet you resist my charms most easily. How can that be if I am so lovely?"

"Fear, milady," he said promptly, and she laughed.

"Fear? Not you, Guy de Beaufort. You are rumored to be a most formidable knight who has won every tournament he entered. Whom would you fear?"

"Your husband."

"Walter?" This time her laughter was incredulous and genuine, mirthful peals like sweet bells. "You jest, Sir Guy! My husband could not fight a dead ferret and triumph. His talents lie more in the wagering than the actual deed."

Scorn laced her amused comments; her low opinion of her husband was obvious.

"Every man has his own talents, milady."

"Yea, but some men have more—talent—than do others, Sir Guy." Heavy lashes lowered over amber eyes; lips pursed in a sultry pout. "I fear me that I am alone, for my maidservant has disappeared, and there is no sign of my husband, as usual. La, I cannot even find my cousin in this crowd."

Guy held out his hand. When she took it after only the slightest hesitation, he smiled. "Since you are unaccompanied, I will squire you safely about the castle."

Eyes lifted to his; her smile deepened. "It would be most appreciated, Sir Guy."

"There is much that can happen to a lady alone in an unruly crowd such as this."

"Only," she said so softly that he had to lean close to hear the words, "if the lady is extremely fortunate."

Her meaning was clear. Guy's pulse quickened. If he wanted her, she was his. *Christus*, but the temptation to ignore sanity, duty, and common sense was great.

Yet the lady was gazing at him with melting eyes, each breath a tantalizing lift of samite and the jeweled pin on her bosom. His gaze lingered on the soft curve of breasts mounding the material. She had been an itch in his cruck since he had met her at Ravenshed.

He blinked suddenly, recalled her earlier words, asked, "Did you say you cannot find your cousin, milady?"

Her head tilted; she nodded. "She was to meet me, but must have been detained."

Guy smiled. It was obvious to him now: Tré had found the lady Jane more tempting than duty. He put his palm over the hand Lissa lay on his arm, pressed her fingers. "I know a place where it is more quiet."

He drew her with him, steered a course toward the lower bailey. Before reaching it, he detoured down a narrow path that led around the foot of the inner walls, where bracken grew in wild tangles along the sandstone talus. Cut into one wall was a postern door that had been sealed shut; it formed an empty arch that was shadowed and hidden from view. Heavy vines looped over it, a drape of green leaves veiling thick mats of red, star-shaped stonecrop that grew in cracks and crevices. The pungent fragrance of cow parsley was reminiscent of a cattle byre.

Ducking into the shaded arch, he pulled Lissa with him, pressed her against the rough stone wall with his weight, and leaned into her. Open-mouthed, eager, she gasped with delight when he cupped her breasts in both hands and squeezed them. Moaning, she arched into his hands; her lips parted as she wet them with the tip of her tongue, igniting a fire deep in his belly.

Impatience made him rough; he touched her, kissed her open mouth, kneaded her breasts as he leaned harder into her. He could not think for the need that rose in him, hot, fierce, driving out thought. Dimly, he knew he should be more careful, but Lissa of Gedling made him reckless.

"Guy . . ." a soft, breathy sigh, "please. . . ."

His hand went to his tunic, lifted the edge, fumbled at the tapes binding his hosen and braies. Against her mouth, tasting her, he muttered, "Are you certain?"

"Yea," she murmured with a provocative smile, "I am most certain, fair knight. What of you?"

Any restraint he still possessed evaporated. He pushed up the rich cloth of her skirts, skimmed a hand along the sleek length of her bare thigh above her garters. Hot, damp, inviting— she spread her thighs.

Shoving his hips forward, he lifted her, pressed her back against the wall to impale her in a single, smooth thrust. Lissa cried out, clutched his shoulders; her legs wrapped around his waist and she buried her face in the angle of his neck and shoulder.

She was light in his arms, legs tangling in her skirts as he took them both to a swift release.

Drained, he stood half-propped against the stone arch, holding her. Slowly, he rose from the haze of repletion to become aware of his surroundings. Lissa's breath was warm against his neck, her arms looped over him still. Her weight was slight, encumbered by soft folds of cotte and surcoat as she hung in his embrace like a silken butterfly.

Shifting, she lifted her head to gaze into his eyes for a long moment; birds chattered loudly in stone niches above their heads.

"You are overbold, Sir Knight." She grazed his mouth with her lips, a feathery caress. "I did not dream you would be so dauntless. . . ."

He inhaled deeply, caught the faint scent of roses, let out his breath in a soft laugh. "I do not have to be asked twice when a beautiful lady beckons."

"So I see." Fingertips played across his cheek; he eased her down his body, a rustle of silk and wool. With her mouth against his jaw, she murmured softly, "You are a gallant knight, indeed."

He released her, stepped back to retie his chausses and adjust the sword and sword belt encircling his tunic. "I thought for a time you did not think well of me."

She gave a flick of her fingers. "La, I did not know what to think of you. Now—I do."

"We should return. Devaux will be looking for me ere long, and so might your husband be searching for you."

Lissa readjusted the caul and cap atop her golden hair, a graceful, feminine act that snared his attention. She leaned out the archway to peer down the line of the stone wall; he followed her gaze. No one was in sight, save a squirrel with a red-plumed tail frisking beneath a ragged tuft of bracken.

When she turned back to look at him, a glint in her eyes shone like newly minted gold. His throat tightened. She was lovely: a brazen angel. *And wed to a Saxon baron.* He bludgeoned his desire into indifference.

Lissa leaned forward to smooth a fold of his tunic, her hand lingering on his chest; seductive lips curved into a promising smile.

"You are very quiet, Sir Guy. Are you displeased?"

"With you?" He caught her hand in his, held it fast as he looked into her eyes. Slowly, he lifted her hand, turned it over to press a courtier's kiss on her pink palm. "Never."

It was true. He was just waiting. Nothing in his life was ever simple. Females were always complication; pleasure always too brief; the luxury of trust nonexistent. He enjoyed Lissa of Gedling but would not trust her beyond the end of his arm.

A soft sigh, replete, extravagant, and she nuzzled his jaw with her nose. "Handsome knight . . . champion of love lists as well as the tourney."

Practiced love talk; he recognized it, used it himself. His thumb slid over the curved bones of her wrist in a light caress. Mouth pressed against heated skin; his words were muffled against her faint pulse.

"This time my lance has won a worthy prize. . . ."

He held out his arm; after a brief hesitation, she lay her fingers on his forearm, accompanied him along the narrow dirt path in the shadow of the bailey wall. In thick brush to one side, a startled plover burst upward in a whir of wings. Lissa shivered in the soft breeze that blew grit and the smells of the fair toward them.

Gray clouds scudded overhead to blot out the sun. Beyond the wall, a loud clatter broke the hush, followed by a Saxon oath.

Guy put out a hand with the intention of guiding Lissa in the other direction. Another curse sounded—a voice he knew too well: *Gervaise Gaudet*. His hackles rose, and so did suspicion.

A finger to his lips, he signaled Lissa to silence. Just a yard or two ahead was the end of the wall; a chink in the stone allowed soft words to filter through. This time he heard them plainly:

"The barons have arrived—all is ready."

"Devaux?"

Gaudet's laugh sent a chill down Guy's spine. He strained to hear more.

"Devaux will be eliminated ere long. All falls into place more easily than I had hoped. The king arrives soon to put an end to it."

"It has taken long enough. . . ."

Strangely familiar, the husky voice was muffled. Both men spoke Saxon English, but he could not identify the second man. Rough stone scraped his jaw as he pressed his ear more closely to the broken stone.

"Yea, but the time is at hand. The woman is here to keep him distracted." Unkind laughter. "She was wed to a Norman baron. I did not think her so foolish. I thought her to be different."

"No woman is different."

Impatience edged the voices, closer now; Guy drew back into the shadow of a low hedge, pulling Lissa with him. His heart pounded loudly, filled his ears and muffled the voices, but he could hear them still. . . .

Menacing Saxon English sounded deadlier than Gaudet's accented tones; like the sibilant hiss of a snake. " 'Tis time to be rid of this poxy sheriff."

"Time and more," Gaudet agreed harshly. "Devaux has too long been a thorn in my side."

A pause, then: "Perhaps the haughty Lady Neville will be of good use. . . ."

Guy felt Lissa's sudden jerk. He gripped her tightly, warned her with a shake of his head. The stone was rough beneath the hand he braced against the wall. Lissa's breath was vibrating in her throat, her eyes wide.

"I do not want to use her," came the sharp reply from Gaudet. "She would be too great a liability."

"It is necessary. Do what must be done. Once Devaux is gone, there will be a position for you as promised."

"No, not a position—the king has sworn I will have what I deserve. . . ."

Boots scraped on the walkway, a shower of small rocks. Guy reacted quickly. He pulled Lissa deeper into the shadows with him, turned, pressed her back against the wall, and buried his face in her neck. The smell of roses filled his nose and mouth; her hair brushed against his cheek, the twisted cords of gold silk caul abrasive.

Footsteps grew closer; there was the sound of Gaudet's coarse laughter, a coarser comment as the men passed.

When they were past, he lifted his head, caught a glimpse of monk's robes before Gaudet and his companion disappeared. He glanced back at Lissa, saw in her taut face that she recognized the danger. His hand tightened on her.

"Do not," he said quietly, "breathe a word of this to anyone, upon pain of your life and liberty."

"Do you *dare* threaten me!"

His fingers circled her delicate wrist, held her when she would have twisted free. "I dare much more than that should you be fool enough to risk us all for the sake of idle chatter, madam."

"What do you think I will tell? That my lady cousin is the sheriff's leman?" Belligerence shadowed her eyes and face. "Do you think I care if she lies with him? I do not."

"It is not your cousin's choice of beds that concerns me. There is danger in knowing too much." He leaned close, ran a hand behind her neck, his fingers spreading to hold her head still. With his nose against hers, he said softly, "It could mean your life if you are unwise, milady."

Her face paled. "I will keep silent, but not because you demand it. I would not hurt Jane."

"See that you keep your pledge."

She pulled free of his restraining hand. "I am not a liar, whatever else you may think of me."

He *wanted* to believe her. Life had taught him better than to trust freely . . . and yet—and yet. . . .

"*You*, Sir Guy, should think of your own skin as well. If the sheriff falls, so do you."

She turned angrily away. His eyes narrowed at her. An unknown quantity had just become dangerous.

19

— 🌿 —

Summer dusk lingered until it was nearly time for Matins to ring the midnight hour. Below the castle, festival bonfires blazed; torches lit purple-hued meadows in bobbing pinpricks of light. Music swirled in eddies of jangling sound. Beyond the edge of town lay Sherwood Forest, a fringe of black lace against pale shadows of twilight and a rounded moon.

Shivering in a cool breeze, Jane watched the midsummer's eve celebrations from the castle wall; the brightly colored silk pavilions shimmered like earthbound butterflies. She rested a hand atop a crenellation, a square tooth between the merlons, ran idle fingers over rough stone while her mind raced.

Priests spoke of the hell's fire that awaited fornicators. She had sinned, lain with Tré Devaux, and was unrepentant. *Gladly* unrepentant. It would take more silver than she possessed to buy enough Masses for the redemption of her soul....

She was a woman alone, reviled if her sin was made public. The church took a dim view of a woman's carnal nature: God's disapproval of fornication was stronger when applied to women than when applied to men. It was a stricture she abhorred—and feared.

She should repent, yet feared emptiness more than she did

damnation. Ah, she was a lost soul indeed, condemned by her own actions, refusing penance.

Uncustomary confusion, filled with uncertainties and fleeting fears; hope lay wounded in the cold light of reason. Did Tré cherish her as anything more than a willing female in his bed?

There had been no sign of it during the evening banquet earlier, no word or deed that marked his esteem. Courtesy, a polite, distant salutation in passing, was all that had gone between them.

I cannot bear it if he avoids me. . . .

"Milady?"

Turning, she saw Enid's pale face in the shadows. Her hands twisted in her skirts, her features revealed a mixture of excitement and apprehension; the maid bobbed a brief curtsy, stumbled slightly in its execution and on her words:

"The lord high sheriff . . . demands . . . requests that thee attend him."

A leap of heart, telltale quiver of hands that Jane hid by clasping them together in front of her.

"Does he, Enid? Where am I to present myself?"

"If it please thee, milady, in the chapel. At Matins."

Blasphemy—another step nearer hell's fire . . . to meet in the chapel. She nodded. "Tell him I will meet him."

Matins, so close now. . . . She crossed the battlement to the tower stairs. Nervous excitement tumbled in her belly. Barely enough time. . . . *Should I go first to my chamber for a change of garments? No, no time for that.* Dena would be certain to delay her, disapproval vibrating in her solid frame, mutters of damnation just loud enough to hear, yet soft enough that she could feign ignorance of them.

Worse—Lissa might be there again, agitated, impatient; fret in her eyes and sharp comments. No hint of what upset her so. Whatever plagued her would surely be told; a confidence shared in time.

Quiet reigned near the chapel, where few went when entertainment beckoned in the hall. Pipe music played, muffled by stone, a lively tune. A light breeze carried a hint of rain, and tempting fragrance emanated from the kitchens, blotted out as she drew near the Royal Mews.

The grass was wet, cushioning her feet, dampening the hem of her kirtle though she lifted it to her ankles. Heavy beat of her heart, stifled breath; when she reached the chapel, she saw a dark shadow barely outlined in the faint light that showed through narrow windows behind.

"My lord?"

"Yea." A step forward spread the bleak light on sculptured bones. His smile was taut, a sideways glance at her, a look of shared intimacy, swift and intense. Pleasure filled her, potent and dark, gratifying and terrifying. "Come into the chapel with me, milady."

He held out a hand for her, and she took it. The warmth of him brought back instant memories of soft whispers and hungry caresses, the luscious sweep of his hand along her thigh and on her breast—

Nervous, she laughed softly. "Do we seek penance?"

"Do we need it?" He glanced at her, eyes too shadowed for her to read. Fingers squeezed her hand lightly. "I seek privacy for the moment. This is the only place absent of revelers."

It was true. The chapel was empty. Ellipses of candlelight flickered; muted sounds echoed from the high ceiling like distant whispers. Incense smelled strongly, accompanied by a musty taint. Round columns supported the roof, spaced far apart and leaving ample room for worshipers to stand.

Near the front was the king's bench; a mockery, since it was well known that King John never took the sacraments. His refusal gave rise to rumors that he was in league with the devil. More likely, he hoped for enough time when death became imminent to buy his way into God's good graces, choosing to hold his coin as long as possible.

"Sit here." Tré indicated the royal bench, ignored her faint protest as he looked down at her. Blunt, without wasting words: "Gaudet summoned you. Is there good reason other than your association with me?"

"Gaudet?" Surprise rippled through her; she shook her head. "I know of none. We barely speak, have no acquaintance with each other. Why would he send me a summons in your name?"

"He seeks to use you against me." He paused, his mouth

tucked inward with wry humor. "Gaudet is more observant and ruthless than I considered. Your danger is greater from him than even from the king. Sir Guy will see you safely back to Ravenshed early on the morrow."

A chill quivered down her spine. She spread her arms, a helpless gesture. "I have no men-at-arms to guard me against Gaudet. I am safer here than at Ravenshed."

He swore fiercely. "Yea, a notable lack. More dangerous now than before. I will send my men to guard you—"

"And cause comment from the king?" She shook her head. "Nay, my lord, it would infuriate King John to have his own castle guard used to protect a widow from him. And—" she added swiftly when his eyes narrowed, "it would draw even more attention to me."

She rose to put a hand against his chest, rich tunic beneath her fingers, ebony silk on one side, gold on the other. Etched in silk thread, a raven with spread wings and one claw lifted. His family crest, the sign of the raven. An omen, perhaps, for Jane of Ravenshed.

"I am safer here, my lord," she repeated softly.

A silence fell, warm and close, as intimate as if they were secluded within wine velvet bed hangings again. The thud of his heart beneath her palm was reassuring. Muscle flexed when he moved, a shift of cool, slick silk against the pads of her fingers exotic and sensual. It was too intense and provocative a sensation within the walls of a chapel, too temporal in a spiritual world.

He must have felt the same; his palm lifted, freeing her, and she tucked her hands into her long flowing sleeves to keep them still. She looked up, studied his face in the dim light.

Tension marked him, sharply defined his features. He regarded her from beneath his lashes, and blew out a deep breath, tone wry:

"It is only your safety that leaves me vulnerable."

"I do not understand—"

"Yes, you do." He did not leave her the polite fiction of ignorance. "Gaudet is not bold enough to strike directly at me. He will use you if he can. You are my weakness now."

Her heartbeat escalated, pounding loudly in her ears. The implications were obvious, profound: *I am valuable to him.*

Encroaching shadows wavered, grew stronger as a gust of wind blew out several candles. Tré glanced toward the door, still shut against the night. His expression changed in an instant, a subtle rearrangement of features into wariness. It was feral, frightening—impressive. She sucked in a sharp breath when his hand dropped to the hilt of his sword, *felt* the change in him, tension in taut muscles.

He glanced down at her, caution in his eyes, words of warning couched in casual tones for listening ears:

"Milady, we will return to hall now that prayers have been offered."

The sense of danger intensified when they left the chapel. Noise drifted from the hall, but there it was faint and muffled, the whisk of wind through tree branches and around stone a low moaning sigh. The smell of rain permeated the air. Her blue samite skirts dragged through wet grass and over the uneven stones of the bailey; wan light from high windows made narrow, gray rectangles as they drew abreast of the hall. Laughter sounded; strains of music provided lively accompaniment. When they paused at the bottom of the steps, she heard the rasp of a sword being drawn.

Tré put a hand on her arm. "Go in. I will join you."

"Nay, I have no desire to brave greedy eyes alone." She shook her head when he swore softly, set her jaw in a stubborn tilt. "I do not go in without you, milord."

Fingers dug into the tender flesh of her wrist. "There is no time to debate the issue, milady. Do as you are bid."

"Arrogant man. . . ." Unwilling, indignant, but cognizant of the danger her refusal could cause if he was distracted, she gave in ungraciously. He released her arm with a smile.

"Go and find Sir Guy in the hall, milady. Send him to me."

A hand in the middle of her back prodded her forward; she mounted the wide, shallow stairs with skirts held up to keep from tripping, glancing back once to find no sign of him. He had gone, faded into shadows.

Discordant sounds assaulted her as soon as she entered the

hall, pausing in a doorway flanked by armed guards to let her eyes and ears adjust. Where was she to find Guy in this throng?

But then he was there beside her, a tall, lean presence that reminded her of Devaux though they were so dissimilar in coloring and nature.

"My lady Jane, you have joined us after all." A low, gallant bow, a sweep of one arm in an expansive gesture that disguised his soft question: "Where is he?"

Taking her cue from Guy, she dropped in a graceful curtsy, one leg bent and her head dipping as she replied, "Outside the hall in the bailey. I know not where. We were followed."

Guy straightened; a broad smile did not diminish the sharp glitter in his hazel eyes. "Your lady cousin seeks your companionship, milady. She won the egg dance, and now strives to win the heart of every man here. Shall I take you to her, or do you see her near the dais?"

"I see her," Jane replied, though she did not.

Guy smiled, murmured something about seeking respite from stuffy air, smoke, and spilled perfume, and was gone, moving past the guards and out the hall door.

Jane took a cup of wine proffered by a servant, sipped distractedly at it while she thought of Tré and elusive danger. Was it more than Gaudet that made him so wary?

Yet the reasons eluded her. . . .

"Jane."

She turned, pewter cup at her lips, lowered it to greet her cousin. Perspiration dewed Lissa's forehead, dampened the pale hair at her temples. Exertion colored her cheeks while sweet, intense perfume surrounded her. Jane smiled at her cousin's enjoyment.

"You have been dancing, I can see—and smell."

"Yea. I won the egg dance . . . when it broke, the perfume went on me as well."

Bits of eggshell speckled Lissa's gown, evidence of the broken egg filled with perfume. Jane reached out, brushed away a few remaining pieces from her shoulder, murmured, "Sir Guy told me you were here."

Lissa looked away, gave a careless shrug. "He is a nithing."

"A nithing?" Jane's hand paused; her cousin's muscles

tensed beneath her fingers. "Not long ago, you were enamored of him."

"I was not." Another shrug removed Jane's hand; Lissa's eyes did not meet hers. "Never enamored. It was a fleeting fancy."

"Just as well, I trow, since Walter can hardly approve if he learns of it." She paused, then added, "Though Walter is hardly a monk."

Lissa's gaze snapped back to her face. Her lips parted, eyes wide enough to mirror the hall in their startled depths. "A monk. . . ."

She sounded so strange, choked . . . Jane put a hand on her arm. "Are you well?"

"Yea." She backed away a step; when she nodded, light danced in the gilt threads of the caul holding her hair. "I am well . . . I must . . . the garderobe. . . ."

Turning away, Lissa left Jane staring after her. Yet, she did not go in the direction of the garderobe but toward the dais. Perplexed, Jane watched as her cousin disappeared behind a latticed wooden screen. It must have been the reminder of Walter that unsettled her. A pity, and little wonder that Lissa would seek love elsewhere when her husband thought more of tavern trulls than he did of his wife.

Music swirled; she moved through the crowd, loath to linger. The hall was thick with barons, knights, wealthy merchants from the town—tables had been pushed back, upended and stacked against the wall to leave the center of the hall clear. A torch dance began. She leaned against a round column, spine pressed into cold stone as a wine-bold knight staggered into her.

"Grant pardon, milady," he slurred, breathing wine fumes into her face. "I'm drunk as a fiddler's bitch. . . ."

Before she could reply, a Saxon voice intervened: "Begone, varlet." With a surprised glance, the knight moved on, steps unsteady.

She looked up, smiled at Gilbert of Oxton. He nodded to her stiffly, red hair aflame beneath torchlight. Two tapers were clutched in his fist; he held out one.

"Join the torch dance, Lady Neville."

She glanced at the ring of dancers forming. Tapers had already been lit, tiny tongues of light flickered erratically. It was tempting; under different circumstances, she would not hesitate.

A regretful smile, shake of her head, and softly: "Nay, I must return—"

"Do you fear your taper will be blown out first?" He smiled at her, waggled the candle. "I recall your victories in past dances very well. You should allow the rest of us a chance for redemption."

It seemed churlish to refuse; she hesitated, cast about for a polite excuse, and was rescued by Sir Guy.

He suddenly loomed at her side, intent, ignoring the resentful glance from Gilbert.

"If you will accompany me, milady, your servant needs you."

"Dena? Is she unwell?"

One shoulder lifted, impatience in his tone as he met her gaze briefly: "I only bring the message, milady."

Jane turned, put a hand on Gilbert's arm, saw his gaze shift away from Sir Guy, deliberate coolness in his eyes as he regarded her. "Gilbert, I cannot stay. Dena is alone here save for Enid, who is too young to be of aid. She is my old nurse—"

"Milady, you owe me no explanation." Stiff words, remote and cordial, disavowing their long acquaintance. He bowed slightly in dismissal of her apology.

Regret formed, but she said nothing beyond a murmur of farewell, then put her hand on Guy's arm. Tension vibrated beneath her fingers; she stole a quick glance at his face, a question trembling on her tongue.

Once they had passed through the doors and out onto the steep flight of steps, she asked it: "Is all well, Sir Guy?"

"Yea. Your servant is fine. The sheriff sends for you." Reassurance imbued the quick smile he gave her.

He gave her no more chance to fret, urging her down the steps and across the bailey to pass under the fitful light of torches and lamps hung on stave walls. A light rain began to fall. He reached around her, swung open a door, stepped back to allow her to precede him inside. Soft gloom closed around her, obscuring most of the chamber.

Inside, a rack of candles provided the only light; she brushed droplets of rain from her sleeves, shook her skirts a bit, sucked in a deep breath. A soft noise snared her attention, and she turned in time to see the door close between her and Guy, leaving her alone.

Her hands clenched in her skirts, and she shivered. Was she to wait?

The smell of spices was strong; a flagon of wine and two goblets stood in the middle of a small table. To occupy her hands and her mind, she moved to pour the wine. It tasted of cinnamon, honey, and ginger—sweet, cloying on her tongue.

The silence grew stifling. At last another door opened across the chamber; she curled her fingers around the stem of the goblet as Tré entered. He saw her, and shut the door softly behind him. A strange tightness constricted her chest, almost painful; her hands felt cold, her face hot. To hide her reaction, she kept her tone light.

"Is all well, milord?"

A lift of brow and one side of his mouth lent him a wicked look. "In Nottingham, all is rarely well."

"No—" She put out a hand to touch him, paused with an awkward shrug. "I meant, I see you are not hurt."

"No. I am not hurt." He unbuckled his sword, set it on the table with a faint metallic rattle. "We do not have much time. The tourney begins on the morrow. There is much yet to be done before the king arrives."

When he paused, she poured wine for him, held it out. He took it, letting his hand brush over hers, heat against ice a scalding contrast. He sipped the wine, studied her in the gloom.

"After the tourney, I have arranged for Captain Oliver to escort you to Ravenshed. He is one of the few here I trust besides Guy."

"Why are you so determined for me to leave?" Her hand shook slightly, so that some of the wine spilled onto her hand. "Am I so unsafe? A burden?"

He still wore the black and gold silk tunic; it fitted him perfectly, spanning broad shoulders and chest, reaching to mid-calf. He moved to take her hand, lifted it to his lips, holding her gaze until she felt light-headed, barely remembering to breathe.

"You are no burden, Jane of Ravenshed." His tongue flicked out, washed heat over the back of her hand where the wine gleamed red. Her breath came more swiftly. Light caught in his hair, dark as a raven's wing . . . she gently touched it. *Like black silk. . . .*

Distracted, fumbling for clarity, she whispered, "Then what am I, my lord, if not a burden?"

He looked up; his thumb pressed into soft flesh, rubbed over her palm. A faint smile quirked his mouth. Darkly beautiful, a sardonic archangel. . . .

"Lovely," he said after a long moment of silence. "And dangerous."

At her quickly drawn breath, he smiled with no trace of mockery, set down his wine. "A danger to any man who would keep you safe. You defy my efforts."

She held her tongue. It would do her no good to tell him that she wanted only to be near, that she did not want to go back to Ravenshed because she could not bear the thought of leaving him. She was besotted; a fool. He had bedded her, yet spoken no words of love, only of need.

And yet . . . and yet, she could deny him nothing, offered no protest when he pulled her to him with a rough sound of frustration, spread his fingers behind her head to hold it still, his mouth brushing over her lips in an urgent kiss. She tasted ginger, cinnamon, and desire. His tongue was a teasing rhythm in her mouth, strokes summoning delicious response. A pulse started in the pit of her stomach, moved lower; spread fire in exquisite torment.

When he lifted his head at last, she curled her fingers into his tunic, held him tightly. The muscles in the back of her knees weakened, yielded. She sagged on his arm, and he held her hard against him.

Against the top of her head, he rasped, "Lovely lady, you undo my best intentions."

She pressed her face into his chest, reaching up, fingers lightly exploring the contours of his mouth, jawline, throat. He smelled of wind and exotic scent; his heartbeat was loud against her ear.

Wild thoughts tumbled through her head, fragments of memory, vague yearnings, uncertainties. He called her lovely, yet female worth was measured by children. She had none. A barren womb, unable to perform a function even the lowest churl could manage with ease. Did he know that?

He has lost a child, a beloved daughter—will he want another? Will he even want me for more than a few moments of pleasure?

Emotions waged war within her, spawned by his touch and nurtured by revealing glimpses of the man beneath the fierce outer shell. Carnal love subtly expanded comprehension of the complex man who held her in his embrace: He was more than just sheriff or baron. So much more. . . .

Her hand shifted, stroked a path over his chest. She felt his muscles tighten as he drew a swift breath. Her skin tingled with awareness of him; her breasts were sensitive, nipples aching and taut where they rubbed against two layers of silk.

He moved, hand sliding from her back to her shoulder, then to her chin to lift her face for a kiss. The movement separated them, allowed room for his free hand to touch her breast. Instant heat blossomed. Her thighs quivered, pressed tightly together to stem the blazing tide. She shuddered.

His breath was harsh against her mouth. Thumb and finger teased her breast, plucked at the nipple as sweet pleasure coursed through her body. A moan, stifled under his lips, signified surrender.

"Yield to me, sweet lady." Husky and yearning: "Yield all to me. . . ."

Tré slid his other hand lower, lifted her skirts to gather them in a fist and draw them up. He leaned into her; his weight pushed her back against the table's edge. Candle glow washed over him, gleamed in his black hair, lit his face in stark play of light and shadow. He bent slowly in front of her, pulled her to him to press his mouth on silk-shrouded breasts.

With a faint sigh, she put her hands in his hair, let strands curl around her fingers. He went to his knees on the wooden floor, both hands at her hips, pushing up blue samite to bare her thighs. Cool air whisked over her, made her tremble. Breathless intimacy as he touched her, finger sliding over damp crevice in slow strokes that dazzled and delighted.

Weakly, she leaned on the table, arms braced behind her, palms against solid wood. Wicked and dangerous, erotic expectation beat through her veins. Then he slid the silk higher, shocking her as he leaned forward to touch his tongue where his hand had just been.

"Oh . . . what . . . are you doing?" Gasping, she grabbed at him, curled her hands in black hair, pushed feebly.

He ignored her, lifted her with both hands to set her on the table's edge, his head between her spread thighs and tongue lashing her intimately, sending spirals of heat through her belly and breasts. Quivering, a gasp of shock and pleasure; she shuddered in reaction.

His tongue delved deeper, sought and found the source of pleasure that rendered her boneless; she collapsed back on her elbows, thighs spread wide in surrender and wonder. Abandoned goblets tilted, fell, spilled wine over the table, onto the floor.

Her entire body felt as if it were scarlet with excitement and chagrin. She should stop him, but all strength she possessed had deserted her. It was provocative and erotic, his head so dark between pale thighs, the wicked rasp of his tongue producing shivering torment. She moaned protest and complete surrender in a single breath, lifting her hips to his seeking tongue.

Sensation coalesced into a tight knot under his heated strokes, a brief moment of unbearable tension that crashed in waves, threatening to suck her under, to drown her in ecstasy. Her moans escalated to a single wild cry of release that echoed from walls and ceiling, surrounding her with the sound of her own pleasure.

Vaguely, she was aware of him over her, blocking light and ceiling, his face sharp with passion. He kissed her cheek, then her forehead, nibbling his way down to her mouth a little at a time, bringing her slowly back from weightless completion.

"My wits have deserted me," he whispered against her cheek. "All around me danger awaits, yet I think only of you . . . of this . . . and this. . . ."

He shaped her breasts in his palms, teased sensitive nipples with kisses and tiny nips of his teeth, summoning heat again. She twisted, agitation curling in her belly; a sense of urgency began to rise, the ache inside her grew strong and sharp. His arousal nudged between her thighs, hot, hard. No more preliminaries before he lunged forward, a rough thrust of his body into hers, breathtaking. She pushed into his movement with back arched.

A groan, a rough mutter: *"Ma chérie. . . ."*

The endearment filled her heart, while his body filled the emptiness inside her. Sweet intimacy, fulfillment of more than passion . . . she needed him. Heart and soul and body were bound together by threads of a desire for more than the easing of a void in her life. She wanted more than mere existence, even if it came with danger. . . .

The cool, hard table beneath her was cushioned in samite, rigid flesh invading her with swift, fierce strokes that took them quickly to release. Her arms lifted, hands curled in his hair, her cry muffled by his mouth crushing her lips in savage fervor.

A moment of suspension when he thrust hard and then stopped, slowly relaxing. His breath was heavy and ragged in her ear. Braced on bent arms, he leaned over her, body still firm inside her though passion was spent. Air spiced with the fragrance of spilled wine wreathed them.

After a long moment, he pushed away, tugged silk over her thighs, rearranged his rucked-up tunic and untied cords. His head was bent, lashes dark against his cheeks, hiding eyes and expression from her.

Awkward, she sat up, shivered a little in the cool air. Outside, rain struck stone, familiar and heavy. She heard it, smelled it, felt it in the damp chill from the open window.

Tré glanced up, ends of his mouth tucked inward. "I do not seem able to keep from touching you, no matter how firm my resolve to stay my distance. You weave a spell to shatter my resolutions."

"Do I?"

"Yea, you do. On the morrow, you will leave with Oliver right after the tournament. No one will mark your departure then or think it unusual. I would have you away from here before the king arrives."

"What do you think John would do? I am a widow, not bound by vow or contract. Ravenshed is mine, my dower gift in lieu of claim to Blidworth. I brought it to the marriage and cannot be divested of it. In his will, Hugh gave it to me in perpetuity."

"My lady Jane, it is not the loss of lands that concerns me." He buckled his sword belt, adjusted it, glanced up at her with brooding eyes. "There is more involved. Gaudet plots. I must be free to dispute accusations or counter his actions without fear of endangering you."

He reached out, took her chin in his palm, leaned to brush her lips with his, lingered for a moment. She stared up at him, curled her fingers around his wrist to hold his hand to her face. Dread loomed.

"My lord—"

"Sweet lady, we must not meet again." Clipped, free of emotion or regret, the words sounded overloud in the dense gloom of the chamber.

Her lips were stiff, unable to form a proper reply; it was not unexpected but shattering. A confirmation of her fears.

"It can be no other way." He paused, stared at her gravely. His words were strained: "There are those who would use your presence here against us both. Should the king learn I have been remiss in my duties by not arresting you for lending aid to outlaws, we would likely have our heads on twin pikes. I do not care to risk it."

She found her tongue in a quiet reminder: "I am not unused to danger, my lord. As flattering as your desire to protect me may be, you seem to have forgotten that I am quite capable of defending myself."

"Are you?" A swift hand caught her before she could move, held her wrist in a bone-crushing vise that summoned a gasp from her lips. "Few men give warning before striking. It would be no different were the quarry a woman—even a woman capable of defending herself."

Stung, she rubbed her wrist when he released it. "I take your point, my lord. I did not realize I must be on my guard with you as well."

It sounded more bitter than she had intended; it did not go unnoticed.

He stared at her from eyes gone gray-green with ice. Softly: "Do not test me."

Misery clogged her throat; she could not reply. Her gaze focused on the wavering glow of the lit candles.

"My lady . . . Jane."

Unwillingly, she dragged her attention back to him. Some of the harshness had gone from his face and voice. He put out a hand; after a hesitation, she put her fingers in his clasp.

"It is for the best. I would mean your death." He drew her closer, tucked a loose strand of hair behind her ear. "I will not come near you again. Spies lurk in every corner, as in the chapel this eve. Be ware of any man who says I have sent him in my name, for he will be lying. Should the time come when I feel it safe, I will come to you then on my own. Guy de Beaufort is the only man I fully trust, and the only other man you should trust."

Hope that had blossomed too early withered inside her, became dust and ashes. She heard her calm agreement, her voice steady, not betraying her anguish.

"I will accompany Captain Oliver after the tourney on the morrow."

His reply was a blur, as was the return to her chamber through the rain. Remote again, safe behind his barrier, he bade her farewell, then faded into the shadows. She heard his boots echo on the stairwell, then nothing but the final closing of the oak door and Dena's familiar voice:

"Milady, I have thy bath ready."

As if arms and legs were pulled by invisible cords, Jane allowed Dena to undress her and help her into the wooden tub, listening to the maidservant recite a litany of the effort it had taken to get Fiskin to find a tub and bring it to the chamber.

She sank down into perfumed water that had already grown cool despite Dena's troubles.

Not even mulled wine eased the chill inside her; she shivered until Dena expressed dismay and tucked her into the wide canopied bed beneath an extra fur.

Finally she was alone, Dena gone to sleep with the other servants on straw pallets cushioning the floor, the chamber still lit by a single candle that flickered in errant drafts.

Sleepy murmurs drifted through the half-drawn curtains to her; Dena and Enid in soft discussion. Outside, it had grown quiet at last. Rain must have doused the bonfires and lively celebrations. It was hushed now, gloom closing around the castle like a fist.

Silence. . . .

Jane wondered why no one heard the screaming of her soul.

20

❦

Morning dawned slowly after the rain. Tré met Guy in the middle bailey. The wet stones glistened; a brisk breeze wafted thick stink from the moat. Sentries paced bridge and wall, bootsteps loud. A cock crowed an undulating salutation to the day.

"Oliver will leave after the tourney ends today."

Guy nodded. "Two of the guards brought in some captured outlaws. Saxons, but none of them were Little John or Will Scarlett. Oliver is set to draw tight the noose. If any man can seize them, he will. He knows Sherwood as well as do the verderers."

"Pray he knows it as well as the poachers. Men have been known to wander into the ravines and greenwood and never be seen again." He frowned, glanced around the bailey, quiet now after a night of revelry, but with signs of stirring at cockcrow.

"I pray the captives we take please King John."

Guy's words were fervent, and Tré's gaze slid back to him. He shook his head slowly.

"John—neither fear of God nor regard for man dilutes his ambition. There is no pleasing him. He does as he wills, takes what he can. He intends to rid himself of me and take my lands, make no mistake about it. It would not matter if I had Robin Hood himself dangling from the gallows for his amusement."

"Yet if the Council of Barons—"

"I have appealed to Geoffrey Fitz-Peter, Earl of Essex, for his aid. As chief justiciar, he has been ordered to return to the church their property that was seized during the interdict. The archbishop is set to return to England, and he takes a dim view of baronies being confiscated. If I can keep my head on my shoulders until my appeal is heard, I may yet thwart the king's intent to hold Brayeton."

"Or you may lose all."

He met Guy's gaze and nodded. "Yea, I may lose all."

Silence descended; smoke from the cooking fires drifted over the bailey. Nottingham was coming to life, the guards already arguing with vendors at the gates. The air was brighter now, the sun breaking free of treetops.

Tré glanced at Guy. Shadows darkened his eyes. Tension was evident in his abrupt movements, an impatience that was unlike him. "Did you learn anything new from the prisoners we took outside the hall last night?"

"Nothing. They have told all they know, I think. Saxon rebels. Paid assassins. They claim they did not know you to be the high sheriff, but only meant to rob you."

Tré snorted in disbelief. "In a chapel? Witless assassins. Nottingham is thick with knights and men-at-arms—thieves would last no longer than fresh meat in a pack of wolves."

"They were sent by Gaudet." Guy's tone hardened. "It would suit me well to see him skewered for this treachery."

"It is only treachery when a man is trusted. Greed and hate prod Gaudet. I doubt he would be loyal to the king if it suited his interests to do otherwise." Eyes narrowed against a shaft of sunlight. Silk pennons and flags snapped in the wind; identifying colors of green, blue, yellow, and red flew over the multicolored pavilions housing barons, knights, and entrants in the coming tourney. "A pity it is not Gaudet who has entered the lists. I would not mind striking his shield in a challenge."

A sea of mud stretched beyond the bailey; on the fringes of the grassy swale cleared for the lists, vendor stalls sprouted in competition with Market Square. A vagrant breeze carried the stench of rubbish.

Guy indicated the lower bailey with a nod of his head. "There were but three strikes on my shield yesterday."

"Only three?" Lightly mocking: "A fearsome champion who intimidates all challengers, Sir Guy."

"One of the challengers is Sir Alfric—a Saxon from Kelham." Guy paused, added meaningfully, "Gaudet's cousin."

"Another cousin . . . they breed like rats. There is too ready a supply of Gaudet's kindred. Have you seen this Sir Alfric?" They walked toward the middle bridge; rain had diluted the moat's stench to a mere hint of odor.

"I have seen him before." Guy stepped over fresh horse dung. On the slopes below, barons began to emerge sleepily from their pavilions. "He is called Alfric the Crusher. A name more likely to incite terror in greenlings than veteran knights."

"Or swooning females."

Guy laughed softly. "If he is the best the Saxons can do, I will need other opponents to save me from boredom."

Tré squinted against smoke as they neared the grassy common below the castle. Smithy fires poured noxious blackness into the air; hammers clanged on iron and steel, armorers plying their trade in anticipation of need.

"What will you tell the lady Jane?"

Guy's question caught him unaware; abruptly, the memory of her pale face and haunted eyes arose. Familiar barriers went up, blocking crippling emotion. The decision was made.

"Nothing," he said, without explanation.

Guy nodded, paused beside a palisade built of new wood. "Captain Oliver will see her safely to Ravenshed. She is well out of this cursed town."

"It is not the town, but Gaudet. I itch to kill him for his treachery."

Guy's good humor returned at even the prospect of Gaudet's demise. "Challenge him to à l'outrance. A match of vengeance would justify his death on the field."

"And listen to the cowled priests mewl of damnation for those who fight in tourneys? I leave that to you."

"I do not need the church hounding me as they do the king."

Tré looked up and across the growing crowd; barricades framed the rectangular patch of grass for the lists, built to hold spectators at bay. Already there were those who staked out their spot along the wooden rails, eager for the entertainment to begin.

Guy took a step away from the palisade. "My fee is paid and my shield displayed. The moneylenders assessed my horse and armor, though I shall be collecting ransoms today, not paying them."

"My wager is always on you, and I have yet had cause to regret it." Tré paused, tilted his head toward the gallery. "I will applaud your victories and collect my winnings."

Guy grinned. "And fret because you watch instead of compete. Shall I carry your favor into the lists instead of one from a lovely lady?"

A crude comment earned his laughter, then Guy departed; it would not be long before the tourney began.

Tré moved past the row of contestants' banners and crested helms set up for view and easy identification during the tourney. Shallow wooden steps creaked beneath his weight as he mounted to the gallery. The new wood smelled pleasant; black and gold velvet hangings were draped from the canopy.

When he turned, Giles nearly collided with him; Tré bent a narrow glance at the steward, who met it calmly.

"My lord sheriff, Captain Oliver bids me inform you that the lady he was to escort is not to be found."

"He is not to leave until after the tourney." He batted impatiently at a dangling tassel, scowled at Giles. "She is most likely not yet ready to leave."

Unperturbed, Giles inclined his head. "Captain Oliver is well aware of the arrangements, my lord. Yet the lady is gone, along with her servants, mounts, and baggage. A guard allowed them out the gate before first light this morning."

Anger ignited, pounded against his temples. He swore softly. Giles did not move. Tré glanced at the lists, already filling with the first combatants. "Send Oliver to me. Find the guard who saw them leave."

Too late . . . the sun is long up.

When Oliver came, he brought the guard, who confirmed that the lady Jane had quit the castle with her retinue.

"Go after them, Oliver." He sat in a high-backed chair under the gallery canopy, hands spread on his knees, and chafed at the duty that bound him to stay there.

Oliver nodded. "They travel with a cart, my lord. We should overtake them swiftly."

"See that you do. Nothing is to interfere with our other arrangements."

Understanding shone in the captain's eyes; he was capable, efficient, staunch. "I will do what must be done."

"Keep the lady secure."

Oliver bowed his head. "That is my first priority."

The captain left the gallery with a clink of sword and mail. Tré propped his elbow on the arm of his chair, appearing indolent. More spectators were filling the wood galleries; laughter rose, silk-clad ladies found seats. Gaudet sat in scarlet solitude; watchful.

A loud cry went up; Tré forced his attention to the lists. Inexperienced knights fought first; bloodshed was frequent, clumsy attempts to batter opponents with lances more common than skillful passes. Impatience surged, tamped down by grim determination. He could not sit there the entire day. Yet to leave would be to invite Gaudet to follow. If Jane's departure was not yet discovered, Oliver would have a better chance to reach her first.

Every move was suspect, every defense inadequate. He chafed, shoved his fist under his jaw, kept his gaze on the field. Lord Creighton arrived, trailed by Gilbert of Oxton. Pleasantries were exchanged. More barons began to fill the galleries. Tension knotted Tré's muscles and his belly. This was not a game he played well; he preferred action to idle waiting. The palm of his hand itched to hold a sword. *I envy Guy his combat.*

At last the first wave of combatants relinquished the field. Impartial judges were stationed at intervals along the grassy swale already littered with the flotsam of the preceding contest. Bits of splintered lances and scraps of bloodied silk testified to bruising encounters as varlets scurried to remove the debris.

Caparisoned destriers pranced down the field; silks and tassels gleamed richly under the benevolent eye of the sun. Riders garbed in mail and heraldic colors held their lances high. The procession was met with thunderous acclaim by the crowds behind the guarded barricades; these were the champions they had come to watch risk all for the prizes.

The ceremonial procession of knights rode along the decorated stands before approaching the silk-draped gallery with solemn ceremony; sunlight glinted on helms and shields.

Garbed in green and gold—the *vert* and *or* of his family colors—Guy drew his destrier to a halt before the gallery. A ripple of excitement ran through the ranks of ladies seated there as he held out the blunted end of his lance. His face was expressionless beneath the curved flange of his helmet, the protective visor lifted. The point of his lance did not waver as he waited.

It was no surprise when the lady tied a length of silk to the lance's end, accompanied by soft squeals of delight from her companions. Few refused; Tré had never known a lady to reject a request for her favor in a tourney.

He raised a brow at Guy's choice. Lady Dunham fumbled with the knot of silk, a wisp of scarlet. No husband was in sight; but Walter of Gedling was rarely near.

Defiantly, Lady Dunham finished tying the silk with a flourish. Guy saluted her with the silk-tipped lance, then backed his steed up to rejoin the procession.

Knights returned to the niches where squires waited to properly arm them for the contests. Pennons fluttered above silk pavilions; shields bore painted bars, chevrons, and fesses in heraldic colors of *azure, gules, vert*; a rainbow. Devices pranced or grinned on curved metal and crested helmets; on some, cadency marks designated order of birth.

Guy de Beaufort's shield bore a star beneath the gold-painted chevron on a field of green, the mark of a third son. No crest adorned his helmet, too likely to snare the edge of lance or sword; armor and accoutrements were kept to a minimum, lethal but not elaborate.

A breeze blew, warmer now: Ladies covered their noses

with scented squares of cloth to block the pungent scent from butchers' stalls and moat. Bright sunlight announced the noon hour. Beside him, Lord Creighton tilted a pewter goblet; light flashed on a ruby ring.

"A decent group of champions, my lord sheriff." The Saxon baron smiled, gestured to the field. " 'Tis said your man has won tourneys the length and breadth of England."

"Yea. Beaufort is formidable."

"Do you care to place a private wager on his abilities against Sir Alfric, the Saxon champion?"

Tré gave him a cool glance, lifted his brow, allowed one side of his mouth to curl up. "I am not in the habit of wagering against Saxons. I find it unpredictable at best, dangerous at the worst."

Pleased, Creighton smacked a hand against his knee, laughed. "Yea, you are more wise than some, my lord sheriff. It is folly to underestimate an opponent, be he peasant or king."

"Or Norman." Tré smiled when Lord Oxton's head jerked around, saw resentment in blue eyes before he looked away.

Seated on Creighton's other side, Gilbert of Oxton wore a surly countenance; Tré remembered his attempt to silence Jane near four months ago, hot chagrin in the baron's face at her tart reply. Enmity hid behind his veiled eyes, but not for the lady. Rumors flew swiftly in a crowded castle; word would fly of a hated sheriff's interest in Hugh de Neville's widow. Servants were a most efficient form of communication, able to see much, and to guess at what they didn't see.

Cheers rose from behind the barricades; a resounding crack of lances and shields came from the field.

He turned his attention to the tourney, restless, impatient to have it over. Still in the recess at one end of the field, Guy waited, mailed gauntlets clenched in a fist, helm tucked under his arm. It would be hot beneath the steel, even with cloth mantling meant to prevent sunstroke in the Holy Land; unnecessary here. Sweat beaded on Guy's forehead and temples, dampened blond hair to a muddy brown. He wiped the sweat away with a cloth given him by his squire, grimaced, looked up, and chanced to meet Tré's gaze.

A grin flashed briefly, acknowledgment and assurance. Guy

intended to defeat Sir Alfric and recoup Norman pride, battered lately by outlaws and royal domination. Redemption would taste sweet—if it was served.

Despite careful plans, precautions taken, a premonition nagged. Jane's unexpected flight from Nottingham bespoke trouble. He felt it, breathed it, dreaded it. All he could do was wait.

21

---🌿---

The King's Great Way cut through the ancient trees of Sherwood Forest, roughly following the banks of the River Leen as it scythed northward around Nottingham Castle. Huge boughs the span of a man's waist thrust over the road to lock leafy branches with other trees, forming a vaulted ceiling of green. Sound was muffled, hoofbeats and cart wheels cushioned by forest debris and mud.

"Milady. . . ."

Jane heard strain in the summons, tugged at her palfrey's reins to glance back at the cart wobbling on the rutted tracks. Dena's face was pale; she clung to the side of the cart with both hands, mouth open and gasping for air.

Alarmed, Jane signaled a halt. Fiskin dutifully drew back on the long leather reins; the rouncy stopped, blew a wet stream of relief from flared nostrils. Tied to the cart's tail, a sumpter loaded with the smaller trunks taken to Nottingham blew an answer.

Wailing, Enid fluttered about her mother like a wounded bird.

"Be quiet," Jane said sharply, and the girl subsided to low moans.

"Dena, what ails you?" Jane leaned from her palfrey to

touch the older woman's sweat-dewed brow. Her skin was clammy to the touch, as cold as a cheese. Gently: "Ah, I should not have hurried you so this morn. Fiskin, aid me in getting her down from the cart."

Between them, they managed to hand down Dena's bulky form and ease her to the verge to rest atop a tussock of long grass. Jane loosened the linen wimple Dena wore while Enid bunched a mantle under her mother's head and gave her a sip of water.

"Pray, forgive me, m'lady," Dena got out. Gray lips quivered; her color was that of cold ashes.

Jane smiled, pressed a palm against her old nurse's cheek. "There is nothing to forgive, Dena. Do not fret. We are here with you."

Outwardly calm and reassuring, Jane acknowledged a pang of uneasiness. With Lord Creighton still at the castle, they were alone on the road, easy prey for outlaws drawn to Nottingham by the lure of the fair and tourney. A cart and baggage guarded only by servants were a great temptation.

"Milady . . . prithee, allow me to rest but a moment and we shall go on."

"Hush now, Dena. Rest." She smoothed hair back from the pallid brow, noted many gray strands among the dark ones. When had she aged so greatly? It seemed only the day before that Dena had been a young mother with broad hips and legs as sturdy as barrel staves; now she looked so frail and old, with new lines in her familiar face, and fleshy jowls that sagged beneath her wimple. She touched Dena's brow. "I shall send Fiskin for aid."

Gnarled fingers curled into the loose wool of her mantle and clung. "Nay, m'lady, do not. This shall soon pass, as it has before."

"Yea, it will pass, but you should be eased and I have no herbs with me."

Gently, she disentangled the old woman's fingers and rose to her feet. When summoned, Fiskin presented himself in front of her, expectation on his features.

"Take the sumpter. We may need the rouncy to pull the

cart. Go swiftly to Ravenshed for Edwin. Here." A fumble at the neck of her kirtle, a deft twist pulled paternoster beads over her head. She pressed them into his hands. "If any man should question you, show him these and say your name and estate plainly. Fly swiftly now."

"Yea, milady." He slid the beads over his head, tucked them beneath his tunic. When the sumpter was unloaded, small trunks stowed in the narrow rear of the cart and on the verge, he mounted nimbly, flashed a reassuring smile, and was gone, kicking the reluctant horse into a brisk trot.

Brief despair eroded her calm; she inhaled sharply. It was one more disaster atop all the rest. One more dilemma to gnaw at her. She hunched her shoulders, curled her fingers into the edges of her mantle. Enid gazed up at her with a complete trust that was dismaying.

She wanted to shout at her: she could neither cure Dena nor save them from calamity.

I cannot even save myself. . . .

Danger lay in that direction, memory stark and painful, too devastating to bear. Shattered hope, lost dreams; truth instead of foolish illusions.

"Enid, go into the wood. Find a hawthorn tree. If there are any, bring berries. Bring me as many as you can."

A distraction, as much for Enid as for herself. She moved to the cart, led the gentle rouncy to a stand of birch. Pale silvery gray bark, black patched and cracked into squares on the trunk; Lady of the Wood with graceful draping branches, a delicate mantle of leaves that drifted in the slight breeze around her.

Perhaps Enid's search would be successful. Hawthorn berries had medicinal properties to ease palpitations of the heart. She sat beside Dena, drew up her legs, and wrapped her arms around her knees. She offered an occasional soothing word as Dena drifted in and out of sleep.

When Enid returned, she brought a few hard berries that were small and not yet fully red. Holding out her hand with a look of hope: "These were all I found, milady. Will they not do?"

Reassurance in her smile, her words were light as she rose to her feet and took the small berries. "We shall pray they do, Enid. Bring the water pouch from the cart."

Whether it was the potion or time, Dena's face began to regain color and her lips took on a normal hue; within a few minutes she was sitting up, albeit shakily.

"I am ready, m'lady." Slurred words, eyelids slightly drooping, certain indication that she was still ill.

Jane hesitated. They were so close . . . Papplewick was not far ahead. Did she dare continue? The palfrey snorted, pricked white ears forward and stomped the grass with its hooves.

Disquiet arose; the forest beyond the road was still and hushed. Not even a bird could be heard in the dense silence. A foreboding filled her, gained strength, as she helped the older woman to the cart. It swayed, tilted, creaked protest as Dena was ensconced on the narrow seat with Enid beside her.

"Milady—" Enid licked her lips, glanced uncertainly at the placid rouncy buckled into the traces. "I have never driven a cart without aid. . . ."

"Take up the reins firmly. The rouncy knows what to do better than you or I. Do not be timid or we will never get back to Ravenshed."

Irritation edged the last words, coupled with a growing urgency to be gone. Jane mounted her palfrey again, nudged it forward. The rouncy took the initiative. The cart lurched forward, the horse following the palfrey like a pet dog.

The cart groaned and rumbled, an occasional jolt from a rut in which the wheels sank almost to the hub. Efforts to free the cart were frustrating, delaying. It would take an eternity to reach the manor. Much better if they abandoned cart and baggage, put Dena on a mount—when Edwin reached them, he would know what to do.

The steady rhythm of hoofbeats and cart wheels filled her ears; her world narrowed to the road, urgency held at bay by grim determination. Her fingers tightened on the reins; the palfrey snorted nervously, sensing her tension. She shifted, slightly off-balance, both feet braced on the small protrusion from the saddle that allowed her to ride.

Another absurd piece of nonsense, to forbid a female to ride astride—unless it was to the hunt. If there were exceptions, why not ignore the dictum altogether?

A cool, damp wind blew from the forest; sunlight was only a thin glow above laced branches. Ahead, where young trees did not cover the road, a large patch of light devoured shadow. Despite her best intentions, she thought of Tré Devaux.

Vivid pain clutched her chest; squeezed breath and hope to nothing. Brief joy had vanished when he discarded her; dispassionate tone, cool words, each one a mortal blow to her heart.

Logic bade her admit the wisdom of his decision: It was dangerous for both of them. Just as dangerous for the castle guard to escort her home, for King John would not view it as justified should he arrive before Captain Oliver returned. A generous gesture from Tré, but one she dared not accept.

The palfrey stumbled, and she grabbed at the high pommel of the saddle to keep from falling. *Curse this cloak!* The hem, heavy with mud, restricted movement of her legs—she bent to free the wool trapped between foot and horse.

In the next instant, the palfrey shrilled loudly, hopped twice, and almost unseated her. She found herself sprawled forward over its neck. Her hands curled into the heavy mane to keep from tumbling to the ground, fingers clutching at leather and coarse hair.

She straightened, and glimpsed the hazy shadows of armed men afoot in the road. Her heart thumped warning just as a man reached for her palfrey's bridle. She yanked it back fiercely. Rearing, front hooves pawed at air as she slid back to land hard and gracelessly in mud.

Enid's scream cleaved the jumbled sounds of snorting horse, pounding blood in her ears, and gasps for breath.

Jésu—outlaws!

It was midafternoon before Sir Alfric and Guy faced each other on the field. Tré watched impassively, while impatience gnawed holes in his outward calm. Already the victor in three contests that day, which had earned him a ransom of destrier and armor from the vanquished knights, Guy lifted a lance blunted by a three-pronged coronal to deflect deadly blows.

Restive, snorting, the massive destrier Guy rode was fresh; it pranced eagerly, huge hooves curiously graceful on the wet earth chewed by the day's contests. Its velvety white hide gleamed in the sunlight; mane and tail brushed the ground with each capering step. Trappings of green and gold silk fluttered while light glinted from the silver and gilt etching of the shaffron and crinet protecting the destrier's head and neck. Single combat was more exciting than the chaos of the melee; it was a form of personal duel that thrilled spectators. That it was betwixt Saxon and Norman champions only whetted their anticipation.

Tré's gaze shifted to Guy, saw him take up his lance, couch it in the shield recess, then fasten to his belt a mace given him by his squire. He positioned himself in the high pommel of the saddle, thrust mailed feet into covered stirrups, and nodded readiness.

At the opposite end of the field, Sir Alfric followed the same routine; they rode into the roar of the crowd and made the obligatory circle around the field, past the spectators' galleries, while the herald announced their names. The destriers pawed the ground, nostrils flaring and muscles bunching with excitement.

Both challengers signaled the judges that they were ready to begin, then tightened grips on lances. The white scrap of linen dropped. Horses leaped forward in a thunder of lethal hooves and flying chunks of mud and grass, eager for the fray.

The first pass was exploratory of the other's strengths and weaknesses; glancing blows of lance to shield were only loud cracks that caused no harm.

Wheeling his mount around at the far end of the field, Guy urged him forward again without pause, gaining a slight advantage on his rival. This time his lance caught Sir Alfric's shield full-force in the middle, knocked him off-balance and nearly unseated him. Both horses staggered beneath the blow. By the time Guy slowed his mount and turned again, Sir Alfric had regained his seat, but Guy won the point.

Tré frowned. He watched as Sir Alfric turned his mount

and leveled his lance; there was an air of wariness in the way
Guy held himself. Fingers that had drummed impatience on
chair arms now fisted around the wood.

"My lord sheriff. . . ."

Giles again, voice a low murmur at his elbow, tactful profi-
ciency behind his chair. He turned, recognized the glint in his
steward's eyes, rose to join him at the rear of the gallery. Giles
put his fingertips together, pursed his mouth.

"The king approaches Nottingham, my lord."

"Now?" Alarm flickered, quickly stifled. "He is early."

Giles nodded, spread his arms. "All is in readiness for
him—save Captain Oliver."

"What word from that quarter?"

Giles did not reply but withdrew a pouch from beneath his
tunic. A slight shake, and a single coin fell into his palm. He
held it out, a five-sided piece of silver. Tré did not need to
take it.

It was the signal for failure. Disaster. A piece of Judas silver.
Gold for success, silver for betrayal. . . .

There was a thundering crash behind him; he turned, saw in
that instant the two destriers collide. Screams rent the air, men
and animals registering pain and anger; spectators groaned as if
one, a collective expression of horror.

Tangled silks, struggling horses, chaos reigned on the field;
another cry went up, this one drawing him to the front of the
gallery with Giles at his heels.

Guy de Beaufort lurched to his feet; blood streamed onto
green and gold silk. Sir Alfric of Kelham faced him as the destriers were snared by scrambling squires. Sunlight glinted on
their drawn swords, murder marked two faces. Steel clanged
harshly. Blow for blow, fierce combat was waged in mud that
sucked at feet and endurance. Harsh grunts filled the air.

The tournament marshal tossed a flag to indicate that the
match was over; a useless gesture ignored, linen trampled by
the two men on the field. A deafening roar rose from the crowd
to drown out the marshal's protest with savage approval.

Saxon against Norman, vicious fighting raged unchecked by
rule or rote. Giles stepped closer to Tré, words a low murmur:
"Beaufort's lance snapped cleanly, my lord sheriff."

A pause as the import of the comment registered, then Giles added softly, "As clean as if cut in twain. . . ."

Provocation. Shattered peace a certainty . . . and the result quickly became clear.

Blades clashed, slid, parted, swung to collide again. A brittle crack split the air as Guy's sword snapped in two, the end of his blade spinning away to land in the mud. Sir Alfric instantly took the advantage; his sword hissed in a wide arc, caught Guy on the edge of his swiftly raised shield, slid along the outer curve to bite deeply into mail and flesh. Another collective groan went up from the crowd, punctuated by a sickening grunt as Guy folded over the pointed blade.

Tré felt it keenly—as if the blade had pierced his own flesh. His knuckles went white on the wooden edge of the gallery as he leaned out, saw the tournament marshal race onto the field and Sir Alfric step back. Rage built, flared higher when Gervaise Gaudet signaled approval to his champion.

He swung around, saw Gaudet glance at him. A triumphant smile fell away; Gaudet took a backward step that brought him up hard against the gallery rail. Men moved away, opening a space between them. Wind flapped the silk edges of the canopy with a loud popping sound. His hand ached, fingers numb where he gripped the hilt of his drawn sword. He did not remember drawing it, but held it up; light skittered along the wicked blade.

"The decree was for blunted swords, Gaudet." Soft, with no inflection to betray the murderous rage fraying both temper and restraint, he swept his glance to Giles. "Have Alfric of Kelham arrested. If Beaufort dies, Sir Alfric will not see another dawn."

Beyond the gallery, chaos held sway; here, silence was thick, heavy.

"It was a fair contest, Devaux." Gaudet's eyes spit fury, but his tone was equally calm. "Your man challenged him first."

"The judges will make that decision when they inspect his broken lance and sword for evidence of foul play."

Now Gaudet's voice rose, words meant to incite anger: "Do Saxons triumph only by foul means in Nottingham, my lord sheriff? Or is it that Normans will not be bested by fair means without crying foul?"

A low murmur ran through Saxon ranks, old resentments rising to the fore. Tré ignored them, focused his attention only on Gervaise Gaudet. He lifted his sword, blade flat and horizontal so that the sharp tip pointed to his scarlet tunic.

Softly, meant just for Gaudet, he promised, "If it is found that the lance was weakened, I will come to you for satisfaction, Sir Gervaise. Mark me—you will not substitute another champion but will meet me in single combat."

"Nothing would give me greater pleasure, Devaux. You have been a thorn in my side too long."

"Beware a hasty tongue. This could be settled now."

Enmity vibrated. Gaudet's hand fell to his sword hilt, tightened into a fist; deliberation in the set of his jaw, hatred in his eyes. . . .

Lord Creighton offered a warning: "My lord, should this not be settled by the justiciar? It is unseemly to quarrel when half of Nottingham watches with eager eyes."

A dash of cold logic on heated temper; Tré inhaled sharply as savage rage abated.

The tumult had escalated beyond the gallery; indistinguishable shouts rose, armor clinked, horses voiced agitation. Guy was carried from the lists on a shield, bloodied hand dangling off one side to drag on the ground.

"My lord. . . ." Unobtrusive Giles stepped forward, a slight incline of his head drawing Tré's attention to the periphery of the castle grounds.

A horn heralded the king's arrival, the royal banner a gold and scarlet beacon fluttering in wind and sunlight. The king arrived with his retinue winding behind him, a line snaking from the castle through Nottingham.

The timing could not have been worse.

22

—❧—

"You took overlong to attend me, Devaux." King John eyed him with irritation; eyes deep-set in sockets beneath a straight slash of furrowed brow were narrowed. Blunt fingers drummed on chair arms, nails bitten to the quick, bleeding in spots. A circlet of wrought gold sat askew on brown hair, reflecting light from torches in a thousand tiny glitters.

"My pardon, sire. I lingered at the bed of Guy de Beaufort."

"So Gilbert told me." The steady, rhythmic drum of fingers on wood paused. "Is he dead?"

"No, sire. A grievous wound, not mortal."

"Ah." The fingers began again, a march of impatience on innocent oak. "We have serious concerns, Devaux."

The royal *we*, invoked to remind a miscreant or errant baron of his place. Tré chose deliberately to misunderstand, a ploy to gain time and assess the king's mood.

"Sir Guy will be apprised of your concern for his fate, sire."

The drumming stopped abruptly, an exclamation: "We do not speak of a landless knight!"

He held his tongue, waited, and John leaned forward. "I speak of the chaos I found when I arrived today. Bickering barons. A match of vengeance despite the church's prohibition. I am newly returned to the holy fold—would you have me set upon by the pope again?"

It was a rhetorical question; Tré addressed the real heart of the king's ire: "Saxon barons fill Nottingham to pay you homage, sire. So do Norman."

"Barons oft meet for treason as well. These do not come to honor a king but to see their favored champions in the lists." John's eyes glittered. "We do not require tributes other than coin. *That* we will have as our just due."

"As you will it, sire."

"Yea, as we will it, Devaux." A slight curl of his mouth was scant comfort. "A timely reminder of your duty to us."

"I have fulfilled my duty as lord high sheriff, sire."

"Have you? Some would say otherwise. Do not reply to that. I know what is said of baseless rumors." He rubbed a thumb across his chin; light glinted from jeweled rings, shone dully on the heavy gold links around his neck. "We are told that you have taken outlaws, killed some, imprisoned others. Taxes have been gathered, men and arms summoned as demanded. Yet there is much still left undone."

Tré waited out the litany. Petty complaints from a profane king.

The king's thumb found its way to his mouth; teeth discolored by age and neglect nibbled at the torn nail. A monarch full of contradictions: known to bathe every three weeks in winter and summer, yet heedless of teeth and nails. Costly jewels worn over stained garments of expensive gilt and embroidered material; intelligent enough to devise the most intricate of intrigues, yet reckless of the mood of his own barons to the point of endangering the entire country.

"Where is the outlaw Little John, Devaux?" He spat out a piece of nail. "Does he languish in Nottingham's hospitality?"

Danger loomed. "Not yet, sire."

"Not yet." Thumb and fingers closed into a loose fist. "Do you even know if the outlaw still lives?"

"He lives, sire." He thought of Captain Oliver, of the silver coin. All would not be lost if the lady was safe.

"On what authority do you have that information?"

Smoothly, with no hesitation: "A man of his height is not easily missed. We ran him to ground. In the fray, he killed some among us and escaped into the forest."

"A different version from the tale I heard, Devaux. Some say you released the outlaws."

"Do some say I dance naked on the church altar as well? I have heard inventive tales put about that would keep the priests busy a year if authors of the tales would confess to them." A careless shrug and faint smile invited the king to share his amusement.

John laughed, a short bark of irreverent enjoyment. "I should like to see you dance naked on the church altar, my lord sheriff. It would certainly entertain the new Archbishop of Canterbury, I vow. Devil take Langton and his ilk. . . ."

Impious king . . . and a providential comparison to earn his amusement instead of his anger.

Rising from the bolstered chair, John moved to a window on the south wall that overlooked the King's Meadows and the River Leen. Purple light smudged the horizon; it grew late. Soon the gates would be closed for the night and stragglers would not be admitted until morning.

John prowled the chamber, moved from window to window with hands clasped behind his back. "I came for the hunt. Before I leave for Clipstone, I want the outlaws hung."

Dryly: "A court council usually pronounces sentence first, sire."

An impatient wave of one hand disregarded such a trivial detail. "They will be hung to warn citizens of their own fates should Little John and his accomplices not be yielded up." He paused, turned with a smirk. "You might have thought of it yourself, Devaux."

"I have not your deft turn of mind, sire."

"Nay, but you have a most facile tongue. I have not forgotten that."

Silence fell; oil lamps sprayed light on walls and floor. The royal apartments were spacious, the king's chamber comfortably furnished. Elaborate tapestries hung on the stone walls, moving slightly in drafts that came through an unshuttered east window.

"Your men approach the castle," King John commented, indicating the window with a tilt of head, eyes gleaming with malice. "It should be most intriguing to learn of their recent activities."

"It is hoped they please you, sire."

"Ah, my lord sheriff, you have pleased me with your persistent efficiency, if not your compliant manner."

"Compliance does not come easily to me."

"Nor to me, Devaux." Harsh laughter rang. "Nor to me. It is a trait we share, this refusal to bend. But I can sustain it, while you must one day bend the knee."

This silence was dangerous; it settled coldly, like winter mist, a clinging shroud that bound his tongue. It was a gesture, no more, yet he could not bring himself to accept the king as overlord when he knew John only waited for the right moment to see him imprisoned and executed.

The rare privacy was interrupted at last when the king's seneschal swung open the chamber door, shattering the silence. The king beckoned. "What is it, Gilbert?"

With smooth diplomacy and a practiced smile, Gilbert announced, "The sheriff's troops have returned from Sherwood with outlaws taken prisoner, sire. They await his presence in hall."

John turned, lifted a brow, eyed Tré for a long moment. "You have exceeded our expectations, Devaux."

And mine. . . .

"If you will grant me leave, sire. . . ." A significant pause, polite anticipation; he stepped away when the king gave an irritated flap of his hand. Dismissal.

"Go. If 'tis the outlaw Little John, we will have the execution early on the morrow, before I leave for Clipstone and my hunt."

"It will be done as swiftly as possible, my liege." Tré escaped into the corridor outside the royal apartments. The torches there sputtered; his boots sounded loud on the stone, echoing in hollow mockery with each step.

There had been no message from the troops in the wood. No word of outlaws or the men-at-arms who waited in the Sherwood environs to capture them. Only that single silver coin from Oliver. His apprehension increased, magnified ten-fold when he reached the middle bailey and recognized the scarlet and yellow livery of Gervaise Gaudet.

Fickle light glinted dully on stone and armor. The only men in black and gold were the guards he'd set; there was no sign of Oliver.

A subtle murmur at his elbow: "My lord sheriff." He turned to see Giles. Shrewd eyes shifted from men-at-arms to him, a pointed glance. "They have taken more than outlaws."

He gripped the hilt of his sword, voice even: "Where are these outlaws?"

"Sir Gervaise awaits the king's presence in the hall."

The press of men about them was constant; he saw in Giles's face more than he wanted. Premonition sent a chill through him.

Amid the clatter of hooves and weapons, he heard raised voices. A bellow of rage was quickly muffled, then another shout of excitement rose. He moved toward the source, Giles at his heels.

Men parted when he pushed through, surly glances were shot his way. Vivid scarlet and yellow livery clustered around a cart. Mailed soldiers dragged several men in chains, but none was of great height. Bedraggled outlaws, mud streaked, weighted down in iron and defeat, were more pathetic than menacing. Unfamiliar faces stared at him resentfully before they were cuffed into moving along toward the motte at the south end of the middle bailey. Below the motte lay caves used as prison cells. Above lay the upper bailey and royal apartments.

Tré glanced at Giles, who repeated, "Sir Gervaise awaits the king in the hall, my lord. He has saved a special outlaw for King John's diversion."

Oblique as always, careful of listening ears, Giles was nearly as valuable as Guy. Loyal competence was scarce. If the steward sensed danger, Tré trusted his instincts: He did not need words to tell him whom Gaudet held prisoner.

23

— 🍃 —

Damp, bruised, shaking from anger as much as the cold, Jane perched on the edge of a bench near the fire. Warmth did not quite reach her, an inviting promise denied. But she would choke before she mentioned her discomfort.

Gaudet regarded her with hooded eyes, a faint smile on his mouth. A negligent wave of one hand summoned a servant to pour more wine into his cup.

"I would offer you libation, milady, but you have said you want nothing from me." He took a sip, raised his brow, and paused with the cup at his lips. "You *did* say that, did you not, Lady Neville?"

Disdaining a reply, Jane stared at the wall behind the dais. Shields were displayed there, black and gold gleaming in torchlight; a raven with outspread wings and a lifted claw, beak open and ravaging, adorned a buckler hung over Tré Devaux's chair. Shire courts were held there to try cases and levy fines and punishment; the high sheriff's responsibility and duty. Would Tré believe Gaudet? He had more reason than most to assume her guilty. . . .

"A pity," Sir Gervaise murmured, smiling at her swift glance of loathing. "It must be in the blood. Tainted by lawless inclinations . . . your uncle was famous for it, was he not? Ah, of course he was. The king hated him, hates him still, no doubt, though he is long dead. Perhaps 'tis good you have not whelped more thugs to plague England."

She felt the blood drain from her face; her hands clenched tightly in her lap, but she held her chin high and still. He would not see that his barb had struck its mark.

"Milady, have you no defense to offer?" Gaudet gazed at her over the rim of his cup, a faint smile still on his lips. "Your silence condemns you."

Turning her head, she gazed at him with such utter contempt that he must have felt it; his hand tightened on the cup until his knuckles turned white. The smile faded, stretched into a taut line. He leaned forward, his words a low hiss:

"Sheriff's leman! See how haughty you will be when the king hears of your crimes. Consorting with outlaws carries a grave penalty. Not as evil to the king as possession of his coffer, however."

False accusation . . . he knows he lies. Yet I am guilty in a way. What will Tré do? He knows the truth that Gaudet does not—will he believe me in this, or think I came here to distract him from outlaws' schemes?

"You should not have been so foolish, Lady Neville. To steal the king's gold is worse than treason. He might have forgiven your alliance with outlaws. He will not forgive the theft of his money."

A dull pounding started in her temples, trickled down to beat against her eyelids. She thought about Dena and Enid alone on the King's Great Way, their terror and Dena's frailty. At least Fiskin was safe, though no doubt bewildered by their disappearance from the verge.

A heinous deceit, concocted by the devil. A collusion with outlaws she did not know, accusation of crimes she did not commit: a well-planned fraud that might see her hanged.

Her neck ached; she held her head still, kept her back straight, refusing to yield to mounting panic. The great hall made her think of a chapel, with wide aisles and thick columns—she wanted to pray but had given her prayer beads to Fiskin. The distraction of the familiar beads to keep count of the pleas for her soul's salvation would have helped.

A door banged behind her, weapons clanked, and Gaudet sat up a little straighter, his gaze shifting to the far end of the hall. The king?

Boots made a heavy sound on stone, crackled on rushes. "You usurp my authority and go too far, Gaudet."

Tré....

She wanted to turn but didn't dare. Would she see anger in his eyes? Disbelief?

"Do I, my lord high sheriff?" Mocking, but a curl of his lip and his tight tone marked his strain. "The king will not think so."

"The king will not hear of it. Release her. She is the widow of a Norman baron, the daughter of a knight—a lady of consequence."

Aware of him beside her, a blur of dark wool and anger, she sat very still. She recognized the tone: dangerous, warning couched in careful enunciation.

"She consorts with outlaws as well as other undesirable knaves, my lord high sheriff. But I believe you must already know that."

Silence descended. She dared a swift glance at Tré. His hand fisted on the hilt of his sword; his features were impassive, revealing nothing of his thoughts.

"A peculiar accusation, Gaudet. How did you arrive at that conclusion?"

"It was easy enough when my men came upon her in the forest with them. They were dividing the king's gold, stolen while we attended the tourney. You planned well, my lord. The lure of gold to outlaws, guards set to watch." A pause, a soft laugh, and the observation: "A rare opportunity for Robin Hood's niece."

She felt Tré's glance and gathering uncertainty; he must remember that day by the Cockpen Oak. Understandably, he would have doubts.

Breaking her silence, she looked up at him and said, "I am not guilty of his charges, my lord sheriff."

An explosion of light in green eyes, quickly veiled by his dark lashes and a hitch of one shoulder in outward indifference. "Guilt or innocence will be decided by the courts, Lady Neville."

Icy fear coalesced, settled in her lungs and heart so that each breath was torture. *If he will not believe me, I am lost . . . lost. . . .*

A hand descended onto her shoulder, fingers dug into wool and flesh, firmly but not unkindly. *A reprieve.* She dragged in air, stared at nothing, not quite daring to hope.

Above her head, she heard him say to Gaudet, "The lady is in my jurisdiction. I will see to her placement."

Hope blossomed into relief—aborted when Gaudet surged to his feet.

"Nay, my lord sheriff, she is not. I have yielded her up to the king's authority. King John has interests in the settlement of her lands."

His hand tightened on her shoulder, urged her to rise before he took a sideways step and his hand fell away. "She will await the king's pleasure in a guarded cell. I will personally escort her."

"Do you think me such a fool?" Gaudet's laugh was angry and astonished. "You will escort her to Sherwood in lieu of putting your whore in a cell—"

"Bide thy evil tongue, Gaudet, for it may yet find rest upon the floor with the hounds."

Soft menace, vibrating fury—a challenge met.

Sheathed steel hissed free of restraint. Jane stepped back, mouth dry, heart hammering against her rib cage.

"Hold!" Imperious tone, royal intimidation rang over the hall as John preceded his seneschal down the wide aisles to confront them. Cold eyes regarded both men, swept over Jane with a flicker of interest, narrowed slightly. "Do you *dare* draw steel in my hall!"

Devaux lowered his blade, inclined his head toward the king. "A momentary diversion, sire."

Cool recovery, urbane smile meant to placate, the mask in place again. Jane marveled at him. From fury to calm in the space of a heartbeat—how did he manage it?

"Diversion, Devaux? Naked swords in my hall is hardly a diversion." John eyed Gaudet, slower to regain his composure at the interruption, fury still simmering in his eyes and rigid posture. "Where is this dangerous outlaw you have brought to heel, Sir Gervaise? Gilbert tells me you have succeeded where Devaux has not, and have Robin Hood's man in custody."

"Not his man, sire." Gaudet sheathed his sword with a brittle clink of steel and iron. "I have Robin Hood's niece, taken in an act of felony."

The king's gaze shifted to Jane, lingered with both malice and amusement. "This lady? You seem familiar to us. How do we know you?"

More calmly than she had thought she could, she replied, "I am Lady Neville of Ravenshed, sire."

"Hugh de Neville's widow?" Surprise marked his face, a brief flicker quickly suppressed. "Ah, your lands lie within the boundaries of the royal forest. Very close to Clipstone, as I recall. Your lands are now in trust for the church, are they not?"

"Mine in perpetuity, sire."

"But no issue. A widow without heirs." The king smiled. "An unfortunate event."

"Yea, sire, so it is."

"Not as unfortunate as the charges Sir Gervaise has levied against you, however." A negligent lift of his hand, and his seneschal put a goblet of wine in it. Jewels gleamed on the bowl and stem, winked in torchlight when he drank.

Jane waited, mimicked Tré's indifference with hands folded in front of her and face devoid of expression. It cost her dearly; knotted stomach muscles twisted painfully, lungs ached for elusive air. A glimpse of other barons moving behind the king was scant relief.

"Such a pretty neck to wear a hemp necklace," John commented as he lowered his cup.

"Hardly necessary, sire," Tré said with a trace of amusement. "Danger lies more in error than in truth. I doubt the lady capable of bearing a heavy coffer from chamber to cart."

Stroking his upper lip with one finger, the king nodded agreement. "Doubtless. Did you find accomplices with her, Sir Gervaise? Robin Hood's men?"

"Yea, sire. Seven stout men, outlaws all. Four were slain, three survive to hang."

"And Little John?"

"My men are in pursuit."

"Excellent. Perhaps we misjudged your abilities. It seems that you have managed well, Gaudet."

As the king smiled, with spite in his eyes and tone, Tré's steward begged leave to speak to his lord.

"Grant pardon for the interruption, my lord sheriff," Giles said smoothly, eyes downcast, "but there is no room for the men Sir Gervaise arrested. The cells are filled with outlaws you brought in to await trial."

Timely intervention, subtle disclosure to remind the king of Devaux's efficiency. Jane regarded Giles warmly.

Gaudet scowled. The king turned toward the dais. "It is late. We are weary. This will be finished on the morrow ere we leave for the royal hunt at Clipstone. Time is scant in these days when barons swear false oaths and commit treason. Gilbert, see the lady to a cell." He paused, fixed Tré with a pointed gaze. "It is expected that she will be confessed and shriven before the morrow. Find a priest to hear her confession."

"She cannot be condemned without trial, sire."

Swinging about, astonishment and rage marred John's face as he regarded his sheriff. "Do you dare admonish us?"

"Nay, sire. I state the obvious with great respect, but vast reservations. Flimsy evidence has been given. Gaudet seeks to mislead you."

Padded shoulders drew up stiffly. "We will decide that."

"I trust when Abbot Thomas arrives, he will be generous enough to lend spiritual guidance and experience of canon law to aid your decision."

Blood pounded in Jane's ears; disaster yawned, a vain attempt to thwart the king that could earn enmity for Tré. She longed to touch him, draw strength from his urbane defiance.

Reminder of the church's new encroachment into English law was not lost on King John. His jaw set. "It is possible he would be persuaded to do so, but he does not arrive until the feast of Saint John's. We have decided to leave early."

"I am certain the abbot will be most grieved to learn that his counsel in the matter of a widow's fate and inheritance is unwanted."

It was implication more than content that snared the king's

attention and earned his displeasure. But the kernel of truth was unavoidable and chafing: The church had an interest in Neville lands as well.

Cold reply, deadly menace: "You importune us, Devaux."

"My apologies, sire. I meant only to lessen your burden and save you from the abbot's disapproval."

A facile explanation, a bland countenance that earned John's narrowed regard and grudging compliance. Abruptly, the king shifted his position.

"Your generosity and dedication earn our admiration." The smile was as patently false as his words, a sop to the barons milling near. "It will not be necessary. We are able to do our royal duty, and will value the abbot's counsel should he arrive in time."

Tré bowed his head in acceptance of the king's edict. "It will be as you will it, sire."

"Of that, there is no doubt." John's smile was tight. He yawned and covered his mouth with a ring-bedecked hand. "We wish to be gone from here by the time Prime bells are rung. Assemble the court and have them ready after Lauds. It should not take long to hear evidence against outlaws caught in the full flush of crime. They can hang while we break our fast."

Callous even for John, this further revelation of his character earned a murmur and rustle among the barons.

Attuned to the mood, the king adapted; sanguine sarcasm edged his decree: "To soothe your offended sensibilities, Devaux, if found guilty, the lady will not hang. It would reflect ill upon the court should the widow of a Norman baron meet the same fate as villeins and outlaws. In our mercy, we will allow the lady to offer penance in a royal dungeon, much as Maud de Braose was permitted to do."

Jane fought a wave of weakness. Classic John: devious, cruel, offering ruin in the guise of leniency. She was to be starved to death, as the Countess de Braose had been.

King John said into tense silence, "Lady Neville, you were found consorting with known outlaws. The penalty for that is death. Can you prove your innocence?"

Desperation lent her strength. "Am I to be presumed guilty

without trial, sire? I am the daughter of a knight, a Norman baron's widow. By law, I am given the chance to plead my innocence before the justiciar."

Invoking the reminder of the law should have swayed the king; greed was too great an influence. Dark eyes glittered. She felt Tré shift beside her, muscles tensed.

John's mandate was harsh: "There will be an inquisition on the morrow, Lady Neville. You may plead your case before *our* justice. When it is done, you will be sentenced."

An angry mutter rippled through the Saxon barons within hearing; Gilbert of Oxton pushed through the crowd. Indignation creased his face as he came to a halt.

"Sire, I do protest. Would you so insult her rank as well as her character by denying her lawful rights?"

John was undaunted. His tone was that of a snarling wolf; feral eyes pierced red-haired Oxton with hot scrutiny. "*We* have been insulted by outlaws long enough. If Robin Hood's niece brought this shame upon her head, then she will face the consequences. What of you? Do you desire to take her place— or perhaps join her?"

Oxton paled, but did not retreat. "Nay, sire. Neither do I wish to see her unjustly condemned."

"That is what an inquisition will determine. Even Saxon law allows for that."

Inquisition. Just the word was enough to provoke stark fear. Hot rods, metal spikes, submersion in water to prove her innocence—if she survived.

Through the mad beating of her heart, Jane heard Tré Devaux voice acquiescence to the king's verdict. Slowly, she turned to look at him, but his face was turned away. Disbelieving, her tongue cleaved to the roof of her mouth in mute terror as Tré offered the king advice.

"Let Abbot Thomas preside at the inquisition, sire," he said calmly. "No man can then say you are to blame for Lady Neville's fate."

"A pretty turn of mind, Devaux. We are tempted to wait upon the abbot's arrival." A pause, a cunning smile. "But if we allow Sir Gervaise to conduct the ritual, we detach from any blame and do not involve abbots in temporal matters."

A sharp order summoned the guard. Jane was flanked by men-at-arms with eyes hidden behind noseguards of steel helms. She gathered her dignity around her like a shield, held her head high as she turned to go with them.

Gilbert of Oxton still offered futile protests; his face was a smear of white, red hair standing up like the teeth of a comb on his head. All was a jumble of sound, a blur of motion and sickening defeat.

Silent, still as the stone columns that held up the high roof, Tré Devaux offered no more argument for her reprieve. Had he abandoned her? She dredged up her courage and looked full into his face—and was glad she did.

24

❧

Shadows lounged like indolent beasts in corners, ranged in corridors, slunk across the middle bailey. Posted guards were solitary figures on the castle walls, phantoms silhouetted against an occasional flare of torch. Gates were closed, no one allowed to enter until dawn; the silence was thick, with all abed.

A faint echo of boots on stone broke the dense hush; Tré paused, frowned, swore softly when he recognized the wraith that separated from deep shadow. He waited until the specter reached him before he spoke, his voice a low rasp:

"What madness summons you from a deathbed?"

Shaky laughter trembled in the air; Guy passed under a fitful spray of moonlight, was reclaimed by shadows. A gleam of pale hair anchored him against the darker wall.

"I knew I would find you here. You go to free her."

He did not bother to acknowledge the accuracy of the statement; time was fleeting. Bluntly, motivated by truth as well as concern, he said, "Begone back to your pallet. You will hinder me, Guy."

"Surly knave." The feeble attempt at humor faded. "You need me."

"I need a whole man, not a half."

"There is enough of me left to lend aid. I am wounded, not dead."

"That can change swiftly enough if we are discovered. You cannot wield a sword, or even defend yourself against the guards."

Guy snapped, "I can slow them with my lifeless body!"

Tré laughed, a wry sound in the dark. "Yea, or you can astound them with your lunacy."

"The king is right—you have a most facile tongue." He shifted, his grin wavering in the gloom. "It will do you no good with me. I have an interest in this as well."

Thin light picked out the linen binding his left shoulder and arm. The hand was thickly wrapped where he had taken the brunt of Sir Alfric's thrust.

Holding up the hand, he added grimly, "It is a wonder I have all my fingers, and may lose one still. Yea, I have a keen interest in thwarting Gervaise Gaudet and his hellish cousin."

Tré nodded, glanced toward the postern door that led to the upper bailey. "If you will not listen to reason, I can use you to distract the guard."

"I will distract him with a dagger, if he is Gaudet's man."

"God willing, he will be my man, not the king's guard. We may hang with the outlaws on the morrow."

Keys clanked; the metallic rasp of lock and tumblers was overloud in the hushed night, as was the creak of unoiled hinges as the door swung open. Cut deep into the foundations of sandstone, bolstered by limestone, damp natural caverns provided ample storage for both prisoners and supplies. Steep stairs led to a newly built undercroft with two stone arches; three guards were posted beneath smoking torches at the far end, with an excellent view of the stairs.

Sound carried in the cavern. Silent, Tré knelt in the dark at the top of the stairs to listen as the guards discussed wenches and dicing almost in the same breath. He shared a quick glance of amusement with Guy; soldiers' conversations rarely varied. The sound of rattling dice echoed. He considered the situation carefully, but there was only one conclusion:

Secrecy was impossible.

These were the king's guards, not his own men, who would never question his command. He felt Guy stir at his side, knew he had come to the same realization.

By releasing Jane, he risked all. The king was no fool. Defying John would earn him a slow and painful death. Yet, if he left her there, it would end the same. He had been dying by slow degrees since Aimée had been killed—until he met Jane of Ravenshed. Lovely lady . . . she had saved him once with her healing hands. Once more with love.

Now he would save her.

Guy put a hand on his arm, shook his head. He met his sworn knight's anguished gaze, smiled tightly. There was really no other choice he could make.

Softly: "Are you my liege man, Guy de Beaufort?"

Stricken, apprehension glinting in hazel eyes, Guy gave a brief nod of his head. His reply was a hoarse whisper: "Yea, you know I am."

"You have always obeyed me. Do so now. Go back to your pallet and do not rise until it is done. Plead ignorance. I want no blame to fall upon you for what I do. First, swear to me you will watch over my lady when I am dead."

"My God . . . Tré. . . ."

"Swear it, or I will curse you with my dying breath."

"There must be another way—"

"Swear it now. Time flies, and I will not have her subjected to torment. *Swear it!*"

Closing his eyes, muscles quaking violently, Guy said softly, "I swear to you I will watch over your lady."

"Good." His mouth twisted; he glanced back at the guards still dicing under the torch. "It comes to me too late that I have been a fool, Guy. Go now, before I have another death on my soul."

Rising to his feet, he slid his sword from the sheath with a metallic hiss that caused one of the guards to peer up into the shadows of the stairwell. As the soldier nudged his companion, Tré moved down the steps.

•　　•　　•

A small sound caught her attention; Jane lifted her head from arms folded over drawn-up knees, staring at the tiny grate in the door. Bars of light were faint stripes in the cell. Furtive rustling in the clumps of straw distracted her, and she glanced toward the shadowed wall with loathing. Rats among the fetid stink of rubbish. . . .

Another sound, closer this time, but outside the cell—a clank, as of keys. She stiffened, dismay coursing through her. Was it time? She had not said enough prayers, offered up enough penance . . . nor had she repented the sin of unchaste love. There was no hope for her. She was damned by God and church, and she could not summon the necessary remorse. Even knowing what she faced on the morrow, she could not find it in her soul to regret having lain with Tré Devaux.

It was a new thing, this raw emotion that took away her breath and scoured her soul. Shriveled hope was reborn . . . blight faded with the recognition that had escaped her—until now.

She had seen in his face what he felt, and knew that he loved her. His lips might lie, but his soul had looked out at her from his eyes. That last scalding glance had revealed more of him than had the past four months.

In that moment when his eyes met hers, she had seen the man too wary to trust or love—and recognized his surrender to it. It was her redemption.

Keys rattled loudly now, jerked her attention back to the door and what awaited her. Closing her eyes, she began to pray again.

"Jane."

Her eyes snapped open at the familiar voice; she lurched to her feet, fear and joy meeting uncertainly. "Tré . . . are you well? The king has not arrested you?"

"The king," he said with a sardonic laugh, "is closeted with a lively trull for the night. She will no doubt give him the pox, which he richly deserves. Make haste. There is not much time."

"Am I being freed?"

"Yea, but not with the king's sanction. Jane—" urgency lent his words weight, "hasten before we are both undone."

The guards had not bothered with chains; her shoes were gone, and straw and cold stone stung bare feet. Ignoring the pain, she limped to him where he stood in the open door, the light behind him leaving his face in shadow.

"I must find Dena and Enid," she said when she emerged into the cold, narrow corridor. Shivering, she looked up at him, and paused, horror-struck.

A livid bruise marred one side of his face, and a gash oozed blood. He saw her glance, grimaced, and put a hand on her arm. "There is only one passage. Avert your eyes when we pass the guards."

The rusty smell of fresh blood filled her nostrils; she nodded silently. It would not be new to her, but death in all its forms was ugly. There was none of the glory men sang songs about, only a sudden absence of life, as if a candle had been extinguished.

Crumpled forms huddled in odd shapes on the hard floor; torchlight flickered over them, gleamed in dark pools spread on stone. A chill scrubbed down her spine, she shivered again. Then they were up the steep staircase and outside. She sucked in fresh air that didn't smell of death, curled bare toes up from the paving stones, and looked at Tré. He was a dark silhouette above her, indistinguishable in the absence of light, save for the warmth of his hand on her arm. Her teeth began to chatter with reaction.

"We m-must rescue D-Dena and Enid."

His fingers flexed tighter, his urgency transferring to her as he pulled her with him up the steep slope of the upper bailey. High walls soared above them, torches faint bobs of light to mark the way.

"I released them before the castle gates closed. They return to Ravenshed. Jane—you cannot return there. It is the first place the king will look when he learns you are gone. Giles waits to see you safely to a nunnery."

Her breath caught. "Are you not going with me?"

"Nay, I cannot. You must know that."

"How would I know that?" Despair rose in her throat; fear offered more protests: "If you stay, the king will slay you."

He stopped, swung around to face her, his hand still on her

arm. Tautly: "I am a baron. My father's grandfather held the lands that John now plunders . . . those lands are *mine*."

"Yea, but they are now lost to you."

Quiet reminder, painful truth; pale moonlight played on his tense features. He blew out a sharp gust of air, his voice low and bitter: "The king may take my lands, but I will not lie down and give them to him. Nor does he dare slay me. The barons would rise up in protest—not for love of me, but fear of dangerous precedent. John knows that."

Desperation rendered her cruel beyond what she had ever dreamed she could be. "Fool—do you think John will care for that? He does not. He will rend you limb from limb without a thought for aught but the revenues from your land. You will make it simple for him if you linger to face his wrath. Do so, and you deserve your fate!"

He did not reply, but pulled her higher up the steep incline. She slid, fell to one knee, bare feet slipping on wet grass and mud. A half-sob of frustration escaped; pausing, he bent and scooped her into his arms, lifting her against him as he continued up the slope. He carried her easily, as if her weight were of no consequence.

His breath was a steady bellows on her hair, warm and smelling faintly of wine. Her hand splayed against wool and muscle; her fingers wadded his tunic in her palm. "I pray thee, my sweet lord, do not give yourself to John."

Grim perseverance was her only reply. Long strides took them swiftly to the upper bailey. His muscles strained as he kept to the dense shadows, moving as stealthily as a cat along the wall.

She wanted to weep, to plead, to rail at him not to be so foolish. It would be futile. She knew that. Her hand moved to touch his jaw in a soft caress. Painful emotion left a raw ache within her; her lips moved against his throat. Her hand on his neck encountered sticky warmth: dead men's blood.

Closing her eyes, she shuddered, said blindly, "I just found thee. Do not forsake me now."

"Ah, God. Jane." He stopped, tightening his grip and raking his mouth across the top of her bare head. Her hair was loose, plaits frayed into tangles down her back, caught beneath the pressure of his arm around her. "I do not forsake thee—there is no other way. If I take flight, there are those here who will suffer for my deeds. Guy is wounded. He cannot withstand a perilous journey. Wounded, too, is captain of the king's guards—Gaudet's men attacked him on the road to Ravenshed. Oliver is loyal. He risked much to return here to warn me. I will not throw such loyal men to the wolves, and especially not to the Angevin wolf."

Despair filled her. She pressed her nose into wool and muscle. How could she ever have thought him false? He was a truer man than most she had known. Now she might lose him; empty days stretched ahead of her, hope and joy extinguished with his death. There would be no chance for happiness if Tré was gone. There were too few chances in life now.

Words muffled against wool and tunic, she said, "If you die, let me die with you."

An involuntary contraction made him hold her closer; unbelievably, he laughed. "So impassioned . . . sweet lady, I do not intend to die. Nor do I intend to let you do anything so foolish."

He swung her to her feet, kept his hand tight on her arm, glanced at the round tower in front of them. Shadows eclipsed the stairwell inside, a coiled entrance to the wall and battlements above. He looked back at her.

"Can you run if necessary?"

Her heart thudded painfully; she nodded. "Yea."

"Once in the stairwell, any sound will carry. The guard will pass in a moment, then we will go."

"Where?" She looked uncertainly from tower to bailey: A rough oval was flanked by the king's apartments, a chapel—unused by John, it was said—guardhouse, and granary. There was no escape there that she could see.

Tré took her hand between his; a taut smile played on his lips. "Do you trust me, Jane?"

No hesitation: "Yea, Tré Devaux. With my life."

A harsh breath, and he pressed his mouth against her palm, then her wrist. He held it there while her pulse beat against his lips, wild and swift.

His gaze shifted, locked with hers, a faint shine in the gloom, distant torchlight reflecting green. Fierce intensity trembled in his voice: "Then obey me without question this eve, for it may well mean both our lives."

She nodded, her throat working to swallow her fear. A whisper: "I understand."

His thumb stroked her skin gently. "I knew you would."

Footsteps sounded above, accompanied by the clink of sword and mail. Tré stepped into the shadows and pulled her with him. They waited until the sound of steps faded and the challenge was answered, guard to guard, a confirmation that all was quiet.

A squeeze of her hand warned her he was ready, and they moved from the bailey into the tower where shadows claimed them. He released her, moved away, furtive sounds in airless gloom the only indication he was still there. Trembling, she heard a faint scrape of metal, then a grating of stone. A rush of air swept over her, musty and smelling of the river.

Tré's hand came out of the blackness at last; he guided her a few steps, whispering against her ear a soft warning to tread gently. She had an eerie sensation like that of falling; two tentative steps found solid footing beneath her, grit powdering the soles of her feet. *Sandstone . . . a cave?*

She was not unfamiliar with the caves of Nottingham; they were everywhere, beneath pubs, taverns, streets, and shops. Used as storerooms, even homes, most were large, but led nowhere. She slid slightly, caught at Tré to stop herself; he tucked her against him, a safe, solid presence.

Deeper they went into the void; she felt her way along with a palm against the wall, the pads of her fingers grazing cool sandstone. Every breath was a heavy gasp that sounded like a smithy's bellows.

Steep decline into absolute darkness, musty drafts—apprehension escalated to smothering panic. Her mouth went dry, palms damp; desperation seeped into her bones.

"Tré. . . ." Faintly, voice a mere whisper, she felt her tenuous balance crumbling as her senses drifted.

He caught her before she fell. Boneless, she was caught up

in his arms as he pressed on. Deeper and deeper until black emptiness went gray, then lightened to dense blue. Clean air gusted, smelling strongly of river and moat.

With the return of perception between dark and light came relief. Her head began to clear, her heart to slow its rapid pace. She heard the sound of water lapping on rock. A sweet breeze drifted over her face, grew stronger. Finally, Tré halted. His voice was low:

"Can you stand now?"

"Yes. Are we near the river?"

"The Leen lies below. Don't look down—I have no desire to fish you out."

"Tré—" She put a hand on his chest to steady herself as he lowered her to her feet. "I cannot swim."

"No, I did not expect you could. Giles waits below with a punt. Make haste, Jane, before the dead guards are found."

A shiver racked her; her fingers felt traces of gilt raven beneath her palm. *Too soon . . . I have not loved him long enough yet. . . .*

Dignity demanded that she depart with grace. Love bade her seek reassurance.

"Will you find me? Will you come for me when the king is gone?"

"Yea, my heart." A finger touched her cheek, then her mouth. Clouds parted, light from a lopsided moon the shape of a hen's egg glistened on the silver-edged rock. He kissed her. Lips moved on hers with unfamiliar tenderness, absent of passion but filled with new emotion. She clung to him, rising on bare toes to press her body against his.

"Do not tarry," she whispered when he broke away, "for I will languish without thee."

"You are stronger than that, Jane of Ravenshed." He took her arms from his neck, pressed her hands together. "Do not forget your oath to obey me. It is time to part."

Seized by a grief that threatened to overwhelm her, she could only nod. Tears stung her eyes, hot and blinding, as she tried to memorize his bruised face.

Then he turned her, stepped to the edge of the smooth sandstone, and called down softly, "She comes."

Before she could protest, Tré swung her out and over the water and released her. The short drop stole her breath; gasping, she landed in the flat bottom of the punt with an ungraceful thud. Giles braced the vessel with a long pole and spread legs, but water still sloshed over the sides and wet her bedraggled skirts.

Through the splash of murky water she heard Tré say, "Guard her well, Giles, and look to yourself."

"Yea, my lord. God be with you."

Looking up, she saw Tré against the rock, moonlight on his face and in his hair. As Giles bent to the pole, pushing the punt away from rock and into the current, she struggled upright.

Stunted bushes climbed the sandstone heights, silver-laced by the moon, waving slightly in the breeze. The same breeze carried Tré's farewell after her:

"I would have loved you well, Jane of Ravenshed. . . ."

Realization struck hard, a knife to the heart, and she suddenly knew the truth: disaster. His life was forfeit.

She scrambled to the back of the punt, her movements rocking it violently. Giles caught her by the arm when she put a foot on the rail.

"My lady—do not render his sacrifice in vain."

He released her, and she slowly sank back into the bottom of the small vessel, skirts billowing around her. As the craft slipped through the water, pole dipping and pushing with a soft *plash* on the river bottom, she stared at the now empty rock where Tré had stood.

Pitted rock, with holes like vacant eye sockets, stared back. And she felt the slow dying inside her, the anguish of loss a vibrant reminder that she would never be the same.

25

—❦—

True Angevin, John reacted predictably. Echoes of the king's rage were heard and felt through the entire castle.

Guy de Beaufort leaned against a wall in the great hall and listened helplessly as John condemned Tré to death.

A shudder racked Guy when the king promised a list of torments to be suffered before the final release of death was granted.

Through it all, Tré gave no indication by word or even the flicker of an eyelash that he heard or cared what was to be done to him.

Goaded, the king at last leaned forward, hands fisted on the arms of his high-backed chair. "You will not be so quiet while the flesh is flayed from your bones, Devaux. It should be entertaining to hear you squeal like an October pig."

A murmur undulated through the throng of barons; it was plain that they disapproved of the king's intent. Guy watched them, saw Adam de Lincoln exchange glances with Walter Foliot. Even the Saxon barons looked disturbed. Did Tré see?

He must have, for he looked at last at the king; his bruised mouth lifted in a faint smile. "Sire, do to me what you will. It is no more than has already been done these past years. So, too, did you flay me with the villainy of my overlord."

"Welburn betrayed the crown as well."

"Yet he is restored to his lands."

John's mouth twitched; his eyes narrowed. "It is so. We have seen fit to restore Welburn to his former lands and title, and grant him lands deseisined from faithless barons. Think you he will cherish Brayeton as greatly as you have, Devaux?"

Tré recoiled visibly. The king smiled with satisfaction and sat back; he beckoned his steward forward. "See it done, Gilbert."

"Yea, sire."

Quill scratched on parchment, the scribe writing frantically to keep up.

At the far end of the hall was a small commotion of new arrivals. The news of Jane's escape and Tré's arrest had not taken long to spread through Nottingham. Guy sucked in a deep breath, steeled himself against a wave of pain. He searched his brain for a solution, anything that would end this before the awful conclusion John desired.

"Sirs," Tré said as he glanced around at the gathered barons, "observe the example I set for you. I have been played false, first by my overlord, then by my king. For this, and the release of a baron's widow whose main crime is owning lands that the king covets, I am to be put to death. Think you that if your lands come under the king's covetous eye, will he not do the same to you?"

Furious, John swung his gaze around the hall, called for an instant judgment. Not a baron moved, except those who stepped back in refusal. Devaux's peers would not judge him. Deseisined he might be, but no baron present wanted to risk the dangerous precedent of conviction without cause.

Heavy silence descended, lingered in grim suspension. A moment's hope sparked; Guy courted it gladly. *If no baron here speaks against Tré, the king must surely free him. . . .*

"I judge him guilty, sire."

The words rang out into the hall, splitting silence and crowd as sharply as a crack of lightning. Men parted to allow the speaker to step through. Guy went tense as his gaze shifted from the approaching baron to the man just behind him— Gervaise Gaudet.

John leaned forward again, a glitter of triumph in his eyes as he fixed them on the baron before the dais. "Speak thy name so that all may hear."

"Walter of Gedling, Lord of Dunham and Kelham," he said. The men around him muttered in disquietude. Dunham met it calmly. His gaze swept the hall, paused briefly, then moved to where Guy stood against the wall. Spite gleamed in blue eyes, mouth thinned with satisfaction. "A baron and a peer, sire, and I judge Lord Devaux guilty of obstructing your justice."

Guy pushed away from the wall; fury vibrated in his battered muscles, guilt spliced his heart. *He knows about Lissa and strikes at me through Tré. . . .*

Before he could speak, another baron came forward; red hair gleamed in hazy light. Gilbert of Oxton claimed the king's attention. "Sire, Lord Dunham does not speak for all barons present. We do not judge Lord Devaux or offer our condemnation. It is our desire that the matter be presented before the chief justiciar at the next council."

Shock rendered Guy motionless. Such support from Saxon barons was unexpected. Nor did it seem to please Gaudet and Dunham, who briefly conferred before turning back to the king. John's scowl was evidence of his own displeasure.

Walter of Gedling took a deliberate step forward, while Gaudet beckoned to the king's seneschal.

Dunham spoke Norman French, fluid words that fell like stones on the ears of all present: "I offer a champion for trial by combat, if it pleases you, sire."

"It would please *me*," Tré said into the silence, and glanced at the king. "I will fight whomever Dunham presents in his place. I am willing to prove my innocence and take back my title and lands."

Despite his ire, it was obvious that the king did not want to risk losing such profitable revenues. He fidgeted, eyes dark slits, and chewed a nail as he regarded the barons. Then he laughed, a harsh sound.

"By God's teeth, it seems you have more courage than logic, Devaux. It would make little sense for me to grant a trial by combat when you are adjudged guilty as my appointed official." Eyes shifted, widened a bit. "Yet, as high sheriff instead of baron, you have no more rights—"

Swiftly, "But I am a baron, sire, deseisined of my lands and title, appointed sheriff only by your decree. It is a fact that cannot be altered or ignored."

"By your leave, sire," Dunham said again, smoothly, with a subtle smile, "a trial by combat would end this farce."

"Yea, and may well set free this treacherous baron," the king snapped. "If triumphant he will join other northern barons who seek to leach my coffers with constant rebellions and refusals to pay proper scutage."

The king's seneschal leaned forward, spoke softly into John's ear, then stepped back. Arrested, the king swung his gaze back to Dunham.

"Speak, Walter of Gedling. We will consider your proposal."

"If Lord Devaux so agrees, a trial by combat with a champion of your choice will settle all, sire."

"I agree." Tré shot Dunham a contemptuous look. "I will fight any man of your choosing."

"To the death— *jouste à l'outrance.*"

"Yea, to the death most willingly, my lord Dunham."

King John sat back with satisfaction in his eyes, nodded. "Then I propose that it be done." He steepled his hands, regarded the hall for a long moment. Then, voice raised, he said, "Sir Guy de Beaufort, come forward as champion against Devaux, and you will be granted lands and title for a victory. Refuse, and royal judgment will be levied against him as high sheriff and treasonous baron."

Tension gripped the hall, held it in thrall to uneasy anticipation. Not yet Prime, it seemed not another person could be squeezed into the crowded aisles.

Appalled, Guy heard Tré's angry protest that he could not be made to fight his own liege man, and the king's smooth rejoinder that it was a free choice, not a command.

"What say you, Guy de Beaufort?" John offered with malice in his eyes. "When you are recovered, will you lend Devaux the chance for redemption? A title and lands are the prize for the winner . . . worthy reward for a victory well fought."

In the space of a heartbeat, Guy saw the implications.

Refuse, and Tré would die a tormented death. Agree, and he would face the man he loved as a brother over drawn swords. It did not take him long to decide.

Stepping forward, moving stiffly with his bandaged arm and hand, he bowed to the merciless king. "I agree, sire."

"You are a fool, Guy." Tré stared out the window of the chamber that was his cell. Anguish clogged his throat, made his words harsh. "I refuse to fight you."

"You swore before witnesses to fight a champion of the king's choice. It is beyond either of us now."

Bitter truth. "I regret not killing Gaudet when I had the chance. He is behind this."

"Walter of Gedling was the monk I heard with Gaudet that day," Guy said heavily. "I thought it was Welburn."

"Odd, that the lady did not recognize her husband's voice," Tré observed.

Guy muttered a soft oath. "Treacherous lady . . . she claims she did not."

"And you do not believe her."

"Nay, I do not." He paused, said acidly, "I should have listened to you. Faithless female betrayed us all—even her own cousin—with her silence. She pleads fear of her husband, when it should be me she feared most."

"Absolution, Guy. Forgive the lady, for she is like most women and cannot withstand the storm."

"I cannot. It took great restraint to keep my hands from her throat."

Rain fell outside; a soft patter on stone, turning the outer bailey to mud. Beyond the town walls, the spires of Sherwood Forest were hidden in gray mist. He thought of Jane, turned to look at Guy.

"Do you have word of Lady Neville?"

"Giles sent word he escorted her to the Blidworth Bottoms, where she insisted he leave her. She is not at the manor, though the king did send his guard there to search. I hope she has sought refuge in a nunnery."

Tré spread his hand on the stone ledge of the window; it was cool beneath his fingers, a reminder that he still had the capacity to feel. Since watching Jane slip away in the punt with Giles, he had thought himself more dead than alive.

"I ask you again," Guy said softly, "to flee England and let the king's rage cool. There are barons who side with you, and will offer you sanctuary."

"Flee like a hound with my tail between my legs? I have never run. It summons to mind my contempt for barons like Robert FitzWalter and Eustace de Vesci who betrayed the king, then fled. I would rather die than live an hour as a coward." He stared out the window. "We are too well watched, Guy. There is no escape, even should I agree."

"The king and barons return from Clipstone Palace on the morrow," Guy said, an abrupt warning that time was running out. "As he must return soon to Bishopstoke, the contest is set to begin within an hour of his arrival here. A priest has been sent for to offer us last sacraments."

"John wastes no time." He turned to gaze at Guy. Strain marked the knight's face; hazel eyes were shadowed, grooves cut deep on each side of his mouth. "Guy. You are still my liege man, bound by oath to obey me. I hold you to your vow to watch after the lady Jane when I am dead."

Silence fell between them; Guy's face reflected sorrow. He shook his head slowly. "I am a landless knight, with naught in this world of my own. My death will be marked by no one. The lady loves you. To take you from her would be far more cruel than anything I have ever done."

A cold chill seized him as he stared at Guy; he knew what was intended. It was intolerable. "Do not defy me. I will not live with your blood upon my hands."

Anguished: "And you think it more easy for me? You have been my liege lord and my friend far too long. *Christus*, I curse the devious mind that set us to this pass, for we are neither one deserving of such torment."

A soft scratching sound behind them summoned their attention to the chamber door. It swayed inward on creaking hinges.

"My sons," came a rusty voice from within the depths of a cowl, "I find you both too willing to die needlessly for the whim of a king. Mortal sins of pride."

Shock rendered Tré speechless. The portly monk stepped into the room, shut the door softly behind him, and leaned against it.

Finding his tongue, Tré said harshly, "It is the duty of a monk to offer redemption, not judgment."

"What if I offer liberty?"

"That is not your prerogative."

Laughter rasped; the monk moved forward nimbly for such a corpulent man. "I have God's authority—and that of the abbot—to see you safely away if you choose life over a vain death."

Tré's eyes narrowed. "Who are you?"

"I am called Brother Tuck by some."

"Why would you interfere?"

The monk slid a pudgy hand beneath his cassock, drew out a small loop of beads. He held it up so that it caught the light from the window, swung softly from his fingers. "I am commissioned by a lady."

He stared at the paternoster beads, remembered them around Jane's neck, nervous fingers toying with each small globe. Slowly, his gaze lifted to the monk's shadowed face.

"I am not a man for exile, Brother Tuck. I prefer death with honor to life with disgrace."

A sigh exploded within the cowl. "She said you would be noble to the point of idiocy. Nay, do not glare at me so fiercely, I only repeat the lady's words. You are offered far more than you know, and more than you will deserve if you are witless enough to refuse. The barons are behind you. There is no disgrace in a temporary retreat to regroup and plan, my lord. Do you condemn to death a loyal knight for the sake of your selfish pride? This man has more grace than do you, if that is true, my lord Devaux."

If he had been slapped, it would not have had more effect. Tré inhaled sharply. He thought of Brayeton, lost to him forever now, yet not as deep a hurt as Aimée's death. For three years, hatred of Pell Ewing had colored his every thought and deed, affected every decision he made, until now it had come to this. He glanced at Guy—loyal, willing to sacrifice all for him.

Noble, she had called him. Tré wanted to laugh at the absurdity of it. He was a fraud. His gaze shifted, focused on the robed monk.

"What would you have me do, Brother Tuck?"

Satisfaction wreathed a heaving sigh. "At last. There may be hope for you, my lord." Fumbling beneath his brown cassock, the monk drew out two bulky garments that shrunk the size of his girth considerably with their removal. "Don these robes, both of you. Make haste. The king will arrive soon. Do you wish to be an abbot or leper, Sir Guy?"

Green, lush and bountiful, swallowed the land for miles. Heavy branches of oak eclipsed the sun, shadows claiming supremacy over filtered light. Muted sound, murmurs of birds broken briefly by the chattering indignation of a red squirrel scampering on fissured bark: Sherwood Forest.

Jane waited, tense with anticipation and fear. The redolence of ground ivy swelled around her. She hugged her knees to her chest, jerkin and hosen more practical in dense wood where branches and nettles gleefully snared loose clothing.

Uncertainty dogged her. It was likely that Tré refused. He did not have the same prosaic view of honor as she did. It came from knowing Robin, who had nurtured a flexible perspective.

"In the tangled politics of England, Jaie, there are many interpretations of honor. I prefer the more practical tendency toward survival."

Peculiar interpretation that had taken him to die in a hot, arid land among heathens. . . .

She plucked miserably at a blade of grass between feet clad in comfortable buskins, winced when her hand brushed the stalk of a stinging nettle. Broad leaves of dock grew nearby, a ready antidote to the bite of nettles that now reddened her skin. Good thing. She had planted herself in a patch of nettles, it seemed, in many ways.

All had unraveled, her entire life fraying like a piece of loose linen. She thought of her parents—of her mother. Clorinda with the raven hair and laughing eyes, a lady and wife. Gone too early from this world, like all others she had loved. Would she lose Tré as well?

Distractions. . . . Idly, she rubbed the flat dock leaf over the back of her hand until the pricking eased.

A high song pierced the air and her head jerked up, heart pounding as she recognized the signal. The small whistle attached to a cloth-yard arrow gave a distinctive warning of approaching visitors. She rose, snatched up her bow and sheaf of arrows, nettles forgotten as she made her way through tangled vines and chest-high bracken.

Will Scarlett found her on the track that was no wider than a man's thigh, a faint ribbon snaking through the dense wood. He met her eyes, briefly, gave a shrug at the question in them. "Little John gave the signal. He sulks still, and does not come near."

She sighed, shook her head. "John only frets for us. It is difficult to know whom to trust."

"Devaux has not lent himself to earning our trust, you must admit," Will said dryly. He looked past her, toward the road. "If Devaux comes here, the king is likely to burn down the entire forest to smoke him out."

"King John loves the hunt far too much to risk a single hart in the greenwood." She inhaled deeply, lungs filling with the sweet scent of creeper. "It has been three days now since Tuck left. Do you think he succeeded?"

"We will soon know."

Jane shifted her grip on her bow, took another deep breath, and went with Will down the steep slope that led to the river's edge.

A faint song slowly became audible, drifting through oak and beech, a pious melody that identified the singer.

Will laughed softly. "Tuck is in rare form. If he has company, they will no doubt be glad enough of silence."

Jane was too agitated to reply; strain trembled in the muscles of her arm, in whitened knuckles where she gripped her bow. Did he come? Or must she offer up prayers for the dead? She closed her eyes, offered instead a prayer of hope. It was echoed in the distant song:

"Gloria tibi, Domine. . . ."

Her eyes snapped open as the Latin words rose to the canopy of laced tree branches; she heard in the joyous melody the sound of success. She splashed into the shallow river, holding her bow over her head to keep it dry, and clambered up the opposite bank without waiting for Will.

Tuck's familiar bulk was flanked by Tré and Guy, the trio dusty and weary. Two knights afoot, a most remarkable sight, wordless explanation for three days of waiting. Boots made for riding, not walking, were covered with mud; monk's and leper's robes flapped about their calves instead of their ankles.

Their unholy aspects should have betrayed them to even the dullest soldier. She stepped out from behind a tree, leaned her bow against the trunk, and waited.

She knew the moment he recognized her. A brief lift of dark brows evinced surprise, swiftly followed by a smile.

My jerkin reminds him of the day at the Cockpen Oak. . . .

Relief momentarily paralyzed her. Beneath the mantle of graceful beech, she was unable to do more than stand in grateful silence. His stride quickened, grew longer to leave Tuck and Guy behind. When he reached her, he did not hesitate, but pulled her hard against him.

She sagged, muscles collapsing with emotion and a sense of gratitude that was overwhelming. His hand tangled in her loose hair, combed fingers through in an almost rough caress, fisted it to hold her head still as her face tilted upward.

"Stubborn lady," he said softly, his familiar rasp a joy to her ears, "you do not yield easily."

"Nay, my lord, I do not. But I did once warn you of that."

He kissed her, hard, almost bruising her lips. "Yea," he said at last, "so you did. I find it inconvenient. Most pleasingly so."

A laugh, hard-won, escaped her, her eyes were wet with dewy moisture. *He is alive and here with me. There is nothing more that I can wish for but this. . . .*

26

—❦—

Darkness folded over them, shrouding the trees in soft sable. A quarter moon silvered air and ground, thin shafts of light piercing the canopy of brush that curved over straw pallet and linen; a cozy bower.

Tré held Jane in his arms. She slept, curled against him, slender hips pressed into the angle of his belly and thighs. Rare serenity threatened to engulf him, peace after the storm.

He had not waited for tender wooing, but took her in rough desperation, as if she would fade to mist before he could hold her again, touch her, taste her sweetness. Now he could not sleep; he could only hold this remarkable woman who had somehow breached his defenses. Tuck was right—irritating as he found the monk—Jane was not a lady to hold in light esteem. It would crush her spirit, blight her soul, if he did not yield to her the honor she deserved.

But what of love? Emotion beckoned him close; inherent vulnerability fraught with danger. He could give his life for her, but his love would destroy her in the end.

He stroked her arm, his hand gentle on soft skin. *So lovely . . . skin like velvet—the heart of a lion. She could have given King Richard lessons.*

His fingers closed on slender muscle; strong enough to

draw a bow, tender enough to heal a thick-headed baron possessed of more gall than wit. Elegant lady, defiant and coura-
geous; she shamed him. He closed his eyes, drew in the elusive
scent of mint.

The night shadows sucked warmth from the forest, replac-
ing it with cool mist that penetrated the bower. His tunic lay in
a heap beneath them, as did her hosen and jerkin. Clad only in
wool hose untied at the waist, he was chilled.

It grew late. He should return to the cave and the men, a
concession to propriety that Tuck had suggested and he had
agreed to. Only the lady protested. He smiled.

There, they were secluded from the cave by trees and the
River Maun; distant laughter rode an air current, faded into silence. An outlaws' lair with men he had fiercely pursued—
open to him now, if not with gladness, with acceptance.

Save Little John.

The giant's memory was as long as his legs. If not for his
lady's grace, John of Hathersage would have preferred to cross
swords instead of break bread with the former Sheriff of Nottingham. He made no secret of it; resentment and distrust
often creased his features, but the giant held his tongue at a
single glance from the lady.

It was understandable.

Tré bent, kissed the heart-shaped whorl of her ear, breathed
softly into it. Loose hair like raw silk cushioned her head,
draped her shoulder; a single strand looped in a gentle curve
around her breast. It drew him to stroke the smooth globe of
flesh, making it quiver slightly beneath his hand and the linen
shirt she wore. Gentle exploration drew his fingers down over
the span of ribs, narrowing of waist, and lush female curve
of hips.

He paused. Fingers splayed over her belly, covered only by
the shirt. Desire again, importuning and insistent, never satisfied. . . . He bent and kissed her, lips finding the pulse beneath
her ear.

Stirring, she turned, a drowsy smile on her lips. His heart
clutched painfully; he acknowledged it with a sigh as he pressed
his forehead against hers. He meant to bid her sleep well, to
leave her lying there alone.

But she reached for him. Clever hands, unerring instinct that drew her to touch him *there*, provoking instant reaction. She sighed; a lengthy exhalation through parted lips was sultry and seductive, eloquent.

Good intentions, the balm of the incompetent, vanished as morning mist beneath bright sunlight. A groan escaped him at her stroking hand, her feathery explorations on his turgid length an exquisite pleasure and delicious pain. He shuddered.

"Lady . . . you undo me."

"Yea, lord, I pray most earnestly that I do."

Fierce heat flared into the driving need to take her again, to crush her beneath him and possess her completely. He wanted nothing between them.

He kissed her throat, her lips, then drew the linen shirt up to her waist. She opened her mouth for him, tasting of excitement. Her hand cupped him, tightened in contractions that drew a groan up from the pit of his belly.

He sat up, pulled her shirt free in a single motion and let it float, white against shadow, to the pallet. Even in the pale moonlight her body gleamed like alabaster. Lovely. Perfect. Rounded breasts, slender hips and thighs, and the sweet promise between—his hand skimmed curved flesh, grazed damp heat, paused to stroke her. He heard her soft sound of pleasure. Deliberate, ignoring the frenzied arching of her hips, he took her to the brink, then stopped.

Writhing, she reached for him, her breath little more than soft gasps. Her hands closed on his wrists, fingers digging into bare flesh with mute pressure, urging him to continue.

He bent, raked his tongue over the beaded peak of her breast, smiled when she gasped again. His hands slid up to explore her body, caressing hills and dips; he used his knees to spread her thighs. She made a little sound of excitement and he kissed her fiercely. He sucked her bottom lip into his mouth, then moved lower, dragging deep kisses over her throat, the valley between her breasts, down to her belly. Her hands fluttered about his head, aimless and as light as sparrow wings against his cheek.

"Tell me," he said huskily against her belly, "what you want, chérie."

She twisted, curled her hands in his hair to hold him. Mute pleas were offered up; he ignored them. His tongue dipped into her navel, laved a damp path over a jutting hip bone. She tasted of soap and mint; luxuries in a wilderness. He had seen the wooden wine cask in the cave, cut in half to serve as a tub. Innovative lady who managed to wrest civility out of incivility, establish refinement in a cave.

"Tré . . . please."

Ragged breath, urgent whisper—he yielded, took her to a collapsing release.

Driven now, he freed himself of hose and braies, bent over her with his weight between her legs. Desperate need, long denied, still denied—he entered her slowly, immersing himself in more than just her body, rocking back and forth until she began to respond. Sweet savagery and gentle brutality rent him from taut control to wild abandon. He used her with growing ferocity, and she answered his potent thrusts urgently.

Shudders enveloped him, sparked his release, a blinding crash that left him spent. He cradled her in his arms, his breath a painful rasp in his throat. Muscles slowly relaxed; he kissed her face and tasted salt.

"Tears?"

A nod of her head, stifled sigh. "I thought you were lost to me. Since I left Nottingham a sennight past, I have not dared to hope. Now you are here." She turned, gazed at him through the shadows. In her eyes shone emotion; love, hope, constancy— all the things he was afraid to feel. All the things he already felt. . . .

She touched his face, a light caress, her words a whisper he felt to his bones: "I love you."

He went still, strangled by reluctant emotion. Never had he said the words to any woman; now they sat heavily on his tongue—a tongue the king had named facile. Fluent in all but these words. He closed his eyes, took a deep breath.

I love you, my lady Jane.

· · ·

Jane drew back the shaft, felt thrumming tension in the taut bowstring before her fingers snapped free; the bolt sped home to pin a slender willow wand to the broad trunk behind with a vibrating *fftwannggg*. Satisfaction rose, spread into modest pride when Tré gave a nod of approval.

"You are more formidable than I remembered, my lady Jane. But then, a bodkin arrow at the throat requires little skill."

Teasing laughter lit his eyes when she turned and lifted her shoulder in a shrug. "It is not so difficult to best a man busy with more pressing matters."

Sprawled on a cushion of thick grass beneath an oak, he regarded her through half-lidded eyes, the faint smile at the corners of his mouth making her heart beat erratically. Sunlight spattered him in a soft golden glow; no black surcoat with a raven on it now, but a jerkin of Lincoln green stretched over his broad chest, barely discernible from the lush green of the forest.

He was one of them now—reluctant outlaw garbed in doeskin and cross-gartered boots to his knees, a sword more comfortable in his hand than a bow. Kept at bay by the others, still not trusted despite her acceptance of him, Devaux was a man out of his element, surviving because his body demanded it.

She knew it, feared it. He would leave the safety of the forest when the time came, and there was nothing she could do to keep him there. The pain eroded her contentment. Yet she would grasp what she could from their time there, wring every tiny shred of joy from her days.

"Where did you learn the art of the bow, chérie?"

An idle question, a distraction she welcomed. She moved to him, folded her legs beneath her, felt his eyes linger on them appreciatively.

"There was an archer who came oft to Ashfield when I was a child, a friend of my mother's. He taught me, though my mother protested." She paused, traced a hand over the soft golden curve of bow that felt like silk beneath her palm, smiled in memory. "When it was seen that I had some skill, my uncle presented me with this. It is of good yew, made from the heart."

"Your uncle." Tré shifted, stretched out a long muscular leg clad in green hosen. "Robin Hood."

Ignoring the hint of derision in his voice, she nodded. "Yea, so he was once called. Robert of Locksley was his true name, then the Earl of Huntington when King Richard bestowed upon him the title and lands in reward for valor and loyalty."

"King John now holds Huntington." Bitter reflection, a taint of loathing and malice to his words. "John, who holds all of England in abeyance." His hand fisted in the grass, tore it from the ground, a frustrated motion.

Silence fell, so impenetrable that she could hear the beat of her heart. Then a lark sent its melody skyward, joyous and ignorant, a balm to ease the tension.

She leaned into him, laid her hand on his jaw until he looked at her, a shadowed, tormented gaze.

"He cannot reach us here, my lord."

His hand closed around hers, held it. "No. Sherwood holds even the king at bay. As it did me. We could remain here until the stars fall from the sky, and none would e'er come near."

He brought her hand to his mouth, lips grazing tiny calluses on her skin. He looked up at her through his lashes, a smoldering gaze.

"Would that be so dreadful to you, my lord?" Her whisper was light, yet fraught with an intensity that did not elude his notice.

He smiled against her palm, nipped gently at fingertips with his teeth, then clasped her hand between his own, large, strong ones, a comfort and a promise.

"Nay, my sweet, not if you were close-by."

He says all but the words I yearn to hear. . . .

A *plash* sounded in the lethargic current of the River Maun, warning of a visitor to the leafy bower where they sat. Tré released her hand, eyes guarded again, wary when Little John hove into sight.

Reserve still lay thickly between them, neither man ready

to trust the other. Jane turned, smiled at the giant blotting out light and tree with his wide frame.

"Has Will driven you from the cave again with his complaints?"

John grunted. "Nay, 'tis the harping songs Alan uses as torment. Rather a day in Nottingham dungeons than more of that." Light eyes shifted to Tré, lingered but a moment before flickering away. "There is word of Ravenshed."

The smile faded from her face. "Not—?"

He nodded. "Aye. Seized by the king, servants driven to the wood. Sir Guy and Will make ready to bring them here."

Tré rose to his feet, a lithe uncurling of supple muscle, and flexed his hands. "It will give me great pleasure to do something other than watch trees grow."

A cool regard measured Tré; John's mouth flattened. "As it will earn us satisfaction to best the Normans."

Hostility quivered in the air; Jane stood up, said in a light tone, "There is room in Sherwood for all. Norman, Saxon, or servant—all who are persecuted unfairly are well come to the greenwood."

Reluctant agreement simmered in Little John's eyes, and he gave a grudging nod. "Aye, 'tis true enough, my lady. The king has bound us together, whether he meant it or not."

Though Tré did not acknowledge the sentiment, it was obvious in the brief tuck of his mouth that he recognized the truth of it. Those outside the king's law were linked by both circumstance and purpose.

John's massive shoulders relaxed slightly; a faint smile turned up his lips. "We have a measure of good wine rescued from Nottingham's cellars, just delivered by Brother Tuck. 'Twas lost on the King's Road, I am told."

Tré's mouth twitched, then eased into an answering smile that was only a bit strained. "It must be the same road that snares venison dressed and roasted for the table. A devious track, with unexpected bounty for the fortunate few who find it there, it seems."

"Yea, so it seems." Bland amusement creased Little John's face, spread into a grin. "A different view from the opposite side of the road, I am told."

"So it is, John Lyttle. So it is. An opportune chance that men of Sherwood are so observant."

Tension dissipated, eased into wary acceptance. Jane dared hope that time would allay Tré's restless desire to leave the safety of Sherwood.

Yet she veered from the inevitable—the knowledge that beyond the greenwood lay both danger and disaster.

27

Rain fell softly on broad leaves; scrubbed the forest of dust, save in the vaulted depths that closed leafy arms against it. Tré knelt at the front of Jane's bower and gazed out; she refused to linger in the cave.

"It closes around me like a fist and I cannot breathe," she explained, and he remembered her flight from Nottingham. A dark night, a brave lady . . . desperation and despair that he never wanted to feel again.

He pivoted slightly on the balls of his feet, looked at her where she sat cross-legged on straw and linen. Misery lined her features, darkened her eyes, was evident in the errant quiver of her lower lip—but unvoiced.

"You know I have to go, Jane."

A nod of her head, tragic eyes looking down. "Yea, I understand."

He smiled tightly. "You are a most dreadful liar. It is as plain as Tuck's big belly that you do not understand at all."

"Yea, you are right." A swift glance up, intensity in her eyes and tone: "You are *safe* here! The king is gone from Nottingham, and Gaudet too busy with his new duties as high sheriff. . . . Soldiers are afraid to come this far into the forest, and even if they did, they could not find us. No, I do *not* understand why you must risk all!"

"I am not a man to live forever in a cave, Jane. There must be an end to this." He blew a heavy sigh, spread his hands on knees covered by rough woolen hose. "Near two months now, and I still am more used to wearing mail than a jerkin. This is not a life for me. Or for you."

At her silence, he looked away, stared beyond dripping trees toward Nottingham. "Tuck brings word from the barons of their willingness to speak at a council in my defense. It is a chance to lift the verdict of outlawry from my head."

"Or a chance to see your head on a pike!"

Vehemence laced her words, spat at him like a cat. He looked back at her, smiled faintly. "Do not honeycoat your feelings for me, sweet lady."

She muttered something inelegant, and put her hands over her face. Soft hair looped over her shoulder, careless plait gleaming on leather jerkin. They all wore green in the forest, shades of Lincoln green and brown that blended with trees and brush to render them nearly invisible. A cautious man could live forever in these trees. Tré understood now how impossible a task it had been to find them there.

He glanced out again at a world of somber verdigris, jade, drab olive; colors washed by dew and mist, an anonymous blur of dense trees and thick vines like walls, a hush that swallowed up light and man with impunity.

It closed in around him with stifling serenity.

"We leave within the hour. Tuck has arranged a meeting with Gilbert of Oxton and Lord Creighton." He paused, heard her muffled sigh, and continued, "The king is at Winchester and poses no immediate threat. We must move swiftly, ere he returns to Nottingham."

A long silence drifted between them. He heard her move at last, a soft shuffle of straw and linen as she came to the front of the bower to put her hand on his arm. Muscles tensed beneath her touch; his hands knotted on a slender twig he picked from the ground to keep from reaching for her instead.

"Forgive my fears, Tré. I would hold you back and have you

be someone you are not, so great is my fear for you." She paused and he glanced at her, recognized the dread in her eyes for what it was.

"I would never leave you willingly, lady mine." The words came out more harshly than he had intended; he cleared his throat, looked away, and tried again. "I do this not just for me but for us. I could never endanger your life by wedding you when the king has a price on my head. John is not averse to using the wives of his barons against them."

Fingers tightened on his arm. "Yea, I know. Go then, with my love and my hope and prayers. I will wait for you here, where I am safe with Little John and Will."

She offered him peace of mind and he took it, turned to bring her into the angle of his arm, tilted her face up for a kiss that was desperate and fierce. Then he set her aside, a hand firmly on her shoulder.

"Do not come to bid us farewell, for I want to keep my memory of you like this, beneath a bower of green vine and sweet flowers."

He meant it, and saw by the wretched light in her eyes that she held back tears. Brave lady, facing him with a wet smile, offering to him what she did not have herself.

It was an image that he held to tightly when they met with Oxton and Creighton.

Shadowed stone and incense enclosed them in the nave of Saint Mary's, a church and sanctuary in Edwinstowe. Tuck's breath was labored, loud huffs that echoed from high ceilings. He tugged at his cassock, eyed the barons and Sir Guy, and said with urgency:

"Be swift, my lords, for we have not much time while I distract the priest with my learned conversation."

Gilbert of Oxton knelt in an attitude of prayer, with Lord Creighton stiffly at his side, both men ill at ease and anxious.

"What news, my lords?" Tré bent beside them, three barons in prayer, guarded by a knight.

"King John met with the justiciar and all the bishops of Winchester on August 4 at Saint Albans. Peace has been proclaimed to all, with strict adherence to the charter laws set out by King Henry." Oxton paused, mouth twisted wryly. "He also enjoined the disuse of evil customs by sheriffs, foresters, and other officers of the crown, as they value limbs and lives, to commit no more extortions and wrongs as they have been wont to do."

"A noble endeavor," Tré said dryly. "Does Gaudet obey?"

"He does not," Creighton growled. Age and anger sat uneasily on the baron's head. Gnarled hands knotted with impotent fury. "New taxes have been levied, more monies demanded. It is at the king's instigation, though he feigns innocence."

Oxton raked a hand through his red hair. "The king committed the government to the justiciar and the Bishop of Winchester in anticipation of his absence from England to fight in Poitou against the French. Now his body of knights refuses to join him. They plead expense already lost in his effort, but John will not pay. That is not all—the northern barons refuse as well. They assert that according to the tenure of their lands, they are not bound to the king in his invasion in France. John sailed to Jersey, but when no one followed, he soon returned in a mighty rage, cursing the day and hour when he consented to the peace." Oxton smiled. "He claims he has been deceived, made a gazing-stock for nothing."

Tré laughed softly; the sound was swallowed in scented gloom, echoed by Guy at his side. "Then the time is ripe to act."

"Yea, my lord, if you hurry." Oxton sucked in a deep breath, exchanged glances with Creighton, and offered a taut smile. "We are behind you, with Adam de Lincoln, Sir Walter Foliot, and Thomas de Gray. We will swear that Lord Dunham lies, a fabrication concocted to further his aims with regard to Gaudet. There is no loyalty in Walter of Gedling—he will throw Gaudet to the Angevin wolf at a moment's notice if he is cornered. We have only to reduce Gaudet, and we have Dunham in check."

"We needs make haste, while the king rides north with his mercenaries and foreign host to bring the northern rebels to obedience," Creighton muttered.

"Yea," Oxton agreed, "but first Gaudet." He flicked a glance at Tré. "The Council of Barons is to be held in two days' time. We stand ready to lend aid when you give the word."

"I am ready, my lords." He glanced at Guy, saw the same emotion in his eyes: anticipation.

Nottingham Castle towered above the town. Familiar walls of sandstone were a formidable barrier. Tré sat with Guy in Pilgrim's Inn below the fortress, sipped ale from a tankard and waited. Had Oliver received his message? Would the captain risk all to lend aid? It would soon be seen.

Beside him, Guy shifted impatiently, growled an oath at the delay that grated on tempers and tolerance. The clang of iron against stone was steady as two soldiers in Gaudet's livery played at ringing the bull. A bull's nose ring dangled at the end of a long rope attached to the ceiling; flung hard, it sped toward the target on the wall.

"Join the game," Tré said, and smiled tightly at Guy's swift, incredulous glance.

One of the soldiers swung the ring again; it whipped through the air, nicked the bull's horn that curved up from a wood brace fastened to the wall, fell away to a groan of disgust. Coin clinked, a wager was won, and the other man stepped to take ring in hand. It looped neatly on the horn at the first try.

Beyond the ward room lay a rear chamber nestled behind a natural chimney of rock. A secret entrance led to passages carved by time and men, conjoining the network of caves.

"Distract them," Tré murmured, "then join us."

Guy nodded. He rose from the bench, walked toward the men, inconspicuous in the rough garments of a woodsman they wore as disguises. He had no noticeable weapons, save a dagger on his belt.

While he engaged the soldiers in a wager, boasting of his prowess yet handling the ring with clumsy hands, Tré slipped unnoticed from the ward room and around the rough rock that formed the chimney. Darkness claimed him; he ran a hand over the surface of the wall, found the latch of the door, opened it, and stepped inside.

Furtive noises like those of scuffling rats drifted down the passage. He waited, breath heavy with anticipation. Everything rested on subduing Gaudet. If he failed in that, he lost all.

He thought of Jane, safe in Sherwood. For now. If he failed, Oxton had sworn to her security.

"I will see to her, my lord," Gilbert had promised with quiet dignity. "Long have I—admired the lady."

It was a burden eased, the knowledge that Jane would be safe.

The door creaked open at last, Guy slipped inside. "I lost my last coin," he muttered, grimaced as the door shut behind him, closing out the light.

The blackness was heavy as they felt along the walls of the passages that honeycombed the rock. There was a steep slope beneath their feet; grit whispered free as boots gained purchase in the dark.

At last, light broke over them, gray and welcome, as they emerged in the tower, Tré glanced at Guy, noted sweat and strain on his brow.

"Now we shall see if we have a chance to live beyond the sun's setting," he said softly, smiled at Guy's soft oath.

The bailey was strangely deserted, with guards atop the walls but no activity near the royal apartments. With the king's departure had gone his vast retinue, leaving behind a welcome silence.

They made their way along the walls, keeping to shadow but with a casual demeanor designed to avoid suspicion. The steep rise of stairs that led to the middle bailey gleamed in the soft light as they descended.

The gatehouse loomed, manned by guards; grim obstacle if Oliver wisely looked to his own neck and abstained from involvement in the fray.

A guard moved from the shadows, pike held across his chest; Tré paused. "Oliver," he said, and the man nodded and grinned, stepping aside to grant them access to the middle bailey and the great hall.

Oliver had not failed him. He would yet win all. . . .

Oliver stepped from an alcove near the hall. "Your swords, my lord."

Tré met the captain's eyes as he took the weapon held out to him. "Should I win the day, George Oliver, you will find honor and security within my halls."

A fleeting grin squared the captain's mouth; blue eyes honest and intelligent met his with candor. "My wife will be most pleased to hear it, my lord. Kath has been pining for a quieter life in the country."

As he buckled on his sword, Guy laughed softly. "It is not a quiet life he promises you, Oliver, but a long struggle ere that day should come."

"It is the way of the world, Sir Guy. A man must work for great reward."

Hefting his sword, Tré said, "Let us go to claim that reward from Gaudet."

Men crowded the great hall; barons come to attend the council were attended by men-at-arms, more than the usual number. Tré recognized Oxton's men, Adam de Lincoln, Foliot, and Creighton among Gaudet's livery. They had kept their promise to him, Saxon barons and Norman, united behind him against common foes—King John and Sir Gervaise Gaudet.

Hoods pulled over their heads, he and Guy threaded a path through the throng. Gaudet sat at the high table on the dais, with Lord Dunham at one side and the Abbot of Croxdale at the other. The mace of office glittered in the light from torches and high windows.

In his element, Gaudet presided over the gathering with a lordly arrogance unsuited to a man of his rank. Scarlet and yellow tunic, a bright splash of color, set him apart from the more soberly clad Dunham and the stark-robed abbot. Jeweled rings glinted; the chain of office around his neck chimed with his movements. A brilliantly plumed bird, gaudy and dangerous.

Barons parted, granted Tré passage with silent permission. He paused by a thick stone column, waited until Gaudet finished speaking in low tones to the abbot and turned to look out at the assemblage.

Then he stepped forward, voice loud in the sudden hush:

"Sir Gervaise, what of the charges brought against you that you have colluded with a baron to defraud the king's coffers?"

Gaudet tensed, glared into the crowd to identify the speaker. "There have been no such charges brought against me. Who speaks?"

"What of charges that you falsely swore against a baron to the king," Tré said then, ignoring Gaudet's question, "and bore false witness against a baron's widow to gain her properties? Properties that belong to the church as well, it is said—a crime against man and God."

Fury marked Gaudet's face. He surged to his feet. "Guards! Find me this man!"

Abandoning the stone column, Tré moved through the crowd to stand near the dais, Guy close behind. Guards used pike and staff to push through tightly packed men, earning harsh looks and muttered oaths.

Oxton signaled for Gaudet's attention. "What of these charges, my lord high sheriff? Do they bear weight?"

"Lies! Vicious lies levied by a man too cowardly to show himself to me or to you—"

Relentless, Oxton pursued it: "Yet I recall the former high sheriff, a baron by right of investiture, denied his rights by law to a trial before justiciar and council."

"My lord Oxton," Dunham leaned forward, a dangerous glint in his eyes, "your memory is impaired. I was here that day, and Devaux waived his rights by agreement to a trial by combat."

"Nay, my lord Dunham," Creighton said then, voice firm to rise above the noise of guards moving about the hall, "it is not as you say. We were many of us here that day, and know full well that Lord Devaux was denied by the king his right to trial before justiciar or even the church. As was Lady Neville, a widow whose dower lands were left to the church despite the king's dispute."

The abbot turned to Dunham and Gaudet, vexation on his face. "Can this be true? I insist that these charges be answered more fully—"

"Do not be duped by the charges of two men with their own

interests," Gaudet snapped. "Gilbert of Oxton is known to lust
for the widow, even though she consorts with the outlaws of
Sherwood. Her uncle was Robin Hood, monseigneur, a wolf's
head, and hardly fit recommendation for her character."

Standing quietly, Tré bided his time; the abbot weighed
charges and countercharges, while controversy raged among
the barons in the hall. A faint smile pressed his mouth. Another council erupting in argument: normal procedure, in his
experience.

Impotent, furious, Gaudet stood behind the table and glared
out over the barons. It was obvious that the tide of opinion had
turned against him, Saxon barons uniting with Norman in a
cause that threatened their personal as well as political lives. If
the king could flout the authority of the church in his condemnation of a single Norman baron, so could it happen to any
baron there who earned his displeasure.

"*Merde!*" Guy muttered at his side, and Tré turned to follow
his gaze.

Before either man could move, a female voice rang out in
clear tones: "My lords! I bring proof to bear in this cause!"

Gaudet and Dunham turned in unison, incredulity marking
their faces. Sir Gervaise recovered first, snapped out an order
to remove the lady from the hall, but was swiftly vetoed by the
abbot.

"Come forward, my lady, and identify yourself before you
render to us this proof you bear."

Tré felt Guy stiffen; he knew the cause.

Moving through the crowd, heedless of the stares, the lady
halted before the dais; her beautiful head was held high.

"I am Lady Dunham—wife to Walter of Gedling, Lord
Dunham, now sitting at the high sheriff's side. Monseigneur, I
bring proof and complaint, with a request for your grace."

"Present it, my lady." The abbot gave a sharp gesture when
Gaudet protested, fixing him with a cold glare. "This is a matter of church as well as crown, as it involves lands deeded to
the church. It would behoove you, Sir Gervaise, to heed my
counsel and allow me to proceed unhindered."

Disbelieving, Tré watched as Lissa gave to the abbot a

much-folded scrap of parchment, bearing, she said, written proof of her husband's plot with Gaudet, and his seal. She did not glance at her husband, though he glowered menacingly.

When the abbot finished reading, he glanced up at the lady. "You bear witness against your husband?"

"I plead succor from the church, monseigneur. Grant me the privilege of sanctuary in a nunnery, for my dower lands. I seek refuge from the harsh hands of my husband, a man of no honor, a traitor to crown and God."

It was a telling speech. He heard Guy inhale sharply when the abbot granted her petition to enter a nunnery. It was unlikely that the church would refuse ample donation for admission to cloistered walls. Unhappy lady. Perhaps she would find the peace she yearned for within serene walls devoted to prayer instead of conflict.

"It is our decision," the abbot intoned, "that the matter of Lord Devaux be reconsidered. I repudiate charges against him, and refer the matter to a council of his peers, to be heard before the chief justiciar of this land at a time agreeable to all."

For a moment, Dunham and Gaudet did not speak, then the Saxon baron bowed his head in acceptance, though his eyes glittered with malice. "At your command, monseigneur, it will be so."

Gaudet was not so easily won, but at a quick word from Dunham gave grudging assent. A vote was taken among the barons, carried by a majority, and Gilbert of Oxton found Tré in the press of men swarming in the aisles.

"It is done, my lord. No justiciar will convict you. There is no proof of guilt—not with barons prepared to swear you innocent of circumstances."

Tré met his gaze, nodded. "Now we fight a common enemy, Lord Oxton, though before it was Saxon against Norman."

A faint smile flickered on Oxton's mouth. "Yea, for the sake of your lady, all has changed." He paused, said softly, "If I had not seen with mine own eyes your defiance of the king even in certain knowledge of your death for freeing her, I may not have thought you worthy of her."

Tré had no answer for that, no explanation that he would

voice, and stood in silence after Oxton took his leave. He saw
Guy move to Lady Dunham, speak to her earnestly. A hum of
talk swirled around him as the council broke up.

It was over. A bloodless coup. *Too easy. . . .*

Restive, a strange apprehension seized him. It must be the
anticipation of a fight, the residue of expected battle still lingering. His blood was high, urgency churning his belly.

Against his left thigh, his sword hung ready; a leather
hauberk was beneath the simple garb of a woodsman. He
needed none of it.

Turning on his heel, he walked toward the double doors at
the far end of the hall. Captain Oliver briefly appeared in the
open doorway, silhouetted against the bright light behind him,
a sturdy reminder of the debt he was owed. It was Gaudet's
men who had waylaid Oliver on the King's Great Way, nearly
killing him and slaughtering most of his troop. Yet he had managed to send the messenger with a warning.

Brayeton would benefit from such good men, as would his
other holdings. Castles needed castellans, dependable men to
hold them in the lord's absence. Once his lands were restored
to him, he would set about fortifying them. Battle with the king
was not over. John would not stop pursuing wars and conflict; it
was his nature. Ever malicious, ever greedy, there was little
hope that the king would be held at bay by edicts from church
or law.

Safety lay in the ability to protect his own lands. He would
not make that mistake again. There was no honor to be found
in a dishonorable man, whether king or baron.

He reached the door, but Oliver was gone. Sunlight was
harsh in his eyes as he paused on the top step and squinted
against it. August had given way to early September but the
days were still warm, drawing from the moat a palpable stench
he had not noticed before in his preoccupation.

Relief began to ease his tension; he thought of Jane. While
he waited for the justiciar's council to convene, he would send
word to her so she would not worry. It was three days since he
had left her; now that the pressing concern was lifted, he could
admit to himself what he had not dwelled on before—he loved
her well.

An elusive emotion found, acknowledged, embraced. A new life, with a woman of great courage at his side. . . .

"My lord!"

His head snapped up, eyes blinked against light, caught a glimpse of metallic reflection, and flung himself to one side. The hiss of a sword cleaving air summoned instant reaction; without thought, he drew his weapon, hilt firm and familiar in his fist as he blindly turned to meet the threat.

Shadows danced in front of his eyes; instinct guided his sword to meet the next downward swing. Metal clashed loudly. Men shouted. He turned, barely kept his balance on the steep stairs that descended from the great hall to the stones of the bailey.

Savage thrusts, parried and turned, concentration bent to keep his footing; he identified his adversary now, the blur of scarlet and yellow. No binding chain of office hung around Gaudet's neck to impede him now, no rings that might catch on hilt or blade; he was there to fight.

Gaudy he might be, but Gervaise Gaudet was a formidable opponent. He fought viciously. The element of surprise was gone with the shouted warning—Oliver?— and now he pursued Tré with fierce intent, relentless blows to force him to the edge of the steep stairs, a crippling fall.

Renewed tension, welcomed; an exultation of released energy and an end to the nagging feeling of danger unmet. It was there, in the form of a man who had declared himself enemy.

Gaudet stepped forward and swung his sword two handed, a mighty blow that would have severed head from neck if Tré had not seen it coming. Sharp blade, slicing through the loose sleeves of his linen shirt, leaving a crimson line of blood to blossom on dull white. The stinging pain was an alert instead of a distraction.

Savagely, he swung in reaction before Gaudet recovered, managed to catch him on one side, heard the clink of mail beneath scarlet tunic, felt the slight drag of the blade that caught on metal and not flesh. Wordless, intent, he jerked his sword free of clinging cloth and links and swung it again, taking the initiative to lunge forward.

It caught Gaudet by surprise and he stepped back. His heel

caught on the step above; he fumbled, wobbled, dropped his guard for just the moment Tré needed . . . a mighty swing of sword, sunlight splintering on wicked blade, the expected shock of connection when it bit through tunic, mail, and flesh to shatter a rib.

Bloodied fingers gripped the blade; an instant's realization lit Gaudet's eyes as Tré stared into his face. A bubble of red frothed his lips, dribbled to the golden tuft of beard on his chin.

"Curse you, Devaux."

Tré freed his blade with a jerk; Gaudet toppled over the edge of the stairs to plummet to cobbled stones in the bailey below.

Breathing raggedly, the pounding of blood hot and loud in his ears, he stood with sword still lifted, slowly aware of growing tumult around him. He looked up, saw Oliver above him, Guy in the doorway. Behind him, he heard the familiar winding of a horn. He turned, saw banners glint beneath bright sunlight, a breeze curling pennons with gold and scarlet colors.

They heralded the arrival of the king.

28

❦

"This pertains to royal jurisdiction, abbot. It is not an ecclesiastical matter." John's lofty pronouncement did not mollify the abbot.

"Sire, this is a matter given over to the Council of Barons. That was done. It should now be heard by the chief justiciar."

It was a nightmare; Guy stood tensely, reeling from the day's events and the untimely arrival of the king. Taken by the king's men, Tré was once more under arrest.

"I have not time for this!" John raged. "I am beset on all sides, with rebellious barons and galling clergy!" As the abbot recoiled in offense, the king paced the rush-strewn floor of the hall. His seneschal hovered nearby, a constant presence. "Gilbert," John snapped, "are the gates locked?"

"Yea, sire. As you ordered."

Tension hung over the hall. The king's mood was dangerous; his temper wavered between satisfaction and frustrated fury.

Rounding on Tré, the king surveyed him with a glitter of gratification. "What say you now, Devaux? You are charged with murder of an appointed official of the king."

Weighted down with chains, bloody, he returned John's stare coolly. "I was attacked from behind, sire. Any man here will tell you that."

A wave of his hand dismissed the claim as trivial. John flung himself toward the dais, snatched up a cup of wine. "It matters not. For that crime, *I* have jurisdiction."

The abbot cleared his throat. "Sire, Devaux is a baron. He is to be tried before a council for even this charge."

The king's glare pinned the abbot, silenced him. Guy's hand tightened on his sword hilt; they had been so close to victory . . . so close. Lissa's evidence against her husband had swayed any baron still unconvinced to their favor. It was done—and now this cursed Angevin spawn arrived to undo it all.

Heartsick, he stepped to the rear of the hall, away from king and chaos. He had to breathe fresh air or he would unman himself there, in front of gathered barons and the king's guard.

A hand reached out to snatch at his sleeve and he paused, peered into gloom with tensed muscles until he recognized Lissa. Pale of face, with hair a golden haze beneath blue wimple, she whispered, "Is the abbot able to stay the king?"

"No. I fear the worst."

"Come with me." She tugged urgently on his sleeve to draw him with her.

He pulled away. "Lady, you have forsworn the secular life for the spiritual. I will not—"

"Fool!" Anger vibrated in the single word, earning anger in return.

"Faithless female, full of tricks—you name me fool when you have played me false?"

"How did I do that? I told you earlier, Walter left me no choice." She glanced around, eyes a faint gleam in shadow. "Come with me. I refuse to discuss this here with you."

Reluctant, angry, he followed her. The bailey was crowded with king's men and barons' men, dissension subdued but tangible.

They paused by the Royal Mews; feathers and falcons fluttered restively. Shadows crept close.

"Tell me what you want of me," Guy said bluntly. "I must return ere the king draws his own sword."

"Softsword? You jest. Listen to me, righteous monk, for I have a message."

"I do not trust any message you may tell."

"Do you not?" She paused; her voice wobbled slightly: "If you do not love your lord, at least love your lady. It comes from her."

"I have no lady."

"No? What of Lord Devaux's lady? Are you not sworn to him as knight?"

He frowned. "You have a message from the lady Jane?"

"Yea. She trusts me, whether you do or not. Oh, Guy—" A pause, fraught with pain and uncertainty, then: "Forgive me just a little. Do it for your lord's sake, if not your own."

The faint scent of roses surrounded her; he thought of her soft skin, the way she felt in his arms . . . the memory of her stricken words and whispered fear, the denials when he asked if she wanted him to rescue her.

"Tell me the message," he said, and she put her hand on his arm and leaned close.

Tré stood stiffly; each movement brought a clank of chains. The king still raged; the abbot and barons offered restrained argument. It was deadly to defy John when this mood was upon him.

Even more deadly to allow him free rein.

His eyes itched; smoke from torches and the main fire wreathed gauzily over heads and guards' pikes. It was likely that this time the king would achieve his aim. A struggle was ended; fickle fate had delivered him into the hands of John. A man's destiny could be delayed but not denied; his father had been fond of saying that. He had never thought it true until now.

Emotionless, he stood flanked by guards; listened to the ongoing argument dispassionately, as if he were not involved. He thought instead of his lady. She would be grieved when word reached her.

Jane, for all my blind folly, I loved you well. . . .

A noise at the end of the hall cut through the babble of barons and king, a sharp voice raised. It quieted again, a ripple as of a rock thrown into water, surface smooth once more. Tré stared ahead of him, thought now of nothing more than the moment. Regret was senseless, futile.

The silence grew tense. Around him, there was a collective sigh, as if something of import had occurred.

He looked up, saw in the king's face resigned fury, heard his mocking: "Another miracle of record, it is plain. Do you walk through walls, your eminence?"

Turning his head, Tré recognized the robes if not the face of the man approaching the dais where John waited with a blasphemous lip curled in defeat.

"I walk through open gates, sire, like most men."

Stephen Langton, the Archbishop of Canterbury. John's nemesis.

At the end of the hall, he saw Oliver and his men, swords and pikes holding the king's guard at bay. Guy looked up, met his gaze, and nodded grimly. Fortuitous arrival—had Guy opened the gates for Langton?

The archbishop's eyes moved to Tré, lingered, then returned to the king. "This man is a baron, sire, is he not?"

"He was." John's eyes narrowed. "Do you *dare* admonish us on a secular matter?"

"It is not a secular matter." He ignored the sharp exclamation, continued, "Lord Devaux is a baron. I have warned you of vengeance against your barons, sire."

"Yea, so you have, all the way to Northampton and now here. Could you not stay in London? The council needs you more than do we."

"If I deemed that true, sire, I would have remained at Saint Paul's instead of given chase to a feckless king who may yet earn more censure."

"You rank a worthy alaunt, your eminence. But you do not chase stags or boar. You hound the *king*. We are not run to ground like prey."

"Do you give up your decision to force your barons to obedience?"

"We do not. Curse them, they defy us with their refusal to pay homage and scutage." Rancor marked his words, taut and heavy.

Langton stepped forward; a glance swept Nottingham's

great hall, the chamber so crowded with barons that not a broom straw could have been inserted between them. His voice lifted, the voice of a man used to command, tempered with compassion yet still imperative:

"Sire, I say to you now that unless this project is at once given up, I will excommunicate every man—save you as the king—should he take part in any military expedition so long as the interdict continues in force. If you have levied accusations against any baron, appoint the day for a trial and it will be done. I do not cease to *hound* you until you grant me your word."

Furious, the king at last yielded. "We set the day as All Saints' Day for barons to appear in court to answer charges of rebellion."

"And this man?" Langton indicated Tré. "He is to be set free at once."

"The charge for Devaux is murder, not rebellion. Not even the church sanctions the unwarranted death of the king's appointed man, we trust."

Tré was not surprised. Devious John, who would grasp at anything to assuage his anger.

"Your eminence!" A body of men stepped forward, earning the king's glare and the archbishop's interest. "We are prepared to swear that Sir Gervaise Gaudet did attack first, on the steps of this hall, and that Lord Devaux was forced to defend himself."

The archbishop turned to John. "I believe that is proof enough for you, sire."

Disbelief, anger, defeat crossed the king's face. He sank into the high-backed chair behind the table, shook his head. "I am beset."

Tré sucked in a sharp breath, suppressed rising exultation. *Too soon . . . elusive victory can vanish before my eyes.*

Even when the chains were removed, he did not give way to relief. He waited; watched the faces spread about the hall, kept his back to the stone column behind him. One hand hovered at his side, palm itching for the hilt of a sword. He would feel better with a weapon in his hand, to die fighting like a man instead of at the king's pleasure.

Illusionary freedom, wavering just beyond his grasp, a promise and denial all in the same breath.

He saw Little John, a head above everyone else, golden hair streaked with gray. Surprise struck first, then instant concern. If Little John was there, then where was the lady Jane?

Jerked from immobility, he left the column by the dais and moved into the crowd, ignored Oxton's outstretched hand that would delay him, shoved past barons who'd come to his aid.

"John of Hathersage," he said quietly, and Little John turned. The dour expression more familiar to Tré was gone; a strange jubilance lit the outlaw's face.

"Aye, my lord Devaux?"

"Where is my lady?"

Deadly quiet penetrated the giant's elation as sharply as the dagger at his side. His smile faded.

"The lady is safe, or I would not be here." Soft dignity, a calm answer.

Tré believed him. "Where is she?"

A faint smile curled Little John's mouth, eyes a proud glitter. "When last I saw her, she stood with an arrow held to Norman throats. It was your lady who opened the gates for the archbishop."

Shock mingled with misgivings; he blew out the breath that expanded his lungs, shifted the dagger. "And you left her there alone?"

"Nay, my lord Devaux, I left her in the best of hands. I assure ye, she has not come to harm."

Mystery shrouded his reply, but impatience to see Jane spurred Tré more than curiosity for the explanation. "If she has come to no harm, why then is she not in the hall?"

"She awaits ye in The Bell, far removed from king and hall. For reasons of her own." John nodded sagely. "She will tell ye what ye want to know soon enough, my lord."

Adrift in a sea of conversation that he did not want to join, Tré nodded curtly. No man tried to stop him as he left the hall, nor was he accosted when he left the castle. It was dusk, earlier now near autumn.

Church bells rang Vespers. Market Square was less crowded; the carcass of a horse blocked an alley, and he went around it, stepping over other malodorous refuse from a tanner's stall.

The Bell crouched over a narrow street, half-timbered and sagging at one end. He swung open the door, stepped into a small common room with low beams and plastered walls that were originally white. It grew quiet as he stood there, men turning to look at him, voices dropping away. He understood. Blood still stained his shirt, caked his wrists where the manacles had rubbed.

"I search for a lady," he said into the charged gloom, and none moved or answered.

Then a bench scraped on the wood floor, a soft familiar voice came to him through the gloom: "Let me lend my aid, sir. I am good at finding ladies."

He did not smile; he could not find the energy or the heart. Not even when Jane paused in front of him, hands on her hips—her best swagger wasted. She wore a hooded jerkin and hosen; a bow slung over one shoulder, arrows jaunty in a quiver at her side.

He curved a hand behind her neck, pulled her to him, kissed her with a grimness born of desperation. A soft sigh of surprise filled his mouth; he swallowed it, deepened the kiss until the cold emptiness inside him was eased. At last he could breathe again; still holding her, he pressed his mouth against the top of her head, nuzzled wool.

Then he released her, glanced up; men stared at them with wide eyes and open mouths that bespoke astonishment at such a display. One man regarded them with a faint smile, different from the rest, his gaze one of wary approval.

Jane snared Tré's attention again with a gentle nudge, a step back to look up at him. "Shall we go home, sir?"

"Yea, I am ready." He inhaled the fragrance of mint. "I am ready to spend the rest of my life with you. You have my heart, now and always. But you must know that."

Soft laughter, then: "I have known that for a while, my handsome lord. It just took you overlong to learn it."

"There are those," came a comment from the light-haired stranger regarding them with indulgent amusement, "who take more convincing than others."

Tré's eyes narrowed. A temper already scoured from too-ready danger rose swiftly. With a hand on the hilt of his sword, he said bluntly, "It is no concern of yours, sir."

"Is it not?" Languid regard centered on him, seasoned with laughter behind blue eyes that looked strangely familiar. "Do not be too certain of that, my lord Devaux."

Before he could respond, Jane put a hand on his arm, fingers curling urgently around muscles taut with strain. "My lord, do allow me to present to you a well-loved prodigal son, returned as if from the grave. A hero lately come home."

The man rose from the bench, careless grace, tall and faintly smiling. "You flatter me, little Jaie. 'Prodigal' suits far better than 'hero.' Were I heroic, I would have arrived in time to lend my arms to hold at bay the Normans at the gate. Alas, you stole my glory with your own feat—a worthy prodigy, I vow, more skilled than I remember the girl I once knew."

"I was a child then. Now I am a woman."

"So I see." Blue eyes flicked to Tré, measured him with an assessing gaze. "A woman for only a worthy man."

Realization struck even before Jane said, "I present to you my uncle, Robert of Locksley, the Earl of Huntington."

Locksley's brow lifted; light hair gleamed. Time and travail marked his face with lines, but he moved like a young man still. Bright blue eyes regarded him steadily, creased with laughter when Tré said softly, *"Robin Hood."*

IV

BARNSDALE IN

SHERWOOD FOREST

HUNTINGTON CASTLE

DECEMBER 20, 1213

29

***

Portions of Huntington Castle lay skeletal and ruined; empty windows like vacant eye sockets gazed at the encroaching forest, walls garbed in vines and creepers wore a leafy mantle of olive against drab shadows.

"The king restored Clipstone Palace with my stone," the earl said in disgust as he gestured at what had once been elegant castle and grounds.

Jane nodded. A painful return after so many years, this visit to happier times where memories lurked in dark crevices and remnants of oak wainscoting. Roofless, open to sky and forest creatures, Huntington showed little evidence of the grand fortress it had once been.

More painful was the bleak light in Robin's eyes as he stood with wind-whipped mantle to view what was left. Hope vanished now, in stark realization of what was lost.

"Will you rebuild, Robin?" she asked at last, a gentle nudge from reverie that brought his gaze to her with a faint smile and hitch of one shoulder.

"I have not enough coin left to build even a cow shed."

"What of the king's promise to repay damages to those barons he has wronged? Will that not be enough to rebuild Huntington?"

"Yea, but agreement has been delayed. There have been two more meetings since All Saints' Day." A hesitation, a shake of his head, then a long sigh blew frost into the air. "I have entered a petition. Until a settlement can be reached, the interdict will not be raised. England is yet without sanction of God at King John's whim."

Wind whipped hair that was still a rich gold, if streaked here and there with gray—familiar to her and yet strange, after all these years, a young girl's memory distorted by time. He was a man, after all, driven by his own demons to fame and folly. Noble, gallant, flawed, as were all mortal men; she admired him now more than she had then, recognizing his generosity of spirit that had risked all without a qualm.

She put a hand on his arm. "There will always be a place for you at Ravenshed. My mother would have wanted you there."

"Ah, sweet Clorinda." He nodded. "I think of her oft still, and the times we had in Sherwood." A grin squared the corners of his mouth. "Did she ever tell you of the time we hid from the sheriff in the Cockpen Oak? He rode right past us. Clorinda put an arrow into the casket of taxes to warn him we watched, and sent his horse down the road with Hugh Bardulf clinging to the neck like a thistle. . . ."

"My *mother* shot an arrow at him?"

Robin's brow rose, faint streaks of gray in the arch. "Yea, she did. Did Alan never sing of those days, little Jaie? Of beautiful Clorinda, a better archer than most men—and some said, equal to Robin Hood himself."

"No. Never." Jane stared at him. Memories teased, of angry protest at teaching her only daughter to shoot a bow, of Robin's laughing persistence. "No one told me."

"Ah, well. After she met your father, she wanted only to please him, to put it all behind her. Clorinda wanted it forgotten that she wore jerkin and hose, that she was outlawed with the rest of us. Yet I thought someone would have told you of it by now." He eyed her for a moment; kind eyes, generous heart, truth offered up as a gift at last. "You have her skill, Jaie, and her strong heart. She was never faint-hearted when she wanted something. Neither are you."

It was a reminder.

Tré was gone again, returned north to Brayeton, leaving her behind in Robin's secure custody. Long nights stretched endlessly as she fretted; he went to reclaim his lands and title, but would he return to reclaim her?

She sucked in a sharp breath that smelled of snow. An idle hand picked at crusted liverwort carpeting a tumbled stone; it crumbled beneath her hand.

Robin's gaze did not waver. "It grows late. Dena will fret if we do not return before dark, and Marian will be irritated that we have been gone so long."

Silent fears, unvoiced and uncertain, gnawed at her peace of mind. Anything could happen. The king's enmity had been incurred, and there was always Pell Ewing, Earl of Welburn—who was responsible for the death of Aimée. If Tré sought vengeance, it could unravel into disaster. At the least, he could be deseisined again—at the worst, slain.

As if reading her dark thoughts, Robin said gently, "He is not a foolish man, Jaie. The king waits like one of his hawks for the least mistake. Devaux knows this. He will not risk all now for the sake of revenge."

"It eats at him, Robin."

"Yea, as it ate at me while I languished in an Arab prison those many years. Vengeance, hatred, rage: futile emotions. Destructive to the man that nurtures them rather than releases them. Freedom comes with the abandonment of empty convictions."

He turned, swept an arm out to encompass the ruins of Huntington Castle. "It is gone, yet I do not weep. I can rebuild dreams of other than stone, and be the richer man for it. An earl or an outlaw, it makes little difference to me, Jaie. I have what no man can take away now, hard learned these past years—serenity. It will stand me in good stead whether in the midst of battle or in the quiet greenwood."

When she did not reply, he came close, tucked her chin in his palm to lift her face to his. "Have faith in him."

Have faith in him. . . . Yea, so I do have faith in Tré, but not in the king or fate.

They left Barnsdale to ride north through the quiet forest reaches. Gray light closed in, drab stretches of umber and dun anonymous in winter's peace. Goosedale and then Longdale were swiftly behind them.

Ravenshed waited, familiar lights welcome beacons on the walls. Chilled from the ride, dusted now with snow, Jane dismounted in the courtyard, greeted Fiskin with a nod and proffered reins.

"It grows cold, milady," Fiskin said as he took the palfrey's reins. "We have visitors."

Curiosity was tempered with dismay; her mood did not lend itself to civility these days and was a constant drain on fading reserves of strength. Now she noted an air of activity overlooked before: men, swathed in layers of wool to keep out the winter's cold, milling near the stables.

"Who is it, Fiskin?"

But he was already at Robin's side, adulation for the famed outlaw earl a constant gleam in blue eyes. Jane stifled a sigh. Head ducked against the wind, she mounted the stairs to the hall.

Warm air washed over her as the door opened, rich with the smell of spices and comfort. Dena scolded, not unkindly, bustled about to take her mantle and brush away the snow.

"Go and sit by the fire, milady. The Lady Marian awaits thee."

Marian. Still beautiful, still elegant, possessed of the same serenity Robin had found. Years in a nunnery had only deepened her faith, sheltered her from life's harshest blows, and lent her more grace. Jane almost envied her for it.

"Do not overtire yourself, Dena," she said as she allowed the older woman to direct her to the hall. It was a futile reminder. Dena ignored all reprimands and set about her duties as if she were still a maid, despite her frailty of body. Her spirit was strong, and that might yet keep her well.

Jane recognized the broad form seated on a bench near the hearth, heard the laughter, and her steps quickened.

"Tuck! And Little John—you are all here!"

They rose, Tuck, John, Will, even Alan of the Dales, a familiar lute in his hand.

"It nears *Christes Masse*, and I am to say the Mass at Blidworth this year," Tuck said with a laugh. "You did not think I would fail to pay respects while so close-by?"

New wine redolent of spices was brought on a tray, Enid smiling at her mother's side. Logs spat smoke and sparks up the chimney, spread warmth in a pool to encompass those on benches. Shadows of gold and gray danced on whitewashed walls. Alan strummed his lute, sang of the fame of an outlawed earl and his lovely lady, to the amusement of all.

Candles burned low, lamps hissed as wicks shortened; a sudden draft bent flames, lifted a dog's head to stare down the length of the hall. Scrambling up, it bayed, undulating tones that riveted those in the hall.

Jane turned, rose from the bench even as the men became alert and tense. Shadows shifted, a voice mocked:

"A merry band, loud as jackdaws and not so lovely to the ears."

Light glinted on gold hair, caught the faint gleam of steel, then washed over the familiar knight as he stepped from the shadows to quiet the baying dogs.

"Sir Guy, you defame us," Robin said, laughing. "Alan may well be grieved to hear your opinion."

Laughter and greetings drifted around her as Jane stood still, waiting, her heart in her throat. Another shadow moved behind Guy, stepped into the light, and she moved instinctively over crackling rushes.

Tré caught her. He held her tightly, smelling of wind and snow. His face was cold, his breath warm against her cheek.

Neither of them spoke; it was enough to embrace. She felt his muscles shift beneath her hands, turned her head to look at him, saw his smile with a painful clutch in her chest. Her tongue would not form the words she longed to say; prayers of relief, pleas that he never leave her side again, vows of love lingered in her heart.

"You are well come, my lord," she said instead, and put her palm against his cheek. "You have been missed."

"Have I?" Intensity vibrated, low and intimate, in his voice and in his touch. "It is good to be here."

"I have longed for the sight of you. . . ."

He put his palm atop her hand, held it to his cheek. "I bring a message from your lady cousin."

"Lissa is well? Does she—"

"Well enough." He glanced toward Guy, a slight shake of his head, then: "She says to tell you she searches for peace as you once told her to do."

Painful memory, Lissa's miserable face, her own earnest pleas that she seek peace within instead of without . . . heeded now at last. "I pray she finds it, though I never thought it would be in a nunnery."

"Safer there for her than where Dunham might yet reach her." Tré's eyes briefly clouded; another glance at Guy told much. "She retreats from more than her husband, I think."

Jane understood. Though Guy smiled and jested, there was an emptiness about him now, as if he had suffered great loss. Perhaps Lissa meant more to him than he admitted.

"Come, milady," Tuck said behind her, "let us greet him as well, ere we grow old."

"Too late for that, Brother Tuck." Tré looked up with a glance and smile. "But not too late for news I bring."

"Come and sit by the fire," Robin invited, "and share it with us."

Tré did not release his grip on Jane, but swept her with him toward the fire, holding her tightly at his side as he shrugged out of his mantle and accepted a proffered cup of hot spiced wine. Cinnamon and ginger seasoned the air, rich and tempting.

Anxious, she scanned Tré for evidence of new hurts but saw none. A quick glance at Guy reassured her that they were both fit and hale. Some of her tension eased, cautious relief creeping in to replace it.

Tré lowered his cup, nodded greeting at these men he had once pursued with grim determination.

"John has at last agreed to repay what is owed. Two sets of commissioners have been appointed, one by the crown, one by the pope, to review the amount of damages the crown must pay to wronged barons."

Lady Marian gasped, turned to Robin with hope shining in her eyes and face. "Huntington can be rebuilt, Robin!"

"Aye." An indulgent smile, a glance at Tré, a speculative lift of his brow. "So it seems. What of you, my lord Devaux? Are your lands secure?"

"They are. I have set Captain Oliver to hold Brayeton until our return. He is a worthy castellan, and Giles is well used to stewardship." He paused, glanced again at Guy with a faint smile. "I have granted one of my holdings to my loyal knight, in gratitude for his service. Behold Guy de Beaufort, Lord of Ravenscar."

Guy accepted their accolades with a grave nod of his head; hazel eyes gleamed in the soft light, a sardonic smile curled his mouth. "My lord Devaux claims gratitude, yet renders to me lands and title he knows I will have to fight the king to keep. He only seeks more northern barons to lend weight to a common cause."

"And will you fight the king should it come to that, Sir— Lord Ravenscar?" Robin asked, tone light but freighted with significance.

"Yea, it will come to that and I will fight." A pause, then softly: "The king does not end his oppression. He has shown his contempt for barons and country by reinstating men proven to be lawless. Eustace de Lowdham is High Sheriff of Nottingham again, FitzWalter and de Vesci restored to their lands as well. The Charter of Liberties promised by King Henry is ignored, and the archbishop frets. Yea, there will be rebellion, you may count on that."

In the ensuing silence, Tuck leaned forward, round face troubled as he asked, "Yet what of northern barons who have sworn again to John? Will they once more forswear their oaths and rebel?"

It was Tré who answered, tone grim: "Yea, as some have done already. Faithless overlords risk much by premature action—John waits like a hawk for a mistake."

An unanswered question hovered, the moment stretching as Jane waited for the subject to be broached. In this dubious peace, Tré risked losing all if he pursued Welburn.

He glanced down at her, eyes a narrow green beneath his lashes. "I have a new overlord."

Silence greeted the news; her heart dropped. Fragile peace destroyed, another weapon lent the king to use against him now. . . .

Knuckles bleached white, her hands gripped tightly in her lap. She heard him, as if from a distance, the familiar rasping tone dear to her now, say, "For overlong I thought of vengeance. I lived it, breathed it. It was meat and drink to me, and I meant to kill Ewing for what he had caused."

It was so quiet in the hall that the popping of a log was like a crack of lightning; Marian jumped, gasped.

"But it would not bring back Aimée. Once, that would not have mattered to me." He looked at Jane, held her gaze. "Now I would not risk my future for what is past."

Tears stung her eyes; her throat ached. Shaky hope rose to form a question, but he answered it before it was asked.

"It seems," Tré continued softly, "that Pell Ewing fled the king's grace once more after being found involved in a plot, and seeks refuge in France. I find it interesting that Lord Dunham is also under indictment for his part in it."

Silence settled; Guy leaned forward, humor curved his mouth. "Are you not going to ask who his new overlord is to be, milady? It involves you as well."

Relief that Tré had not killed Welburn erased any other concern, but she nodded. "Yea, it would be intriguing to hear what baron will now have Welburn's lands."

"They have been granted to the man who petitioned the king for them as a payment for loss of lands and castle—the Earl of Huntington."

For a moment, Jane did not move. Disbelieving, her gaze shot to Robin; he smiled, hitched a shoulder. "I seek to expand my holdings, and Yorkshire is lovely, I am told. Is that not what you told me, Lord Devaux?"

"Yea, and I did not lie. Yorkshire is most lovely, near as lovely as Sherwood."

Tré rose to his feet, held out a hand. "Milady, with the interdict ended, marriages can once more be performed by priest and monk. If Brother Tuck is willing, I would wed thee on Christmas Day."

No hesitation: "Yea, my lord, I will wed thee before man and God."

His hand closed around her fingers, held tightly. "Before man and God, Jane of Ravenshed, I swear my love."

Bleak sunlight pierced scudding clouds to play over the steps of Saint Mary's Church in Edwinstowe. Sentiment brought them there to wed; Robin had wed his lady Marian on those very steps.

Holly and ivy wreathed Jane's head, tucked into a silk band that dipped over her brow. Clad in a blue gown that flowed around her body, she looked more lovely than Tré had ever seen her.

Tuck cleared his throat, almost regal in his clerical robes. "Then let him come who is to give away the bride. . . ."

Robin, garbed in the raiment of an earl, came forward with Jane on his arm. She looked at Tré, eyes blue-shadowed beneath her lashes, love gleaming so that his heart pounded loudly, nearly drowning out the wedding liturgy.

". . . And let him take her by the right hand, and let him give her to the man as his lawful wife, with her hand uncovered, as she is a widow."

Solemnly, Robin placed Jane's right hand in Tré's; long fingers, bare and lovely, trembled on his wrist. She held his gaze, and he saw in her eyes his past and his future. It made him clumsy, so that he fumbled as he slipped the gold band on and off three successive fingers of Jane's right hand, as required by ritual—in the name of the Father, the Son, and the Holy Ghost—then finally slid it onto her left hand and held her fingers tightly in his.

The smell of mint pervaded his senses and prevailed over the spicy scent of spruce trees beside the church. It was calming. Now the words came easily to him, the pledge heartfelt:

"With this ring I thee wed, with this gold I thee honor, and with this dowry I thee endow. . . ."

Jane knelt at his feet, head bent, glorious hair gleaming in the morning sunlight. He lifted her up, held her hand in his to take her into the church for the blessing.

Shrouded in silence and incense and surrounded by former outlaws, they were united forever. Later would come the blessing of the wedding chamber, the marriage bed that would seal them as wedded in the eyes of the church.

Necessary rituals for man and God, but not for him. He had sworn to Jane of Ravenshed long before now, in his heart and soul. Nothing else was required to make his contentment complete.

Outside the church waited Jane's loyal household; they waved sheaves of wheat in blessing, a sign of fruitfulness as benediction for the marriage. Oxton and Creighton stood on the fringes of the crowd, signifying with mute presence their approval.

Tré lifted Jane onto the back of her snow-white palfrey, bedecked for the occasion in garlands of late flowers and wheat. With his hands still about her waist, he looked up at her, cleared his throat of sudden emotion, and sought a light note to the solemn moment.

"Perhaps Tuck should have made you swear not to take up arms against me again, Lady Devaux. I find you formidable."

"Do you, my lord husband?" A smile wavered on her lips, eyes a bright sheen in winter sun. "As I do find you to be. I pray our son does not have your daunting nature."

"Should we have a son, I am certain he would have his mother's sweet temper."

"Son or daughter, my lord, we will know by Midsummer's Day."

For a moment he stood frozen, looking up at her, at the uncertain smile on her mouth and the hope in her eyes. "You are certain of this?"

"Yea, my heart. 'Tis my wedding gift to you . . . a child of our love."

A lute strummed softly, chords rippling through the air as Alan began to sing.

And so the sheriff and his lissome bride
Went hand in hand to forest bower,
While birds sang approval in merry Sherwood,
And 'twas a most blissful hour. . . .

It was a promise made and kept, a new beginning for both of them—for all of them.

TO MY READERS

In researching *The Baron*, I visited Nottingham and the surrounding area, tramped paths through Sherwood's forest and meadows, walked the ruins of Rufford Abbey, and even found the ruins of King John's Palace at Old Clipstone. It was a remarkable journey. Edwinstowe still exists, as does the church of St. Mary's, where legend says Robin Hood and Maid Marian were wed. A short walk from Edwinstowe is the Cockpen Oak, now known as the Major Oak, a nineteenth-century name for the huge, gnarled old oak that is said to be the oldest living tree in England. There is conjecture about this tree, some saying it was a sapling during King John's reign, and others saying that it is fifteen hundred years old. Apparently, a very similar oak in this spot did, indeed, offer shelter to outlaws and sheriffs alike. Sherwood Forest is still mystical and beautiful, lending substance to the tales of spirits living inside the ancient, twisted trees, for faces do seem to peer out from the mottled bark.

Medieval barons would laugh at our modern concept of barons as bluebloods. That virtue was left for royalty to boast. Many barons gained land and title by right of sword, marriage, or royal largesse in gratitude for a favor. Those who inherited title and lands were fortunate if they managed to hold them.

For *The Baron*, I used *John Lackland*, a wonderful book I

found at a library sale, as a framework on which to base many events. It gives detailed information about the king's activities. Apparently, it was not without precedent for John to appoint his barons to an office. A noted case was that of William de Braose, who was deseisined of his lands granted him by the king, appointed Constable of Limerick, deposed, then appointed again. It is historical fact that Stephen Langton chased John to Nottingham to halt him from enacting vengeance against the northern barons. Contemporaries of the time recorded date, deed, and words, found in *John Lackland*. An invaluable assistance.

While I strove to stay true to medieval times, of course, the language had to be modified to be readable. Language is not the only difference. Medieval perceptions were quite different, guided by the church, molded by brutal warfare and short life spans. Yet they were not miserable all the time, and if they lived in what we regard as squalor, to them it was normal. Even the peasant had his pleasures. Rivalry between Saxon and Norman did not end easily. It has still not ended in some ways. As example: I could find little information on William the Conqueror at Westminster Abbey, where he was crowned king in 1066, but there were entire shelves of books about the conquered Saxon king, Harold. I was informed by the sales clerk—very politely—that William was *Norman*, as if that explained it perfectly. It did.

For the depiction of the tournament, I used as my reference several accounts that varied only slightly. The barrier known as the tilt, which separated the jousters from one another and is so popular in movies, was not conceived until the fifteenth century; thus, there were inevitable collisions between knights. The rituals are as accurate as I could find them described, though of course I took author's liberty with the actual wording.

Descriptions of Nottingham Castle are as accurate as research can show. I have a wonderful little book I bought at the castle, *Nottingham's Royal Castle* by Andrew Hamilton. It has detailed drawings and descriptions of the castle since it was first built, listing dates when improvements were made. For descriptions of thirteenth-century Rufford Abbey, I found a book there, *Rufford Abbey and Country Home*, which is put out by Nottinghamshire County Council. Some of the abbey still stands.

Nottinghamshire is just riddled with caves, many lying beneath the city of Nottingham like a vast honeycomb. The castle cave and entrance used in this story does exist, but I won't regale you with my adventure in exploring it. Suffice it to say, going down was a lot easier than coming back up. By all accounts, outlaws of the time lived in caves that abound in the area, where they could conceal the entrances and remain hidden from discovery.

I would like to thank Mike Stacey, a charming gentleman employed by Weaver's Wine Merchants in Nottingham, who gave us a lovely tour of the wine cellars and was the first to tell me of the extensive cave systems beneath the town. It was in the cave below Weaver's that *The Baron* first took full form, as Mike shared his extensive knowledge of history with us.

The present castle is not as high as the first Nottingham Castle, due to a former resident's desire to lower the sandstone bluff on which it stood, but it is still imposing. Some of the original eleventh- and twelfth-century walls are still there, as well as the gatehouse. I must thank castle employee George Oliver of Hucknall for his delightful help and advice in navigating the castle grounds. I hope I was as helpful with my guided tour of Graceland for him and his wife, Kath.

The Rock Yard still exists below the castle, known since the seventeenth century as the Brewhouse Yard. It has an excellent museum, though they no longer brew ale. The Pilgrim's Inn exists much as it did in King John's day, cut into rock at the castle foot, and still has the ring and horn game. I made several return trips for good food and to soak up atmosphere. Established in approximately 1189, it was renamed The Trip to Jerusalem in the eighteenth century. Until recently, it was thought to be the oldest English inn still in use, but new information has come to light and a challenger for the title is The Bell, also in Nottingham.

Until 1835, Nottingham was divided into two boroughs, one Saxon and one Norman, represented by two sheriffs. I must thank Perry, Lord of Thorpe, for his invaluable assistance in giving me the real names of the sheriffs during that time. Eustace de Lowdham was sheriff in 1213, though his name was also spelled Ludenham. I took the liberty of using the Lowdham version, as that is the name of a village near Gunthorpe. It made sense that it was the same. He was demoted, then reinstated as sheriff, which worked in perfectly with my story. Philip Mark was high sheriff during the same era. He has the distinction of being named in the Magna Carta as one of the dishonest officials to be banned from continuing his depredations. What an honor for posterity!

Ravenshead (Ravenshed) and Blidworth figured largely in the tales of Robin Hood. Will Scarlett's grave is at Blidworth, and Brother Tuck's hut was located two miles away, at Ravenshead, near the fountain where he is said to have first met Robin Hood. (The title of Friar was not used until the fourteenth century and probably originated with the use of *Frère*, French for "brother.") I visited Blidworth, which is also the traditional home of Maid Marian. It is a charming village not far from Old Clipstone and the ruins of King John's Palace. I used the thirteenth-century boundaries of Sherwood Forest as my guide, though it is now much diminished, comprising only 450 acres. Sherwood Forest was not then, nor is it now, just wooded tracts, but includes fields, meadows, and villages. One can still walk paths through woods and meadows, or ride horses on the trails and think of bygone days.

While staying in nearby Gunthorpe, I prevailed on my wonderful hosts, Clive and Pip Harris, to take me to Robin Hood's Cave in Walesby. I was enchanted by the sandstone cave and the River Maun that meanders a gentle path through fields and wood, and felt as if I could actually see traces of the outlaws who had once used it as a sanctuary. Though it is now much washed away by time and erosion, and not nearly as deep or hidden as the Robin Hood's Cave in Cresswell Crags, I chose to use this location for my story. The majority of this story takes place within a twenty-five-mile radius of Nottingham, for Ravenshead is eleven miles north of the city, and the Cockpen (Major) Oak only sixteen miles north. Gunthorpe, where I stayed in The Toll House bed-and-breakfast on the River Trent, is only eight miles from Nottingham.

While reading old tales of Robin Hood, I found references to Clorinda. Maid Marian did not show up in the ballads and tales until about the fifteenth century. Before then, Robin Hood's lady was a raven-haired lass wearing a Lincoln-green jerkin and laced buskins to the knee, and was named Clorinda. I chose to interpret her relationship with Robin Hood my way, for she was said to be expert with the longbow and thus a fitting mother for my heroine.

As for Robin Hood himself, he may have been an actual outlaw or a composite of a number of outlaws. There are many entries in old ledgers referring to Robert Hodde, Robert Hood, etc. It is a matter of record that outlaws were called Robin Hood, much as we use the name John Doe today. Whether this was a coincidence used by minstrels to earn a penny or two, or because of the first Robin Hood, is now all conjecture. I have my own theories.

Last, Barnsdale Forest lay just north of Nottingham, between the city and what is now Bestwood Lodge, and should not be confused with another Barnesdale much farther to the north in Cumberland. Interestingly, it has recently come to light that Huntington was once an earldom in the forest of Barnsdale just outside the town of Nottingham in the thirteenth century, so tales of a local Earl of Huntington have even more validity than before.

To quote John Selden, Keeper of the Records in the Tower of London in the seventeenth century: "There is more historic truth in many of the old ballads than in many modern histories." I think he was on to something.

I hope you have enjoyed my story, and also enjoyed a vicarious journey through the beauty of the English countryside, which still echoes the heart of medieval times.

ABOUT THE AUTHOR

JULIANA GARNETT is a bestselling author who makes her home in Memphis, Tennessee, when she is not in England or Scotland researching her next medieval tale. Her love of the era of knights, dark villains, and damsels in distress began when she was a child reading stories of *Robin Hood*.

In *The Baron*, Ms. Garnett wrote about one of her favorite characters, the Sheriff of Nottingham. She freely admits to watching "Prince of Thieves" a dozen times, not for admiration of the noble Robin Hood, but fascination with the sheriff. It is her opinion that on occasion, villains make the best heroes . . . she hopes that you will agree.

You can write Ms. Garnett c/o Bantam Books, or visit the author on her Web site at www.ladyofshallot.com

From one of romance's brightest new talents comes four breathtaking medieval epics of danger, temptation, and forbidden desire

JULIANA GARNETT

THE QUEST
___56861-2 $5.50/$6.99 Canada

THE MAGIC
___56826-0 $5.99/$7.99

THE VOW
___57626-7 $5.99/$7.99

THE SCOTSMAN
___57627-5 $5.99/$7.99

Bestselling Historical Women's Fiction

❧AMANDA QUICK❧

____28354-5 SEDUCTION ... $6.99/$9.99 Canada

____28932-2 SCANDAL .... $6.99/$9.99

____28594-7 SURRENDER .... $6.99/$9.99

____29325-7 RENDEZVOUS .... $6.99/$9.99

____29315-X RECKLESS .... $6.99/$9.99

____29316-8 RAVISHED .... $6.99/$9.99

____29317-6 DANGEROUS .... $6.99/$9.99

____56506-0 DECEPTION .... $6.99/$9.99

____56153-7 DESIRE .... $6.99/$9.99

____56940-6 MISTRESS .... $6.99/$9.99

____57159-1 MYSTIQUE .... $6.99/$9.99

____57190-7 MISCHIEF .... $6.50/$8.99

____57407-8 AFFAIR .... $6.99/$8.99

____57409-4 WITH THIS RING ..... $6.99/$9.99

❧IRIS JOHANSEN❧

____29871-2 LAST BRIDGE HOME ... $5.99/$8.99

____29604-3 THE GOLDEN
                BARBARIAN .... $6.99/$8.99

____29244-7 REAP THE WIND ..... $6.99/$9.99

____29032-0 STORM WINDS .... $6.99/$8.99

Ask for these books at your local bookstore or use this page to order.

Please send me the books I have checked above. I am enclosing $_____ (add $2.50 to cover postage and handling). Send check or money order, no cash or C.O.D.'s, please.

Name _____

Address _____

City/State/Zip _____

Send order to: Bantam Books, Dept. FN 16, 2451 S. Wolf Rd., Des Plaines, IL 60018
Allow four to six weeks for delivery.

Prices and availability subject to change without notice.   FN 16 4/99

Bestselling Historical Women's Fiction

⚹Iris Johansen⚹

____28855-5 THE WIND DANCER . . .$6.99/$9.99
____29968-9 THE TIGER PRINCE . . .$6.99/$8.99
____29944-1 THE MAGNIFICENT
                ROGUE . . . .$6.99/$8.99
____29945-X BELOVED SCOUNDREL .$6.99/$8.99
____29946-8 MIDNIGHT WARRIOR . .$6.99/$8.99
____29947-6 DARK RIDER . . . .$6.99/$8.99
____56990-2 LION'S BRIDE . . . .$6.99/$8.99
____56991-0 THE UGLY DUCKLING. . .$6.99/$8.99
____57181-8 LONG AFTER MIDNIGHT.$6.99/$8.99
____57998-3 AND THEN YOU DIE.... $6.99/$8.99
____57802-2 THE FACE OF DECEPTION. .$6.99/$9.99

⚹Teresa Medeiros⚹

____29407-5 HEATHER AND VELVET .$5.99/$7.50
____29409-1 ONCE AN ANGEL . . . . . .$5.99/$7.99
____29408-3 A WHISPER OF ROSES .$5.99/$7.99
____56332-7 THIEF OF HEARTS . . . . .$5.99/$7.99
____56333-5 FAIREST OF THEM ALL .$5.99/$7.50
____56334-3 BREATH OF MAGIC . . . .$5.99/$7.99
____57623-2 SHADOWS AND LACE . . .$5.99/$7.99
____57500-7 TOUCH OF ENCHANTMENT.$5.99/$7.99
____57501-5 NOBODY'S DARLING . . .$5.99/$7.99
____57502-3 CHARMING THE PRINCE . .$5.99/$8.99

Ask for these books at your local bookstore or use this page to order.

Please send me the books I have checked above. I am enclosing $_____ (add $2.50 to cover postage and handling). Send check or money order, no cash or C.O.D.'s, please.

Name _____

Address _____

City/State/Zip _____

Send order to: Bantam Books, Dept. FN 16, 2451 S. Wolf Rd., Des Plaines, IL 60018
Allow four to six weeks for delivery.
Prices and availability subject to change without notice.